# In Plain Sight

## ALICE DANIELS

# IN PLAIN SIGHT

## AN IVY RIDGE NOVEL

### ALICE DANIELS

Editing: Aria Harding

Cover Design by Jillian Liota, Blue Moon Creative Studio

*For my fellow late bloomers, friends with social anxiety, or the ones who are just too scared to put themselves out there. May we find our person.*

*And for my very own Grandpa who I took so much inspiration from for Gramps. I love and miss you so much. Your Ali-oop.*

PLAYLIST

After The Storm- Mumford & Sons
All I Wanted- Paramore
Banks- NEEDTOBREATHE
Close To You- Gracie Abrams
Eternity-Alex Warren
Everybody's Got Somebody but Me- Hunter Hayes,
Jason Mraz
Everything- Alex Warren
Faithfully- Journey
Hollow (Acoustic)-Belle Mt.
I Like Me Better- Lauv
In Your Love- Tyler Childers
Lost in The Wild- WALK THE MOON
Ordinary- Alex Warren
Outro- M83
Pain Is Cold Water- Noah Kahan
Pretending- Lea Michele, Cory Monteith
The Prophecy- Taylor Swift
Risk- Gracie Abrams
Run- COIN
Safe & Sound- Taylor Swift, Joy Williams, John Paul White
Starting Over- Chris Stapleton
Sunscreen- Ira Wold

Sway- Kacey Musgraves
Take Me As I Come- Evan Honer, Wyatt Flores
Troubled Waters- Alex Warren
The View Between Villages- Noah Kahan
Waving Through A Window- Ben Platt
When He Sees Me- Kimiko Glenn
When I Look At You- Miley Cyrus
WHERE WE ARE- The Lumineers

*To listen to whole playlist, scan the code!*

# CONTENT WARNING

Dear Reader,

**In Plain Sight** contains subjects that may be triggering to some. This content includes on page scenes depicting Hannah's struggles with anxiety and social anxiety. There is also medication use (as prescribed), panic attacks(on page), graphic sexual content, medical content, drug trafficking investigation, police investigations, death of a minor by overdose(on page), gun violence and shooting of multiple characters resulting in surgery and blood loss, parental death (off page), mentions of grandparent death **(I promise it's not Gramps for those who may be concerned)** pregnancy (side character).

This book includes explicit language and graphic sexual scenes. Reader discretion is advised.

Take care of yourself. Your mental health matters more than a book.

# AUTHOR'S NOTE

Dear Reader,

There are a few things you need to know before reading Hannah and Thomas's love story.

First being that this is fiction. The circumstances that send Hannah and Thomas to a safe house is not how an investigation would happen in real life, and I understand that. But, please note that this is their story, and it's just that, a story. Fiction. So, I hope that you can suspend reality for that brief detail, because this is how their story was meant to be told.

Second, Hannah's story is very near and dear to me. Her experiences with social anxiety are my own. Social anxiety and anxiety in general is different for everyone, and this is the way that mine presents itself. Some things seem so daunting that the thought of going on a date with a person you really like sends you into such a tailspin that you have to pull over on the side of the road and throw up. (Yes, that did really happen.)

So, please note that while it may not seem realistic for

someone to have these feelings or thoughts, please know that this is the way some people function, and that's okay.

Also worth noting, a nurse, paramedic, and lawyer were consulted in regards to certain scenes in this book, but a few liberties were taken.

I hope you enjoy In Plain Sight.

xoxo, Alice

---

## HANNAH

The radio on the dash beeps, alerting us to another dispatch. I swipe the radio off the hook, beeping into the call.

"OD, roughly seventeen, male."

I curse under my breath. I glance over at my partner, Miles, who flicks on the lights and sirens.

"Unit 13, responding." I listen to the little information that the dispatcher gives us, internally logging it. Moments later, we're pulling up to the scene, a dilapidated house that slants to the left, barely standing up.

Police are already doing compressions on the boy. I snap gloves onto my hands, grab my pack and run toward them as soon as the rig slows to a stop. Miles will get the gurney and more Narcan, but for now, I need to get over to the patient and evaluate.

The officer doing compressions is one I'm familiar with. Thomas Cunningham. His face is red, eyes focused only on the young boy lying on the ground in front of him. I kneel beside him on the crunchy gravel and rest a hand on his broad shoulder, ready to tap him out.

Thomas grunts out his vitals in between compressions. When he last had a pulse, how long he's been doing compressions, and when the last dose of Narcan was. I tap his shoulder again, urging him to let me take over. The second Thomas's hands pull away, putting my all into making his heart beat again. Rocks burrow into my knees, sending sharp tingles of pain through my legs. I ignore it, focusing on the task. I count to myself, watching the small portable monitor next to his head, willing there to be cardiac activity on the screen.

Time passes. I don't know how long with my own flight-or-fight activated, but it's long enough that Miles taps me out, taking over as we fight to get this kid breathing again. After another minute, we load him onto the stretcher and into the ambulance. Miles and I switch again while he drives the rig to the hospital. Thomas climbs into the back with me, calling out orders for his teammates to follow us with his vehicle, as his K-9 German Shepherd, Arson, is in the backseat.

I give my everything to this kid, willing for him to breathe again. I'm so fucking sick of this. Too many kids have died on my watch in the last two years, and I don't fucking want there to be another one.

"Two minutes," Miles calls from the front. "Any rhythm?"

A bead of sweat rolls down my neck as I call out, "No."

I hear him curse under his breath, and feel the jolt of rig speeding up. "Come on, kid," Thomas says, his voice low and pained as he manually checks his pulse. "Switch."

Nodding, I step back, trying to catch my breath while also checking his lines and the monitor. The vehicle jerks to a stop, and Miles flies out of the front seat.

The back doors open as the nurses run toward us, and I

call out status report as I help move the stretcher down to the ground. They take him back, and I feel my adrenaline starting to fade. I don't say out loud what I'm thinking—that at this point, they aren't going to get him back. His body has given up. We've been doing compressions for so long, that even if they manage to get a rhythm back, his brain might not recover. There is no life left inside him. He's only seventeen. He's barely old enough to drive, and now he doesn't even have a life left to live.

I pull off my gloves with a *snap*, throwing them into the garbage can by the entrance. Taking a moment to breathe, I find a sink and scrub my hands and arms clean. I typically won't know if a patient has made it or not, that's one of the things I have to come to terms with often as a paramedic, but right now, it sucks.

A body comes up behind me, standing at the sink next to me. "Hey," Thomas murmurs, washing his hands. "They called it."

Even though I had a feeling they would, that doesn't stop the sinking feeling in my gut.

Unsure what to say to him right now or how to help when he's rightfully emotional over yet another loss, I simply nod. It doesn't help that I'm awkward in social situations. Performing my job or talking to my coworkers about cases I've worked on are a piece of cake, but mundane tasks like ordering a pizza, making doctors appointments, or small talk can send me into a full blown anxiety attack. Thomas should fall into the first category, since we've worked on scene for many of the overdoses over the last few years since the drug trafficking ring made its way into our small town. But, unfortunately for me, the fact that I find him extremely attractive and have little experience in that department, makes me anxious about his starting a conversation with me.

Thomas is nearly a decade older than me. Nine years and five months if we're being specific. And god, now I sound like a psycho stalker. I'm not. I swear. I'm just really good at remembering birthdays.

"I'm sorry," I blurt. "He was young."

"Too young," Thomas responds, ripping a paper towel off the automatic dispenser hung from the wall. He turns and leans against the stainless steel sink and looks directly at me.

Crap, there goes my stomach, giving me all sorts of butterflies and swirling feelings. And of course, my face turns red as soon as his attention is on me. Can't forget that. It's *super* great. I can't tell people how I'm feeling, but my face sure as fuck can.

In a way, I hope I'm still flushed from doing compressions so my blush isn't so evident, but I'm not usually that lucky.

"I should get back out to the rig. Miles is probably ready to get back out."

"What time are you off this morning?" Thomas asks, surprising me. He stands nonchalantly, running a hand through his loose blonde waves and hooking his thumbs in his Kevlar vest. Doesn't he know how hot he looks when he does that? And why is he asking what time I'm off?

"Um—"I stutter, "Six."

"Some of us are meeting up for coffee if you and Miles want to join us. Just for a debriefing. We try to do it after a rough night, but it hasn't been happening lately like it should. You're more than welcome to join. I'll text Miles the plan."

I swallow the lump in my throat. "Okay, sounds good." I wave an awkward goodbye and stumble over my feet as I turn to head back to the ambulance bay.

*Stupid, stupid, stupid, Hannah.* He's probably laughing at you in his head right now over the fact that you can't even walk straight. It's probably why he's never invited you out before now.

"You okay?" Thomas calls, and I internally die *just* a little more.

"Fine," I squeak, holding up a thumbs up as I dash out the sliding doors.

I climb into the ambulance, and pull my seatbelt over my body. "Ready?" Miles asks.

Nodding, I fiddle with my fingers in my lap. "Thomas is going to text you about some coffee breakfast thing this morning." I tell him as he drives out of the hospital parking lot.

"Oh, is he?" Miles prompts. Miles is also ten years older than me, but he's taken on more of a big brother role if anything with me.

To someone that doesn't have social anxiety, going in and picking up a coffee or food order is no big deal, but for someone like me, that might be the hardest thing they do that day. Throw in the fact that I also have good old generalized anxiety disorder, and I'm a real treat. Miles, along with the help of my therapist, have helped me so immensely that now I can do things like that, mostly without a second thought.

Miles has also become a safe person for me. If there's a work event and he says he will be there, then I can go, no problem. If he's not there? Count me out. Like I said, it probably sounds stupid. But for me, that's my reality. I can't just... turn it off, or make the thoughts in my brain go away.

"Are you going to go?" Miles asks, turning onto a highway. We don't have a call right now, so we get to drive until we do.

"Are you?" I turn the question on him. He narrows his eyes, glancing over at me briefly.

"Hannah," he starts. "You can go alone. You don't need me there."

I sigh. "I know I don't *need* you. It's just easier for me if you are there." Miles knows my issues, and he and I are pretty close, despite never hanging out outside of work. When you spend as much time together as we do in close quarters, it's hard not to get close. I still have some things I mask when I'm with Miles, as well as things I overthink or worry about, but it's getting easier with him. It also helps that he understands certain things that make me uncomfortable. He's been trying to help get me out of my comfort zone, while also not pressing me too hard.

"I have to check with Lochlan. He wants to head up to the cabin this weekend since it's our last shift until Monday."

I nod, while internally trying to come up with ways I can get out of going now that he probably won't be there.

"You still should go, Banana," he says, using the nickname he knows I hate. It's the most basic nickname for someone with the name Hannah. "I know it's hard. But I bet you can do it. You know Thomas and some of the other guys well enough now."

Miles also knows about the teensy weensy little crush I have on Thomas. Crush is such a stupid word. He's attractive. I would love to get to know him more, but I don't know if I'll ever make the first move. And I doubt he's attracted to me.

What can I say? I'm a mess. I'm a twenty-seven-year-old woman with severe social anxiety that prevents me from going on dates, a virgin, and I've never been kissed. Lovely, right? I'm totally dateable, I know.

"I'll try," I tell him, not really committing myself to it, though. A sideways glance from Miles tells me he's not buying my blatant lie.

"Hannah," he says my name slowly. "You really don't need me to come."

"I know I don't," my voice grows higher pitched. I do know that, and I hate that I feel that I need him. Things are just *easier* if I have a person I trust there.

"So you'll go," he states.

"I will think about it," I correct.

Miles sighs, and his phone lights up in the center console with a text. "Can you check that?"

I nod, grabbing it and asking for his code. The message is from Thomas.

THOMAS CUNNINGHAM

Hey, breakfast at the diner after shift. Meet at six-forty-five. What's Hannah's number? I should have asked her at the hospital for it. I want to shoot her a message about it too.

"What did he say?" Miles asks.

I swallow the lump in my throat. "He said breakfast is at six-forty-five at the diner and asked for my number."

"So, give it to him?" Miles responds.

"Right," I mutter, typing a response, and tagging my contact card in the conversation.

Thomas sends a thumbs-up in response, but nothing else. My cell phone doesn't buzz with a text right away, and thankfully, dispatch radios us, distracting me from waiting for a text that probably won't come.

2

————

## THOMAS

What a crappy night. I take a deep inhale of air as I pull into the police station to finish up a few things before breakfast. Arson, my K-9 German Shepherd, who I've had since he was a year old, is in the backseat, wagging his tail as the station comes into view.

"I know, buddy," I say to him. "We made it." My phone dings in the center console with a message from Miles, one of the paramedics on duty last night.

MILES

> Hey man, I won't be able to make it this morning. Lochlan wants to head up to the lake and start our weekend early, but Hannah should be there.

ME

> Good deal. Have a great weekend, tell Lochlan I said hi.

I don't know why I never had Hannah's number until earlier this morning, but I hope she comes. She doesn't come out much, unless Miles is there, and I hope she knows we don't bite. Yeah, she's a lot younger than the rest of us, probably about ten years, but I don't mind that. We're all adults, and working in a high stress job.

To be honest, I would much rather curl up in my bed right now than go out for breakfast with everyone, but like I said, it was a crappy night, and I think we could all use a little pick-me-up.

I stride into the station with Arson at my side. There isn't much activity here this early in the morning, and I'm thankful for it. I pull up a chair at a table in the common area, and start filling out the paperwork I know can't wait. Thirty minutes later, Arson paws at my leg, desperate for his morning meal, and my stomach grumbles in response. I toss a scoop of food in his bowl, and he starts scarfing it down. A look at the clock tells me I have ten minutes until breakfast, which gives me enough time to walk the few blocks down to the diner.

"Morning, Thomas," Henry greets me as he walks through the door, thermos of coffee in hand. He is one of the detectives we brought on for the drug trafficking case. "I just finished up at the scene from this morning."

"Anything notable?" I ask, though I have a feeling it's going to be the same answer as always, no.

He shakes his head somberly. "Nothing."

I pass him the file folder with my report and information, and he takes it with a nod. "Off for the rest of the day?" he asks.

"Yep. Off to breakfast, then I'm crashing. I'm off for a few days after this."

"Good for you."

"Can Arson hang out with you while I'm at breakfast? Judy down at the diner doesn't like it when I try to convince her to let me bring him in."

"Hmm, I can't imagine why," Henry says with a chuckle. "Of course. I'll grab his bed and a water bowl from down the hall and he can hang with me."

"Thanks, man." I offer him a goodbye, then give my dog a scratch behind the ear. Of course, Arson follows me nearly out the door until Henry calls him back to his office. I hate leaving him behind, but if I try sneaking him into the diner again, Judy's never going to forgive me.

The sun is starting to rise as I stroll down the cracked cement sidewalk of my hometown. I like to go on walks in the mornings or evenings after my shift anyway, so this will count as my walk. I like to do it as a way to sort of give my brain time to process, or think about things I witnessed or experienced on the shift.

I live in a small town, so I won't deny that I don't see nearly as much horrible shit as I might working in a higher population area, but that doesn't mean I don't deal with some vile shit. It almost makes it harder when you learn things about a person you've known your whole life and it changes the way you look at them.

I reach the diner right on time, and glance around the near-empty room. A few older gentlemen sit at the bar chatting over their coffee, and Judy flits around, getting ready for the morning rush.

I don't see anyone from the crew in the diner, so I pick a round table big enough for our group, and take a seat. Judy strides over with a menu even though I don't need it, plopping one in front of me and setting an empty mug in front of me.

"Morning, kiddo," she greets as she fills the mug with rich smelling coffee. She not so sneakily peeks under the table at my feet. "No Arson this morning?"

"Figured I'd get scolded if I did," I tell her with a laugh.

"You'd be right," she snarks. "He's a good pup, though."

"That he is."

"The usual?" Judy asks, not even looking at me. She glances up as the bell above the door chimes and I follow her lead. Hannah walks in, shoving her hands in the front pocket of her hooded sweatshirt.

I shake my head. "Yes, but not yet. There's a few people joining us." I stand, waving at Hannah until she sees me. Her cheeks burn red as she strides over to the table.

Judy mutters her agreement, walking off as I pull out a chair for Hannah. "Morning," I say, sitting back down as she settles in next to me. "How was the rest of your shift?"

She shrugs, not looking at me as she scoots her chair slightly away from me. "It was fine, one chest pain, and one fall assist at the nursing home. Nothing too crazy. Where is everyone?" Hannah looks up as if she expects everyone to have suddenly appeared.

"Don't know," I reply. "I can check and see. I'm pretty sure Leo and Steve said they'd stop by." I pull out my phone and note the missed texts from both of them letting me know they won't make it.

Judy drops a mug in front of Hannah and fills a cup of coffee for her without Hannah even having to ask.

"Well, I guess it's just us," I announce, noticing the way Hannah tenses. "The other guys can't make it."

"Oh," Hannah mumbles, taking a slow sip of her coffee.

"Do you want a minute to look at the menu, or should we order?"

"We can order," she states abruptly.

"I'll have my usual, Judy." I smile and pass her my menu.

Hannah glances at the menu briefly and swallows harshly. "I'll have a bowl of oatmeal and rye toast." Her voice shakes and when she hands the menu back to Judy, I note the stiffness in her body. Her breakfast choice is interesting to me as well. It's not something I'd order for myself at a diner known for their breakfasts, but who am I to say anything?

"How are you feeling after last night, er, this morning?" I ask Hannah.

She shrugs, some of the tenseness still in her shoulders. "Fine. Just another night I guess. It sucks, but it is what it is, right?"

I nod. "Right, but I mean, if you ever need someone to talk to, I'm here," I offer. As if I'm one to talk. I've been trying to be fine, to process things on my own, but I'm close to a breaking point. It's why I suggested this group breakfast this morning. I needed someone to confide in.

Hannah chokes on the gulp of coffee she took, and starts coughing. "Shoot, you okay?" I ask while I pat her back and offer her a napkin.

She waves me off, and clears her throat a few times. "Sorry, swallowed wrong."

"No worries, as long as you're okay."

"Fine," she says. "Are you doing okay after last night?" She looks up and I finally get a full glimpse of her face for the first time since she sat down.

Her long blonde hair is pulled back into a ponytail with a few pieces falling out over her ears, pieces that probably fell out during her shift. Her blue eyes are bright despite our long night and the sheer exhaustion she must be feeling. There are flecks of gray in her eyes that I've never noticed before, and a smattering of freckles dance across her nose and cheeks.

It feels like I'm seeing her for the first time, even though I've known her for years now. She's a damn good paramedic, has been since her first day. She has good instincts, and people in town love her.

I'm brought back to the conversation at hand when Hannah notices me staring. She quickly wipes at her face as if she has something stuck to it, and brushes the loose pieces of hair back.

"I'm fine," I tell her. "Like you said, it sucks, but it is what it is."

The real truth of it though, is that I'm not fine. No one wants people to die, and no one wants to be the one to tell the mom of a seventeen-year-old kid that their child is dead.

So, why aren't I confiding in Hannah?

"Actually," I state, ready to spill my guts to this girl, but Judy slides our plates in front of us, and walks away without asking if we need anything else.

"Actually?" Hannah asks, picking up her spoon and poking at the globular-shaped oatmeal in the bowl. I don't miss the slight grimace as she lifts a scoop to her lips and swallows it down harshly. Damn, she's not even going to put brown sugar or milk in it?

I shake my head, ignoring her questionable oatmeal choices. "Never mind," I state, hunger overtaking me now that my food is in front of me. I dig into my meal of hash browns, eggs, and ham, and change the subject. It doesn't escape my notice again that Hannah is barely eating, picking at her oatmeal, and is that... rye bread? Who likes rye bread for breakfast? Did she really mean to order that?

## 3

## HANNAH

He needs to stop looking at my gross oatmeal. I mean seriously; he knows it's disgusting; I know it's disgusting, but he doesn't need to keep staring at it like it's going to hop out of the bowl and eat him. Though, maybe it will. At this point, I don't know.

I didn't want oatmeal this morning, but when Judy was hovering over me, snapping her gum in her mouth impatiently, I ordered the first thing I saw. Oatmeal and toast. Then, to add insult to injury, when she asked what type of toast I wanted, I said rye. *Rye?! I hate rye.* Why didn't I order wheat?

So, here I am, picking at my breakfast. Except, if I'm really honest with myself, if I had ordered something I wanted, would I have eaten it in front of him anyway? I hate eating in front of people. My brain likes to overanalyze every look from someone, as I consider if I'm eating too much, because people love to judge the amount of food that a fat person eats.

Ugh, I hate myself. Why can't I be normal? Why do I

have to think about every bite I take in front of him or anyone for that matter?

I pick at my bread and eat a few more bites of my oatmeal, feeling jealous of Thomas and his plate of hash browns, eggs and meat. I would have loved to order something like that. I will probably make myself a peanut butter and jelly sandwich when I get home, because this oatmeal is not it. Even if I tried to spruce it up with some brown sugar or milk, I'm not sure it can be salvaged.

"What does the rest of your day look like?" Thomas asks a few minutes later.

I shrug. "Probably sleep. I'm off the next few days, so I'll take a nap today, and try to get back on a normal sleep schedule since I'm on days next."

"Me too," he agrees, taking the last swig of his coffee. "It's my niece and nephew's first birthday party tomorrow, so I need to get some sleep so I can be a presentable human."

"How many nieces and nephews do you have?" I ask curiously. After growing up in our small town of Ivy Ridge, I know he has a few brothers, and over the years, they've all found their partners, or gotten married. It's adorable, and honestly, I don't know why someone hasn't snatched up Thomas yet. If I could, I would.

"Three nieces, one nephew, and another nephew due in August. Lots of kids lately. My parents are loving it." He smiles softly, an almost proud look crossing his face.

"I bet. It seems like fun."

"What about you? Any nieces or nephews?"

I shake my head. "Nope. My older sister is married, but I don't think she and her wife are planning on having kids."

"What about you? Do you have a partner? Kids?"

His question is innocent, genuine even, but it stings a bit that he knows so little about me. It shouldn't, it's not as if I'm a memorable person in town. I shake my head. "No. Single."

Thomas looks across the small table at me, and his blue eyes blaze, something I don't recognize. "Well, I'm sure you'll find someone, if that's what you want."

"You too," I mutter, though I'm trying hard not to swallow my tongue.

Judy swishes over to us, dropping the bill onto the table. Thomas swipes it before I can, and I hold out my hand. "Give it to me when you're done. I have cash for my half."

"Nope," Thomas states. "I've got it. You can get the next one." He winks and flashes me a grin, showing off the slight gap in his front teeth that I find so insanely adorable.

I can't help the swoon that rocks its way through my body. He shouldn't be saying these things to me, because now, I'll probably romanticize the heck out of this one inter-action for months. Like I said, *pathetic*.

"Right," I say through an awkward laugh.

He pays the bill despite my second attempt at paying my half, and we walk out the door together, watching our town slowly come alive with the morning activities. I'm nearly dead on my feet, and simply cannot wait to get to bed at this point.

"It was nice talking with you," I tell him. Because I'm weird and don't know what else to do, I offer out my hand to shake.

Thomas smiles his easy-going grin again and shakes his head. "Nah, we can hug it out, freckles."

Oh god.

He leans in and wraps his arms around me in a tight, amazing hug. I can't even think because one second I'm staring at him, the next, I'm face first in his chest, breathing in his insanely good smell. He smells like that candle scent at *Bath & Body Works*. Mahogany Teakwood? I don't know. He smells fabulous. I stand awkwardly until I remember to wrap my arms around him.

His arms tighten around my shoulders, and wow. He really is a great hugger. The type of hug where I feel like I can let everything go, and maybe feel like the weight of the world is off my shoulders. Even if it's only for a minute, the relief is indescribable.

He releases me, though I could stay in his arms forever. "See you next time, Hannah." Thomas turns, shoving his hands in his pockets and heading down the sidewalk toward the police station.

I stand there, awkwardly, watching him for longer than I'm sure is appropriate, before getting into my car and attempting to process the last hour of my life.

I just had breakfast with a man I'm extremely attracted to, and I didn't spontaneously combust. And he hugged me? And... hold on. Did he call me freckles?

## 4

## THOMAS

Pulling my vehicle up outside of my younger brother Beau and his wife, Marley's place, I allow myself a minute to sulk in my feelings. All three of my siblings are married or with their forever person and have families of their own, and then there's little old me. Single, living alone in my boring apartment with my dog who is more human than most animals. I haven't even had a real date in well over a year. Not that that means anything. I've gone through so many failed talking phases on dating apps it's almost comical at this point. The loneliness is eating at me, and I'm growing impatient. It feels as if a part of me is missing.

Who knows, maybe I'm meant to be single. For a while I was okay with it, but now, I see how happy my siblings are and I can't help but feel jealous. I want what they have. I want my person, I want the relationship, the marriage with a house and a dog and two and a half kids. I'm thirty-six. I'm aging, and I want to find someone to spend my life with. Ten years ago, I was convinced that I'd find my person right away. Now, I'm unsure if it will ever happen.

Arson nudges my arm away from the steering wheel.

"Alright, buddy, I know you're excited to see the kids. Let's go." At my words, he stands from his sitting position, his tail wagging furiously.

I get out, letting him hop over the console and onto the gravel driveway.

It's hard to believe that Marley and Beau's twins are already a year old. They, along with Lennie, my older brother, Jason's daughter, and Fallon, his girlfriend's daughter, Presley, are all getting so big, so fast. It's crazy. Time won't slow down. Jason and Fallon were both single parents who met back in college, and found their way back to each other last year.

Speaking of Lennie and Presley, they sprint across the lawn toward my vehicle once they see that I'm here.

"Uncle Tommy," Lennie yells, a wide smile taking over her face. Her dark brown hair is in two long braids over her shoulders, and she's wearing a purple bathing suit with pink flowers all over it. Presley is in a similar suit, only hers is blue with yellow flowers. Her dusty blonde hair is shorter, but also in braids. "We've been waiting *hours* for you."

"Hours?" I reply, throwing a hand to my chest dramatically. "How did you ever survive waiting that long?"

Presley scratches the top of Arson's head, and he moans in delight over the extra love that she's giving him.

"It was really hard," Lennie states. "But everyone is waiting for you. Come on!" She waves her arm, and both she and Presley take off in another sprint toward the backyard. Arson takes off and follows them, beating them to the back where everyone sits. It's beautiful outside. The sun is shining, and it's not too hot or humid, so it should be a perfect afternoon. When I round the corner of the house, I see my entire family sitting in lawn chairs on the porch and around the patio table under the umbrella.

My sister-in-law, Josie, takes up two chairs, one for her body, the other to elevate her legs. She's almost eight months pregnant with my next nephew, and absolutely miserable. Her red hair is up in a messy bun, and she's wearing a tank top and cotton shorts. My brother, Andrew, stands behind her, holding a fan over her face as it blows cool air on her.

Beau has one of the twins, Arlo, on his hip and is talking to him, while Marley holds Ariel's hands, letting her practice walking. Fallon sits on Jason's lap next to Josie, while my parents and Gramps sit across the table from them. I feel bad about being late, but I couldn't sleep last night, and only fell asleep at seven-thirty this morning, giving me about six hours of sleep. I texted Beau to let him know I would be a little late, and he understood.

Flipping back to a day schedule after a night rotation is always exhausting. I can never get back on the right track.

"Hi, honey," my mom greets, standing up from her chair to give me a hug.

"Hey Ma." I hug her back. My dad greets me with a head tip, and I pick the chair closest to my Gramps to sit. I reach over and squeeze his shoulder. I've always been extremely close with my gramps, and was equally close with my grandma before her passing. Gramps has been the constant in our family. The one to make us all laugh when times are hard, and support each of us on each journey we take in life.

"How's work been?" my dad asks. I can see the subtle question in his eyes that he wants to ask, but he doesn't. By now, the news is out that there was another teenage death the other night.

I shrug. "Another overdose."

He winces. "How old?"

"Seventeen," I say with a sigh. The memory of his mother wailing in my arms after we notified her of his death hits me square in the chest. "He told his mom he was going to a friend's house for the night, and instead went to a party at an abandoned house."

"I'm sorry, son. I know this investigation has been weighing on you," my dad replies. My mom offers me a sympathetic smile.

Luckily, Gramps changes the subject. Though it's not exactly in my favor. "Heard you were out with a girl the other morning." He grins, the familiar mirth shining in his eyes.

I raise my brow as I glance over. "You gossip more than anyone I know, old man."

He guffaws loudly, clutching his hand to his chest. "What can I say? I need to keep tabs on all my kiddos."

Shaking my head, I chuckle. "Let me guess, Fred is the one who told you?" I thought I saw Gramps' best friend sitting at one of the counter spots, but didn't think much of it at the time.

"Sure did. He's one of my spies."

*I'm not surprised.* "Is he really a spy if you gave up his position?"

"He's not a very good one anyway. Though he did give me some valuable information. Told me you were out with a pretty blonde."

"I was out with a pretty blonde," I admit. Hannah's gorgeous. Totally my type, curvy, sweet, kind, and gorgeous blue eyes that look like they could tell you a story if you looked hard enough, but I doubt she'd ever go for me. I mean, we work together, and I'm probably too old for her taste. "But it's nothing. Her name is Hannah. She's a paramedic I work with. We had plans with the rest of the crew on shift the other morning to go out for breakfast and decompress, but Hannah is the only one who could make it."

From across the table, Marley pipes in, "Oh my god, I *love* Hannah. I mean, I've really only met her the one time, but she was so kind, and so good at her job."

"She's an amazing medic," I agree. Shortly after Marley found out she was pregnant with the twins, she passed out while at her photography studio. Beau called me in a panic because he knew I was on duty and could help get medical services dispatched over there quickly. Hannah was the paramedic on duty that day.

"She did really well calming both of us down," Beau says, coming to stand behind Marley, wrapping his arms around her midsection.

Arlo toddles over to me, holding his arms up, fingers grabbing at me. I pull him into my lap, blowing a raspberry on his cheek. He squeals and giggles, sending a burst of warmth through me. Ariel shoves at her mother's arms, desperate to get to me after seeing the joy on her brother's face. Soon, I have all my nieces and nephews in my lap and by my side. The twins are in my arms, while Lennie and Presley stand on either side of me, cooing and teasing the twins. I spot Marley sneaking out her camera, snapping pictures of the interactions. I'll have to get some copies of the photos later.

"Yeah, like I said, she's great," I state, returning my focus back to the previous conversation.

"So, it's settled then. You should ask her out," Gramps declares.

I let out a stuttered laugh. "I can't ask her out, Gramps."

"Why the hell not?"

"Because," I state, taking a deep, fortifying breath. "I'm

sure she's got guys lining up to take her out, and I'm a lot older than her. She's not interested."

"You won't know until you try," Andrew states from where he sits by Josie, now rubbing her feet.

I shake my head again. "I really don't think it would be a good idea. I mean we work together. Wouldn't it be awkward when we break up?"

"Who said you have to break up?" Josie says, affectionately rubbing her baby bump. "I mean, really, the chances are fifty-fifty. I say, cross that bridge when you come to it. If you're interested in her, go for it. The worst thing that could happen is she says no."

"Yeah, and then what? The awkwardness of seeing her nearly every shift would be enough to make me want to crawl in a hole. And when did this turn into a conversation about my love life? It's a birthday party." I gesture to the zoo animal themed tablecloth.

"No one else is here yet," Beau says, shrugging off my attempt to change the subject.

I let out a heavy sigh. "I'll think about it, but honestly, I don't see it ending well for me."

"Manifest good things," Fallon states as she sits down next to me. Lennie leaps into her lap, and Fallon pulls her into her arms. It's been incredible watching how seamlessly Fallon and Presley weaved their way into Jason and Lennie's little family. Fallon kisses the top of her head and whispers in her ear.

As more people start to arrive, I continue to think of Hannah. It's like my family mentioning it has flipped a switch. I've always been attracted to her, all her curves and natural beauty, but in all honesty, I never thought I'd have a shot with her, so I tamped it down and kept it platonic. But after having the first real one on one conversation I've ever had with her the other morning, and my family putting the bug in my ear, I can honestly say I'd love to get to know her more. She's so closed off, so quiet and reserved, but has the best smile, and a genuine, kind heart. I've seen it when she interacts with her patients. I'd love to see what she's like behind her walls.

## 5

# HANNAH

"Grandma, I'm home!" I call into the house as I kick off my shoes in the entryway. My sister's car is parked out front, so I know she's here too.

"In the kitchen, Han," my sister calls. I should've known she would be the one to answer. My Grandma's hearing is long gone outside of a five-foot radius, and she hates wearing her hearing aids at home. Well, she hates wearing them outside of the house too, so really, she just hates them altogether.

I round the corner into the familiar space to see my sister, Julia, standing beside my grandma. "Hi," I greet, heading over to give them both a kiss on the cheek, and Julia a hug. "Where's Tiff?" I ask, wondering where her wife is.

"She's on her way. Got stuck an extra hour at work on a new contract."

"Good, I haven't seen her in a while."

Tiff and Julia have been married for just over two years, but together since college. Watching their relationship bloom from being best friends to realizing they were actually in love with each other was cool. I, of course, got all of the freak out calls and texts from Julia when she realized she was actually bisexual. It was honestly magical. Grandma knew Tiff from the many nights she had come to the house with Julia as a friend, and when they walked in holding hands, she glanced down, smiled, and asked Tiff what she wanted for dinner. There was no questioning, no anger, only acceptance and happiness for my sister and her partner. Julia was so worried about what Grandma would say about her bringing a woman home instead of a man, but Grandma was only happy for her.

I know not all people are that lucky to have the immediate acceptance, but my sister and I have been pretty blessed with our Grandma. Our parents would have been the same. They would have wanted us to be happy, no matter what.

"Hannah, can you grab me the cream?" Grandma asks. I nod, and pull it out of the fridge, handing it over to her. "Say, do you have anything you'd like to tell us?"

I tilt my head. "What do you mean?"

"Well, I was at my grief group the other day, and I heard Earl Cunningham talking to Fred McAllister." She waits for a beat, like she's waiting for me to catch on. Of course I know who they are. Earl Cunningham is Thomas's grandfather, and Fred, well, Fred is the town gossip.

I motion for her to continue, raising my brow. I grab plates from the cupboard and set the table as she speaks. "Fred was telling Earl all about how his grandson, Thomas, was out with a young blonde girl who is a paramedic. Would you happen to know anything about that?"

Turning so she can't see the swift reddening of my face, I swallow harshly. "Nope. I don't."

"Oh my god," Julia says, her voice raising an octave with

realization. "Did you go on a date with Thomas Cunningham?"

I forgot that my sister graduated with Thomas. She knows him, probably better than I do. They were in the same friend groups. I think maybe they were even in the same prom group. Crap crap *crap*. This is horrible. What if Julia thinks he's too old for me, or worse, what if she hates him from high school? Though, I'm not sure how anyone could hate him.

"No!"

"Liar! Why didn't you tell me?" Julia rounds the table to stand next to me. She takes the plate from my hand, plopping it onto the hardwood table.

"There's nothing to tell!" I shriek. "It wasn't a date. It was two co-workers decompressing after a very bad night. It wasn't even supposed to be just us. The rest of the crew on duty were supposed to join, but no one did. There is no story, no date, no nothing!"

"Hmm." Julia crosses her arms and her deep brown hair cascades over her shoulders with the movement. I can tell she totally doesn't believe me, but I think she will drop it for now.

"I say go for him," Grandma says, shocking me.

"Grandma!" I shout. "He's Julia's age. I can't. And even if I wanted to, he'd never go for someone like me."

Julia pinches my side.

"Ouch, what the hell?" I cry.

"Uhh, what's goin' on?" Tiff says, appearing in the kitchen in her navy blue pantsuit and short blonde pixie cut.

"We're convincing Hannah here that she's beautiful and any man deserves her."

"I second the shit out of that," Tiff states. She walks

over, pulling my sister in for a quick kiss, and a whispered hello before stepping over to pull me into a hug. I melt into my sister-in-law's arms. "Hey sis." She's called me that pretty much since day one. I adore Tiff and have always felt safe with her.

"Hi," I say into her neck. "I need you to save me."

"Quit asking her to save you," Julia says. "You don't need saving. You're fine."

Pulling back, I dramatically gasp. "Rude."

"I'm just trying to make sure you know how amazing you are. I know dating is hard for you, but if you wanted it, Thomas, or any man would be lucky to have you, Han."

My eyes burn with tears that I won't shed. "Thanks."

"Time to eat," Grandma calls, setting down the homemade chicken alfredo onto the table.

## 6

## THOMAS

Sliding the pair of Captain America boxers up my legs, I chuckle to myself. My brothers have teased me about this since I was a kid, but it works like a charm. Every time I need a little bit of good luck, or think something good is going to happen in life, or just need good vibes for the day, I throw on a pair of superhero boxers. It's not just one pair. I have a few that I cycle through, and over the years, I've had to get new ones, but they've never lost their power.

Some may say it's the placebo effect, but I think it's good old-fashioned manifestation. They've never steered me wrong, though. The day I was accepted to the police academy? I had on Hulk boxers. The day I got Arson? Iron Man. The list goes on and on, and it's not just me that gets the good luck. The day Andrew met his now-wife, Josie, I wore them. I wasn't sure why, but something about the day compelled me to wear them, and look at the two of them now. Happily married with their first baby due soon.

I can keep going, but honestly the boxers prove themselves every time. Which is why I'm wearing them today. We both are on shift, and I'm hoping I'll be able to see her.

I'm not asking Hannah out yet, but I want to test the waters with her. Maybe flirt a little, and see what happens. If I don't get a good reading on her, then I won't ask her out, but with me wearing the boxers, I think it will be a good day.

I load up Arson into the backseat of my police cruiser, and get ready to start the day. I have a renewed sense of excitement about going to work today.

After a call with the FBI to discuss the potential of bringing them in to aid in the ongoing trafficking situation, I get on the road. There was a lot of discussion about attempting to get some undercover guys in there and really see what happens on the inside.

The start of my shift is nothing special, a few traffic stops, and one domestic disturbance that turned out to be a dog barking excessively. My radio beeps an incoming call, and I hone my attention to it.

"Elderly male, eighty-six, fall, no injuries, just needs an assist to stand. Location, Park Woods Independent Living."

And just like that, my mood drops. Because that's where Gramps lives. I know it's him. Goddammit. We've been telling him to stop being so goddamn stubborn and start using a walker when he gets tired.

"1831 responding," I say through gritted teeth into the radio. Fire would usually respond before police in a situation like this, but knowing it's Gramps has me responding anyway.

"Copy that. Officer?" the dispatcher says with a questioning tone.

"Yes?" I respond.

"He said he's fine, if that's any consolation. Just needs you to help him stand. He used his life-alert."

Well, that's one positive. He's been refusing to wear it

lately, but who knows how long he would be on the floor if he didn't have it on.

"Copy. Thanks."

Another voice radios in. "Unit thirteen responding to assist."

*Hannah.*

Her voice is soft, but strong at the same time. She's secure in her work, never has been timid or shy when it comes to her job. It's something I can appreciate about her.

I breathe out a sigh of relief.

At least if he was lying about potential injuries, I'll have other professionals to back me up in convincing him to take a ride to the hospital. Like I said, he's a stubborn man.

Less than five minutes later, I'm throwing my vehicle in park outside of the independent living facility. I leave the car and the air conditioning running for Arson, and tell him I'll be back shortly.

I run through the automatic doors and head down the hall toward Gramps' room. A few of the residents move out of the way as I shuffle down the hall. When I reach his door, I knock once and push inside. "Gramps?" I call as I glance quickly around the kitchen.

"In the bedroom," his low voice calls.

I rush down the hall to find him sitting on the floor beside his bed. He looks unharmed, and honestly, a little content to be sitting on the floor. "Causing trouble again, I see?" I ask with the little humor I can manage to muster right now.

"As always, kid," he says. I crouch down in front of him, glancing over his aged body to assess him for any injuries. He looks okay. He's in his long pajama pants and white undershirt, white-gray hair a tousled mess from sleep.

"Hurting anywhere?"

He shakes his head. "I told that nice lady that talked to me on my fancy necklace that I was okay, and to tell you not to worry."

"She told me," I tell him. "You know I'm not going to not worry, though."

He lets out a heavy sigh. "I know. Worth a shot, kiddo."

"Seriously, Gramps. Do you hurt anywhere? Hips? Arms? Legs?" I insist.

"Just my ego," he says, slightly defeated.

"EMS!" A booming male voice calls from the door.

"Back here!" I yell.

The shuffling footsteps and swishing of pant legs gets louder with each step they take toward the bedroom door. Miles enters first, with Hannah close on his heels. They both have blue medical gloves on their hands, first aid bags resting on their shoulders.

"Mr. Cunningham," Miles greets him. "Pleasure to see you again, wish it were under better circumstances."

"You too, kiddo," Gramps says.

I step back to let them do their jobs, all while trying not to stare at Hannah. She has her hair in a braid, and a few stray pieces are falling into her freckled covered face. My fingers twitch in my pocket to reach out and push them away for her.

"Earl, are you having any pain anywhere?" Hannah asks as she takes a set of vitals.

"Nope," Gramps states. "Though my heart hurts a little."

"Your heart?" she asks, grabbing her stethoscope to listen. My own heart rate picks up. Why didn't he say anything sooner? Is his pacemaker not working? "Are you having any shortness of breath?"

"No, I'm fine. My heart hurts knowing that Tommy is

lonely," Gramps says with a dramatic sigh, clutching at his chest.

I groan, pinching the bridge of my nose. "Gramps, you can't joke about your heart."

He waves me off. "Pish posh. I just want my grandson to find someone. Say, Hannah is it?" he asks, pointing at her name badge.

Hannah laughs a little uncomfortably. "Yes, that's my name."

"Are you single, Hannah? You'd be perfect for Tommy."

She coughs, and her cheeks flame red. "Gramps," I scold, widening my eyes at him and slashing a finger across my throat to try and get him to stop.

He simply chuckles, ignoring me. "It's okay if you're not. Do you have any single friends, or a sister, perhaps?"

Hannah chokes on a soft laugh. "My sister is married, and I don't have many friends, Earl."

"Does that mean you'll volunteer?"

"Jesus, Gramps." I rub my face. "You can ignore him, Hannah."

Thankfully, Miles saves us both from this awkward interaction. "Well, Earl, if you're not having any pain, should we help you get standing?"

"Yep," Gramps says as Hannah takes the blood pressure cuff off.

"Everything looks okay?" I ask her.

She turns to face me, a soft smile on her lips. "Yeah. His blood pressure is slightly elevated, but I think that could be from the stress of the fall. Once we get him settled in his chair, I'll check it again."

Miles and Hannah wrap a transfer belt around his waist and help him into a standing position, where he uses a walker to get over to his chair. He doesn't use his walker often, but maybe he should be using it more now. I get him a glass of water, and after a few minutes, Hannah checks his blood pressure, giving me a thumbs up when it's normal. Gramps declines any new pain with movement, which makes me feel better.

His fall could have been a lot worse, and it has been worse in the past, so I'm glad this was easily handled. "Gramps, I should get back out on the road. Call me if you need anything, okay?"

He waves me off. "I'll call your dad and bug him. Or I'll call one of your brothers. You're working."

I sigh. "I know, but still."

Hannah checks in with Gramps one last time before they pack up their things. I give Gramps a quick hug, and then leave him alone in his apartment. I hate leaving him, but I'll send one of my brothers over to sit with him. Maybe Jase can bring his girls over to spend some time with him.

I pull out my phone and send a message in the family group chat with an update, and already, my dad says he will head over. I let out a sigh of relief and tuck my phone away.

"Thanks guys," I tell Hannah and Miles as we reach the ambulance and my vehicle.

Hannah smiles, her cheeks turning pink. "It's our job, Thomas."

"I know, but still. Thanks for putting up with him asking all about your personal life." I wave a hand. "He can be... a lot, but he means well."

She shakes her head. "It was sweet. My grandma is the same with me."

"Glad to know I'm not alone."

Miles claps me on the shoulder. "I'm happy he's okay. The last call I had with him as a patient was not a good one."

I swallow the sudden lump in my throat. "Nope, that was not a good day."

"He came back strong though," Miles replies.

"Yes he did." The memory of seeing Gramps in the hospital after brain surgery assaults my mind. I never want to see him like that again. I know he's getting up there in age, but in my mind, he's going to live forever, even though that might not be the case.

"We should probably get going," Miles states, gesturing to the front of the ambulance.

"Same. I'll see you guys at the next one," I state, offering them both a wave.

I'll likely see them again today, or in the next day on another call. Starting the day off with Gramps falling was not ideal, but I think once I get my head back into gear, I can get a feel for Hannah.

Gramps definitely interfered a bit, but who knows, maybe it will work in my favor?

I SPEND the rest of the day secretly hoping for a medical call so I have the chance to see Hannah again, and when one doesn't come, my spirits fall a bit. For a second, I think that maybe my superhero underwear has lost its touch, but then, I realize that the day isn't over yet.

I pull into the driveway as my idea fully forms in my head. If I can start a conversation with her, who knows where it will go? Grabbing my phone from the center console, I start a new message to her.

ME

Hey Hannah

I wanted to say I was sorry for my Gramps earlier. He can be a lot, but he really does mean well.

I wait for a beat, hoping she responds right away. She doesn't, but I don't let my hope fade. She's probably just getting home from work too, and might not be on her phone.

It was a long day today, I had a meeting with Henry, and they're considering bringing in the FBI for the drug trafficking investigation. We have a few guys who are also in training for some undercover work, so it seems like things are finally happening with the investigation.

I feed Arson and stare at my phone sitting on the kitchen counter, almost willing it to buzz with a new message. A few more minutes go by until my phone finally buzzes.

HANNAH

No need to apologize, really. He's adorable.

Okay, *breathe*. No need to panic or get too excited. I need to keep her talking. It's been a long time since I've talked with a woman I'm interested in, so I'm out of my game.

ME

He's the best.

I try to come up with something else to say, but she responds quickly, the bubbles appearing and another message taking their place before I have a second to think of something,

HANNAH

He seems like it.

Time to change the subject, keep her talking.

ME

How was the rest of your day?

The bubble appears and disappears a few times as I change out of my work clothes and into a pair of sweats. I flop down onto the couch as I wait for a message back.

Either she's typing a novel, or she doesn't know what to say. In the times I've interacted with her, she's pretty tight-lipped, so maybe she just doesn't know what to say.

HANNAH

It was fine. We had a stroke code, and a few other calls, but nothing too bad. You?

I let out a sigh of contentment. She's keeping the conversation open.

ME

Lots of traffic stops. Pulled over one of my teachers from elementary school for going seventy in a fifty-five today. That was a blast from the past.

HANNAH

I bet that was funny. Did you give them a ticket?

ME

Had to. She got a warning a week ago from a different cop, in the same spot.

HANNAH

Are you serious?! You would think she'd learn

ME

Definitely not

I have a lot of repeat offenders, believe it or not

Holy crap. It's working. She's talking to me. Granted, it's about work, but still. How can I keep it going, maybe change the subject? Maybe I should ask about her sister. She said she was married earlier, didn't she?

Arson climbs onto the couch, plopping his head into my lap and snuggling in. I offer him a few head scratches while waiting for Hannah to reply.

HANNAH

We have a few frequent flyers too, they call any time they breathe weird, or have a sniffle.

ME

Definitely the worst. I know I've seen some stuff in my time, but you guys see way worse.

HANNAH

Weirdly, I've gotten used to it.

ME

Same.

Now's the time. Change the subject, keep the conversation going.

---

## 7

# HANNAH

**W**hy is Thomas texting me? My heart flutters steadily in my chest as I read over our messages thus far. I thought the conversation was at a natural end, but he just sent another text.

THOMAS

> Ivy Days is next weekend. Are you going to
> go to any of the events?

My stomach swoops. Why is he asking? The little voice in the back of my mind reminds me not to overthink it. I've always wanted a reason to go to more events at Ivy Days, but always talked myself out of it, besides the craft fair with my grandma.

ME

> Maybe? My Grandma likes to go to the
> craft fair, so I'll probably take her. I'm also a
> bit of an old lady and like the craft fair as
> well, and antiques. I don't typically go to
> the street dance or anything, though.

THOMAS

You should. It's a good time. Even if you go just for the band. You don't even have to dance.

I swallow the lump in my throat.

ME

Maybe. I'll think about it.

Let's be honest. I won't go, even if I want to. I would love to go to the street dance with him. It sounds like fun, I just don't know if I would actually be able to go. My brain might shut down, tell me lies about myself, and make it so I'm too anxious to go.

It's happened anytime I've tried to go on a date. Once, I tried to meet up with a guy who was super nice. We'd been talking for a few weeks after matching on a dating app, and he invited me to coffee.

I was so anxious that I got so nauseous I puked on the way there. I had to pull over and throw up on the side of the road. I got vomit in my hair. I called Julia sobbing, and bailed on the date, asking for a rain check as I wasn't feeling well. He ghosted me the next week. I get it. It's not fun to be bailed on at the last minute, and he probably thought I was lying.

THOMAS

Seriously, I hear the band is super good this year.

I can be your dancing buddy

This is escalating way too fast. Is he asking me on a date? There's no way. He's probably simply being friendly. Even if I think Thomas is hot as hell, there's no way I could ever have a shot with him.

Crap, and now I've been staring at my screen for so long, he probably thinks I forgot to reply, or am ignoring him. Do I flirt? I don't know how to flirt. Maybe I need to call Julia.

ME

Haha, I'm sure it's fun 😊

That was chill, right? Kind of a non-answer? Oh, who am I kidding? I need my sister. I swipe out of the messages with Thomas, and open Julia's contact, calling her. I put the call on speaker and wait. Thankfully, she answers on the third ring.

"Hey, Han, what's up?" her familiar voice chimes.

"Oh thank god," I breathe. "I need help."

"What's going on? Is Grandma okay?" Instantly, her voice grows wary.

"She's fine." I wave off her words. "I don't even know what's happening right now, but Thomas Cunningham is texting me, and I need help interpreting the messages."

"He's texting you?" she shrieks, her voice growing louder with each word.

"Yes! Now, shut up so I can read you these messages."

"Okay, okay," she says, lowering her voice and listening as I read our conversation thus far.

The bubbles appear again as I reach the bottom message, the one I sent most recently. "He's replying," I say with an anxious whine.

"Han, I totally think he's interested in you!"

"No!" I shriek. "He's not. I need you to help figure out what he's doing, because why would he randomly be texting me?"

Julia takes a deep breath, and the exhale sends static through the line. "He's interested in you, Han. He has to be.

I know I don't have much experience with men, but I really think that's what it is."

"Oh god, he replied," I state, bile rising in my throat as I view the message.

THOMAS

> It's a blast. But I'm sure it would be more fun if you were there! We could invite people from the station too, if you didn't want it to be only us.

I read the message back to Julia. "See, he's not interested. He's just being a friendly guy."

"Orrrr, he's trying to make sure you're comfortable. He might have caught on to the fact that you get a little nervous around people."

"A *little* nervous is putting it lightly," I say, with a hint of snark.

"Maybe you should talk to Kimberly about this," Julia says, referring to my therapist. "She will be more help than I am."

I groan. "I know, but I need help right now, and my next appointment isn't for another week, Jules."

"Okay, okay," she concedes.

"What do I say back?"

"Well, do you want to go to the street dance with him?"

I pause for a moment. "I think I do," I respond. "But Julia, I can't go alone."

"Let me check the calendar. Maybe Tiff and I can come down for the weekend."

"Oh god, that would be amazing," I breathe, some of my anxiety lessening. "Wait, what should I say?"

"Tell him you will go. You can do this, Hannah. You'll

regret it if you don't. Even if he wants to see you as a friend, this will be so good for you. Exposure therapy, remember?"

I take a deep breath. "Right. Okay, I can do this." I type out my response.

ME

That would be fun. Could I invite my sister and sister-in-law, too?

His reply is almost instant.

THOMAS

Of course, the more the merrier! I'm sure my brothers will be there with their significant others.

I let out a sigh of relief. If Julia and Tiff are there, then maybe I can do this. I just need someone by my side. Right?

ME

Great, it sounds like fun.

THOMAS

I think it will be.

8

———

## THOMAS

The superhero underwear did their job after all. Talking with Hannah that little bit was enough to make me feel on top of the world. However, I know this, I'm not wearing my special underwear until that night though. Gotta save their power for the good stuff.

There's still a week before the street dance, but I want to talk to her more, maybe even see her again before then. I debated whether or not to keep texting her after last night, but I can't help it. I want to talk to her more, show her I'm interested in her. I've just finished my shift, and am sitting on the couch when I send her another text.

ME

Hey, Hannah. How was your day?

I fiddle with a loose string on my sweatpants, feeling oddly nervous as I wait for a response. I shouldn't be nervous, yet I am. Ever since I opened myself to the idea of a relationship, of the potential of something more in my life after nearly giving up hope, I let myself dream for a moment, and it's her. She's all I can think about.

HANNAH

It was good. I had the day off, so I ran a
few errands, and took my Grandma to an
appointment. What about you?

I smile as I read her message. It's nothing special, but it's a conversation.

ME

Work, thankfully not too busy of a day. Now
I'm snuggled up on the couch with my
bestie.

HANNAH

Your bestie?

I chuckle to myself. She probably thinks I'm curled up on the couch with one of my brothers or a guy from the department. I snap a photo of Arson as he lies on his back, sleeping with his stuffed bear in his mouth, and send it off to Hannah.

ME

He's pretty lazy when he's not on duty.

HANNAH

Oh my god, I can't get over how cute he is.

ME

He's a lover, that's for sure, but he knows
how to protect, too.

HANNAH

He must have had a busy day today if he's
that tired.

ME

Nah, I threw the ball for him in my backyard
for like thirty minutes. That burnt his energy
real quick.

HANNAH

How long have you had him?

ME

Since he was a pup and in training. He's always been there for me.

I look down at my dog again, thankful that I've had him to fill some of the void of loneliness for the last five years.

HANNAH

Do you have any other pets?

Fuck, I'm so happy she's actually continuing the conversation.

ME

Nope, just him. Though, I think he'd be fine if I got a cat or something. My sister-in-law, Josie, has a cat, and he loves her. Do you have any pets?

HANNAH

Nope, but I always wanted a dog. We never had one when I was a kid, and then after my parents died it would have been hard on my Grandma to care for a pet, and me. Now, I don't have the time. Trying to train a puppy while working twelve-hour shifts sounds difficult. Maybe someday, though.

ME

You can borrow Arson if you want. He's potty trained, and a great cuddler.

HANNAH

Haha, I'm sure he would much rather stay with you, but thanks for the offer.

ME

I'm serious

Sometimes, my brother Jason will take him for a few hours, and his daughters will run him ragged and then he curls up on the couch with them for hours during their princess movie nights. It's adorable.

HANNAH

I'm sure it is, but it's okay, thanks for the offer

ME

Next time we end up on a call, I'll make sure you get some Arson loving.

HANNAH

I'd like that

I try to think of something else to bring up, to continue the conversation, but I'm drawing a blank. I can't think of anything. I'm about to start looking up conversation starters on the internet, when the bubbles appear on the screen again.

HANNAH

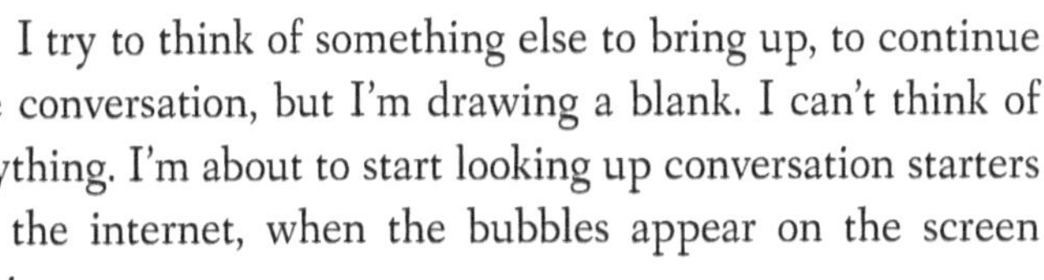

Do you work tomorrow?

Hmm. Do I flirt? Or do I be normal? Maybe a mix of both.

ME

Sure do. Why? You want to see me?

HANNAH

Oh, um, I was curious if I'd see you out and about. I work days.

ME

Yep, I work days too. Not that I'd ever wish something bad to happen to someone, but maybe I'll get to see you tomorrow. Cause I want to see you.

There isn't an answer for a long few minutes, and I worry I've gone too far. I can't seem to get a read on her, on what might be too far, or just enough. I'm a natural flirt, and I'm holding myself back a bit, not wanting to scare her away.

HANNAH

I'd never wish bad on someone either, but I'd like to see you too.

I throw my fist in the air when her message comes through. Hell yes.

# HANNAH

Oh god, did I really send that message? I'm so nauseous. Is this what flirting feels like? The constant urge to vomit and pass out all at once while butterflies swirl in your stomach and your heart races? Or maybe this is a new kind of anxiety attack that I've never experienced before. That could be it.

"Hannah, breathe," my sister reminds me through FaceTime. After Thomas sent the message about wanting to see me, I started to panic. As only a big sister can, she helped me through it, and even helped me flirt a little bit back. If that's considered flirting.

Thomas hasn't replied yet. It's been over a minute. His responses are usually pretty much instant, so why is it taking so long? Did I do it wrong?

"He hasn't responded," I tell her, my voice shaking in my anxiety.

"Maybe he went to the bathroom," she says.

"Or maybe it was too much!" I shriek. "I am not built for this, Julia. This is why I don't date."

"There's no way that was too much," Julia says with a scoff. "That was tame compared to most flirting."

My phone buzzes, falling over from where it was resting on my water bottle.

THOMAS

We can't wait to—hopefully—see you tomorrow.

My breath catches in my throat when a picture of him and Arson comes through with the text. His blonde hair is tousled over his forehead, a few pieces hanging in his eyes, and his blue eyes are bright with excitement. My favorite part of the photo though, is the goofy grin he's wearing, showing me two of my favorite features of his, his dimples and the gap in his teeth.

He's so hot and so adorable all at the same time that I have to take a few seconds to compose myself.

"Han? You're blushing. Like, way more than normal. You good?" Julia rambles in the background as I stare at the photo. "Oh my god, did he send a dick pic? Is that what you're staring at? I will kill him."

"What?" I shriek. "No, he didn't send a dick pic! It was a picture of him and Arson, and it's... Julia, he's so cute," I groan, flopping onto my couch.

"Have you replied?" she asks, her voice at a much calmer level now.

"No, what do I say?"

"That he looks cute, exactly what you told me."

"I can't say that!" My heart rate climbs again.

"Yes, you can! Get your flirt on, girl!"

I groan, throwing my arm over my eyes. "I feel sick."

"You're dramatic."

"Yeah, well so are you," I retort.

"Where do you think you got it from?" she teases. I flick off the camera, and grab the phone again. I swipe out of the photo, giving it one more stare as it gets smaller in the text thread.

I take a deep breath, and type.

ME

Fingers crossed. I can't decide who's cuter, though, you, or Arson. 😌

I hit send before I can think twice about it, and swallow the bile rising in my throat. This shouldn't be this hard. It's a good thing I'm seeing my therapist soon.

Like before, his reply is quick.

THOMAS

Arson, definitely. 😄

After talking with Julia for a few minutes, and a few more messages with Thomas, I decide I can take it from here. We hang up, and Thomas and I spend the next hour texting back and forth about nonsensical things. It gets easier with each message that I send, and I start to think that maybe I can do this. Maybe I can go to the street dance and dance with him.

## 10

# HANNAH

In the week since Thomas sent me the photo of him and Arson and I tried my hand at flirting, we've been texting every day. It's mostly been casual, some flirting here and there, but nothing too crazy. Somehow, we haven't seen each other in person since then either.

I'm ashamed to admit that I'm worried it will be much easier to talk to him over text than it will be in person. The thought of seeing him in person, having to hope that the interest from him transfers from over the phone into real life is daunting. I spiral every time I think about it.

There was a day this week when police were on scene to assist during an accident, but Thomas was called away before we could do more than wave at each other. Now, we've been working opposite shifts. I'm coming off a stretch of three night shifts, and I'm absolutely exhausted, but I forced myself out of bed so I can take Grandma to the craft fair and then head to the Ivy Days street dance.

I'm hoping that the time with Grandma will help calm me, because right now, I'm not doing well. Poor Julia has been the recipient of many frantic texts, but I don't want to bother her today. She's working most of the morning, and then she and Tiff are coming down for the weekend, mainly as moral support for the street dance tonight.

"Sweetie, what do you think of this?" Grandma asks, pulling me out of my internal thoughts. She's holding a handmade oven mitt in her palm for me to see.

"That's cute," I state, but I'm not really focused on it.

"I think it would look nice with my fall decor," she says, adding it to the pile of things she plans to buy from the vendor.

"I agree." She has already asked me twice if I'm feeling anxious, and I felt bad, but I had to lie to her. She always sees right through me, and I don't think I'm ready to tell her that Thomas has been texting me, and how I'm not totally sure what that means.

Once she pays and has her items in a small brown bag, we continue to make our way through the fair. A few rows down, a sudden floral smell overtakes my senses. It's not too strong, but enough to draw my attention to it. Grandma tells me she's going to look around by herself, and she will meet me at the front in a bit. I wander toward the smell of the flowers as soon as I'm alone.

A pink tent stands over the booth with a large variation of flowers and stems in buckets. Josie Cunningham stands in the center of the tables, talking with another fair-goer. When she sees me lingering at the front of the booth, she offers me a smile and a wave, holding up a finger to let me know it will be a moment.

I've met Josie a few times since she opened up her business here, and she's always been so nice every time I stop into her store to get an arrangement for Grandma.

I look around at all the different flowers she has, leaning down to smell some of them. She has a "build your own bouquet" section, complete with ribbons and vases as well.

Josie looks absolutely gorgeous. She's wearing a light blue sundress that accentuates her baby bump. Her red hair is tied up in a ponytail off her neck, and she has a beautiful pregnancy glow to her. From what I've heard, she's due with her and her husband's first baby sometime at the end of next month. I couldn't be happier for them. I remember hearing about their love story too. She moved to town and opened her business, and shortly after, got set up for a blind date photoshoot with Andrew, and the rest is history.

I'm lost in my thoughts as I look at the flowers in her booth, until there's a tap on my shoulder. "Hey, Hannah, right?" Josie asks. I turn to face her, and she's wearing a light-hearted smile.

I smile back, and can already feel the heat rising in my cheeks. Like clockwork, the social interaction with someone new, even though we've met a few times makes my cheeks flush a deep cherry red. "That's me," I say, chuckling awkwardly as I wave.

"Thomas told us you're joining us tonight at the street dance?" she questions. It takes me by surprise that Thomas has told his family about me, for some reason. I get the sense they're close, so it shouldn't.

"I am," I confirm, twisting my hands together.

"And your sister, too?"

"Yes, she and her wife are coming after they finish work."

"Great, it will be so nice to meet them as well!" Josie smiles, her eyes bright.

A new voice appears from behind us. "Petals, they ran out of deep-fried Oreos, but I got you a funnel cake with ice cream on it, instead."

Josie turns, her face lighting up at the sight of her husband carrying a plate with a huge funnel cake toward us. "Thank you, honey," she says, reaching for the plate and stretching on her tip-toes to kiss his cheek.

Andrew turns his cheek so her lips land on his, and they kiss. I turn my gaze away, feeling like I've intruded on their moment. I distract myself with a green leaf from one of the eucalyptus stems beside me.

"Anyway," Josie says, pulling my attention back to her. She sits down at one of the tables she has, and directs a small portable fan on her. "Thomas was saying how excited he is to see you tonight."

I can't help the smile from spreading across my lips, and I look at my feet. My heart thumps loudly in my ears. Despite hearing it straight from Josie, it doesn't stop the self-deprecating words from playing in my mind, or flying out of my mouth. "I'm sure he was just saying that."

Andrew is the one to respond. "Thomas has never been one to 'just say' anything." I lift my eyes from my feet to him.

Their features are so similar, yet so different. They have the same shape of eyes and nose, but their eye color, hair, and body type are completely different. Andrew is muscular, his arms toned from his work as a woodworker, but Thomas is broad. He's thick, his biceps toned and strong, much like the rest of his body. At the same time, he's soft, someone I'd love to rest my head on and fall into the comfort of his body.

I shake myself free of thinking of Thomas's body. I should not be doing that when speaking to his brother and sister-in-law.

"Right," I say, though I'm still not so sure I believe him. He's shown me that he's interested, but my own issues make it so hard for me to believe that Thomas has an interest in *me*.

My name is called from the booth across, and Grandma is waving me over. "I uh—" I gesture to my grandma. "I have to go. I'll see you guys later."

Andrew and Josie say goodbye while I head toward Grandma. I take a deep breath as I approach her, and she shows me a quilt one of her friends made. I try to calm my racing heart and wipe my sweaty palms on the front of my shorts as I start to overthink my outfit. It's four now, so there's only three hours before we're supposed to meet. I didn't think this through. I should go home, shower, and make sure I'm not sweaty and stinky after walking around in the heat with Grandma.

My phone buzzes in my back pocket, interrupting my internal crash out.

THOMAS

Looking forward to tonight. Make sure you've got your dancing shoes on, freckles.

Oh god, oh god. Okay, *breathe*, Hannah. I need to calm myself. "Grandma?" I turn to her, and she offers me a smile.

"Ready to go, sweetie? I think I have everything I need." *How does she always know?* Ever since I was a kid, she's been the one to know I'm overwhelmed from being in a crowded space or with new people, sometimes before I even realize.

"Yes, please," I murmur, running a hand through my hair.

I CAN'T DO THIS. I'm still panicking. Julia is set to arrive any minute, and it's a good thing, because I'm about thirty seconds from convincing myself I'm not going. I'm sitting on my bed, my bath towel wrapped around me. I've been staring into space since I got out of the shower ten minutes ago , my mind whirling with all the things that could go wrong tonight. I mentally tick off the list in my mind.

First, he could see me.

I mean, it's a pretty real fear. He could see me, realize he, in fact, does not want to spend time with me, realize that I'm not as pretty as he might have thought, and look the other way, pretending that I don't exist.

Talk about humiliating.

Second, he could try to touch me again. What if he hugs me and it's awkward? Oh god, he could try to kiss me.

Now, that could be a good thing, unless I panic puke on him, then in that case, it would be very, very bad.

Third, I could forget how to speak.

I could turn into a jumbled mess, and he might think I'm having a stroke. He'd call 911, and all our co-workers would come, and then I'd be more embarrassed.

Knocking on my front door halts my thoughts. "Coming!" I call, rising from the bed and stumbling to my front door. I unlock the deadbolt, pull the door open, and throw myself into my sister's arms.

"I can't do this," I say, my voice coming out shaky.

Julia sighs as she tightens her arms. "Yes, you can. We are here for you, but I promise you, Hannah, you can." I exhale a heavy breath as a hand rubs up and down my back. Tiff is here too, thank goodness.

"Come on, sis. Let's go get you dressed," Tiff says, her voice soothing.

Julia pulls back, resting her hands on my shoulders after she brushes my hair from my face. "You've got this."

They lead me back into my bedroom where my closet has all but thrown up on my bed. Clothes are strewn everywhere in my attempt to find an outfit for tonight, because what I had on earlier is not working. Nothing else I tried on worked either. I feel too frumpy. I can see too many of my rolls.

"I couldn't decide," I explain, gesturing at the pile.

"I can see that," Julia replies, already pulling out a few items. "Sit." She gestures to my bed.

"Your hair looks great," Tiff says. "I love how you curled it."

I reach up to tuck a hair behind my ear. I curled my blonde hair and threw it into a half-down, half-up bun, with a few pieces hanging out to frame my face. "Thanks."

"Now, we want to go for comfort and cute, since you're going to be dancing," she eyes me expectantly, like she knows I want to protest, "and it's warm out."

She pulls a light-purple sundress from the pile. "What about this?"

I shake my head. "I don't want my thighs to chafe, and my undershorts ripped last week."

She tosses it aside. "Veto." She picks up another item, a pair of light wash denim shorts, and a lavender bodysuit with a scoop-neck tee that I bought on impulse, but have never worn. "This is perfect."

I shake my head, reaching out to grab it from her. "No, I don't even know why I have that."

"At least try it on," Julia says, holding it up above her head as I continue to reach. "If you totally hate it, then we will veto it, but you bought it for a reason."

I sigh, stopping my attempts to grab it. "Fine." I thrust out my hand to grab the outfit from her, and shoo both her and Tiff from my room while I change. Once I finagle the buttons closed at the crotch and slide it up and over my hips and shoulders, I pull the shorts up, buttoning them over my belly button.

When I look at myself in the mirror, my first instinct is to start picking out the things I hate about the outfit. It's too tight, you can see every roll in my stomach and back, my fupa is outlined in the shorts, you can see the cellulite on my thighs, but then I stop.

Instead, I try to do what I've been working on in therapy. I admire myself. I look great in purple, it brings out the blue in my eyes. The shorts fit me perfectly, and even make it look like I have a little bit of an ass, something that usually is flat. My cleavage looks great too, the scoop neck offering a hint more than normal, but I'm not mad about it.

I rest my hands on my hips and take a deep breath. Yes, I like this. Especially if I throw on my white high-top Chucks. It's a basic outfit, nothing fancy, but it's comfortable and cute, exactly what I need for tonight.

I open the door, and Julia and Tiff stand there waiting. They both smile when they see me, but Tiff is the first to speak. "Yeah, you're wearing that."

"Agreed," Julia states.

I let out a sigh, and nod. "I like it."

"Now, you just need a little mascara to make your lashes pop, and you're perfect," Tiff says, heading into the bathroom. "No need for more. We can't hide your freckles."

I smile, the good kind of butterflies fluttering in my

stomach as I think about how Thomas has called me "freck-les" more than once now.

"No, we can't," I agree. I'm still terrified for tonight, but a good outfit and having my sister and her wife being my hype women helps.

## 11

## THOMAS

Fuck, I'm excited for tonight.

I roll the lint roller over my light blue cotton shirt and khaki shorts, silently cursing my dog for shedding as much as he does. I swear, I could brush him four times a day, and he'd still shed enough fur to make a whole other dog. I have on my favorite pair of Spider-Man underwear in preparation. Gotta have all the luck I can get tonight.

I look back to where Arson is lying in his dog bed, saying a quick goodbye before I'm out the door.

On the drive over, I think about tonight. Sure, it's probably not a true first date even though I'd like it to be, but it's a start. I can tell that Hannah is a bit skittish, but I want to show her that I'm nothing to be afraid of. I want to be there for her.

I send her a text letting her know that I'm on my way, even though it's a less than five-minute drive to my brother Jason's brewery, where the street dance is being hosted on Main Street.

When I find a parking spot and climb out, I'm greeted by the sight of Marley and Beau getting out of their vehicle as well. They cross the street toward me, holding hands. "Hey guys," I say, leaning in to offer them each a half hug.

"Hey you," Marley responds. "Excited for tonight?"

I don't hold back the immediate grin that slides onto my face. "Yep. I think this could be good."

Marley squeezes my arm. "I think so too. I'm excited to spend some time with her, get to know her. Though, we won't impede on you getting to know her. That's the priority."

"Thanks, Mar." Marley is the best little sister. I mean, she's technically not my real sister per se, but before she and Beau finally became more than best friends and got pregnant with the twins, she grew up next door to us, and has always been around. Andrew, Jason and I have always called her our sister, but Beau never did. It makes sense why, though. He's been in love with her since the start. Now, they get to have their happy ending.

"Jason and Fallon are coming, right?" I ask, pulling my phone out to check if I have any missed messages from them. "The grandparents are watching all the kids tonight?"

"Yep. When we dropped the twins off at your mom and dad's, Presley and Lennie were already there, dressed in their princess gowns," Marley says. "It was adorable. They had little tiaras ready for Ariel, and even grabbed one for Arlo when he wanted to join. The babies didn't even care that we were leaving."

"Well, that's fucking adorable," I say as we slowly approach the barricaded area on the street outside of the brewery where the band will be and the dance is held. Out of the corner of my eye, I spot Jason and Fallon sitting with Josie and Andrew at one of the patio tables. Thankfully, it's big enough for our group plus Hannah and her sisters when she arrives. Raising my hand to wave,

I head that way while Marley and Beau get drinks from the bar.

My eyes scan the area as it becomes more crowded, searching for her face somewhere in the sea of people.

"Dude, sit down, you're making me nervous," Andrew remarks, gesturing to an empty seat beside me.

"I can't," I reply. "I want to see when she gets here." I'm also antsy and feel like I need to move.

"I have never seen you like this before," Josie says. "It's cute. She was nervous today too."

I jerk my eyes from the crowd to Josie, who is sitting with her feet in Andrew's lap, rubbing her bump.

"She was?" I ask.

"Yep. She stopped by my booth today at the fair. I told her how excited you were for tonight, and she couldn't seem to believe it."

"Why not?"

Josie shrugs. "Who knows? She thought maybe it was something you were just saying, that you didn't really mean it."

I shake my head. "I mean it. I mean, I barely know her, but I can already tell, she's a great person. We've been texting, and we have so many things in common. She's such a sweet girl that I get excited every time her name comes across my screen."

"I agree," Josie says. "We told her that you don't say things like that lightly, and that seemed to help."

I don't get to respond because at the edge of the crowd, I see her. Fuck, she looks beautiful. Her hair is framing her round face, her purple top hugging her curves and lighting up her bright blue eyes. Those eyes catch mine from across the patio and it's like I'm pulled to her. My feet carry me through the tables toward her. Hannah's face is red as she talks to her sister, Julia, who I recognize from high school. Another woman, who I assume is Julia's wife, stands on her other side.

When I reach her, I barely glance at Julia and her wife, only to greet them half heartedly. I only have my attention on Hannah now.

"Hey," I say, losing myself in her gaze.

"Hi," she says, her voice shaking.

I'm at a loss for words, completely in awe of her. "You look beautiful."

Her cheeks adorably grow more red at my words and I want to reach up and cup her cheeks to soothe the heat.

Hannah looks down at her feet. "Thanks, but it's nothing special. It's just something I had in my closet."

I reach out and lightly grasp her forearm. "Hannah, you're something special. You look beautiful. You'd look beautiful in a paper sack if that's what you wanted to wear."

Her eyes grow wide as she looks up at me. She clears her throat. "Thank you. You look really nice, too." She gestures to me with her free arm.

"Thanks, freckles," I reply. I'm glad she didn't cover her freckles with makeup tonight. I love seeing them. I turn my gaze to the rest of the world again, seeing that her sisters have stepped aside, giving us a moment. "Should we introduce everyone?"

Hannah nods, and I move my hand from where I was holding her arm to slide down, and offer her my hand. She hesitantly takes it, and I lead her toward our table, waving her sisters over to join us. Internally, I'm cheering. She's holding my hand, and it feels incredible. "I hear the band is good," I say as we walk, trying to make easy small talk with her.

"Are they local?" Hannah asks, glancing at the banner as they set up.

"I'm not sure," I say, shrugging. "We will have to ask Jason, he's the one that hired them."

"Oh, he did? I suppose that makes sense, since it's his brewery."

"Do you want something to drink?" I gesture to the bar with my free hand.

Hannah shakes her head. "I'm really not a drinker, to be honest. I'll have one every once in a while, but I don't like the way it makes me feel, or the taste."

"Fair enough. How about water or something?"

"I brought my emotional support water bottle," Hannah says, gesturing to her sister. "Julia is holding it in her bag for me."

"Perfect," I reply as we reach the table. My siblings are all smiles as they take in my hand holding hers. Julia and her wife step up beside Hannah.

I introduce Hannah to each of my siblings and their partners, even though I'm pretty sure she knows them, and vice versa. Julia introduces her and her partner, Tiff, and they head off to get a drink at the bar.

I reluctantly let go of Hannah's hand and pull out a chair for her and she sits stiffly, a nervous energy surrounding her. She folds her hands into her lap as she turns to face me when I sit down beside her.

"How has work been?" she asks.

I shake my head. "We aren't going to talk about work."

"W—we aren't?" she stutters over her words. I shift in my chair so I'm closer to her.

"Nope. We talk about work every day we have texted, and when we are at work. I want to learn more about you, Han. I've watched you for over a year now, and finally got the nerve to talk to you, so I want to talk to you about anything but work."

She inhales sharply as I lean in, her breasts rising with the intake of breath. I glance around the table to see if anyone is watching us, but my siblings are all engrossed in their own conversations, and Julia and Tiff are back at the table, sitting by Jason and Fallon, in deep discussion about the beer and seltzer he makes.

"Uh—" Hannah stops, taking a deep breath. "Do you like cheese?"

I pause, my mind going blank at the unexpected question before it hits me.

**D**id I just ask him if he liked cheese? Oh, holy shit I did. It was the first thing I could think of, and now I'm going to have to explain the plot of an early 2000's rom-com to him.

It doesn't help that I've already been awkward. I didn't know what to say when he complimented me or grabbed my hand, which felt amazing. How can a simple touch light my insides on fire?

The blank stare on Thomas's face makes me cringe.

"Are you—" he pauses. "Did you just quote *She's The Man?*" His brows raise and the dimples appear on his cheeks.

"You know that movie?"

"*My favorite's gouda,*" he quotes.

"Oh my god," I say with a small laugh. "I can't believe you know that movie, and quote."

Thomas gestures over to Marley. "It's one of Mar's favorite movies, so she made us watch it all the time."

"It's one of mine too. It's so funny. I don't even know

why I said that. I couldn't think of anything to say, and it slipped out."

"I mean, I thought it was pretty great," Thomas says, his lips curving into a smile.

I take a deep breath and decide to be honest. "I'm not going to lie. I've been super nervous about this."

Thomas reaches over and takes my hand. "How come?" He squeezes my palm gently, and instead of spurring my nerves, it helps to calm me.

"I'm not good at this," I say, letting out a breath. "Meeting up with new people is hard for me. I mean technically, you aren't new—I've known you for a while—but I don't *know you*, know you. Does that make sense?"

"I think so," he replies. "What can I do to make this easier for you?"

"You're doing it. My social anxiety can be really hard for me, but I'm working on it with my therapist, and I'm getting better. Things that used to be hard, I can do now, no problem. Exposure therapy is hard, but worth it."

"Did I pressure you into tonight?" Thomas asks, the worry evident in his voice.

I shake my head. "No, you didn't. I'm not going to lie and say I didn't freak out a bit, but it helped that I could bring my sister." Thomas glances over to Julia, still talking with his brother.

"I'm not good at... dating." I quickly stumble over my next words. "Not that this is a date or anything. I didn't mean to assume that."

Thomas squeezes my hand. "Hannah, this is a date. You aren't assuming anything. Maybe I should have been more clear about it, but if you're okay with it, then that's what this is."

My mouth goes dry at his words, and I nod, unable to speak.

"Good," he says. "We can take this at whatever pace you need, but Hannah, I've been dying to get to know you, and I can't wait to see where this goes."

I nod again, still lost for words.

From behind us, the band starts playing a classic rock song, and people rush to the street to start dancing. Thomas lets go of my hand and rises to his feet. My heart thumps wildly in my chest as he stands before me. He holds the same hand out to me. "What do you say, freckles, want to dance?"

Tentatively, I slide my palm into his, reveling in the warmth and steadiness that he provides, and agree. He pulls me to my feet and leads me onto the street, where the crowd has already started to grow with each passing second.

I've never been to a street dance before, but I understand why people love them so much. The joy and excitement is intoxicating. Everyone is happy, singing along to the classic songs, and dancing their hearts out, whether it be with a partner, a group of friends, or by themselves.

"I'm not a great dancer," I admit as Thomas turns to face me.

"Neither am I, but that doesn't mean we can't have fun," he says, and the grin that follows makes me shiver. His sparkling blue eyes focus only on me as we reach the opposite edge of the crowd. Thomas drops my hand, and slowly slides his hand around my waist, resting on my hip as he pulls me into him. Goosebumps scatter across my skin at the sensation of his hands on me, and I inhale sharply.

"Is this okay?" he asks, his eyes searching mine.

"Yes," I respond, trying to keep my breathing steady. With his other hand, he slides down the length of my arm to lift and rests my hand on his shoulder. Exhaling a shaky breath, I revel in the feel of his broad shoulder under my palm.

I let myself breathe for a moment and try to slow my racing, panicked heart. I can do this. I will not throw up. People do this every day. This is nothing. I'm just touching his shoulder, it's not like I'm sucking his dick, right?

Oh god, now I'm thinking about sucking his dick.

I clench my thighs to quell the sudden pulsing heat between them, and try to refocus on what is currently happening in front of me.

Thomas wraps me up in his embrace. My free hand flies up to his other shoulder, and just like that, we're wrapped in the other's arms. Thomas slowly begins to sway, all while staring into my eyes, keeping me captive with his beautiful eyes.

Thomas holds me close as he hums the old Journey song, every so often singing the lyrics lowly. He has a great voice, smooth with a hint of a rasp. It's perfect for the song, and all my focus fades into the lyrics of the song.

The song fades into a new one, this one slower. We move to the beat, our bodies growing closer and closer to each other. Our chests are pressed together, and my fingers link behind at the nape of his neck. My anxiety is shoved further down as I do what I can to stay present in this moment. I count down from five, slowing my breathing and closing my eyes to focus on the steady beat of his heart.

We dance for another song until Thomas notices Andrew waving us over. "The pizzas we ordered must be here," Thomas explains and sadly drops his hands from my waist. The loss of his touch saddens me more than I care to admit.

We head back to the table and sit down. My sister sits

beside me in an open chair, and I swallow down my nerves over eating in front of all these people. I shove the thoughts that they'll judge the amount I eat away, and take a slice of sausage pizza from one of the boxes.

Thomas sits beside me and takes a few slices for himself. We eat together while he peppers Julia with a few questions about what she's been up to since high school, and it sinks in how much older than me he is. I knew there was a nine-year gap between us, but it didn't truly hit until now.

Thomas rests his hand on my left thigh, his palm warm as I shiver from his touch. It's such a casual touch that I don't even think anything of it. I'm learning that he's a touchy guy. He's pretty much been touching me from the moment I got here.

I don't mind it, though. I thought it would stress me out or be too much, but with him, it feels comfortable.

After talking with everyone and finishing the last of the pizza, the band plays the opening notes of a ballad. Thomas squeezes my thigh. "Want to dance again?"

I nod, and we stand.

"We're going to hit the dance floor again if anyone wants to join," Thomas says to the group.

The table lets out a few yeses, and soon everyone is standing with their partners and heading to the dance floor. Watching all these happy couples gives me a pang of jealousy deep in my chest. I want the comfort of someone, and yes, Thomas is with me right now, but I can't let myself go fully into thinking we're already a couple or something. There's still that fear that he's going to let me go once he sees how much of a mess I am.

Thomas wraps his arms around me again as we merge into the sea of people, soothing my fears for now. We sway again, and this time, he pulls me into his chest. My ear is pressed against where his heart is, and I can hear the steady beating of his heart. Thomas bends his head down to rest on the crown of my head.

It's calming, and it helps me ground myself when I feel myself slipping into anxious thoughts. I close my eyes, soaking in this moment. When I open them, I spot Julia and Tiff a bit away from us, and they glance at me with sweet smiles.

Julia mouths, *"He really likes you."* Tiff nods in agreement.

I smile in return and close my eyes again. I can't believe I'm actually doing this, that this is finally happening.

We dance for a bit longer, pulling apart to dance to the more upbeat songs, and Julia steals me away from him when one of our favorite songs plays, and we jump and dance together, and that helps me loosen up even more.

At the end of the song, Julia embraces me in a hug. "If we leave, are you going to be okay?"

I nod. "Yes. Thank you so much for coming. I don't think I could have done it without you."

"Yes, you could have," Tiff says, pulling me from Julia's arms.

I shrug, not agreeing or disagreeing. "Either way, thank you."

A moment later, everyone joins us in the little circle we've created. "I think we're going to head out," Andrew says, gesturing to him and Josie. "Thanks for inviting us, Tommy."

The two men clap each other on the back, and Thomas hugs Josie, pressing a kiss to her cheek. Jason, Fallon, Marley and Beau follow suit, and everyone is saying their goodbyes a moment later. It's amazing to see how close they are as a family. I'm so thankful that I have Julia and Tiff, but as a kid I always wanted more siblings, some closer to my age. With how close in age they are, the four brothers had each other to lean on as kids, and it shows with how close they are now as adults.

"Do you want to stay for a bit longer?" Thomas asks, leaning down to whisper in my ear.

I think for a moment. "Yeah, maybe a few more songs?"

"Absolutely, freckles."

## 13

## THOMAS

I couldn't have asked for this night to go better. Sure, our first date might not be what others would prefer, what with having our families with us as more of a group date, but I think this was what we needed. And I've gotten plenty of one-on-one time with Hannah as it is.

When she told me about her social anxiety, it made things really start to click. I want to do what I can to make her comfortable with me and my family. I want to learn all about her.

Two songs later, I regretfully pull away from her. Having her in my arms for most of the night has been a dream. "Ready to go?" I ask, taking her hand in mine again.

I don't miss the way her body stiffens. I wasn't implying anything by my words, but I wonder if she thinks that I was.

"I can walk you to your car," I say, hoping to clear it up. Her body is still stiff, but some of the tension visibly eases.

"I'm on one of the side streets," Hannah says, pointing her free hand down the street.

"Thomas!" My name is called from across the street. I turn to see Henry, and slow my pace.

Looking down at Hannah, I ask, "Do you have a minute? I want to make sure everything is okay."

"Of course," she replies. "That's Henry Thorson, right? He's the detective they brought on to help with the trafficking situation?"

"Yeah. I've been working pretty closely on the case with him."

I keep Hannah's hand in mine as we walk toward Henry. "Hey, man," I greet him.

"Hey, I wanted to update you on something quick before your shift in the morning. I was going to call tonight when I got home, but then I saw you."

"Sure, what's up?"

Henry glances between Hannah and me. He widens his eyes at me. I reluctantly let go of Hannah's hand, immediately missing the feel of her. "Can you give us a minute, freckles?"

"No problem," she says, stepping aside and walking thirty feet down the sidewalk. I'm glad she's staying in my line of sight.

"What couldn't you tell me in front of Hannah?" I ask, honestly feeling a little irritated with my friend.

"We found a trail," he murmurs, eyes glancing around like he thinks someone is about to pop out from behind the buildings.

"What do you mean, a trail?"

"For the trafficking ring. We found the name of the leader."

My gut churns. This is the first lead we've had in months, and we have to take advantage of it. "Holy shit," I breathe, glancing behind him to check on Hannah.

"His name is Charles Cook, but he goes by Chaz.

Tomorrow, we're going to set up a game plan on how to infiltrate and take them down."

A renewed sense of motivation swirls inside of me. This is the break we've been waiting for. If we can arrest him, we can hopefully put a stop to the trafficking happening in the town. We've had more drug-related deaths in the last five years than ever before. I can't handle another teenager dying from an accidental overdose. They've been lacing their shit, killing these kids before they even have a chance to live.

I reach out, clapping his shoulder. "Finally," I breathe.

"It's not over yet," he states. "In some ways, this is only the beginning. Cut off one head, and two more will appear, or so they say. We're in for a long ride, my friend."

I offer him my hand. "Yeah, but we've got this."

"We do," he says. His brow is set in a determined line. "I'll let you get back to your night. Is that Hannah Pearson?"

I offer him a smile. "Sure is. If I have anything to say about it, she'll be my girl soon, so don't even think about it."

Henry chuckles. "Congrats man. I've met her a few times in the field. Nice girl."

I look at her again as she stands on the sidewalk waiting for me. "Yeah, she is."

Henry and I walk together to meet Hannah. "Thanks, Hannah," Henry says. "I'll let you get back to your evening." He offers us a parting wave, and turns down the side street, heading to his truck that I can see on the opposite side of the road.

"I'm down this road too," Hannah says.

I take her hand again. "I had a great time tonight."

With a deep breath, Hannah replies, "I did too. It was a lot of fun."

"Think I can convince you to do it again sometime?"

A hopefulness blooms in my chest, because fuck, I want to do this again. I want to spend all the time I can with her.

I catch the blush creeping up her neck, even in the low glow of the moonlight.

"Yeah, I think you could convince me," Hannah says with a smile. We arrive at a small silver sedan that must be hers. I don't want to let her go yet.

"This is me," she says, and I squeeze her palm a little tighter. My heart pounds in my chest. Fuck, I want to kiss her so bad right now. Is that going to be too much for her?

"Hannah," I breathe her name, my voice dropping an octave.

She lets out a breathy sound as she leans back against her car. "Thomas?"

I take a step closer to her, reaching out to rest my free hand on her hip. "Can I kiss you?"

She swallows thickly, her pupils dilating. She doesn't speak for a long moment, and I think she's going to turn me down. It would suck, but I would obviously respect her decision. Tonight has been a big night, and I'd rather not push her too far.

"Yes," she surprises me by saying. Her voice is shaky, and my hand on her hip trails up her body, to the base of her neck, then to cup her cheek.

"Are you sure?" I say, dropping her palm from my other hand. I move it so both hands cup her cheeks.

"Thomas, I need you to kiss me before I chicken out," Hannah replies, and I chuckle. Her palms rest on my chest, and I can barely feel the shaking in her hands.

She's so adorable.

I lean in, more ready than I've ever been in my life for a kiss. Our noses brush, and I can feel the faintest hint of her rapid breaths on my lips as I get closer. I'm about to press my lips to hers when I hear the shouting.

Hannah pulls away first, her breathing increasing even more. "What was that?"

I pull her into my chest, turning her so she's angled behind me. "I don't know. Stay behind me," I tell her.

The shouting gets louder and louder, the voices rising in pitch and anger with each word. I can't understand a word of it until I catch Henry's voice.

"Put your gun down!" he yells, and my heart drops.

"Hannah, get in your car and duck," I tell her, throwing open the backdoor and shoving her in. "I'll be right back."

"Thomas, wait!" She tries to stop me, but I can't. Something is going on, and I need to help Henry.

I reach around my body to grab my gun, and come out empty-handed. That's when I remember I chose to leave it at home tonight. Fuck. I should have at least brought Arson, he could take the fucker down.

I quietly close the door behind Hannah, glancing back to see her tucked into her backseat like I told her. Good girl.

Crouching down, I rush as fast as I can in the direction of Henry's vehicle. It's not lost on me that I'm making an idiotic decision. No gun, no protection of any kind, but I have to get to him, have to help in any way I can.

When I'm fifteen feet away, I see Henry standing with his arms held in surrender. His gun is in the holster on his hip. I take in the man in front of him, holding him at gunpoint. I slow my breathing and try to take in any features I can of the man with the gun. He's about five-foot-ten, wearing dirty blue jeans. Black work boots that are nearly ripped to shreds. White t-shirt that's ripped on the bottom corner, covered in dirt. He's got a black mask covering his face, no visible facial hair. Hair is hidden.

Caucasian, unable to see eye color. Snake tattoo on his right arm. I try to make out the words inked alongside the belly of the snake, but I can't. I'm too far away.

"This will teach your crew about getting too close to Chaz," the man says, his voice quieter now, no longer a yell. I know what's going to happen before it happens, and I stand, running toward Henry to throw him out of the way.

The gunshot is quicker than I am.

I watch the gun recoil in his hand, and the shot hits Henry before I can take two steps. Henry drops to the ground, clutching at his shoulder. As soon as the man sees me, he holds the gun up to me. Blood pools around Henry's shoulder as he lies on the ground, motionless.

Instead of running, the man turns his attention to me. "Should have known you wouldn't be far behind him. Seems you two have been working together a lot, haven't you, Cunningham?" he spits my name out with a venom that sends a shiver down my spine. Fuck, this isn't good.

I flick my eyes down to Henry at my feet, and check the distance between my raised hands and the gun on his hip. It's too far for me to move fast enough, get the gun, aim, and shoot him before he could shoot me first. I'm caught between a rock and a hard place. He could shoot me, and it would be over in a second.

Sirens wail in the distance, and I take a breath. I have to keep him occupied for another minute or two until they get here. Someone had to have heard the gunshot and called it in.

"How do you know who I am?" I ask.

"You and that motherfucker have been hunting us, and you thought we didn't know?" He chuckles menacingly. "Of course we knew. We know everything."

"So now what? You kill us and call it a day?"

He lets out a cackle. "No. I think I'll let you live. Let you have the knowledge that we know who you are, where you live, and we are watching your every move. Let you stew in fear for a little longer."

"Why?" I ask, unable to hold the question in.

"It's fun to watch."

I inch closer to Henry, who lets out a low groan on the ground. Thank fuck, he's alive. For now, at least.

The distant sound of a door opening and closing sends my heart racing. Please, no. Please, please *please* let it be anyone other than Hannah.

"We've been watching you already for weeks, even tonight, while you were on your special date with that paramedic. What's her name again?"

I don't take the bait, but my gut churns with the knowledge that they've been watching Hannah tonight. That means it's not just me in danger, it's her, too. It's *all of my family*.

The sirens get closer, and the man takes another step closer to me, gun pointed directly at my chest. One wrong move, and it's over.

"I'll leave you with this," he says, wobbling the gun in his hand. "You're next. Thorson is as good as dead, so my job here is done."

I move one inch closer to Henry, listening to his shallow breathing. The dumbass hasn't realized I'm close enough yet, but the second his guard drops, I'm onto him.

"Do you really think you're going to make it out of this?" I ask, my voice steady. "To me, it sounds like half the county is on their way here. Are you really going to be able to run?"

"The whole point was never to run. I know I'm not getting out of this alive. The point is to tell you to watch your back, cause soon, you'll end up bleeding on the ground like him."

With that, I move as quickly as I can, reaching down to grab the gun from Henry's hip. A shot fires, but I'm not hit. Instead of firing again, the man turns and runs down the street. I lift Henry's gun, click off the safety, aim, and fire at him as he runs. He jerks, clutching at his arm, and running out of sight before I can stand to chase him.

"Fuck," I curse, turning my attention back to Henry. I flick the safety on, set the gun by my leg, and move to assess Henry.

His shoulder is bleeding like a bitch, but thankfully, it looks like it's too high up to have hit his heart. I can't be sure it didn't hit an artery, though. I put pressure on the wound with one hand, while sliding my other hand to see if the bullet went through. When I don't feel an exit wound, I curse under my breath. This just got a bit worse.

A voice calls my name, and I look up to see Hannah running toward us, a bag in tow. "Thomas," she calls again.

"I told you to stay in the car," I tell her, scanning behind her for any more threats.

"You need help." I can see her shift from fear to all business. Fuck, she's amazing at her job. Dropping to her knees beside me, she checks his pulse, and once she feels a heartbeat and sees his chest moving as he breathes, she tears open her bag, dumping out the contents. She grabs a pair of gloves and puts them on, ripping open a package of gauze and switching out with me. I let her continue to apply pressure while I open more gauze for her.

"Did you call it in?" I ask.

"Yes, they should be here any second."

We work in silence, and I check Henry's pulse. The

rapid thumping under my fingers helps me take a deep inhale of breath, feeling the proof of life beneath me.

Henry groans again, this time, trying to sit up. "What the fuck?" he grumbles.

"Stay down, man." I push on his other shoulder to get him to lay back down, as the ambulance arrives on the scene. I let out a sigh of relief when two familiar faces climb out of the rig. Henry loses consciousness before they reach us.

Hannah starts calling out information. "GSW to the left shoulder, heavy blood loss. Thomas, what was his pulse?"

I blink as I watch her work. "I-uh, I didn't count."

She nods, and turns back to the paramedics. "Respirations are shallow and labored."

They transfer him onto the gurney, throwing an oxygen mask over his mouth.

Hannah steps aside to let them work, and I reach for her arm. "Are you okay?" I ask her, my panic starting to rise as the adrenaline shifts.

"I'm okay," she assures me, snapping her gloves off and dropping them to the ground for now. "Thomas, are you okay?" Hannah reaches out, resting her hands on my chest. Her touch is grounding.

"I'm okay," I say, hopefully in a convincing tone. Physically, I'm okay. Mentally though? *What the actual fuck?*

I don't even know how to start processing what has happened. The most important thing right now is that Hannah is here, she's okay, and I'm okay, and Henry is getting the help he needs.

Minutes pass as they work to get Henry's bleeding semi under control before heading to the hospital, but it's not long before they're loading him into the back of the rig and taking off.

I hold Hannah, not even caring that I'm covered in blood.

Officers that I recognize filter into view. My chief appears in my line of sight, and I let out a deep sigh.

"Jesus, Tommy. You okay?" Chief asks.

"Yeah. I couldn't get a good view of the guy, though. He had his face covered," I tell him. "I have to tell you everything while it's fresh, Chief."

"Alright," he agrees. "Let's get you two cleaned up. Hannah, you okay?"

Hannah nods. "I was hiding. I could barely see what was going on."

"We'll still have some questions for you, if you can come down to the station."

She agrees, and Chief leads us to his vehicle. I slide in the back with Hannah as I try to process the last fifteen minutes.

## 14

## HANNAH

My hands shake in my lap as we ride in the back of the police car to the station. Thomas is sitting as close to me as physically possible without having me in his lap. He didn't even bother putting on his seatbelt.

He's covered in blood. There's even some on his face and in his hair from when he tried to push some of his blonde strands out of his eyes. Though, I suppose I am too. My hands aren't quite as covered, but my arms and thighs have blood spattered all over them. It's stupid in hindsight, but my clothes are ruined, and I loved how good I felt in them tonight.

Now that we aren't at the scene, I start to lose my grip on reality. I stayed calm for as long as I could and did my job to save Henry, but now, I'm slowly deteriorating.

The police station comes into view, and it all hits me like a freight train. My vision narrows, my pulse skyrockets, and my breathing goes shallow.

I keep it together as Thomas helps me out of the back of the car, and into the station. He leads me to the women's bathroom to clean up, and as soon as he drops my hand, I push through the door, and collapse to the ground as it shuts behind me.

Should I care that I'm sitting on the floor of a dirty police station bathroom? Yes. Do I have it in me to care right now? *Not a chance in hell.*

I sit against the wall, staring down at my blood-covered arms and try to breathe. Sobs wrack my body, and the gut-churning fear eats at me. I was more scared tonight than I have ever been in my entire life.

Scared that something was going to happen to Thomas, scared that I wouldn't get to him in time, scared that I would have to watch the light leave those beautiful blue eyes.

I dig my nails into the flesh of my thighs, begging my body to stop, to feel something other than this fear. Nothing is working, nothing is pulling me from this haze. I stand on shaky legs and run to the sink, turning the water on hot and scrubbing at my arms and legs, doing anything to get the blood from my skin.

The water is so hot it burns, but it reminds me I'm alive. I'm here.

When I'm clean, I look up into the small mirror above the sink, and see my face. The small amount of mascara I had on is smeared all over my red splotchy cheeks, and I splash the water onto my face, hissing at the sting of the burn.

I can't get myself under control. I can't regulate right now, and this has to be one of the worst panic attacks I've had in years, maybe ever. The last one I had this bad was the night my parents died, and my Grandma had to have the hospital give me medication.

I sink back down onto the ground. I need to calm down. I can't go to the hospital right now, can't bring that attention to myself. That's too much, then everyone will ask me what happened, more so than they already will, and I'll have to tell them I'm a nervous wreck.

I pinch my skin, dig my fingernails in again, do anything I can to help me calm down.

"Hannah?" Thomas's voice is a familiar sensation between heavy thumps of my racing heart in my ears. A hard knock on the door is a feeble attempt at pulling me from the haze, but I'm flung right back into it as soon as the knocks are done. My name is called again, maybe more than once, before I hear the words, "I'm coming in."

Hands grip around my arms, pulling them free from my scalp. I didn't even realize I'd started digging my nails into my scalp until now.

"Hannah, breathe. You're safe, I've got you," Thomas's voice says, but it sounds like he's underwater. "What can I do to help you?"

I shake my head, unable to get words out.

Thomas wraps his large arms around me, pulling me into his lap so I'm straddling him, and he squeezes. Tight. So tightly that it almost hurts to breathe, but it helps. God, does it help.

After a long minute, my breathing slows, and the whooshing in my ears fades until it's only the steady thumping of my heart, and Thomas's low voice rumbling against my chest.

"You're safe. I've got you. Keep breathing, there you go, baby. You're doing it. Keep breathing." His words are so soothing, and soon, I'm following his patterned breathing as he inhales and exhales slowly.

My head is pressed into his neck, and my tears slow.

"Thank you," I croak, after long minutes of no more tears.

Thomas nods slowly. "It helped me too."

I start to extricate myself from the tangle of limbs we are in, and Thomas holds me closer. "Just another minute. I'm sorry I didn't come in sooner."

I shrug. "It's okay."

"Does that happen often?" he questions.

"Not anymore, no. Usually, I can control it before it gets that bad, but tonight..."

"Tonight is out of the ordinary."

"Yeah, you could say so," I say, letting myself laugh softly. "Are you okay?"

I feel his head moving. "Yes. Now I am, knowing that you're safe, and in my arms."

There's a knock on the door. "Tommy, are you guys okay in there? Do you need EMS?"

"No," Thomas calls out. "We'll be out in a minute. Just calming down."

"Could everyone hear me?" I say, cringing.

"No. I was the only one out there until Chief came by to grab us, and then I went in. Chief could have heard, but he knows it's been a rough night."

I nod into his chest. "We should get up." I slowly stand, shaking out my aching, tired limbs. After my panic attacks, my body always feels wrung out. My extremities tingle, and I feel like I've run a marathon, something you would *never* catch me doing.

Thomas stands and opens the door. Chief is leaning against the wall, a somber look on his face. "You two doing okay?"

Thomas replies first, "As okay as we can be. Any update on Henry?"

"He's in surgery. They're optimistic. The bullet missed any major arteries, and looks like it missed bone, too. He should be okay."

A heavy sense of relief settles in my body.

"We will interview you separately for now, okay?" Chief asks, and I nod, not sure of the usual procedures.

Thomas cringes, but doesn't say anything. He squeezes my hand as I'm led into a separate room.

"Do you need anything, Han?" Thomas asks before he leaves. "They'll bring you some water, but I can stay, if you need me?"

I shake my head. "I'm okay. I won't be long, anyway. My story is much shorter than yours."

Thomas grimaces. "If you need me, tell them and I'll be there, no matter what. Okay?"

"Yeah," I reply, and he pulls me into his embrace. I sink into the hug, focusing on the steady beat of his heart. He's calm. I can do this.

He pulls back after a moment and leans down. His lips caress my forehead, and I feel the heat creeping up my cheeks.

"I'm right next door, freckles."

## 15

## THOMAS

"Is Hannah okay?" I ask for what seems like the millionth time. We've been separated now for an hour, and I'm worried about her. I cleaned up as much of the blood as I could in the bathroom before coming in here, but I haven't left this room since.

Elena, nods. "She's finishing up shortly, I think." Elena got here with a crew from the FBI a bit ago, and they promptly announced that they'd be taking over the investigation.

"Then I can take her home?" I ask, ready to stand up from the chair.

Elena cringes, her dark brows furrowing. "Officer Cunningham," she says slowly. "There's something you need to know."

My heart sinks with the change of her tone. Did something happen to Hannah? Did she have another panic attack? I rise from my chair, ready to stride out of this room to find her, consequences be damned. "What happened? Is Hannah okay? Is it Henry?"

"They're both fine, but Thomas, please sit down." She gestures to the uncomfortable chair I've been sitting in.

"What is it?" I press, my anxiety still heightened.

"We found a tracker on your personal vehicle. Do we have permission to do a sweep of your house?"

My stomach sinks. "Yes. Arson, my K9 is inside, but if you send one of our guys, he will be fine."

Elena nods, picking up her phone and sending off a message. "You've been working on this case for a while, is that right?"

I nod, folding my hands in front of me. "Since day one. I was the one who made the connection that we were dealing with a trafficking situation."

Elena takes notes, soaking up all of the information I offer her. I've been working on this for years now. I've been one of the most involved officers in the department. I begged for help until they finally sent Henry my way. We couldn't find the link we'd been searching for. Anyone we interviewed knew the barest of information, or the friends of kids that passed away got the drugs from a friend of a friend, and the trail always ran dry.

I tell Elena all of this in depth, even going as far as having her pull files and cases that are pertinent to the investigation. After another hour, Elena steps out of the room to give the information I gave her to the other detectives.

When she comes back in, her eyes are downcast, and she can't look me in the eye. "I hate to be the bearer of bad news, but with the information you've provided us and the circumstances, the FBI believes it would be best that you be placed in a safe house for the time being."

My world spins, this already small room seeming to

close in on me. "No, you can't. I need to stay here. I have to make sure my family and Hannah are okay."

"They will be. At this time, we don't have a reason to believe that your family or Hannah are in danger, of course we will monitor them closely, and should they need to be moved, we will," Elena explains.

The thought of any member of my family, of *Hannah* being harmed because of me is enough to send a cold chill through my veins.

"He threatened her!" I yell. "He threatened Hannah. He knows who she is."

"We're aware, but like I said, they will be well protected here. It's you we're most concerned about at this time, Thomas. They clearly have a vendetta against the people working directly with the case and want to eliminate that as best as they can."

"I can't leave Hannah behind. I saw that glint in his eyes when he brought her up. She's in as much danger as I am."

"I understand you care for her, Officer Cunningham, but unless you two are engaged or married, we don't have any real reason to send her with you," Elena says, folding her hands in front of her on the steel table.

I take a few deep breaths. She might kill me for this, but this is the only way that I know she will be safe, that I can be the one to protect her. "She's my fiancée, Elena. She has to come with me."

Elena sits in stunned silence, her eyes widening as she takes in my words. "She's your fiancée?"

"Yes," I state firmly, my hands balling into fists under the table. "It's new. We weren't telling anyone yet, not even our family knows."

Elena lets out a weary sigh. "That changes things." She stacks up her paperwork into a neat pile. "I'll be back."

"Can I at least see my fiancée?" I ask, laying it on thick.

She sighs. "I'll check."

I let out my own sigh of relief.

She lets herself out of the room, and I'm left to my own thoughts. I can't believe I said that Hannah was my fiancée, but it slipped out. The thought of them making her stay here, working in the field when shit like this is going down, and the dealers clearly know who she is, and know that hurting her would hurt me? Yeah, I can't handle that. I would never live with myself if something happened to her and it was because of me.

I don't want to go to a safe house, but if I have to, then I have to. Fuck, I never thought something like this would happen to me. I've heard stories of guys who've had to go into safe houses before, but I always brushed it off. They have a reason for sending me away, so maybe I should really take it seriously.

A few minutes later, the door opens, and Elena strides through. "She's in the next room. I'll give you two a few minutes."

"Thank you," I breathe, already rushing to the door.

I pull it open and rush down the hall and fling the door open, my eyes searching for her. As soon as I see her, my heart sinks. Her eyes are red, cheeks blotchy. She's clearly been crying again.

I move as fast as I can to cross the small room and pull her into my arms. She lets me wrap my arms around her and hold her tight to my chest. "Shhh, Hannah. You're safe. I'm here."

She nods, but it's not enough, I need her to know I've got her. I pull slightly away and cup her cheeks in my palm. Those watery blue eyes hold me captive. "I have to tell you something," I say, hoping like hell she will go along with this.

"They're sending you to a safe house," she says, her breath catching, like that's all I have to tell her.

I shake my head. "Us. They're sending us to a safe house."

Hannah's brows raise. "What? No, they said I wasn't going, that there wasn't a reason for it."

"Technically, there isn't. Except, we're engaged."

## 16

## HANNAH

"Engaged?" I repeat the word back. "We're not engaged, Thomas, we aren't even dating."

Thomas looks up at the ceiling, closing his eyes. "I need you to trust me, Hannah. Can you do that?"

"Thomas what are you—"

"I told them we're engaged," he interrupts me.

I let his words simmer in my brain, and I don't know what to say. He told them we were engaged? Why would he do that? We barely know each other. There is no way anyone would believe that we are engaged. It's not believable. I mean, we only had our first date tonight, and with how much this town talks, everyone will know it's fake.

"Why did you do that?" I ask, my voice shaking.

He drops his gaze to mine. His hands are still cupping my cheeks, and I try to slow my breathing. "The only way they'd let you come with me is if we were engaged, or married."

Thomas hesitates for a long moment, studying my reaction before continuing. "The thought of anything happening to you makes me sick, Hannah. I need to know you're safe. I promise I'm not trying to scare you, but the man who shot Henry was watching us tonight. He saw you, and knows you're someone important to me."

I don't think about myself at this moment. "What about your family? Then they clearly know your family too," I stammer.

"I know," he soothes, rubbing his thumb across my cheek, swiping tears I haven't realized have fallen. "Elena has assured me that my family is safe, but Hannah, I can't go, knowing you're here alone."

I try to process the way tonight has undoubtedly changed my life. I could tell him no, that I'm not going to go along with it and stay home. I have to look after my grandma, I have a job, an apartment, a life.

Something is holding me back from telling him no, though.

"Okay." My voice shakes as I speak.

"Hannah," he breathes my name. He rests his forehead against mine, and his breathing shutters. His palms shake as they grasp my cheeks. It hits me then. He's as scared as I am. It feels like earlier when he was about to kiss me, only this time, the stakes are higher. His life's in danger. Heck, maybe mine is too.

My fingers twist in his shirt, his warm body heat radiates through the material to caress my skin. "Can I kiss you now?" Thomas asks again. This time, it's more of a plea than a request.

I nod, even though I'm terrified.

I suck in a sharp breath when he tilts his head, and my eyes fall closed as I anticipate what will happen next.

My fingers thread in the cotton of his shirt, my heart pounding in my ears. Then, his lips caress mine. It's a slow movement, but it sends goosebumps flaring across my skin. I lean into the kiss a bit more. He's still taking the lead, but I'm allowing him to.

Thomas's lips are soft and gentle as he opens my mouth with his, and his tongue slides against my lower lip. I hold my breath, unsure of what I'm supposed to do. I mean, you see kisses all the time in movies, read them in books, but it's not like there's a manual on how to kiss someone properly. Right?

I try to keep my brain calm, to keep me in the moment, but I can feel the anxious thoughts creeping in at the edges. *You're not good enough. Why does he want me? He's going to regret this.*

The door flies open behind us, and Thomas pulls back, removing his lips from mine.

*I just had my first kiss in a dingy room at the police station.*

A dark-haired woman enters, followed by the chief. "We've received approval from the safe house that they'll be ready for you. You'll have two hours to pack your things and make any arrangements. Hannah, we've already alerted your boss to the situation, and made him aware that you will be out for an extended length of time."

The reality of the situation slowly dawns on me. It's one in the morning. If I have two hours to pack, I won't get to say goodbye to my sister, Tiff, or my grandma. I won't get to fully explain to them what's happening. My breaths come in quick succession, my thoughts going hazy again.

Thomas has me pulled into his arms before I can fully process it. He speaks low so no one else can hear. "What do you need, freckles?"

"Ice," I murmur. I need something to ground me right now, and while Thomas's embrace is helping, it's not enough right now. This is all happening so fast.

"Can I get a cup of ice?" Thomas asks, or rather, demands. The door opens and closes again, and I swear I'm getting emotional whiplash from the last few hours.

I went from having one of the best nights ever, to being sent into protective custody with the man who gave me my first kiss mere minutes ago. I feel lost, spiraling out of control.

Thomas cups my cheeks, and I can vaguely sense him telling me to breathe with him while we wait. I follow his instructions, and it helps, but it's not quite enough.

"Here's the ice," someone says as the door opens and closes. One of Thomas's hands leaves my face to grab the cup of ice, and he holds it between us. I take it from his hand and bring it to my lips, tipping it and letting one of the small cubes slide into my mouth.

I rest it on my tongue, letting the painful cold help ground me, and calm myself. I don't know what it is about ice, but it helps me, more than any medication or other technique has.

After a few minutes of the ice melting in my mouth, I can breathe normally again, and my head feels semi-clear. There's still intense anxiety surrounding the situation and what's to come, but for now, I feel better.

"Sorry," I murmur, taking another ice cube into my mouth.

"Hey, don't apologize," Thomas says, swiping a tear from my cheek. "Are you ready to sit down? I think Elena has some more information for us."

I don't miss the way he cringes, as if he's hoping talking about the inevitable won't spur me into my third panic attack of the night.

We sit down in the uncomfortable metal chairs, and Elena holds out some paperwork for us. "We have an older couple that lives on a farm in southern Missouri that the FBI has on standby for situations like these. He's a former agent, and knows how to keep you safe. We've contacted them, and they are available to take you in for the time being."

Thomas rests a hand on my thigh, stroking his thumb on the bare skin there, and squeezing gently. My clothes are still covered in dried blood, but thankfully, my skin is clean. It's enough to send goosebumps fluttering all over my skin.

Elena pauses, letting the information sink in before she continues. "While there, you are to have no social media, no contact with your families, except through the burner phone that we provide you. We will bring you to your house once we are done here and give you time to pack. An officer will be with you the whole time to keep watch." She slides a basic cell phone across the table.

"Can we call our family now?" I ask, needing to talk with them. To explain.

"Yes, you can use the station phone to call, but you cannot give them any details on what happened tonight, only that you are safe, and need to go away for a while," Elena says, her voice steady and firm. "If you tell them any details, you risk compromising their safety too."

I nod quickly, knowing I would do anything to keep them safe. Thomas squeezes my thigh again. He reaches out and grabs the phone from the table, shoving it in his pocket. I stand, taking the cup of ice with me as I do.

"Can we use an office?" Thomas asks, his brow raising. His blonde hair is still a disheveled mess from today, but at least now there isn't any blood in it. He must have cleaned up after I did.

"Yes, that's fine," Elena agrees. Thomas takes my hand

in his, and leads me down the hall toward the offices that are empty in the middle of the night.

He opens the door to the furthest one down, and I take in the room. It's nearly empty aside from the basic desk, with a few scattered file folders on it, a computer and a desk phone. Leading me to sit in the chair, he kneels beside me, tucking a hair behind my ear.

"Do you want to do this alone?" he asks, and while I appreciate the gesture, I don't think I can do it alone.

"No, please don't leave me," I beg. "I don't know what to say."

"You can do this, but if you need me to, I can take the lead," Thomas says. My heart pounds. I've always been on the other end of the call, the one receiving bad news, so to be the one giving it tonight is hard.

"Is this really happening?" I ask. I know that it is, but I need to be sure. If I have to call the people I love most in this world, and tell them I'm leaving for an unknown length of time, then I need to know this is real.

Thomas frowns, brows turning down. "You have no idea how much I wish this weren't happening, that this wasn't the way we would be getting to know each other, Hannah. But, it's real. It's happening."

I nod. That was the confirmation that I didn't want, but needed. I have both Grandma and Julia's numbers memorized, so I dial Julia first. I put it on speaker, because I'm not sure I'd be able to hold the phone to my ear with how badly my hands are shaking.

Honestly, I'm not even sure where my actual cell phone is.

The line rings and rings until I'm not sure she will pick up, but then at the last second, my sister's voice comes across the line. "Hello?" she sounds breathless and anxious, though I suppose I would be too if I were getting a call from an unknown number at almost two in the morning.

"Julia? It's Hannah," I greet her.

"Oh my god, Hannah, where are you?" Julia asks. "We've been worried sick. You weren't answering our calls or texts." In the background, I hear rustling and a whispered, "It's Hannah. No, I don't know, I just answered." There's a pause, and then, "You're on speaker."

"I'm sorry," I tell them. "I didn't mean to worry you."

"What happened? Why are you calling from this number?" Julia asks.

I take a deep breath, and Thomas squeezes my hand, giving me a nod. "I'm at the police station. I'm safe. I can't tell you what happened, but I'm safe. I have to leave town for a while," I explain.

"What?" she clamors, and I can hear Tiff trying to calm her in the background. "I'm going to kill him. What did Thomas do?"

"Thomas didn't do anything," I rush to say, trying to protect him from any of this. "He's the one keeping me calm and safe."

"Where are you going?" Tiff asks. "Do you need a lawyer?"

I shake my head, while also knowing they can't see me. "No." My voice breaks on the word. "I can't tell you where we're going. I don't really even know."

"We?" Julia asks, her voice high and shrieking. "What do you mean, we?"

I look at Thomas, unsure of what to say. Thankfully, he jumps in. "Julia, it's Thomas. They're sending us away while they get things under control, but I promise, on my life, that I will do everything in my power to keep Hannah safe. That's all this is, a measure to keep us safe."

Tiff is the one who responds. "And you don't know when you'll be back?"

Thomas looks over at me, and grimaces as he shakes his head. "No. They don't have a timeline yet."

Julia sobs in the background, and my heart clenches as my own tears stream down my cheeks. "I'm sorry," I murmur. A hand slides around my shoulders. "We don't have much time, and I have to call Grandma."

Tiff calms Julia down enough for us to say a teary goodbye with promises to call as soon as I can. If I thought that call was hard, this next one is going to be worse.

I take a minute to breathe, popping another melting piece of ice into my mouth. I dial Grandma's number, hoping I don't give her too much anxiety over this.

She answers on the third ring, her voice groggy in her sleep. I can already hear the tense edge to her tone. "Hello?"

"Grandma? It's Hannah," I say the words through my tears.

"Hannah? What's going on?" The anxiety in her voice picks up. Just like that, I lose my ability to speak. It's like weight has been placed on my windpipe, and I can't breathe.

"Mrs. Pearson, this is Thomas Cunningham," Thomas pulls my head into his chest, and I let out a muffled sob. "Hannah is safe."

"Thomas? What—I'm so confused," Grandma says.

"We were witnesses to something tonight, and unfortunately, they've decided it's best for us to be sent to a safe house." He pauses for a moment to let my grandma process. "I'm not at liberty to tell you where, but I need you to know that she's safe. She's been anxious tonight, rightfully so, but I'm doing my best to keep her calm, and helping her anyway I can."

Of course, Grandma, being the woman she is, and the one to be there for me every step of the way during some of my worst panic attacks and social anxiety diagnosis, jumps into protective mode. "She will tell you she's okay, and she's not. Make sure she's eating and drinking enough. If she's picking at her nails, she's anxious. Ice can help ground her when it's bad, as well as tight hugs."

Thomas nods, as if he's logging all this into his brain. "Yes, ma'am."

"Hannah, sweetie? Can you hear me?"

"Yes," I squeak. "I'm here."

"I love you, sweetheart. Call me when you can. Thomas will take good care of you, I'm sure. If he doesn't, he can expect hell to rain down on him," Grandma says, her voice deepening with the threat. I can't stop the bubble of laughter that surprises me, creeping up my throat.

"Thanks, Grandma. I'm sorry."

"You have nothing to be sorry about. You have to go and keep yourself safe. I love you."

"I love you, too," I say, and we hang up the call. Thomas holds me against his chest while I sob, my heart aching. I don't know how long we will be gone, and I'm so worried about them, but she's right. We have to go to keep ourselves safe.

I pull myself together. "I'm sorry, you have to call your family, too."

Thomas shrugs. "I'm only going to call Jason. He'll pass it on to the rest of the family. It would take too long for me to call everyone."

"But what about your parents? What about—" My stomach sinks as I realize something. "Andrew and Josie's baby is due soon. What if you miss it?"

"Hannah, it's okay," Thomas says, but I can sense that

he's realizing this at the same time as I am. "I'll meet the baby when we get home, and it will be fine."

"Will it, though?" I cry. I pull away from his arms, rising to my feet and pacing. "How is any of this okay?"

Thomas does the same, standing to his full height and following behind me. "It's not. I shouldn't have been selfish and told them we were engaged."

I shake my head. "No. It's what's best. I wouldn't feel safe if I weren't with you," I blurt before realizing the words have fallen from my mouth.

"Really?" Thomas asks as I halt in front of him.

"Yeah. I thought about it, saying no, and staying home, but the thought of you having to do this alone, and being here, with no way to contact you and know if you were okay, was worse."

Honestly, it's surprising to me, but if there's one thing I know about my social anxiety, it's that I can cling to people. So yes, maybe Julia or Thomas finds this out of character for me to suddenly be okay with going to a safe-house with a man I hardly know, but for some reason, my anxiety is making me latch onto him, and I'm okay with it. Maybe it's a trauma bond, or maybe I truly trust him.

Thomas wraps me up in his embrace again. I have never been in such close contact with someone like this. Sure, in my family we are huggers, but not to this extent. I've never been touched like this before, and I can't help but crave more.

His voice rumbles deep in his chest as he speaks. "Why don't you have them bring you home while I make the call I need to, that way you have a little extra time to pack. I'll pick you up in a bit, okay?" he asks, his voice raising.

I get the feeling he wants to make his calls alone, and I

can understand that. I don't want to leave him, but I will if it's what he needs.

"Okay," I say, removing myself from his arms. "I'll see you in two hours, then?" I confirm.

"Yep." Thomas leans forward, pressing a gentle, yet firm kiss to my forehead. "See you soon, freckles."

I leave the room, shutting the door behind me and taking a deep breath. I stride down the hall, and Elena catches me.

"Hannah, are you ready to go get your things?" she asks, her voice gentler than it was in the other room.

"Yeah. Thomas is calling his family, and will meet at my apartment later."

"Great, let's go."

## 17

## THOMAS

My hands tremble as I watch Hannah leave the room. I don't want to call my family, but I know I have to. I can't just disappear. I think calling Jason is the best option. He's the most level headed of us brothers, and will be the best one to spread the news.

I fight the urge to rub my eyes. My contacts are getting dry and I can't wait to get them out and throw my glasses on. I hate driving with my glasses on, but I don't think my eyes will last another hour in these contacts.

Elena told me that we'll be escorted down to Missouri, but as soon as we are at the safe house, we will be on our own. They'll follow us in an unmarked vehicle and keep watch on us. I can take the first shift of driving and hopefully Hannah can get some sleep, and maybe we can switch after. I might be able to do the full stretch without sleeping, but I know that wouldn't be the safest option.

I dial my brother's phone number, ignoring the guilt I feel about waking him in the middle of the night. It rings and rings until his voicemail picks up. Shit. I dial the number again, and it continues to ring. On the third ring, he answers.

"Hello?" His voice is thick with sleep and there is a rustling along the line.

"Jase, it's Thomas," I reply, my throat thickening with unexpected emotion.

"Thomas?" he grunts. "What time is it? Are you okay?"

"I'm okay," I confirm, swallowing. "Something happened, though. I can't tell you what, but I have to leave town for a while, and I don't know when I'll be back."

"Shit, what?" He sounds much more alert now.

"Jase?" Fallon's faint voice questions in the background.

"One second, sunshine," Jason soothes. "Thomas, what do you mean, you have to leave town?"

I run my hands over my face, fighting back tears. "Hannah and I witnessed something tonight when we were leaving the street dance, and it was decided that we be sent to a safe house for a while."

"Where?" Jason asks.

"I can't tell you," I reply. This fucking sucks. "I need you to tell everyone that Hannah and I are safe. Oh, um." I pause for a long moment. "Also, we're engaged, if anyone asks."

"You're engaged?" he stutters. "You two just had your first date. You can't be engaged."

I sigh. "Jason. I can't give you any more details, but if anyone asks, yes, I'm engaged."

"What the fuck did you do?" he asks, his big brother aura coming out.

"I didn't *do* anything, Jason," I growl, growing defensive. "I need you to tell everyone that I will call when I can, but I won't have my phone. I don't have time to call everyone tonight, and we have to get on the road."

"Is Arson going with you? Do I need to pick him up?"

"No, I'm taking him with me," I state, though it was never discussed. My dog goes with me, no matter what.

Jason sighs through the line. "Fuck, dude. Is there really nothing else you can tell me? You know Mom is going to lose her mind."

"I know," I say through gritted teeth. "I can't, though. I'll call you all when I can, but for now, this is all I can offer you."

"Alright. Be safe. We love you," he says, and I can't stop the burning pricking my eyes. I try to write it off as the contacts causing me trouble, but the tears that fill my eyes don't lie.

"Love you, brother." We say goodbye, and I hang up the phone, and dig my hands into my hair, tugging at the mess of strands. That was harder than I thought. I won't be able to see my family for who knows how long. The thought of leaving everyone behind, the thought of not being able to explain to my nieces and nephew why I can't be around, is like a punch to the gut. Then there's the thought of not meeting Andrew's first child the moment I can. What if something happens during the delivery and I'm not here? What about Gramps? What if he falls again, and this time gets hurt?

My anxiety ramps up, but I slow my heart before it can get any worse. No, this is what I have to do to keep myself safe. If something happens, they'll find a way to get a hold of me, and I'll come home, consequences be damned.

For now, though, this is what I have to do to protect Hannah. To protect me.

I stand from the swivel chair, and head toward the closed office door. Time to get home, get my shit, and get back to Hannah.

BARELY TWO HOURS LATER, I'm shoving my suitcase into the vehicle that Elena arranged for us to drive to Missouri. Thankfully, I had enough time to shower before I packed. My suitcase is packed to the brim, with everything I could fit in there. I've thrown my blankets and pillows in the back as well, and grabbed all the things Arson would need. His dog bed, food, and his favorite toys take up a corner of the trunk.

My eyes are no longer burning thanks to the glasses resting on my nose. Exhaustion seeps into my bones, but there's nothing I can do about it now. I'm still waiting for the two cups of coffee I chugged while I was packing to kick in.

I have one last trip inside to grab Arson and one more bag, and then I can get to Hannah.

After they did a sweep of my house earlier, they had officers posted around the block, and I had the Chief inside with me while I packed up. I admit that it's nice to know he's been here watching.

I head inside, throwing open the door and scanning the room for Arson. He's sitting by the couch, head tilted in confusion. "Ready, buddy?" I ask. He gives me a weird look, surely confused by the sudden urgency to pack as much of our things as possible, including his toys.

"You have to be on your best behavior, man," I tell him, throwing the duffle bag on my shoulder and grabbing his leash from the door. I don't need a leash often with him, but it will be nice for stops along the way. "Hannah is a nice girl, so you can't mess this up for me with your dramatic attitude." I glance down at him. He rushes over to me as soon as he sees the leash in my hand.

I complete my final walk through of the house, making sure the lights are all turned off. I open the front door, and Arson flies out, running onto the front lawn to use the bathroom as I turn around and lock the front door behind me.

Letting out a heavy sigh as the lock clicks, I try not to think about how long it could be before I'm home again. My house isn't much, but I've lived here for a long time, so it's home.

I whistle for Arson, and throw my final duffle into the trunk. He hops up into the backseat, and I climb in, noting that Chief has started his vehicle as well.

Chief pulls out onto the road as I'm pulling my seatbelt on, leading the way to Hannah's apartment. I hate that the first time I'm going to her place is like this, but there's not much I can do about that. I'll have to make it up to her in the future.

It's a short drive, maybe five minutes, before we're pulling up in front of the complex. Chief climbs out, holding up a hand for me to stay put. I nod, but really, I'm itching to get out and get Hannah myself.

I note the other squad car across the street, and wave to the guy inside of it. I can't quite tell who it is, but we're a small department, and I know everyone.

Moments later, Chief is striding out of the complex, holding a few pillows and blankets, as well as rolling a suitcase behind him. Elena and Hannah follow, Elena with a small bag, and Hannah with a backpack and another suitcase. It looks like she planned the same way I did and brought a lot in case we are there for a while.

I slide out of the car and meet them at the trunk. Reaching out, I grab the wheeled suitcase from Hannah's hand, our fingers brushing in the transfer. I can't control the shiver that passes through me at the small touch.

Once everything is loaded, Elena stops us, giving a few last-minute instructions. "The Graffs are expecting you. Don't stop on the way unless you absolutely have to for gas or food." She pauses, pulling an envelope from her back pocket. "Here's a pre-loaded card with enough money on it to get you there, and a few hundred dollars in cash for anything else you might need.. There's an address to the Graff's in the envelope. Enter the address in the GPS. You're not in witness protection, so you don't need new identities, but keep contact with anyone outside of the Graffs to a minimum. You never know when it comes to dangerous people."

Hannah shudders beside me, and I reach out, taking her palm in mine. Her hands are ice cold.

Elena glances at me. "You have the burner phone?"

"Yes," I confirm.

"We will contact you when it's safe to return home. Hopefully it's only a week or two, but it's hard to say in situations like this. You'll have an unmarked escort following you." She points to the black Suburban to my right. "If they note anything of suspicion, they will turn on their hazards. When they are done escorting you, they will flash their headlights three times. Make sure you keep your eyes open and watch your surroundings. We've checked all the vehicles multiple times for trackers, but they can be hard to find sometimes."

"Thanks, Elena."

"Be safe," she says as a parting gesture. Chief gives me a final nod, and turns to head to his vehicle, leaving Hannah and I alone.

"I'll take the first shift, okay?" I start by saying, but

Hannah isn't listening. She's frozen, staring up at the sky, her normally bright blue eyes dull and hard to read in the darkness. I squeeze her palm. "Hannah?"

"You're sure this isn't a dream, right?" her voice is so quiet I can't be sure I heard her.

"As much as I wish it were, it's not. Let's get in the car, freckles." I guide her to the car, opening her door and making sure she's in and buckled before shutting it.

I take a deep breath and round the vehicle, opening the driver door. There's a loud screech that puts my mind into overdrive. I reach to my side, gripping the handle of my gun and assessing what's happening before me. Hannah has her palm pressed to her chest, but there's a wide grin on her face. Arson has his front paws on the center console, and his head is resting on her shoulder. There's a visible wet streak across her cheek.

She breaks out into a fit of laughter as I take in the scene before me, slowing my racing heart. I drop my hand from my gun, and climb into the car. "Arson, get back, dude."

He flops away from Hannah into the backseat, curling up. "I'm sorry," I tell her. "I forgot to warn you he was in here. Are you okay with him?"

Hannah's laughter softens, but she still chuckles a bit. "Of course I am. It's not like you were going to leave him home, right?"

I shake my head. "No way."

"Sorry I screamed," Hannah says, her mood sobering. "I'm so on edge, it freaked me out to suddenly have this giant thing on my shoulder."

"It's okay. He's a big lover, but the best fighter when he needs to be. He'll protect you from a fly if you need it."

Hannah turns a little in her seat. "You're a good boy, Arson," she croons.

I swear, I witness my dog fall in love with the woman in real time. He preens, turning his head to the side and giving her the wickedest puppy dog eyes I think I've ever seen him pull. His tongue lolls out to one side, and he literally grins. This motherfucker is going to steal my girl.

"He's a little shit, that's what he is." I narrow my eyes at my dog, who acts like I don't exist.

"Oh, quiet," Hannah says, turning back to the front.

My heart has finally slowed, so I settle into the seat, pulling out the envelope and finding the address for the Graff's house. I enter it into the GPS, cringing internally when the estimated time of arrival says eleven hours and thirty-five minutes.

Hannah looks over at me, and she gives me a curious glance. "I didn't know you had glasses," she states.

I reach up and adjust them. "Oh, yeah. I don't wear them often, mainly at night, or times like now, when my eyes get dry and itchy from wearing my contacts for too long."

"Makes sense," she replies, folding her hands in her lap.

"When I was at the police academy, I had to make the switch, because I would be running and doing drills, and they'd fall off my face and I'd be blind as could be. The guys gave me so much shit."

Hannah giggles, and the sound is like music to my ears. I shift the vehicle into gear, and her laughter dies. "We've got this, Han," I say, reaching over to take her palm again as I pull onto the road. The unmarked suburban follows behind us at a close distance, keeping an eye on us.

She lets out a slow breath, grabbing her water bottle from her backpack on the ground. She opens the lid and slides an ice cube from inside into her mouth.

I move to take my hand away, realizing how much I've

been touching her for the last few hours. Perhaps it's been too much, especially since in reality, we don't know each other all that well. I've always been a physical touch guy.

Only Hannah doesn't let me get far, her grip tightening on my hand, keeping it locked in hers. I keep my grateful sigh in my chest, but relief seeps through my bones.

"Music?" I ask.

"Not right now, if that's okay. I think it would be a little too much."

"Fair enough. Let me know if you change your mind," I tell her. I grabbed one of my old iPods from my closet in my rush while packing, and made sure the car has a few adapters as well. Since we can't have our personal phones, hopefully there's some good music on there.

As soon as we are out of the town limits, the true reality of this situation sinks in. Thankfully, I have eleven hours and fifteen minutes to process it.

# 18

## HANNAH

I gasp and my eyes fly open as I jerk awake. The sun is rising in the distance, and the only thing I can see in front of me is the freeway. I flick my eyes to the rearview mirror, seeing the unmarked vehicle behind us. Still keeping watch.

Thomas's hand squeezes my palm, and there's a nudge on my shoulder. "You're okay, Han." His voice is low and soothing.

"Sorry," I sit up straighter. "I didn't realize I'd fallen asleep. How long have I been out?"

"Maybe thirty minutes," he tells me. Arson pushes at my shoulder again, and I turn in my seat, letting go of Thomas's hand.

"That's it?" I question with a yawn, scratching at the top of Arson's head.

"Yeah. If you want, we can pull over at the next rest stop and get you a bed set up in the backseat. I'm sure you're exhausted."

I'm shaking my head before he finishes. "No, I'm fine. I'm sorry I fell asleep. I can take a shift if you want to sleep in the back?"

Thomas also shakes his head. "Nope. I'm good."

I narrow my eyes.

He chuckles. "Seriously, I'm fine. I had two cups of coffee before we left, and I'm used to nights of no sleep. This is a walk in the park."

"Sure," I say sarcastically. Yeah, I've done night shifts with no sleep, too, but that doesn't mean driving with a lack of sleep is easy.

"Do I sense some sass from you, Hannah?"

"Nope."

"Sure," he drawls, returning my earlier comment. "You up for some music now?"

I shrug. "I guess, but radio stations suck. Where are we, anyway?"

"Passed through Ankeny, Iowa while you were asleep, so we have about seven hours left according to the GPS." Thomas reaches into his front pocket and pulls out a small silver item. "I grabbed this at the last second since I figured we'd want music, and I agree, radios suck."

He holds out the older version of an iPod for me to take. "I haven't had an iPod since high school," I respond. "Do you really still use this?"

"No," he says with a chuckle. "I'm old, but I'm not that old. I use my phone for music, but since neither of us have ours, I figured I would grab this."

I plug the device into the adapter, and it powers on. I scroll through some of the music, finding a lot of old rock and country on here.

"Finding anything you like?" he asks after a minute.

I'm about to say no when I find something particularly funny. Without saying a word, I press play. The first notes fill my ears, and I carefully watch his reaction, unsure of what I'm looking for, but knowing there's a reason behind this song being on his iPod.

"What is this?" he questions, his brows furrowing before a bright red creeps up his neck, even the tips of his ears flushing as he realizes. "Shit, is this *Glee*?"

I burst out laughing, perhaps the lack of sleep and stress making me a bit punchy, but never in a million years would I have expected Thomas to have not one, but multiple *Glee* songs on his iPod. "Yes," I shriek.

Thomas groans, "Dammit, Marley."

"How is this her fault?" I question through laughter as the song continues to play. "Thomas, this isn't even like a popular *Glee* song that everyone knows was on *Glee*. This is a *Glee* deep-cut!"

"Marley used to make us watch it with her! I can't help it if some of the songs are good, Hannah!"

"I never said they weren't good, I just never expected you to have them on your iPod," I laugh. It feels good to laugh so unabashedly. The last—not even twelve hours— have been so chaotic and anxiety ridden that I needed this.

The song ends, and my body lags again. I'm so exhausted, but I know I can't sleep anymore. One, it's not fair to Thomas to expect him to drive the whole way. Two, I don't know if my brain will be able to relax again. It did before, so maybe it will, but at the same time, I don't want to sleep. What if I fall asleep and something happens? What if they've been secretly following us the entire time and choose the moment I fall asleep to attack? Cause an acci- dent or something worse?

A shiver rocks through my body, and I try to stop the spiral. I focus on the music instead, throwing an old country album on.

## 19

## HANNAH

The drive is tortuously long. It doesn't help that both Thomas and I are so brutally exhausted that we can barely think straight. We don't talk much, only singing along to songs that play from his old iPod.

When the GPS says there's an hour of the drive left, the Suburban following us flashes their headlights at us, veering to an exit and leaving us to our own devices.

Not long later, we take an exit off the freeway and drive onto side roads, passing through small town after small town, until finally we end up on a seemingly endless gravel road.

When Elena said we'd be in a remote location, she wasn't kidding. I haven't seen another house or even another car now in over ten minutes, the only thing my eyes can see is trees and woods. Arson has his head smashed against the window, his slobber all over the glass as he watches for animals.

"In eight hundred feet, turn left," the GPS voice announces, and I can finally see a structure in the distance. Thomas turns onto the road, and we continue. Nerves bubble in my belly. What if the people hosting us are horrible people? Are we staying in their house? I never thought to ask specifics, but now, it's all I can think of.

Will Thomas and I be expected to share a room? A bed? I suppose so. We're technically engaged, so I presume they're thinking we will share a bed.

*Oh god, why didn't I think about this sooner?*

The dirt road curves, leading us to a small farm with a red barn sitting on the opposite side of the property from the house. It must be a hobby farm, because I don't see any signs that it's a dairy or cattle farm.

More woods line the far edge of the property, with a trail leading deeper into the trees. Thomas parks the vehicle, and reaches behind him to grab the leash for Arson.

An older woman steps out onto the front porch. She looks straight out of a movie with her long gray hair pulled into a low bun on her neck, and a pale blue apron covering her front.

A man steps out behind her in a worn flannel and jeans. His dark hair isn't fully gray, but speckled with strands and pieces that give him a salt and pepper look. If I had to guess, I would say they are in their early seventies.

Thomas hooks Arson's leash with a *click*, and Arson climbs up onto the center console of the vehicle, waiting for him to get out. Thomas looks over at me, and it's visible how exhausted he is. We've both been awake now for over twenty-four hours, and it shows. His blue eyes are bloodshot behind the lenses of his glasses, with deep dark purplish circles under his eyes. The familiar brightness and excitement that usually fills his gaze is gone, now a dull glow.

"Hopefully once we get settled, we can get some sleep," Thomas says. "Are you ready?"

I nod, reminding myself to breathe. Like I told Thomas

last night, meeting new people is hard for me, and this is no exception. I overthink every little thing, from my hair or body, down to the way I interact with people. It's brutally exhausting. I still haven't stopped overthinking everything with Thomas. The only people who I am fully comfortable with are a thousand miles away.

Thomas gets out of the vehicle, Arson bounding with him. I take one moment by myself before I get out, my feet landing on the gravel driveway. The sun is hot, and it's aggressively humid out, like walking into a sauna.

I glance around, the faint sounds of animals in the barn drawing my attention to it. Chickens mill about the area, pecking at the ground and clucking at each other.

Thomas waits for me at the front of the vehicle, and I move to stand by his side. We walk toward the couple, who have made their way down the steps and onto the driveway to meet us. Arson nudges at my hip a few times, probably sensing my anxiety, and I reach down, rubbing his head.

"Hiya folks," the man says.

"Hi, Mr. Graff?" Thomas questions. The man nods, and Thomas visibly lets out a sigh of relief. "I'm Thomas Cunningham, and this is my fiancée, Hannah Pearson, and our dog, Arson." I withhold my shock at him introducing me as his fiancée. I mean, technically, to everyone on the outside, that's what we are, but it was weird to hear him call me it. He also referred to Arson as ours. Arson nuzzles into my thigh as if to agree with his dad, so I pet him a bit more.

"Nice to meet you two," the man says. "My name is Ron, and this is my wife, Dottie."

"Thank you for doing this," Thomas says, reaching out to shake their hands. "I can't tell you how much we appreciate it."

"Absolutely," Dottie replies, a warm smile crossing her

face. "We are happy to be a safe space for you in your time of need."

"Thank you," I murmur, finally finding my voice. Dottie glances over at me, her smile so genuine. It seems that she can see right through me as she holds my eyes for another long moment.

"Why don't we give you folks a short tour, and then we will leave you to settle in," Ron says. I expect him to lead us into the house, but instead, he gestures to the UTV parked by the barn. "We'll take the side by side down to the cottage."

"Sounds good," Thomas responds, glancing over at me. I offer him a little smile, hoping to convey that I'm okay. It probably comes across as a grimace, because Thomas furrows his brows in concern. "*You okay?*" he mouths.

I nod frantically, trying to show him I'm fine, but my aggression only makes him more concerned. He looks me up and down, and takes my hand before I can step away. He gives it a squeeze, and I squeeze back. Thankfully, that helps him realize that I'm alright.

Dottie and Ron climb into the front row of seats, leaving the back row to us. Thomas climbs in one side, closing the door and buckling while I do the same. Arson sits between us, his tongue lolling out of his mouth as he glances around in excitement.

Ron starts the engine, and then we're off. He slowly drives by the red barn, pointing inside. "We have kind of a variety of animals here as you can see. There's chickens, a donkey, a cow, some goats, and an emu. Dave, the emu, is around here somewhere. He has free rein of the land, so he pops up now and then. You'll meet him at some point."

"Dave?" I can't help but ask. Also, what the heck is an emu? Isn't that like a smaller version of an ostrich?

Dottie chuckles. "The grandkids named him. They named all of our animals, so they all have some interesting names, to say the least."

Thomas laughs in return. "My brother has a dog named Travis, so I get that."

Ron drives us around their property, briefly explaining some things we need to know, until he reaches the woods, and the beginning of the trailhead. He directs the UTV down the trail, the sunlight dimming under the shadow of the trees.

"Back here, is the cottage. When we bought our house back in the seventies, it was a tiny shack. Over the years, we've cleaned it up, added an addition, and now families stay there when they come to visit, but it's also a great spot for us to lend a helping hand for folks like you," he explains.

"It's tucked away about a mile down the path here, but there's electricity, running water, everything you might need. We stocked it with groceries, cleaning supplies and pillows and blankets. Anytime you need something, give us a shout," Dottie says. "It's a nice little spot for you guys to have some privacy, as well as safety."

The trees part up ahead, leading us to a clearing with a small wood cottage on the far edge of it. It's definitely small, but also so cute. It has a small front porch with a wooden swing hanging from the overhanging roof.

"This is adorable," I say.

"There's a small pond, and it's even swimmable," Ron points to the pond across the clearing.

"Wow, that's great," Thomas responds.

"Come on, let's show you inside," Dottie says, climbing out of the UTV.

We all follow, heading up to the front door of the

cottage. The door opens with a slight creak, and Ron gestures for us to enter.

The interior is small, with the kitchen on the far side of the room. It's nothing special, a small fridge, stove, sink and a few countertops. The pots and pans hang from one of those fancy things from the ceiling, and a small vase filled with wildflowers is on the countertop. There aren't any cupboards, just planks of wood lining the room with bowls, plates, cups, mugs and seasonings organized on them.

To the right is a staircase leading up to a lofted level. I think I spot a bed up there, but I'm not sure. It's hard to tell from this angle. To my left is a sectional couch facing the TV hanging from the wall. In the opposite corner, a small wood fireplace sits on a ledge.

Dottie brings us further into the cozy cottage, telling us where we can find everything, and showing us the bathroom off the kitchen. She and Ron lead us upstairs to show us what is, in fact, the bedroom. There's a queen-sized bed up here, made up with what appears to be a handmade quilt. My stomach flips with the confirmation that we will be sharing a bed.

I can sense Thomas's eyes on me with that confirmation, but I refuse to look at him right now. Thankfully, the light is dim up here, so I'm hopeful he can't see how red my face is.

We head back downstairs and outside for Ron to show us a few more things, but honestly, I'm not paying much attention. I'm too lost in my head, which isn't even functioning properly with how tired I am.

How long will we be here? A week? A month? A year? Will Thomas get sick of me in that time? Will he wish he never said we were engaged? The questions ricochet through my brain, and I lose my grip on what's happening in front of me, zoning out on a knot in a piece of wood in the siding.

My mind whirs through possible interactions and scenarios, each one ending worse than the last, until there's a soft tap on my shoulder. "Hannah, are you okay?" Dottie asks, her soft voice pulling me back to the present.

I shake off the thoughts, offering her a small smile. "I'm fine, just a lot going on is all."

"I'm sure. You two look like you need some sleep. I can tell Ron we need to call it quits. This can all wait until tomorrow." I try to stop her, to tell her we're fine, but she shushes me. "Ronnie, we need to let these kids get some sleep. Let's go get their car so they can unload and get settled. This can wait till tomorrow."

Ron straightens from where he was showing Thomas a drainpipe. "You're right, I'm sorry."

Thomas waves him off. "It's fine, really."

They won't hear any of it, though. "Stay here," Dottie goes as far as saying. "We will go get your vehicle."

They don't let us protest before taking the keys from Thomas and heading back to the main house in the side by side.

Thomas and I stand there a little dumbfounded as we watch them leave. "I'm exhausted," he finally says. "Come on, freckles. Let's wait inside."

The air is muggy and humid, so I'm thankful for the two window air conditioning units, one in the living room, and one upstairs. The coolness feels wonderful on my skin, and I kick off my shoes and sink into the comfortable couch right away.

Thomas unhooks Arson's leash from his collar, and

Arson bounds over to me. He settles at my feet, running his face along my shins, pressing his nose hard. "Hi, buddy," I say, scratching his neck. "What do you think of the cottage?"

He nudges me again, as if he is trying to tell me he likes it.

Thomas sits down beside me, reaching out to rub Arson's nose, too. "Sleep?" he questions.

"I kinda want to shower again, I feel really grimy, but then, yes."

"Ditto," Thomas rubs his eyes under his glasses. "I can't even think straight."

"Hmm," I can only mutter in response. The sound of the trunk opening pulls me from the haze momentarily, and Thomas and I both stand to head out and help grab our things.

Ten minutes later, Dottie and Ron have helped us with our bags, giving us a few final notes, and their phone number with instructions to use the landline and call them if we need anything, promising to stop by tomorrow to check in.

With them gone, I'm left feeling awkward, unsure of what to do next. Thomas and I bring our bags upstairs, but after, it's like a guessing game. We don't know what to do, or what to say, so it's awkward, this weird tenseness in the air.

"Do you want to shower first?" Thomas asks, gesturing down the stairs.

"Sure," I reply, quickly digging into my bag for a pair of shorts and shirt I can change into as well as my bathroom things.

I rush downstairs, closing the door behind me, and hurry to turn on the fan. I start the shower, climbing in before it's even had a chance to get hot, letting out a quick squeal, and settling once it warms.

The shower is like a reset button. This has all felt like such a dream that I didn't really process things until now, but it is truly settling in. I'm in the middle of nowhere in Southern Missouri, with a man whom I barely know under the guise of him being my fiancé. I already miss my Grandma, and wish I could text my sister and beg her for advice, but I can't. I'm all alone with only Thomas to lean on. A man that for a long time, I've had feelings for, but never planned to act on.

A man that was my first kiss not even a full day ago. So much has happened that I don't know how to process it.

Instead of trying to process, I go numb. It's like there's nothing left of me, I'm simply a shell. I go through the motions of washing my hair and body, making sure I'm fresh and clean. I get out of the shower before I use all the hot water, not wanting Thomas to freeze.

I dry my body and apply a thin layer of lotion before dressing and towel-drying my hair. I run a brush through it and brush my teeth again before exiting the bathroom.

Thomas is sitting on the couch, his head flopped back onto the wall. Arson's head rests in his lap, and he snores softly. I wish I had my phone. It's a cute moment, and I'm sure Thomas would appreciate a photo of it, but oh well.

I slowly walk over to them to try and wake him, but I trip over my own feet, stumbling and nearly falling to my knees. I catch myself before I do, but embarrassment floods my veins anyway. Arson startles awake, waking Thomas in the process.

"Wha—" Thomas stutters, sitting up, eyes glancing around the room.

"Sorry," I say quietly, my cheeks flaming. "I wanted to let you know that I'm out of the shower."

He rubs his chest. "Oh, thanks."

I nod and spin on my heel, heading up the stairs. All my stuff is on the right side of the bed closest to the stairs, so I pull back the comforter and climb in.

I sink into the bed, my body going lax and eyes shutting within seconds. The bed and pillow are so comfortable that I barely even have time to remember I brought my own pillow from home before I'm drifting.

SOMETHING SHAKES my leg and I move my limb away, grumbling. Grandma never lets me sleep past nine on weekends, and it's annoying as heck. There's another shake, this time on my shoulder. "Grandma, stop, I'm tired," I mumble, pulling the covers over my eyes.

"Hannah, it's Thomas," his voice is low as he talks quietly. The bed dips at my hip, and I shoot up straight when I remember where I am. I'm not at Grandma's for the weekend, I'm in the middle of nowhere, Missouri, with Thomas Cunningham after we witnessed an attempted murder, and a threat on Thomas's life.

I breathe hard as all the memories flood my brain. "Hey, you're okay," Thomas says, resting his hands on my shoulders. Arson is tucked at my side, sound asleep, missing all the activity. He must have joined me at some point.

"What's going on?" I ask, running my hand through my still damp hair. Huh, maybe I hadn't been asleep very long.

Thomas's hair is wet, a piece hanging down over his forehead. My fingers itch to push it up and away, but I refrain. His black square glasses are sliding down the bridge of his nose, and he takes his hand from my shoulder to push them back up.

"I'm sorry to wake you, but you should sleep on the other side," Thomas says, gesturing to the untouched side of the bed.

I rub my eyes. "Why?" I don't have a problem moving, but I'm curious.

Thomas sighs, looking up at the ceiling. "I don't want to scare you."

My gut churns, and I give him a warning look. "Thomas..."

"Fine," he breathes. "On the off and completely unlikely chance that there is a break-in, if I'm on this side of the bed, I'm closest to the stairs, and where the intruder would enter. I brought my gun with me, and would have it in the nightstand."

"Oh," I state. It makes sense. If there is an intruder, he's the most equipped to deal with it. Well, besides Arson.

"I promise I didn't mean to scare you," Thomas rushes to say. He reaches up with one of his hands, tucking a piece of hair behind my ear gently. "I'm trying to keep you safe, Han."

I nod, shifting so I can stand. "I know. Thank you," I say. I want to say more, to tell him how much I appreciate his kindness and him taking care of me, but the words die in my throat. I slide out of the comforter and off the bed. Arson wakes with a loud grumble as I round the bed, switching the pillows so Thomas doesn't have to sleep on a wet pillow from my damp hair.

I climb back into the bed on the opposite side as Thomas pulls the blinds on the one window up here. It's darker than it was when I first fell asleep, so I'm assuming he closed the blinds and curtains downstairs too.

A lot of light still peeks in, but it's plenty dark enough to fall back asleep with how tired I am.

Thomas moves around the small upstairs, and I drift off quickly, too tired to overthink anything else at this moment.

## 20

## THOMAS

Hannah's chest rises and falls slowly as she enters sleep. I feel guilty for waking and confusing her, but as soon as I walked up the stairs and saw her fast asleep in the spot closest to the stairs, I knew I had to wake her. Perhaps it's the caveman in me, but I brought her here to protect her, so I'm going to do my damndest to do that, and if that means making her sleep on the far end of the bed, then so be it.

I don't want to admit that the minute she crawled into bed on the opposite side, relief flooded my entire body like a warm caress.

I let her fall into a deeper sleep with Arson at her side before I crawl into bed. She doesn't even move as the bed shifts, letting me know that she's out like a light.

Her soft snores are another indicator that she's passed out. That in itself is a relief. I could tell how tired she was, the deep purple circles under her eyes darkening with each passing minute. I turn onto my side, and I wish so badly that I could pull her into my embrace, to hold her and know that she really is safe and in my arms, but I can't do that. I can't cross the unsaid boundary I know she's not ready for. Sleeping in the same bed as her already has to be a big step for both of us.

I didn't think to offer and sleep on the couch, though thinking about it now it would've been a first line of defense, but all I could think about was not leaving her side.

Arson cuddles up in the middle of us, letting out a huff, like he's content now that both of us are in bed with him. "Good boy," I whisper, giving him a head scratch. Sleep takes me fast, my body too exhausted to consider fighting it.

A CLATTER WAKES me from a deep sleep. I sit straight up in bed, hoping my brain catches up as I nearly fall out of bed. The bed is empty to my right with no sign of Hannah, or Arson. I rise to my feet, ignoring the stiffness in my muscles. I reach for my gun from the side table, hoping I won't need it, but thankful I have it.

"Shit," a voice comes from downstairs, amidst another clatter.

The heavy weight on my chest eases as I recognize the voice. A soft woof sounds, and Hannah shushes him. "Shh, Arson. Your dad is still asleep."

He woofs softly again, causing Hannah to shush him again. "I know you're hungry, I am too, but I don't know where your food is, and I don't think bacon is good for you, buddy."

He starts doing the thing he does when he's really feeling dramatic. The only way I can describe it is howl-talking.

"Arson!" Hannah whisper-shouts. "You're going to wake him up!"

I chuckle under my breath as I walk down the stairs. "It's okay, freckles, I'm already awake."

Hannah squeaks, clutching her palm to her chest. Arson bounds over to me, continuing his dramatic howling. "I know buddy, I'm sorry, I'll get you some food."

"I let him out when I woke up not long ago."

"Thanks," I reply and grab his bag of food from where I left it earlier in one of the closets, scooping him a bowl of food and placing it on the ground for him. He devours it ravenously.

"What time is it?" I ask, noting the pitch black outside.

"Three in the morning." Hannah glances out the square window above the kitchen sink. "I woke up and figured I may as well make some food, I was starving. They left the kitchen fully stocked for us."

"Wow," I respond. "That's nice of them." I stride up behind her, taking the pan from her hands and setting it on the stovetop. I start the burner, noting the carton of eggs sitting on the counter.

"Are you hungry?" Hannah asks. "I can make some for you, too."

"I can help."

We work together in silence, me, cooking the bacon, her, grabbing some plates from the shelves and setting the table. She grabs juice, butter, bread, and fruit from the fridge, and cuts some of the fruit up for us.

I wasn't hungry right away when I came down, but now that the food is cooking, I'm starving, my stomach growling. "How do you want your eggs?"

"Any way is fine," Hannah replies, mindlessly buttering toast.

"Over-easy?"

"Yep."

I make the eggs, grabbing the two plates from the table to plate them, and bring them, and the bacon over to the center of the table. We slept for just under twelve hours. Hannah sits down next to me at the table.

"How did you sleep?" I ask. There are so many things that we should talk about and discover more about each other, but I want to focus on right now.

"Fine," she murmurs, pushing her eggs around her plate. "I slept really hard at first, but then was restless, so I came down here. I'm sorry I woke you up."

"It's okay, I really don't mind." I shovel some food into my mouth. "Arson can be annoying once he has something he wants."

"He's still cute, though," Hannah responds, finally taking a bite of food.

"Last week, he yelled at me because I didn't take him with me over to my brother's house. He was pissed when I came home smelling like his dog, Travis."

"How dare you," Hannah says with a mock-gasp. "That is a huge betrayal."

"You'd think I'd left him home alone for days. I was gone for maybe two hours."

"Clearly, he loves his dad." Hannah laughs softly.

"We're a good team. I've had him since he was a puppy. We bonded instantly and went through the training program together." I scratch the top of Arson's head as he sits at my side, drool dripping from his mouth. "I love him. Even if he's disgusting."

"Ew," Hannah mumbles, glancing at him.

"How are you holding up?" I ask, deciding to bite the bullet.

"I'm fine," she replies, dropping her gaze back to her food.

I've been around enough women in my life to know that her saying she's fine, means that she's actually not.

"Hannah," I state, reaching over to rest my hand atop her palm.

"I'm fine, Thomas, really."

"I'm not," I reply.

Her head snaps up, eyes meeting mine. "You're not?"

"Of course not," I say with a lackluster chuckle. "I watched a friend get shot, was scared for your life and mine at the hands of a gunman who is part of a drug trafficking ring, had to give a statement to police, tell my family I'm going into hiding, and leave my life behind for an unknown length of time," I finish with a heavy breath. "I don't think anyone would be fine after that, and it's okay not to be."

"Right," she mutters, using her fork to push her food around her plate. "I don't know how to process this."

I nod, hoping that if I stay quiet, she will continue.

"It all feels like a weird dream. I don't know how to do this, Thomas. It's all so much. Being in a fake relationship, being in hiding... How do we process it all? "

"I don't either, but we can work through it together, yeah? We have a lot of time on our hands. We can work through this, get to know each other, and hopefully before we know it we will be back home." I reach across the table to rest my hand on top of hers. She stiffens for a brief second, then relaxes into my touch, even turning her hand to grasp mine.

"I'm here for you, Han. I want you to tell me everything, even if you think it's nothing. And not only to keep you safe or be your friend in this situation, I want to get to know you, so that when we go home, we can pick up where things left off. We might be pretending to be engaged, but that doesn't mean that my feelings for you are pretend."

She inhales sharply, her blue eyes widening in shock. "You don't have to say that," she says. "We barely know each other, Thomas."

"So? I still know that I have feelings for you, Hannah."

"We're just tired."

I let out a soft sigh. I thought we were making progress, but now, it feels like we're backtracking. I'll just have to show her how real my feelings for her are instead. "Are you finished? We should get some more rest. I know I'm still tired."

Hannah nods, silently standing from her chair to scrape her mostly uneaten plate into the trash. I watch as she goes about tidying the kitchen, so I stand, helping her clean up. We clean in silence, and I can feel the shift as Hannah shuts down. I anticipated this, knowing how hard the last twenty-four-plus hours have been, but that doesn't mean it doesn't hurt any less.

After she wipes down the table for the third time, I know I have to put a stop to this. "Hannah, it's clean. Let's go to sleep."

She looks up at me, and those blue eyes swirl with emotion. "Okay."

"I'll be right there the whole time. We're safe."

With an unconvincing nod, she hangs the wet washcloth over the sink and dries her hands. I let out Arson one final time and when I look back, Hannah is already heading up the stairs. My gaze travels down her delectable body, but I move my eyes from her ass, because even though it looks fucking amazing in those tiny sleep shorts, now is not the time to get an erection.

Arson and I follow her up the stairs, and I pull the

sheets back on my side as she rounds to the other side. She climbs into the rumpled bed, lying on her right side and facing the wall. "Goodnight," she whispers, and fuck she sounds so broken, so sad, that I don't know what to do.

"Hannah," I whisper, kneeling on the bed to lean forward and place my hand on her shoulder. "Talk to me. How can I help?"

She shakes her head. "I'm fine, Thomas. Really. I'm tired, that's all."

I don't believe that for a second. She shifts so my hand falls off her shoulder. I can't push this anymore. I lie down on my right side, pulling the sheets up over my body. I watch her, waiting for her breathing to even out so I know she's asleep. Instead, sleep takes me first.

## 21

# HANNAH

My body trembles with unbridled anxiety. I've been sitting up in bed against the headboard for two hours, waiting, listening, and watching. Thomas fell asleep the moment his head hit the pillow, and you would think that my brain would have settled by now, but it hasn't. I can't stop thinking about how easy it would be for someone to break in. They could come in from the other side of the woods, totally avoiding the Graff's house altogether, and sneak in without us even knowing.

Sure, we could put up a fight between Arson's attack instincts and Thomas's gun, but still, I am sure we would be outnumbered. And what help am I? I'm a burden. Thomas would be worried about me, and distracted, so he makes for an easy target.

How can he possibly be asleep right now? Hasn't he considered these potential things happening? Shouldn't we be awake and on the lookout?

Thomas rolls over in his sleep, the bed shifting as he adjusts. He snores loudly as he does, and Arson pretty much copies him, letting out a weird moaning noise as he scoots closer to me. As if he can sense my distress, Arson blearily opens his eyes, and shifts to be nearer yet.

He shoves his head underneath one of my hands that is picking at the skin of my fingernails. He plops his entire body across my midsection, and the weight of his body calms my labored breathing.

I pet his soft head, and having physical to do helps soothe my increasing anxiety. Even though it helps calm my racing thoughts, it does nothing to help me sleep. The potential of things happening with us asleep are still too great to risk one of us being asleep. This way, if I hear something, I can wake Thomas up right away.

I sit and stare into the dark night for another hour until the sun slowly starts to rise. With the light rising in the sky, my anxiety dissipates. If they were going to ambush us, during the night was the best time. There's too much risk of being seen during the day. At least that's my thought process.

Arson is still sleeping in my lap, and I slowly sink down so my head is on the pillow, sleep finally taking over.

A SOFT WHINING wakes me up. There's a heavy weight on my chest, and it slowly dawns on me that Arson has been lying on my chest since I fell asleep early this morning. The sun is high in the sky now, illuminating the small cabin easily.

The smell of coffee stirs my senses even more. I sit up, and Arson rolls off me, jumping off the bed and onto the wood floor. His nails clack against the wood as he tippy-taps his toes in a combination of excitement and probably the need to pee.

"Alright, buddy, I'm coming," I tell him. The sheets beside me are pulled up neatly, the spot Thomas was in empty.He must be downstairs with the coffee. I can't believe I slept through him getting out of bed. I wonder what time it is?

Arson bolts down the stairs, running to the front door as soon as he hits the floor. Thomas chuckles. "Gotta pee, Arson?" As I make my way down the stairs, I see him stand from the couch, set his coffee mug on a side table and head to the door to let Arson out.

"Morning, freckles," he greets as he sees me.

Self-consciously, I run my hand through my hair, sure it's a mess of waves and tangles since it was wet the first time I fell asleep, and when I finally fell asleep the second time, I was still a little restless. I tug my shirt down a little too, hoping it's covering me up.

"Morning. What time is it?" I ask, glancing around to spot a clock. The oven is an old-style stove with no clock on it.

"About nine. Sorry if Arson woke you. I've been trying to get him to come down since I woke up at seven, but he wouldn't leave your side," he explains.

"Oh, it's fine. I needed to get up anyway. Can't waste the day," I say with an awkward laugh.

"You can sleep as late as you want," Thomas says. "We have a lot of sleep to catch up on."

I shake my head. "I'm good now." I don't fully believe myself, though. I can feel the pressing tiredness behind my eyes, my body heavy with exhaustion. Thomas glances me over like he doesn't believe me either. He lets Arson in the front door, who dashes over to me again, like he only left my side because he absolutely had to.

"Coffee?" Thomas asks, gesturing to the half-full pot in the kitchen.

"Yes, please." I move in the direction of the steaming pot.

"Sit, I've got it." He shoos me over to the couch. I flop down, pulling my legs up and crossing them underneath me.

"How did you sleep?" he asks as he pulls a cup down from the shelf.

"Fine," I respond. Probably a little too quickly, because Thomas eyes me warily.

He doesn't question me though, instead asks, "Cream and sugar?"

I nod, and he pours a generous amount of each into the cup, giving it a stir. He heads back over to me, handing me the warm mug of steaming coffee. He surprises me when instead of sitting down next to me, he first leans down, pressing a long kiss to my cheek.

"You look beautiful this morning." He sits beside me, closer than I anticipated. I fight the urge to shift away.

I take a sip of my coffee, hoping that it helps explain the sudden heat coursing through my body instead of trying to blame it on his proximity to me. "Thanks," I murmur, instead of telling him I surely look like a potato.

Arson snuggles into my side. "What are you going to do today?" I change the subject away from me.

"I figured we could head to the main house and get to know Ron and Dottie. I want to do some work for them while I'm here. Whether that be repairs, helping feed the animals, whatever, I want to make myself useful. I'm not great at sitting around."

I nod along. What am I going to do? It's not like I have any special skills to offer them while here, I mean unless someone gets injured, but it's not like I want them to get hurt so that I have something to do.

"Would you want to join me?" His brows lift in question.

"Yeah, but I don't have much to offer them."

"Stop that," Thomas says.

"What?"

"You offer a lot, even if you think you don't. You're so smart, Hannah."

I shrink back into the couch a little, taking another sip of coffee to disguise the heat racing through my veins again.

We sit in silence as we finish our coffee.

"I'm going to get dressed. Should we plan to leave here soon?" Thomas asks as he stands up from the couch.

"That works," I respond, drinking the last sip of my coffee. Hopefully this helps me wake up a bit. Thomas heads up the stairs, glancing back at Arson who has not moved from my side on the couch.

"Are you coming?"

Arson huffs, snuggling further into my side. I snicker as his fur tickles my arm. "I get it buddy. I want to stay and snuggle with her, too, but you got to snuggle her all night," Thomas says.

My stomach swoops at the words. *He* wants to snuggle with me? I clear my throat and shift. "Arson, go with your dad." I gesture to Thomas standing on the stairs. Arson glances up at his dad, and huffs again, ignoring him.

I'm not going to lie, it feels good having Arson at my side, almost like he knows I'm anxious and need his protection. "He's fine, if you're okay with him staying." I pet his smooth fur.

"Of course," Thomas responds. "I didn't want him to be annoying you, that's all."

"Not at all. I like it."

"Alright, then." He continues up the stairs, and I hear the shuffling sounds of him rifling through his bags. "One unfortunate thing about not having our phones is not being able to check the weather at the drop of a hat. I don't even know what the weather in Missouri is like," he calls.

"I'm not sure, either." I raise my voice a bit so he can hear me. "It looks sunny out. I can see if there's a weather channel on TV or something."

"Nah, we can live on the wild side for today." A second later, he's striding down the stairs in a pair of gym shorts and a shirt. The deep navy Ivy Ridge PD shirt clings to his chest, showcasing his broad shoulders, thick pectorals, and the softness of his stomach. The shorts broadcast his thick thighs, something I didn't expect to be a turn on, but apparently, I have a thing for thick thighs. Noted.

A tingling feeling settles between my thighs, something new and unexpected. Thomas glances at me, and down to my hand. "Are you done? Can I take your cup?

I nod, my mouth dry and my brain unworking. I stand from the couch, Arson clambering down after me, and dart past Thomas throwing my thumb over my shoulder in a gesture toward the stairs. "I'll go get changed."

Arson dutifully follows me, and I almost feel bad that he's following me so much, rather than hanging by Thomas. Without waiting for an answer, I rush up the stairs and scan the area for my suitcase. Thomas must have moved it last night so that it was on my side of the bed after I fell asleep the first time, as it's in the far corner of the loft.

I grab a pair of comfortable jean shorts, change out of my pajama shorts into them, and exchange my top for a sports bra and a band shirt from a concert Julia and I went to last year. I run a brush through my snarled hair, and grab a claw clip from my bag, twisting it up and off my neck. I slide on some socks and my tennis shoes before heading back downstairs. Arson plods beside me, his nails clacking on the wood stairs.

Thomas is sitting back on the couch, quite literally twiddling his thumbs. He stands when we reach the floor, and I gesture toward the bathroom. "I need to brush my teeth. I don't think Ron and Dottie would appreciate my coffee and morning breath."

"Eh, I'm sure that's the least of their concerns."

I laugh as I head into the bathroom, trying to ignore my rising nerves over our second meeting with the Graffs. With time, I'll hopefully get used to them, but right now, I'm not there yet. How much time will we have here, anyway? Hell, I'm barely comfortable with Thomas, and the man is supposedly my fiancé. I take a few deep breaths as I close the bathroom door behind me. There's a press against the door as the latch is about to click though, so I open it, and find Arson peeking in.

"Buddy, I need to go to the bathroom. I can do this alone, okay?"

The look Arson gives me is the absolute definition of puppy dog eyes. His deep brown eyes seem to call out to me, pleading for me to reconsider, and I swear he makes his lower lip tremble as I slowly close the door on him again. Guilt swarms me, but he will be okay for two minutes without me, right?

I relieve myself, brush my teeth and hair, and put on a layer of deodorant, exiting the bathroom in only a few minutes. Arson is still sitting there when I open the door, and he looks irritated with my audacity of leaving him. "Stop it," I tell him.

"Arson, leave the girl alone," Thomas calls. He whistles, and at the sharp tone, Arson is at attention, bristling over to Thomas's side in an instant. Thank goodness. Arson is such a good boy, but I feel bad that he was choosing me over his dad for a while.

"Ready," I announce as I enter the main area again.

"Off we go." Thomas opens the front door and rests his palm at the small of my back as I walk through.

Warm summer heat smothers my body. The area is mostly shaded from all the trees, but there is still a lot of sun peeking through. It's muggy and hot, but thankfully a light breeze is present, ruffling the leaves and blowing strands of hair into my face. The pond over in the distance is looking more and more appealing with each step we take on the path. I try to recall if I brought a swimsuit, but I was so frantic while packing that I don't remember half of what I packed.

Something I didn't notice yesterday is the set of swings hanging from a tree. They're simple, rope hanging down and connected to wooden planks, but it looks relaxing, like something out of a romance movie.

Thomas still has his hand resting on my back, guiding me through the trees. The path is mainly gravel, so I'm not worried about tripping over sticks or anything like that. The silence is nice, though, and I don't have the compulsion to fill it with conversation. It feels natural.

Arson is about fifty feet ahead of us, his nose pressed to the ground as he scopes the land. Every time he gets a little too far, Thomas lets out a quick whistle and Arson returns to him, tapping his thigh before going out again.

It's fascinating watching the two of them together.

Arson is a well-trained dog with sharp instincts, and it's cool to see him use his nose to search for whatever scent is hounding him.

We make it through the woods into the clearing that shows us Ron and Dottie's house and barn. Ron is outside, a throng of chickens following at his heels.

"I'd bet anything that the chickens want whatever is in that bag," Thomas says with a laugh. Arson darts toward the chickens, and I shriek.

"Oh my god, he's going to eat them!" I panic.

Thomas whistles, and Arson stops in his tracks, circling back to us without hesitation. "No, he won't." Thomas laughs.

Arson boops my thigh this time, surprising me. He sticks by my side now, heeling to me.

"Morning," Thomas calls to Ron.

Ron raises his free hand to wave, and a few chickens cluck in protest as he veers off course to meet us. They follow him with increasing speed, and I shift closer to Thomas. It's not like I need protection, or am scared of the chickens, but if they're hungry, you never know what they might do.

"How'd you folks sleep?" Ron asks. The chickens cluck and bawk at him. A few even go as far as peck at his boots, spurring him to grumble, "Alright, you menaces, here."

He scoops a handful of grain, tossing it onto the grass. The chickens go wild, fighting and fluttering for a bite to eat.

"Well, thanks," Thomas says. "You didn't have to stock the kitchen for us, we could have gone shopping today."

Ron shakes his head. "Nope. The less you two are seen outside of this land, the better, right?"

Thomas sighs, nodding. "I suppose that's true. Regardless, it's appreciated."

"No thanks needed." Ron waves him off. "Come this way. I'll introduce you two to the rest of the animals."

He leads us into the barn where I spot Dottie in one of the far stalls, hoisting a full shovel of manure into a wheelbarrow. I wrinkle my nose at the smell. I'm not sure it's a smell someone could get used to.

Dottie calls from the corner. "Morning, you two!"

"Morning," we reply in unison.

"Did ya eat?" she asks, shoveling another sloppy scoop of manure.

Thomas looks a little green in the gills as he swallows thickly. "Sure did. Thanks, though."

Dottie nods. "Good, good."

Ron leads us further into the barn. To my right is a stall that has a few goats inside. A speckled black and white one perches up onto the railed fencing. I shriek, stepping back in shock, a little scared it's going to haul itself over and hurt me or something. Ron chuckles, reaching over the barrier to scratch the goat's neck.

"This here is Oreo," he says. He points out a few more of the goats in the stall. "And here is Popsicle, Cookie, Snickerdoodle, and Pudding."

"I wonder if your grandkids like sweets?" Thomas chuckles, reaching over and wrapping his arm around my shoulders. Right, he's my fiancée I have to play the part. I lean into him, and even though it's warm as hell in here, his touch sends a shiver through my body.

"Blame that one," Ron says, pointing to his wife. "She always has to make the kids sweet treats when they come. And then, she yells at me when I try to sneak a bite."

"Because it's for the kids!" Dottie yells in return. "I

want you healthy, especially after that scare a few years ago, my love."

Ron leans forward, whispering conspiratorially. "I'm healthy as a horse. I had a checkup a few weeks ago. Doc says I'm fine after a mini-stroke about three years ago."

My heart clenches as the memory of my mom receiving the call about my grandpa's stroke flashes through my mind. My hands clutch at each other, and I pinch myself, reminding me to stay in the moment.

*Do not get lost in your mind.*

Pinching helps as I focus back on Dottie's teasing remarks toward her husband.

Thomas glances down at me while they're distracted, his eyes seeking and curious. I offer him a smile that probably looks fake as hell. He raises his brows, but I ignore his silent question, instead turning back to the Graff's.

The stall that Dottie stands in is connected to an outdoor pasture, and the sun streams in through the open door. She clicks her tongue a few times, and the sound of clomping hooves has me curiously leaning forward to see.

A golden-red Highland cow saunters into the now clean pen, rubbing its forehead against Dottie's hip. "Oh my god," I whisper.

"What?" Thomas replies, voice edging toward concern.

"It's so cute, holy shit," I continue whispering, my feet moving toward the stall at their own volition. Thomas's arm slides off my shoulders as I move.

Dottie sees my growing smile and lifts the cow's head. "This is Fern," she says. "She's about five-years-old, and very friendly."

"I love cows," I reply. I probably look and sound a little odd at the moment, but I couldn't care less. I've always loved cows. I mean, you can drive a mile outside of town and see a bunch of them at any farm, but there's something about having one right in front of you to make it even more exciting.

"Didn't you hear them yesterday when they said they have a cow?" Thomas asks, sliding back up beside me.

I shake my head, my eyes wide as I take in this adorable creature. "No, I was so focused on the emu," I state. I tentatively reach out my hand as I approach the stall. "Can I pet her?"

"Absolutely," Dottie says, a smile crossing her face.

I hold my palm out and Fern shoves her head into my palm without hesitation, jerking her head back and forth when I freeze, almost like she's making me pet her with the motion, rather than me moving my own hand. A giggle bursts from my lips. "Oh my god, she's so cute I can't handle it."

"She likes you," Dottie says. A nudge at my leg pulls my attention away from Fern. Arson is rubbing his entire body against my legs, nearly shoving me into Thomas at my side.

"Someone's jealous," Thomas says with a laugh.

"Oh, buddy, it's okay," I croon, removing my hand from Fern to pet Arson. He leans into my touch with his whole body.

"Dave is around here somewhere," Ron explains. "His stall is here," he points to the stall across from Fern's, "but he tends to wander the property."

"Should we go inside? I can give you a brief tour," Dottie remarks.

"Sure," Thomas agrees. I give Fern one final pat on her head, and follow Thomas. His hand moves to rest on the small of my back again as he leans down to murmur in my ear, "Watching you be excited over that Highland cow might have been the cutest thing I've ever seen."

My cheeks burn. "No, it wasn't."

"No, it really was adorable. You got so excited, it made me think of my niece, Lennie, when she sees Arson for the first time in a few weeks. Pure joy."

I swallow, trying to hide the slight embarrassment. I did get a little over-excited. I can't help it, though. I love animals, especially cows.

## 22

## THOMAS

Hannah is so cute. For a moment, I thought she was getting lost in her head in the barn. I watched as she pinched herself in what seemed like an attempt to bring herself back to the present, and her eyes took on this lost quality that scared me, but seeing Fern helped.

Hannah walks beside me, with Arson on her other side as we follow Ron and Dottie toward their front porch. A sudden, rhythmic thumping echoes louder as it gets closer, and Ron turns on his heel, sticking out an arm without even looking. A blur of dark feathers flies through my vision, and Arson barks, stumbling back into my legs.

When the motion stops, I can fully take in this ginormous bird. It's taller than my six-foot frame, with beady bright brown eyes and a sharp-looking beak. Ron has his hand around its neck, not tightly, but enough to hold him back. The bird makes a noise that can only be described as an echoing thumping from deep in his chest.

"This is Dave," Ron explains, pushing the giant bird back. Hannah presses herself into my chest, and my arms reflexively wrap around her. She cowers into me at the sight of the large bird in front of us. "He can be a little territorial, but once he gets to know you two and Arson, he will be your best friend, I promise. Now go on, get," he says to the bird, who surprisingly listens, darting off toward the barn.

"He can be chaotic, but he's a sweetheart," Dottie says. She waves us toward her, heading up the creaking wooden steps. I unwrap myself from Hannah's body, moving my palm to rest on her lower back again. We walk up the stairs as Dottie opens the front door for us.

When we walk in, a blast of cool air hits my skin, sending a shiver across my body. The entryway is small, with family photos hanging on the walls, as well as a few religious verses in fancy script.

We kick off our shoes and follow them into the kitchen. The kitchen has a lingering scent of coffee and bacon, the perfect combo. Ron gestures to the table, pulling out a chair for Dottie and Hannah. Hannah sits, glancing up to make sure I'm sitting next to her.

It's moments like this where I can really see her anxiety shine through. She mentioned to me earlier that she feels most comfortable when she's with someone she knows well. I hope that now, and hopefully in the future I can be one of those people for her, and not only because she has to lean on me, but because she *knows* she can.

I sit down beside her, scooting the chair closely so our thighs are almost touching. I put my arm around her shoulder, and notice that she relaxes ever so slightly.

"Coffee?" Ron asks, coming to the table with the pot and a few mugs.

"Please," I confirm, and Hannah nods. He pours us all cups, and grabs the cream from the fridge, and a little container of sugar. Hannah pours a generous amount of cream into her coffee, adding a small scoop of sugar, while I do the opposite. Lots of sugar, not a lot of cream.

It's these little details about her I log into my memory for the future.

"How long have you two been together?" Dottie asks as both Hannah and I take our first sip of coffee. Hannah sputters over her drink, and I pat gently between her shoulder blades.

"Sorry," she says between her muffled coughs. "Swallowed wrong."

To be fair, I wasn't totally expecting her to ask that question, nor is it something that Hannah and I have discussed, so I choose to wing it. "A few months. But, a lot of our relationship has been very private while we got to know each other. We only very recently got engaged." I clear my throat at the end, hoping it conveys nonchalance, which I definitely don't feel right now.

"A whirlwind romance," Dottie says with a swooning sigh. "Sounds familiar, doesn't it, Ronnie?"

"Sure does," Ron replies, leaning over to kiss his wife on the cheek.

Hannah has stopped coughing now and is leaning back in her chair. She's looking at Ron and Dottie with fondness, a look I haven't seen on her face before.

"We met when I was nineteen and he was twenty-two," Dottie explains. "Three months later, we were walking out of the courthouse with a signed marriage license. When you know, you know. Everyone who says it's too fast, or that you don't know each other well enough is simply jealous. Love comes first, and the rest will fall into place."

Ron looks at his wife with so much love and adoration that I have to swallow the sudden lump in my throat. That is the kind of love that I want, and it's something that I hope I can have with the girl sitting next to me.

"That's beautiful," Hannah says, her voice soft with emotion.

"I have a feeling your love story will be just as beautiful," Dottie says.

"Thank you," I reply, completely genuine. "Are all the photos of your children?"

"They are," Dottie replies proudly. "We have four children. Two boys, two girls, and eight grandchildren."

"Wow," Hannah breathes. "All of your kids have children, then?"

Ron shakes his head. "Our youngest, Fletcher, is still single. He plays hockey for a team in Minnesota. Maybe you'll meet him. He's coming for a visit in a few weeks."

"Wow, that's awesome," I state. I'm curious to know what team he plays for, but Ron changes the subject, so I'll ask later.

"How did you guys become a safe house?" I ask.

Ron chuckles under his breath. "It's a long story. I was in the FBI for most of my working years, and a lot of that time was spent traveling. This place, my home, my family, was my safe haven. When I retired, I knew I wanted to be able to provide that for people like you folks, so ever since then we help when we can. Sometimes the timing doesn't work out, but we've helped quite a few people throughout the years."

"Wow," I breathe. "That's amazing. Thank you so much. You've helped so many people."

Ron shrugs. "It's the least I could do."

We continue to chat for a while, and when I look at the clock next, it's nearly noon. Arson has been sitting at our feet the whole time, but I can tell he's getting antsy to get outside and explore, so it's probably time to head back.

Hannah also looks like she's dead-on-her-feet exhausted. "I think it's time we head back to the cottage, don't you, freckles? We are still getting caught up on our rest."

"Oh, of course," Dottie tuts, rising to her feet and collecting our mugs. Hannah stands slowly, letting out a yawn as she does.

As we head to the front door, I remember part of the reason I wanted to chat with them in the first place. "Say, do you two need some help around the farm while we are here?"

Ron raises his brow. "No, no, we are fine," he responds. "You should take this time to relax, spend time with your love."

I shake my head. "I mean, I'm going to take advantage of the time with her, for sure," I say, taking Hannah's hand in mine and leaning down to kiss her temple. She tenses briefly, and I take note of that reaction before continuing, "but I also know it will be nice to put myself to work a bit. I can help with whatever you need. Cleaning stables, working on machines, handyman work, you name it. I like to be busy."

"In that case, I may take you up on a few things," Ron says with a chuckle, reaching out his palm to shake mine.

"My grandpa was a woodworker, so I grew up helping him in the shop. I'm good with my hands." I raise my hand in a weird semi-jazz hand.

"Ooh, maybe Thomas can fix my jewelry box," Dottie says, her voice raising in excitement.

"Absolutely," I state. "My brother took over the business, so he'd be better at it, but I can patch it up, no problem."

"I would appreciate that," she replies. Arson whines quietly at my feet, and I take that as our cue.

"We should probably head out before this one ruins your rug." I gesture to the front door. "Thanks again. I'll stop by tomorrow morning and get to work."

They try to protest, but I wave them off as Hannah and I walk out the front door. Arson darts to the first tree he spots, relieving his bladder.

"They're so nice," Hannah mumbles as we get further from the house. Arson follows, running ahead of us on the gravel path toward our cottage.

"They are," I agree. My hand is still entwined in hers, and I'm hesitant to let go. I love every second of contact that I can have with her, and the thought of letting go hurts. "Do you want to take a nap? I think I need another few hours of sleep before I can fully feel like a human again."

Hannah nods. "Yeah, a nap sounds good."

I decide to bring up the couch. "If you want, I can take the couch from now on. I should have done that in the first place, but I was too tired to think straight last night."

Hannah's blue eyes dart up to mine in an instant. "Why would you take the couch?"

"Because you would probably be more comfortable sleeping alone?" I think back to the way she tensed earlier in the kitchen. I didn't mean to insinuate anything other than that I was excited to spend more time with her, one-on-one, but perhaps it came across differently.

She shakes her head. "Don't be silly."

A flush burns my skin. Oh, does that mean she likes the thought of sleeping by me? The real question is, do I push a little and flirt? Or do I be cordial and thank her?

What can I say? I've always been a bit of a flirt.

"Aww, freckles. Does that mean you liked snuggling with me last night?" I watch the blush creep up her freckled chest and feel the slight twitch in her palm.

She clears her throat. "It makes more sense to share the bed, that's all."

"Hmm," I murmur. "We can kick Arson to the floor tonight. He's a bed hog."

That gets a chuckle and a smile out of her. "Yeah, he kinda is. He was plastered to my body all night."

"I feel bad, because that's how he usually is with me," I say. "Ever since he was a puppy, he has been a velcro sleeper."

"I didn't mind," Hannah says. "It was kinda nice waking up with him all over me this morning. I don't have any pets, and clearly I've not cuddled before, so it's not like I know what it's like."

"You've never been cuddled?" I ask, my curiosity blooming. I had an inkling that Hannah might be inexperienced, but I don't think I fully realized just how inexperienced she is. "And why do you say, *clearly?*"

She shakes her head, kicking at a rock at our feet. Arson chases it as it skitters across the gravel. "I'm not exactly dating material," she says condescendingly.

"Um, yes, you are," I retort.

She glances up, her eyes narrowing. "Thomas, you have to be lying."

I pull her to a stop by our entwined hands. "Why would I lie about something like this?"

She shrugs, turning her gaze away, almost as if she's embarrassed.

"Hannah, you have to know I'm serious. Everything I've said or done to you has been out of my pure desire. I don't lie, and I would never lie to anyone, let alone you, about this."

She doesn't look at me, and my irritation grows. I let go of her hand, and I don't miss the way she almost shrinks in on herself. We're through the clearing now, our little cottage visible just barely in the distance. We're completely alone.

Hannah picks at her fingertips, ripping the skin raw, and even without that tell, I'd know she's anxious.

I grab her hands, stopping their assault on her fingers, and pull her toward me. I reach out, caressing my fingers up her arm and across her shoulder, and then slowly up her neck until my thumb and pointer finger are gripping her chin. I tilt her face upwards, forcing her eyes to me.

"Stop that," I tell her.

"I can't," she says, and those blue eyes well with tears. "I can't, because no one has ever wanted me before. The date you took me on? That was my first real date, and the whole time, I was questioning myself, wondering if I'd made it all up in my head and you just wanted to be friends. I've never made it past a talking stage, because all guys want with a girl like me is sex, and if I'm too anxious to meet up with someone, then clearly, sex is off the table."

Tears run down her cheeks, and I swipe them with my fingers, moving my hand to cup her cheeks. "Baby, please don't cry," I coo, pulling her into my chest.

She shakes her head in my chest. "I'm fine."

"No, you're not. I know I have to earn your trust, but I want to be here for you. I want to get to know you, Hannah, more than I've ever wanted to get to know someone. I don't want you for sex, or anything else. I want *you*, the person."

Hannah sniffles against my shirt, pulling back. I take her chin between my fingers again. "I'm sorry if I've ever made you feel like I only wanted you for sex, or if you feel that I brought you here for that purpose."

She shakes her head rapidly. "I've never felt that way, not with you. I know you didn't. I needed to tell you that, because... I don't know what I'm doing. I don't know how to be in a relationship, even if it's fake. I don't know how to talk to people most of the time unless it's in a work context. So for me to jump from a first date to a fake engagement has been a lot, and it might take me some getting used to, but I want to get used to it. I want to get to know you too, Thomas. I do."

"Good."

"I feel like I should tell you something," Hannah says, surprising me.

"You can tell me anything, freckles." My heart ramps up in my chest as I think about what she could possibly want to tell me.

She takes a deep breath, holding it and closing her eyes before releasing it. "When you kissed me the other night, that was my first kiss."

A bucket of cold water could have dropped on me and I wouldn't feel as cold as I do right now. Regret floods my body. I should not have kissed her in that room. I should have waited, but the thought of not feeling her lips for another moment, not feeling that connection with her, was so painful that I thought maybe if we shared that connection, I'd feel better. I made it about myself. "Fuck, Hannah, I'm so sorry."

"You're sorry?" she questions, laughing softly. "You have nothing to be sorry about. You asked, and I said yes."

"But—" I choke on my words, running my hands through my hair. "We shouldn't have had our first kiss in a gross interrogation room, Han. Our first kiss should have been somewhere meaningful, or something better than that. *I* should have made *your* first kiss special."

"Thomas." Hannah rests her palm on my chest, and now it's her turn to calm me down. "You made my first kiss special because it was *you.*"

My heart clenches in my chest, and *fuck* I need to be closer to her. I step forward, my palm resting on her cheek, then slide it down to cup the nape of her neck underneath those blonde waves. "Can I make your second kiss even better?"

Her eyes grow wide, and her mouth drops open, a soft gasp escaping her lips. "Yes," she breathes after a long moment.

I bend down, resting my forehead against hers. I can feel the rapid beat of her pulse under my finger on her neck, and I hold in my chuckle. I love that I can make her react like this, because I'm right there with her. I can feel my own pulse thrumming rapidly in my chest, moving as fast as a hummingbird's wings.

"Ready?" I ask, my voice husky as it drops an octave.

"Yes."

Her confirmation is all the answer I need before my lips drop to hers for a second time.

## 23

## HANNAH

My second kiss is much better than my first one.

Thomas sweetly cups my cheeks in his large palms as our lips press together. For the first time in maybe... ever, my mind goes completely silent as I lose myself in this. His warm body leans into mine. My palm presses against his chest where I feel his steady heartbeat, the rhythm keeping me grounded .

His tongue slides out, tracing my lip in a slow seductive taunt that sends goosebumps across my skin. I clutch at his shirt, my fingers digging into the cotton. My lips part as Thomas slips his tongue into my mouth, our bodies melding together. It's everything I've ever dreamed of as he moves one hand down to my waist, pulling our hips together. I never want to leave this moment, this exquisite feeling of wholeness where my mind isn't running a mile a minute and telling me to overthink every action or word out of my mouth.

Thomas pulls our lips apart for a moment, letting us catch our breath before pressing two more kisses onto my lips in quick succession. His thumb caresses my cheek, moving back and forth in a soothing motion. When we part, he barely moves, resting our foreheads together.

"That was better than our first kiss," Thomas states, not leaving room for much argument, not that I'd argue. I wholeheartedly agree as I nod against his forehead.

"Yeah, it was," I breathe.

Arson chooses that moment to force himself between our legs, pushing us apart in an effort to gather our attention. "Sorry, Arson," Thomas says with a chuckle. He smooths his finger across my cheek one last time before dropping his hand. We turn, and Thomas slides his palm into mine, squeezing gently.

"I know we've been through a lot the last few days, and this isn't conventional by any means, but I'm excited to see where this takes us," he says, giving me a goofy grin, showing off both of his dimples.

I take a deep breath as we start walking the gravel path again. "I am too," I admit, realizing that despite all my current anxiety over every inch of my life, I can't wait to see what happens next with us. Even if it's only for a short time until we go back to our real lives.

He squeezes my hand. "Good. Can I tell you something crazy?"

I raise my brow in question. "Sure?"

"I have this weird thing that I like to do."

I wait for him to elaborate, and he doesn't for a long moment, so I prompt him. "Okay?"

He takes a deep breath, chuckling on the exhale. "You're probably going to think I sound ridiculous."

"I promise I won't," I reply. My curiosity is officially piqued, and I need to know what he's about to say.

"I have lucky underwear."

Okay, that is nowhere near anything I could have anticipated him saying. I let out the smallest of giggles as I reply, "What makes them lucky?"

"I suppose it's not one specific pair, and maybe it's more of a superstition rather than anything, but I think they're lucky." He pauses, waiting for me to say something, and when I don't, he continues. "Anytime I need a little bit of good luck, or think something good could be coming, I throw on a pair of my superhero underwear. I have a bunch, but I only wear them when I think I need the extra boost or good vibes. I wore them the day I got accepted to the Police Academy, the day I got Arson, and I wore them on our first date."

He glances down at me and smiles. "I can keep going, but I think history has proved itself."

I can't stop myself from asking, "Even though what happened that night was the worst?"

He shrugs. "I mean, that's a fair point, but it also brought us together in a way."

"I suppose you could look at it that way."

"I'm a glass half full kind of guy, freckles."

"I'm gathering that," I respond as we reach the cottage, heading up the wooden steps. Thomas opens the door with his free hand, and Arson darts inside. He guides me inside, and the cool air on my skin feels nice. "How do you decide when to wear them?"

"Sometimes it's a vibe, or if I know something might be happening that I want to manifest good luck for, I'll wear them." He shrugs, letting go of my hand to close the door.

"That's a lot of trust in some underwear," I respond, heading to the kitchen to grab my water bottle and fill it. A nervous jitter runs through my body. How are we so casually talking about his underwear?

"It is, but they've never failed me," he says confidently.

Arson is already curling up on the couch, flopping down with a low groan. "He acts as if he just worked an eight-hour shift with three foot chases," Thomas says, gesturing toward his dog.

"Oh, to live the life of a dog," I say with a smile. The exhaustion is hitting me again, and even though we got a good amount of sleep between yesterday and today, sometimes when things are extra emotional, it makes me need the sleep.

"I'm beat," Thomas says.

"Me too."

"Come on, let's get some rest."

I finish filling my water and follow him toward the stairs. When Arson sees where we are going, he jumps off the couch and bounds upstairs. I can hear the soft thud as he hops onto the bed. Thomas chuckles, and lets me start heading up the steps first. He follows close behind me, resting his palm on my right hip. His simple touches are so sweet, and it's helping me to realize how serious he is about all this, about me. It's reassuring.

Arson is curled up smack dab in the middle of the bed waiting for us. I grab a change of clothes, knowing I won't be able to sleep in jean shorts. I run back downstairs to change and use the restroom, and by the time I make it back, Thomas is shirtless in bed. I can't see what he's wearing for bottoms, but seeing him shirtless sends a shiver through my body.

Now is *not* the time to get turned on. As much as my body may want and crave him, my mind is not ready yet.

I round to the other side of the bed and pull back the sheets, this time remembering to grab my pillow from home from my suitcase and throw it onto the bed. Thomas turns onto his side, so he's facing the middle of the bed. I tentatively crawl into the bed, and Arson shifts so he's not in my space.

I move to lie on my left side and face Thomas. He reaches out, cupping my cheek again before leaning toward me. He takes my lips in a swift, sweet kiss, like we've been doing this for years. It's comfortable, safe.

"I make no promises that I won't end up cuddling you in my sleep now that I'm not sleeping like the dead, so it's your last chance to make me take the couch," he whispers, tracing his fingers over my skin.

I shake my head. "No. I want you here."

"Then here I'll stay," he says, that familiar smile crossing his lips.

My eyes grow heavy almost immediately, and thankfully, sleep takes me fast.

## 24

## THOMAS

Hannah is still fast asleep when I wake up, so I crawl out of bed as silently as I can. I try to get Arson to come with me, but of course, he wants nothing to do with me. He curls up closer to her, leaving me in the dust.

I head downstairs, grabbing a granola bar from the pantry and sliding my shoes on before heading outside. My watch tells me it's past four o'clock in the afternoon, and the sun beats down on the pond in the distance. It's probably a good thing I woke up when I did, because I want to get back on a normal sleep schedule as soon as possible. Even though I switch between working night shift and day shift often, it doesn't make switching back and forth easier by any means.

I make my way over to the swings hanging from the trees, and sit carefully on one, slowly swinging back and forth.

I haven't really taken the time myself to process this. It feels like I've been running for the last two days, my body functioning on pure adrenaline only, and now that we're in the safe house, I can let myself feel the weight of this situation. Worry eats at me as I think of Henry. Did he make it out of surgery? What is his healing process going to be? So many unanswered questions settle in my gut.

The case that I've spent so much time and emotional effort on is now in the hands of others, and I don't know how to reconcile it. I know that for my safety it's best that I'm here, but it is hard being so far away when I've put so much work into the case.

I feel useless here, knowing that back home the department is down two people in the middle of an active investigation that just took a turn. Henry was spearheading the investigation into finding the head of the trafficking circle, and now they have a name and potentially even more after Henry was shot by one of Chaz's lackeys.

What if someone else is on their "list"? Or, with me being gone, will they replace me with someone else to kill?

Not only am I worried about my fellow co-workers, but I'm also petrified for my family. Having no contact with them is brutal, especially with Josie being due with the baby in the next few weeks. I played it off earlier, but I fucking miss my family already, and it hasn't even been two days. What if something happens to Gramps when I'm gone? Will they try to contact me?

God, this sucks. It's selfish of me, I know it is, but I'm so thankful that I have Hannah with me. At least I know that she is safe and healthy. That's one person I would have worried most about, especially with her being a prime witness to the shooting.

A dragonfly appears in my line of vision, circling for a moment before landing on my shoe. Some small memory tugs at the back of my mind, perhaps something from my childhood at the sight of this dragonfly. Its blue, almost holographic coloring shines in the sunlight.

I shift my foot so I can get a better look at it. I move

slowly, hoping I don't scare it off, and thankfully, it stays put. When I get a look at it from a different angle, the niggling memory hits me right in the face.

Grandma Irene loved finding the symbolism in little things, and she scattered these things through the home she and Gramps shared. Butterfly figurines, sunflowers when they were in season, and bouquets of a variety of flowers in the vase on the kitchen table, each with a different meaning, which she always made sure to explain to us.

She passed away back when I was in my early twenties, but I remember so many details of her that I'm surprised it didn't hit me right away. The dragonfly stays put on the toe of my shoe, and maybe it's stupid, but I feel like this dragonfly is trying to show me something, tell me something.

She had a dragonfly brooch that she'd wear every Sunday during family brunches. It was blue, like this one, and she would always explain to us that they symbolize change, and that change, while it can be scary, can also be good. She would tell us how open she was to change.

Perhaps this is a sign from my grandma. Life is changing for me, right this very moment, and even though I think I'm open to it, maybe it's a reminder that even though change is scary, it can be good.

So yeah, this change is scary as hell, and missing my family and my life is hard, but I've also got this amazing woman by my side who could change my life for the better, and I can't wait to see what that change could bring.

## 25

## HANNAH

He's fast asleep again.

The dark is freaking me out. It's nearing five a.m., and I've been awake all night, despite hoping that my anxiety last night was a one off. The sunrise is peeking through the trees, illuminating the sky and sending light through the blind-covered windows. I can't sleep, and it's not because I'm not tired. I'm exhausted, but I still can't get the irrational fear out of my mind that as soon as I fall asleep, they'll strike.

Arson snorts, rolling over and waking up. When he sees me awake, he wags his tail, shaking the bed. "Shhh," I shush, but he grows more and more excited. "Alright, fine."

I throw my legs out of the bed and go downstairs, Arson following closely behind. I open the front door, rapidly glancing around outside for anything that looks different or suspicious. I don't see anything, so I open it wider for Arson, who beelines to the nearest tree.

Once he comes back to me, we head to the kitchen where I get him a scoop of food out of the bag Thomas placed in the hall closet. Now that I know where it is, I am more than happy to feed him when I'm awake and Thomas is not.

I make a pot of coffee, adding a generous amount of creamer and a scoop of sugar once I pour myself a cup. I sit down on the couch and curl up in one of my blankets, grabbing my book from the side table. I only had a few minutes to grab everything when we left, but I made sure to grab a few of my comfort novels so that I at least had something to distract me. I read the first few pages, letting the familiar words and story pull me out of reality.

Two hours later, Thomas groans. "Hannah?" he calls, his voice gravelly with sleep.

"Down here," I reply. He appears moments later, wearing only a pair of cotton shorts. I can see the outline of his cock through the fabric, and I swear to god, it makes my mouth water. I've never had such a physical reaction to another person before. This man is so attractive, and that doesn't even account for his personality.

"Good morning," he greets. One side of his lips pulls up into a smirk, triggering one of those dimples to pop on his cheek.

"Morning," I say, trying to hide my flushing cheeks and the sudden heat flaring through my body. He has his glasses on again, which are slowly becoming my favorite accessory. I've always had a thing for hot men wearing glasses—*cough, cough, Clark Kent*—but seeing Thomas wearing them might be my undoing. His blonde hair is sticking up in random points around his head, and as he runs his hand through it, his arm muscles flex. I gulp, looking down at my book. The couple in the enemies-to-lovers novel were about to tear each other's clothes off, so maybe that's why I'm feeling so flustered. That has to be it, right? It has nothing to do with how attracted I am to Thomas. Nothing to do with how I'm more attracted to him than I've ever been to someone before.

And his hands, *oh god*. They're so big, and he has those veins that pop from his arms and the back of his hands, which is every medic and nurse's wet dream. Thomas catches me staring at his hands as he pulls his shorts up. His soft stomach and muscular pecs are covered in a light dusting of chest hair, and fuck, why do I want to run my fingers through it?

This is dangerous.

Thomas strides over to me, bending down to slide his hand across my cheek, threading his fingers in my hair. "What are you reading?" he asks. His voice still has a slight rasp from sleep in it, and it is so incredibly sexy that I almost forget to answer the question.

"A book," I reply, to which he chuckles, planting a kiss on my forehead.

"What's it called?"

I've read this book no less than ten times. I could recite the prologue from memory, as well as many quotes from it without a glance at the page, so tell me *why* my mind goes completely blank, the title flying out of my mind instantly.

Instead of telling him the title, I hold the book up between us since he's still leaning toward me, our foreheads nearly touching. I show him the cover of the couple embracing each other with the title in a cursive font on it.

"Hmm," he murmurs, leaning back to get a look at it. "Seems intriguing."

"Yep," I squeak.

Thomas lets out a low chuckle, rising to his full height and striding toward the kitchen. "How did you sleep?"

I fight a yawn as I reply with a lie, "Fine." I don't need to place this burden of my lack of sleep on him.

"I slept hard, even though we slept so much yesterday," Thomas says as he pours himself a cup of the brewed coffee. "Apparently we needed the sleep."

"Yeah," I agree noncommittally. Changing the subject, I say, "I fed Arson this morning, so he's good to go."

"Thanks, you didn't have to do that," Thomas replies.

"You really think he would have let me not feed him? Remember the first night?"

"Good point. Either way, it's appreciated."

"No problem," I respond. "What time are you heading to work with Ron?"

"Probably a half hour or so. Are you coming?"

"Sure, maybe I can help Dottie with something around the house."

Thomas sits down beside me with his coffee. "That will be nice. They seem like really nice people."

"I agree. Dottie kind of reminds me of my mom. She always wanted to make sure everyone was fed, cared for, and happy. It hurts in a way, but it's a good reminder of her, too." I'd been thinking that yesterday during our breakfast with her and Ron, but saying it out loud really drives home how true it is. Dottie is older than my mother ever will be, but I can imagine my mother making sure the house is always ready for guests and grandchildren.

Julia might never want kids, but it's something that I've always wanted. When dating was sort of out of the cards, I kind of gave up on the prospect of having kids, but it's still a dream of mine.

"That's really awesome. I'm glad that she reminds you of her," Thomas says, pulling me out of my internal thoughts.

"I agree. My parents were the best. They had their faults, of course, but I loved them. I was close with them, I trusted them more than anyone, and losing them hasn't been easy, even though it's been ten years since their death. I'm lucky that I still have my grandma, but I know that losing her some day is going to break me. After my parents' death, she became my rock. Sometimes I think she, Julia and Tiff know me better than I know myself. "

"It seems like they love you a lot. Would you mind telling me how your parents died?" Thomas questions, his brows furrowed as he holds my attention.

I shrug. "They were in an accident. A drunk driver crossed the median and hit them head on. I was fifteen. They were at a wedding in the Cities."

"Now that you say it, I think I remember hearing about it." Thomas's blue eyes lock with mine, and they're loaded with sympathy.

"Word travels fast in situations like that," I respond. "A lot of my anxiety has stemmed from that. It sounds stupid," I chuckle to myself. "But a big anxiety trigger for me is when the phone rings. It's not so much anymore, but if it's an unexpected call, or from someone who wouldn't normally call me, I get so anxious I nearly throw up. Phone calls equal bad news in my brain."

Thomas takes my book from my lap, setting it on the side table. "That's not stupid. It's a trigger."

I shrug. "It is, but I've worked through a lot of it, so now it's not quite as bad. Ironically, all I can think about right now is how badly I wish I had a phone and it would ring so I could talk to Grandma or Julia."

Thomas takes my hands in his. "That's my fault, I suppose."

I rapidly shake my head. "No, it's not. I've said it already, but I'm glad I'm with you. I'd be a wreck with worry for you if I wasn't, Thomas."

He sighs, his body deflating a bit.

"I wish I had my phone for the same reason that you do, to speak with my family, that's all. Not because I wish I was home, or mad at you for taking me here with you," I reiterate, and finally, I see some of the guilt leave his eyes. "Okay?"

Thomas nods. "Okay."

"Should we head to the main house?" I ask, shifting on the couch.

"Probably."

I stand from the couch and stride to the kitchen, pouring the remnants of my coffee into a travel mug and filling it again with fresh coffee and another splash of creamer. I grab another travel mug for Thomas, and grab his mug from his palm as he walks to me.

"This feels so domestic," Thomas remarks, leaning down to kiss my cheek. "I like it."

I laugh. "I like it too."

## 26

## THOMAS

Something isn't right with Hannah. She's absolutely exhausted, and I can't seem to figure out why. We caught up on all the sleep we missed from the drive and night of the shooting, so I don't know why she's so tired.

She's been asleep on the couch since we got home from our day with the Graffs at six-thirty. I worked my ass off today, shoveling out pens, helping Ron cut down a tree, and even going so far as climbing onto the roof to patch a leak.

Hannah spent most of the day inside with Dottie, helping her bake a few casseroles for a local woman who lost her husband recently in an unexpected accident. Then, she sat on the front porch and read her book while Dottie ran to town and dropped the casseroles off.

I was patching the roof of the barn while she was reading, and I caught her nodding off a few times.

It's barely past nine now, and she's sound asleep. I don't want to wake her, but I also don't want her to sleep on the couch for the same reason I moved her to the far side of the bed the first day. I need to be the first line of defense.

Maybe if I slowly pick her up, I can get her up to bed without waking her. Then, tomorrow if she's still tired, I'll talk to her about it.

I stand from where I'm sitting on the couch and bend over her. I slide my arm under her neck and the other under her hips. As gently as possible, I stand, pulling her into my chest. Not only does Hannah immediately stir, she screams.

Her voice is hoarse as she screams, her limbs flailing. One arm swats at my face, while the other pushes on my chest. My glasses go flying off my face as she scratches.

I don't move to let go of her, though, and maybe I should. "Hannah!" I shout, hoping I can break through her screams. "It's me!"

She breaks from my hold, her feet hitting the ground with a thunk. Her eyes fly open as she bangs at my chest. I reach out, clasping her wrists in my hands to stop her assault. "Baby, it's Thomas!" I yell again.

Her eyes widen, pupils dilating as she fully takes in my face. Tears well and stream down her cheeks as she sobs, her body softening as she sinks to the floor.

I sink to my knees in front of her, wrapping my arms around her shoulders and letting her sob into my chest. The entire time I hold her, I whisper in her ear, letting her know I'm here, that she's safe, that I will never let anything happen to her.

She melts into my body, her sobs heavy and brutal. I want to step away for a moment to get an ice cube, something I know helped her at the police station, but at the same time, I don't dare step away from her.

Instead, I hold her as she cries, hoping that I'm enough to calm her right now. Another few minutes pass, and she calms, her breathing slowing enough for me to feel comfortable pulling away.

"I'm going to get you an ice cube, okay?"

When I shift away, she clutches at my shirt tighter and whimpers, "No."

"I'm sorry, Hannah. I shouldn't have tried to move you when you were asleep. I wasn't thinking," I whisper.

"It's not your fault. I shouldn't have fallen asleep. I... I thought someone was taking me." Her voice is hoarse from her screams as she speaks into my chest.

It's probably a good thing we aren't closer to the main house, since her screams might have sent them into a spiral of worry.

"Fuck, I'm sorry. You have been half asleep all day. Are you getting sick or something? You're exhausted." I caress her head, smoothing her hair and running my hand over the skin of her neck, subtly trying to check her temperature.

She shakes her head against my chest. "I didn't sleep last night."

"What do you mean? You climbed into bed with me." I replay last night in my mind, fully remembering her climbing in beside me.

"Yeah, I got into bed, but I didn't sleep," she murmurs. "As soon as you fell asleep, I sat there."

"How come?"

"My mind wouldn't let me. It didn't let me the first night either. I'm not afraid of the dark, I never have been, but something about it the last two nights has been terrifying to me. I mean, we have no idea who's out there. They could be waiting until it's dark to make their move, Thomas."

"Hannah," I murmur, wrapping my arms around her and tucking my head into her neck as I breathe her in. I try to say something more, but she cuts me off.

"Someone needed to be awake in case they found us. Someone needed to be prepared."

All I can think of at this moment is how badly I let her down. I didn't even know she wasn't sleeping. I got up fairly early this morning, and when she was already awake, I thought that maybe she was an early riser. I didn't suspect a thing until she nearly fell asleep every thirty seconds today.

"I'm so sorry, Hannah. I should have known something was up." I keep stroking the back of her head, hoping I can soothe her somehow, someway.

She leans back, moving away from me as she hurriedly swipes at the tears on her face. "I'm fine. I don't know how to safely use a gun, but I figured if I was awake, if I heard something, I could wake you."

"We are safe here, Hannah," I tell her, reaching out to wrap my hand around her wrist. "You can sleep, and know that." I glance at my feet, noting Arson pressed up against her calf.

"How do you know that?"

"The FBI wouldn't have sent us somewhere we weren't safe and if we were in danger, they would move us. We're not near any major roads or highways, and we haven't seen anyone else besides Ron and Dottie since the day we got here."

I reach down and scratch Arson's ears. "Plus, even if he's in a dead sleep, Arson will wake up to anything, and trust me when I say he will bark his head off to let us know before something happens. Promise."

Hannah stands and sinks onto the couch, dropping her head into her hands. I grab my glasses from the floor and place them on my face before I sit down beside her. I slide my arm around her shoulders and pull her into my side. Her body shudders as she sobs. "I'm sorry," she murmurs. "I don't even know why I'm crying."

"Probably because I scared the absolute shit out of you tonight," I reply, pressing a kiss to her temple. I can't help but touch her right now. I need it to ground me. "I probably did more damage than good then."

She shakes her head as she leans into me, opening her eyes. The whites of her eyes are bloodshot and stained red, the blue a vibrant shade, totally contrasting to the redness. "I'm sorry," she repeats.

"Stop it," I say, cupping her cheek with my other hand, turning her face to meet me. Our foreheads are touching, breaths intermingling as I wipe away her tears. "You don't need to apologize. The only thing we need to do is figure out a way to help you sleep."

She nods against my forehead, squeezing her eyes shut as she inhales deeply through her nose, and exhales through her mouth slowly.

"Do you want me to sleep on the couch so I'm down here in case?" I ask, even though that's the last thing I want to do. I want to be by her side.

"No," she rushes to say. Taking another long breath, she continues, "I need you there with me."

"Okay." *Thank god.*

Without another word, she stands. "I'm going to get ready for bed."

"Wait—" I reach for her, clasping her wrist in my hand. "Hannah, wait."

"I need a minute, Thomas. Please." She spins to face me, her eyes pleading, hands twisting in front of her.

I nod, letting her go. She heads upstairs, coming down a moment later with her pajamas and shower supplies. She closes the bathroom door behind her, and a minute later the shower starts up.

Alone, I lean forward, resting my elbows on my knees and dropping my head into my hands. I am so frustrated with myself that I didn't even take care of her well enough to make sure she was okay. I know she has anxiety, and I know this is a tough situation, so what the hell is wrong with me that I didn't think to take an extra step for her?

## 27

## HANNAH

The hot shower helps soothe my tight muscles and calm the remaining anxiety. It feels better, knowing that Thomas knows I didn't sleep last night, or much the night before. We've barely been here three days, but it feels like much longer, probably due to my lack of sleep.

I wash my hair and body thoroughly, giving myself the extra time I need. In all honesty, I had no intention of sleeping tonight, so now that Thomas knows, I have a feeling he won't sleep unless I do.

My fears seem silly when I lay them out. We are quite literally in the middle of nowhere, and I have a giant police dog sleeping at my legs. He and Thomas will do anything they can to keep us safe. I know that, rationally, but I don't want them to have to protect me, that's the problem. I don't want the potential attack in the first place. *That* is what scares me.

I rinse out my hair and step out of the shower into the cool air of the bathroom. I shiver as I wrap myself in the towel.

There's a knock on the door, then Thomas's voice. "Hannah?"

I clear my throat before answering, "Yes?"

"I'm going outside with Arson for a few minutes."

"Okay," I reply, and I hear Thomas's heavy footsteps as he leaves the cottage, the door opening and closing behind him.

I search my toiletries bag for the bottle I need. I haven't taken this in a long time, but it might be the only thing that can get me to sleep tonight. I am not going to take it without talking to Thomas first, though. The medication helps when I have extremely bad anxiety attacks, but I don't like to take it because it can make me very drowsy which would help in my favor at this time.

I find the bottle of hydroxyzine and set it on the counter, staring down at the small pills. It's not true, I *know* it isn't, but I don't like to take these because it makes me feel like a failure. Like I wasn't strong enough to calm myself down, and now I need help. Asking or needing help isn't a failure, and I've been trying so hard to remember that, but sometimes, I can't get past it.

Staring at the bottle, I towel-dry my hair and brush it before twisting it into a French braid down the middle of my head. I throw on my shirt and cotton shorts and hang the towel up on the hook behind the door.

The sound of the door opening and closing echoes in the main room, and I take a deep breath before exiting the bathroom.

Thomas is hanging up his red flannel on the coat stand as Arson bounds toward me. I lean down, giving him scratches as he croons his pleasure. Meanwhile, Thomas stands in the doorway, rocking on his heels with his hands in his pockets.

"How are you doing?" he asks.

"Better," I answer. I head to the couch, sitting down and gesturing for him to sit as well.

He sits down beside me, reaching over to take my hand. I let him, and he notices the bottle in my left palm. "What's that?"

"This is my hydroxyzine. It's my rescue med for when my anxiety gets so bad that I can't control it, or when I can't sleep. It usually makes me really drowsy, and I don't take it often, but I think I should take it to help me sleep." I pass the bottle to him, and he takes it carefully, glancing at it and reading it.

I don't care that he knows what medication I take. I'm on a daily medication too, and if he wants to know what med that is, I'll tell him. I don't have to share these private details with him, I know that, but I *want* to. I want to be open and honest with him.

"In all honesty, I should have preemptively taken it last night. And who knows, maybe I won't have to take it every night. Maybe I only need it to get over the first hump and then I'll be fine. But I have the option, and I should have used it sooner," I say, fighting the urge to apologize again. I should have been taking better care of myself, and I wasn't.

"If it helps you sleep, then I'm all for it, freckles. I don't want you to be anxious."

"I don't want to be anxious either." I grab my water bottle from the side table, and take the bottle from Thomas's palm. When our hands touch, there's a zing that shoots its way through my body, and I have to remind myself that now isn't the time. I open the pill bottle and shake one out into my palm, throwing it into my mouth and swallowing it with a gulp of water.

All I can think about at this moment is how my therapist would be proud of me. She might be worried about me, what with me literally disappearing before our appointment that was scheduled for yesterday. It's taken a long time for me to get to the point in my mental health journey where I can allow myself to accept my need for the medication. Maybe I should have known to take a pill sooner, I'm doing it now, and that's the important part.

With the medication taken, I relax a little. Arson cuddles up against my legs, and I bury my fingers into his soft downy fur. I sink into the couch as Thomas wraps his arms around my shoulders, pulling me into his chest.

"I'm proud of you," he whispers, tilting his head down to kiss my forehead.

I can't stop the snort that escapes me. "Proud of me? For what?"

"For taking care of yourself. Even if you didn't realize you needed it before, you realized now, and I'm proud of you for taking it instead of avoiding it, and trying to fight through the anxiety. You admitted you needed help." His thumb caresses my shoulder back and forth.

"I know I'm not, but I feel like a failure."

"Not even close," Thomas murmurs, kissing my temple again. I sink into his touch, letting my head fall onto his shoulder, my cheek resting against his chest.

"Thank you," I say. My hand moves from Arson's fur to rest on Thomas's chest, feeling his steady heartbeat. We sit like that for a while until my head starts to feel heavy.

"Are you ready for bed?" Thomas asks.

I nod into his chest.

"Come on, freckles." Thomas slides his arm from my shoulders, gently helping me to stand. That familiar burst of anxiety swells in my chest, but it's easier to dampen now.

Thomas's hand clasps mine as he leads us up the stairs

toward the bed. Things around me are slowly becoming familiar. From the way his hand feels in mine, to the cottage around us. The way the creaking wood sounds as we scale the stairs, to the squeak in the door hinges.

We reach the bed, and Thomas pulls back the comforter, guiding me to my side before pulling the sheets over me and rounding the bed to his side. "I'm going to change, and I'll be right back, okay?"

I agree, and he grabs some clothes from his bag, rushing down the stairs as Arson hops up next to me, flopping down behind my calves. He snuggles right in, groaning in relief as he relaxes.

Not even two minutes have passed when Thomas climbs the stairs again. My eyes grow heavier by the second, and I'm glad he's back. He gets into the bed next to me, and instead of keeping our distance in the bed like we've done the last few nights, he instead scoots to the middle of the mattress and pulls me into him.

He lies on his back and moves me so my head is on his chest, my right arm draped across his stomach.

Thomas runs his fingers down my face as he whispers, "Goodnight, Han."

I mutter *goodnight* as sleep slowly takes me. As I fall into a restful sleep, I feel his caressing touches on my skin, my cheek, the bridge of my nose, and down my arms. It's soothing, and maybe I should have let him hold me sooner, because this makes me feel better than anything else could.

## 28

# HANNAH

I swing slowly back and forth, letting my bare feet drag through the grass. Dusk is slowly appearing behind the trees and clouds as I wait for Thomas to finish his chores for the day.

It's hot today, over eighty-five degrees, and humid again. The air doesn't cool down in the evening's here like it does in Minnesota.

It's been six days since the night I took my anxiety medication and slept through the night for the first time since being here, and since then, we've been busy. Thomas has all but turned into a full-fledged farmer with Ron, waking up early to help him with the morning chores, and helping him with little things throughout the day.

Meanwhile, I've been spending my days with Dottie. She's taught me how to cook a lot in her kitchen, as well as shown me how to master some sweet treats. I haven't gone into town with her yet. I'm not sure if we are supposed to, so I figure it's best to stay back and play it safe.

I've been sleeping better, too. I'm not sure if it's the medication that I've been taking, or the fact that I've fallen asleep in Thomas's arms every night, but I'm sleeping, and no longer plagued by the constant anxiety and worry over falling asleep at night. It's still there, but the medication and Thomas help quiet some of the noise.

Every morning when I wake in his arms, it helps me put in perspective how real he is. He cares for me, that much is apparent. I care for him too, and I'd be lying if I said I hadn't been feeling more and more heat rising between us, in a good way. It all feels a little too good to be true, especially since our so-called engagement is fake. It doesn't feel fake in those moments.

He's so good looking, I have to remind myself that he has said he's attracted to me. It can be hard, especially for someone who's never been on the receiving end of this type of affection before, but I'm starting to crave his kisses, his touches, to the point where I am ready for more, but I don't know how to take that step.

Even thinking about him, how it might feel to have him hovering over me as he's inside of me, his hands on my bare skin, sends a tingle of pleasure right to my pounding core.

How do I show him I'm ready? That I want to slowly take another step? By now, he's surely figured out I'm a virgin, even though it's never been blatantly said. But with my admission of his lips being the first to kiss me, as well as my telling him he took me on my first date and that I'm not good with people, he must know.

Do I take the first step? *Can* I take the first step? I've felt his hardness against my back and my stomach every morning we've woken up, and seen the way his eyes linger on my body and my face. There's a lustful heat in his eyes in every gaze and longing look.

The pond in front of me glistens in the sunlight, the water shimmering as the soft wind moves it. The sound of crunching footsteps pulls me out of my thoughts as I turn in the swing to find Arson ambling up to me, Thomas a few steps behind him.

Sunlight seeps through the trees behind him, making him glow with an ethereal look. There's dirt on his arms from a hard day's work, and his hair is tousled and mussed.

"Hard day?" I ask as he approaches, sitting on the empty swing beside me.

"Not bad, just hot," he says, swinging toward me. He reaches out with one hand, the other holding onto the rope as he cups my cheek, kissing me sweetly. "How was your day, freckles?"

My belly flips as he moves his hand from my cheek, sliding down my neck and my arm, to finally rest on my thigh, his thumb stroking my bare skin.

God, his touches are enough to drive me wild.

I clear my throat, feeling the burn of my neck and cheeks. "It was good. Dottie taught me how to make home-made chicken pot pie. There's some inside waiting to be heated up for dinner."

"That sounds amazing," he says.

"It's really good."

"Ron was telling me that their son is coming to visit in a few weeks," Thomas tells me.

"That will be nice," I reply, but my gut churns inside. More people to try and interact with.

"Mhmm," Thomas says, but I get the feeling he isn't really focused on a conversation as he eyes me closely. His hand has moved up toward the apex of my thighs, grazing the hem of my shorts. I'm wearing denim overalls and an orange tank top underneath. I glance down to watch his hand as he grips my thigh, squeezing gently, making goose-bumps prick across my skin.

A simple touch is enough to make my core clench and heat burn low in my belly. Thomas leans forward in the swing, taking my face in his other hand and kissing me. His lips expertly trace the curve of my bottom lip, teasing it open and deftly swooping his tongue inside. I let him take the lead, as always, as I lose myself in his kiss.

When he pulls away, I have to hold back my whimper of want at the loss of his taste, his warmth.

Thomas chuckles softly. "There, did I get you to stop thinking for a minute?"

I pull further away from him, quirking my brow as I work to steady my breathing. "What do you mean?"

"The moment I mentioned the Graffs having a visitor, you shut down. I've learned that when I kiss you, your brain shuts off. Did it help?"

I swallow, my throat suddenly dry. "Yeah, it did."

Thomas leans forward, kissing me once more, chaste and quick.

"Good. Now, why does the Graff's son coming stress you out?"

I shrug, not really wanting to dive into it.

"Hannah, you can tell me. That's what I'm here for. I want to be your sounding board, your person, someone you can lean on."

I turn my eyes to the pond in front of us, watching the glistening water as I try to form words. "It sounds stupid."

"No, it doesn't. Whatever it is, I'm sure it doesn't."

"I told you that meeting new people is hard for me."

Thomas nods, taking my hand and urging me on.

I take a deep breath. "When I meet new people, my brain tells me that they are picking apart every piece of me. I overthink literally every aspect of an interaction. From the way my voice sounds, to the way I say a word, or the way I walk when I'm throwing something in the trash. It's exhausting."

He squeezes my palm, showing me he's listening. I'm distracted for a brief moment when a dragonfly buzzes into my line of sight, landing on a nearby rock. Thomas glances over, his eyes widening as he takes it in. He looks back at me after a moment, his eyes full of some emotion that I can't place. When he doesn't say anything, I continue.

"It's so frustrating overthinking everything. I wish I could be normal, but I can't."

"Normal is boring," Thomas says. "You're doing amazing with Ron and Dottie. They love you, but I can understand that it's hard when you have these things running through your mind. Is there something that I can do to help you in this?"

I shake my head. "You're doing it. I like having someone by my side, even though my therapist wants me to do things on my own. A year ago, I couldn't even go into a coffee shop to pick up an order on my own. Now, I can sit and read a book for an hour and not freak out. There's still the constant noise in my head that people think I'm weird for reading a book alone in public, or what I'm eating or drinking is too many calories, but it's progress. Miles and my therapist have helped me a lot."

"Miles, like your partner at work, Miles?"

"Yep. When you are stuck in an ambulance for twelve-hour shifts with someone as kind and talkative as him, they help you break down your boundaries."

Thomas chuckles. "Yeah, that sounds like him."

"I always forget that you went to high school with him. Well him and my sister." I glance down at where his hand is on my thigh. "Are you sure it's not weird for you that you went to high school with my sister and we're... y'know?"

"Engaged?" Thomas supplies.

Heat flushes my cheeks. "We aren't really engaged, but you know what I mean."

"For all intents and purposes we are," Thomas says, offering me a wink. I can't stop the smile that crosses my face. "But to answer your question, no. Our age difference, or the fact that I went to high school with your sister, doesn't bother me. Does it bother you?"

I shake my head rapidly. "No, not at all."

"Good," he replies. "Because age is just a number, baby." He raises his brow, and his dimples pop with his cheeky, gap-toothed grin. Every time he calls me baby, a butterfly flies in my stomach, tickling my insides.

I can't stop the laugh that slips out. "That was horrible," I giggle. The dragonfly that was in view on the rock the entire time flies away, leaving our gazes following after it for only a moment.

"What can I say? I'm a charmer," he replies, looking back at me. "But really, it doesn't bother me. I like you for who you are. You're beautiful, kind, and a damn good kisser."

I swear, my skin is going to burn off with how hot it flames. "I am not," I counter.

"Yes, you are."

"Stop lying."

Thomas inhales sharply. "I'm not! Saying you're a bad kisser would be like saying you have ugly eyes. A lie. Anyone can see that. The blue is so bright it's almost irides-cent, with a hint of gold around your pupils. Though, I wouldn't want anyone else to kiss you to prove my point. I'll keep you to myself, thank you very much."

With that, he takes my lips in a bruising kiss, this one different from any of our other kisses. This one is passionate, his lips roughly moving with mine as he tries to prove his point.

He leans his swing forward, one hand on my thigh, moving to rest on the base of my neck above my breasts. I'm sure he can feel the heavy pounding of my heart and the heat of my skin, but I don't care. I'm learning his touches, learning the way he moves and breathes, letting each new thing I learn engrave itself in my brain.

I let myself lean into the kiss, trying to do something I never thought I would. Take the lead. Only instead of meeting his lips, I feel the moment we lose balance. His swing shifts abruptly, causing us to pull apart and him to flail, arm waving as he tries to catch his balance.

Laughter bursts from my chest as I open my eyes and see him, eyes wide as he leans back, his fingers white-knuckling the ropes connected to the tree. His blue eyes are wide as he looks at me. "On second thought, maybe we should go inside if we're going to get lost in each other."

Heat burns inside as his words hit me. He wants to get lost in each other? Does that mean what I think it does? Thomas stands from the swing, holding out his hand to me. Heat burns in his gaze as he rakes his eyes up and down my body. When I stand, he pulls me into him, his arms wrapping around my waist, fingertips caressing the top of my ass.

If a simple graze of his fingers over my jeans-covered butt sends a zing of excitement through me, what will I do when his bare hands are all over my body?

"Let's go inside. I'm starving," Thomas says, squeezing my hips. I don't miss the double entendre in his words as he slides his hands around my belly to take my hand.

Arson follows us, and with each step we take closer to the cottage, my heart pounds harder and harder.

When we get inside, Thomas groans at the scent of the

chicken pot pie. "Fuck, that smells incredible. Did you eat already?"

"I did. It's pretty good."

"Can I eat and take a shower? Then, what do you think about watching a movie?" Thomas asks, gesturing to the couch.

"Sounds great," I say, my voice cracking on the second word.

Thomas smiles, and I know he can see right through me. I *want* something to happen tonight. I don't know how to act around him, how to show him I'm ready, yet still terrified all at once.

"Great," he replies, heading to the table to dish up.

This gives me a little time to prepare. Or panic. Or both? Oh god. I point to the bathroom, already feeling the heat in my cheeks. "I'm going to shower if that's okay? I'll be out by the time you're done eating."

"No rush," he says, waving me off as he sits down at the kitchen table.

I stride into the bathroom, closing the door behind me and locking it. Once I'm behind the closed door, I really feel the panic creeping in. I lean forward on the counter, taking deep, long breaths.

I can do this. I want to do this. I've wanted this connection with someone for years now, so why am I freaking out? Oh, right. Because it's *Thomas Freaking Cunningham*, the man who I never thought would ever go for me, and now I'm fake engaged to him in the middle of nowhere in a cute cottage and about to let him touch me in ways I've never been touched before. Right. That.

I take one calming breath, and turn on the shower. This will help me chill out, and then I'll be fresh and clean. Yes, okay, this I can do.

I let the water heat up, and shed my clothing, climbing into the hot spray and letting it calm me.

Once I've shaved and washed up, I get out, towel-drying my hair and braiding it before putting lotion all over my skin and wrapping myself in the robe I left in here. I open the bathroom door, and Thomas is sitting at the kitchen table still, plate empty, with Arson at his side.

"It's all yours," I say, gesturing to the bathroom, and heading to the stairs. Once the door clicks shut behind him, I let myself breathe.

## 29

## HANNAH

Fifteen minutes later, I'm sitting on the couch, waiting for Thomas, dressed in a comfy t-shirt and my favorite cotton sleep shorts. He's still in the shower, so Arson and I are hanging out. I have my book in my lap, but I haven't read a page, too excited, too nervous about what's to come.

Thomas comes out of the bathroom a few minutes later wrapped only in a towel. His skin glistens with water still clinging to his body, his hair flopping over his face and in his eyes. He raises his arm to push the hair from his face, and in doing so, shows off his strong biceps.

*Oh sweet lord, he's trying to kill me.* That's what this is. He knows I can't resist him if he teases me like this. *Fuck,* he's hot. The thickness of his chest, the softness of his belly, it's all doing me in. With every step he takes, his thick thighs shift the towel, and I swear I can see the outline of his semi-hard cock.

"Forgot my clothes," he says with a laugh.

Words don't come to me, only a soft squeak. Thomas catches the noise, giving me a subtle wink as he passes by, heading up the stairs with the towel clinging to his ass.

I'm not going to survive this, am I?

I shrink into the couch, taking a long inhale of air. Arson glances between the two of us, flopping onto the dog bed in the corner.

A moment later, Thomas comes back downstairs with his hair towel-dried, and a pair of loose shorts and a shirt on. He has the towel slung over his arm, and he heads into the bathroom to hang it up before coming back into the main area and sitting on the couch beside me.

I shift myself to give him more room, but he doesn't let me. Instead, he wraps an arm around my waist, pulling me into his body. A small squeak leaves my mouth, but I relax into him. I move my book from my lap and set it on the arm of the couch.

"That's better," Thomas mumbles. "Movie?"

I nod into his chest.

"What are you feeling?" he questions.

"I'm up for anything," I say with a shrug.

Thomas turns on the TV and searches the channels, finding an old movie from the eighties that's about to start. "Okay?" he asks.

"Yep," I reply, trying to keep my breathing and heart under control. Throughout the first twenty minutes of the movie, Thomas's fingers trail up and down my arms, my side, the curve of my hip, constantly touching me.

When his fingers twist in the end of my braid, sliding up to the base of my neck and cupping it gently, I shiver. His large hands do something to me.

"Do you know how beautiful you are?" Thomas whispers, drawing my attention to him with the hand to my neck, making me look into those bright blue eyes.

I swallow thickly, words failing me.

"Because you are. Every time I look at you, I find

another thing to love. Your eyes, because the shade of blue reminds me of a lake in the summer. Almost navy with flecks of gray. Your freckles, because they're a road map, directing me to another part of you. Your lips, because now I know exactly what you taste like, and every time I walk away from you, I would do anything for one more kiss."

He caresses my cheek as he looks into my soul. "Your body. I love how soft it is. How each dip and curve is a new place for me to touch, to worship. Your hair. I love the way it feels when I run my fingers through it. So silky smooth."

I'm completely in awe. If I let him, he'd keep going, I know he would. He'd probably find a way to describe my kneecaps, but I stop him before it gets to that point, sitting up and taking initiative.

I get to my knees at his side, sliding my hand up his chest and tilting his chin to face me. "Thank you," I murmur, bending in close until our noses brush. Without any further hesitation, I kiss him.

At first, it's sweet, a thank you to him for making me feel better than anyone ever has. Then, it turns passionate, the heat between us burning brighter than it ever has. My hands are on his face, feeling the scruff of his beard on my skin, my palms tingling as it scratches.

Thomas's hands slide down my arms to my waist, hooking around and scooping me onto his lap. My legs open, allowing me to straddle his wide thighs as I hold myself up over him. His large hands grip my waist tightly, our mouths never breaking apart as he devours me, fully taking over the kiss that I once led.

My thighs start to ache from holding myself up, but I don't care. This feels more amazing than anything I've ever felt. I let one hand tangle in his damp hair while the other presses into his chest, his warmth radiating. I lean forward, pressing my breasts into his chest, loving the feel of his body connected to mine.

Thomas grunts into my mouth, and I panic, moving to shift off him, fearing that I did something wrong. "Don't move," he mumbles against my lips.

Even though my pelvis is barely resting on him, I can feel how hard he is getting. I let out the smallest whimper, because holy hell, that is hot. Knowing that I'm the one doing this to him makes my clit throb and wetness seep into my panties.

Is this really happening? I'm not positive that I'm not in a dream, but all the same, I let myself bask in the heat of this moment.

Thomas tries to pull my hips down, but I don't move, my body still frozen, hovering over him. "What are you doing?" he mumbles.

"You told me not to move," I say breathlessly.

"Yeah, you were trying to get off of me when I wanted you to sit on my lap, baby," he argues.

"I'm sitting on your lap."

"No, you aren't. You aren't putting any weight on me." He kisses the line of my jaw, down my neck as he tries to pull me down again. I resist, holding myself up.

"Hannah, sit." His command sends a *zing* through me, and I lower myself onto him an inch. "Not enough," he growls, pulling me further.

It's harder to resist this time, and he settles me fully onto his lap, letting me feel the hard heaviness of his erection between my thighs. I squirm, trying not to put my full weight on him, but he holds me firmly down. "Stop it."

"I don't want to squish you," I mutter, heat flooding through my system.

"You aren't. I want this, want to feel your pretty pussy grinding against me, baby."

My pussy pulses and a gush of wetness floods my panties at his words.

"Oh," I breathe, my body melting into his.

"There you go," Thomas murmurs, kissing my pulse point and pushing my braid to the other side to suck on the sensitive skin of my neck. "That's what I wanted."

My hips slowly rock as if they have a mind of their own, or some natural instinct kicks in. Thomas's hands shift from around my waist to the top of my ass, squeezing gently and kneading the softness there.

He rocks his body along with my hips, his hard length flush with my pussy. There's only a few thin layers of fabric between us, and as intense and overwhelming as this is, I can't wait for there to be nothing between us.

My heart beats wildly in my chest. For once in my life, it's not anxiety, though. It's lust, heat, and anticipation. My clit is rubbing just right with the seam of his shorts, his pants and the hardness of his cock giving me the right amount of friction and movement.

I've never felt an orgasm rise this fast, not even when I would use my vibrator at home, but the familiar pleasure begins to tingle in my core, and build more with each passing second, with each rock of our hips.

My head falls onto Thomas's chest as his mouth continues to suck and press gentle kisses to any piece of skin he has access to. "If you keep moving those hips like that, you're going to make me come, freckles."

I sigh heavily, my body tight and coiled like a spring, waiting to release. I want him to come. I want to feel his release, feel what I can do to him, so I don't stop.

## 30

## THOMAS

I'm about to finish in my pants.

There's no stopping it, and I don't even care. Having Hannah grind on me is driving me wild. I'm having to hold myself back from tossing her down onto the couch and touching her everywhere, but I know that wouldn't be right of me. She said I was her first kiss, which means there may be many other firsts we might share together too. I'm not going to take that honor lightly.

I love it. Love that I get to be the first one to touch her like this, to show her what it's like to feel this good, to feel this connection to another person.

My hips thrust up into her covered pussy, and god, I can't wait to be inside her. Can't wait to feel her slick pussy clench around me as she comes.

"How does it feel, baby?" I grind out, clenching my teeth to hold back my impending orgasm.

"So good," she mumbles, her face still buried in my chest.

I pull her up, kissing her mouth again before slipping one of my hands under her shirt. "This okay?" I ask.

When I get an affirmative, "Okay" I continue, feeling the softness of her belly under my palm, the warmth of her skin, and the curve of her as I trace my way up to her breasts, memorizing every single inch of her.

My hands meet the roundness of her breasts, and I groan, because holy fuck, this is going to send me over the edge. Hannah practically thrusts her breasts into my open palm, so I squeeze gently over her thin bra, feeling the peaked nipple under the fabric.

"Hannah," I sigh her name as the base of my spine tingles, and my balls tighten. "Fuck, I'm going to come, baby."

Her movements grow stuttered and shaky as she tenses, letting out the softest of whimpers as her eyes squeeze shut, and her body loses itself in her pleasure. God, I can't wait to make her be loud, really let herself go in her pleasure. I can tell she's holding back right now, and I need more from her. Need her moans, need her loud cries as I make her come.

With that thought, my cock explodes into my pants as I finish, my cum soaking my boxers and shorts instantly. It's such an intense orgasm that I lose focus for a moment, my eyes hazy as I come back to my brain. Hannah is rocking slowly, her hands tangled in my hair, and as soon as our eyes lock, we crash together in a relentless kiss. Fuck, she's everything I've ever wanted and more.

When we reluctantly pull away, Hannah glances down between us, scooting herself up and off my legs. I don't want to let her go, but I have to. She slides to a standing position, glancing at her feet and avoiding eye contact. "I'm going to get cleaned up," she murmurs, jerking a thumb toward the bathroom.

"Hold up," I say, standing and pulling her into my arms.

"You okay? I know that was probably... a lot. I hope I didn't rush you."

She vehemently shakes her head. "No, you didn't rush me. I was ready. I don't know what came over me, but it was fun."

"So, you wanna do it again sometime?" I ask with a flirty wink.

That blush I love so much creeps up her neck and cheeks again as she nods. "Yeah, I do."

"Me too, freckles."

She heads into the bathroom, and I dart upstairs to grab yet another fresh set of clothes. When I get up there, I spot Arson lounging on the bed. He glances up at me, giving me an irritated look. "You didn't have to come up here," I tell him.

He gives me another look, as if to say, *Yeah, like I wanted to see that.*

I shrug. "Thanks for the privacy." *Okay, time to stop talking to your dog, Thomas.* I grab a fresh pair of boxers and opt not to grab a new pair of shorts. I have a feeling we will be climbing into bed soon anyway.

After sliding the fresh boxers on, I head downstairs, throwing the cum-stained ones into the washer right away. "Han, do you want me to throw your clothes into the wash? I'm starting a load."

"Yeah, give me a second," she calls from behind the bathroom door. The door opens a second later, and Hannah comes out wearing only a dark grey robe. It's thin enough that I can see the teardrop shape of her heavy breasts without her bra, her nipples poking through the fabric.

*Annnnd* I'm about to get hard again.

I clear my throat, glancing down at her hand instead,

where she holds out the clothes. "Thanks," she murmurs. "I'm going upstairs to change."

"Okay. Are you ready for bed?" I drop the clothes into the washer, adding some soap and pressing the start button. "Or did you want to finish the movie?"

Hannah is yawning when I turn back to face her. "Never mind," I answer my own question, leaning forward to take her hand and kiss her cheek. "I think it's time for bed."

She only nods, yawning again as she heads up the stairs. With the washer running, I head into the bathroom one last time myself, taking out my contacts, putting my glasses on and brushing my teeth. I give Hannah a few more minutes upstairs to herself before loudly clomping up the stairs, giving her ample warning that I'm on my way up.

It's moments like these that I wish I had my phone, or a camera of some sort. Hannah is already under the covers, and Arson is tucked up into her. They're basically spooning, and I'm man enough to admit that I'm jealous of my dog.

"Arson, you're in my spot," I say, and Hannah laughs.

"He's fine," she says, petting his belly.

"No, he's not. I'm officially kicking him out."

Hannah looks up to me, her eyes softening as she takes me in. "I should tell you something," she says.

I wait for a moment. I have an idea of what she might say, but I want her to feel comfortable enough to say it.

Her eyes are downcast, but peek up at me with uncertainty as she speaks. "I'm a virgin. I'm sure you knew, what with you being my first kiss, but I felt that you needed to know... officially, before things go any further."

I take in the flush of her cheeks, and offer her a smile. I'm not going to make a big deal out of this, because it's not.

It's a silly label that society has made feel like a curse if you are a virgin past the age of twenty-one.

"Thank you for telling me," I reply, feeling honored that she feels safe enough with me to divulge that to me. "I like that I get all your firsts. It's an honor, and I won't take it for granted, freckles."

Instead of dwelling on it, she changes the subject. "I love when you wear those glasses," she admits, and I about melt.

"Lucky for you, I need them to see," I say with a laugh, shooing Arson to the end of the bed.

"You look hot," she murmurs. "I like you without them, too. But there's something about them that I love."

I get into the bed, tucking myself under the covers and shifting so I can pull her into my chest. "You could wear a paper sack and I would love it," I tell her, and she giggles, smacking me on my chest.

"Stop it."

"I'm simply telling you the truth." I let out a sigh, sinking my head into the pillow as I hold her closer. "This is where you belong. In my arms."

Hannah tilts her head up, her fingers trailing circles on my bare chest. "I think you might be right."

I kiss her, hoping I can convey all my emotions in one simple kiss. My feelings are so strong for this woman, that I would do anything to keep her as long as possible. And I hope it's forever.

## 31

## THOMAS

"When do you think we can contact our families?" Hannah asks once I join her on the wooden swings after taking a dip in the pond with Arson. She closes the book she's been reading and sets it on her lap, looking over at me with a soft smile. Arson lounges in the grass in front of us as he dries off, his fur glistening with water droplets. He's shaken out quite a few times, but he has so much fur that he's still pretty wet.

My stomach twists. "I checked the burner phone this morning, and there is still nothing," I admit. We've been here for nearly two weeks now, and while they never gave us a concrete answer on when to expect news, I'd hoped we would have heard something by now.

Hannah sighs, her body deflating.

"I'll text Elena when we go inside. Surely, they have information for us by now," I say, wanting to rid the look of sadness off of Hannah's face.

"Okay. I'm just worried. I mean, what if something happened?"

"If something happened, they would have contacted us, no question," I reply, reaching out to take her hand. Her palm is warm, the heat sending a zing up my arm.

"You're sure?"

"Positive."

A set of padding, rapid footsteps distracts me from our conversation. A look at Arson shows that he's in the same spot, looking as confused as I am. All of a sudden, a blur of feathers flies by us. Hannah shrieks, and Arson stands up in a staggered movement, letting out an attempt at a snarl that turns into more of a heavy inhale.

Arson is left in the dust as Dave the emu blazes by him. He's so confused, it's almost comical. He's been around the giant bird a bit at this point, but he's still not fully used to him. His tail is wagging, so he's not too terribly stressed out by the abrupt entrance and exit of Dave.

"Well, that was something," Hannah chuckles. I look behind us to see Dave chilling on the tree line. He's looking at us with such curiosity, and he starts moving closer to us.

"Oh, here he comes," I say with a laugh.

Hannah turns to look behind her. She smiles as Dave saunters to us, his feathers fluttering in the soft breeze. Dave stops right behind Hannah, tilting his head in curiosity before his long neck cranes downward to rest on her shoulder.

"What do I do?" she asks in a whisper. "Do I pet him?"

"Sure?" I laugh, reaching out to pet him. He makes a low thumping noise deep in his chest.

"What was that?" Hannah's eyes widen. I touch his soft feathers, smoothing my hand over them.

"I think that's the noise they make. Ron was telling me about it the other day. I had no idea. I thought maybe they clucked or squawked or something, but it's that low thumping sound. It's super weird."

"Huh," Hannah says curiously, moving her hand slowly to pet Dave.

Arson walks over to Hannah, flopping his head on her lap. I'm not sure if he thinks he needs to protect her from the emu, but he's in protection mode. I love that he is as protective of my girl as I am.

As swiftly as he arrived, Dave flits off and back to the main farm area. Hannah reaches her palm back down to Arson. "Aw, were you jealous, pretty boy?" she croons.

Arson groans as she scratches under his jaw.

"I'll take that as a yes. I think they could be friends once they get more comfortable around each other," she says.

"I think so too," I confirm. "He just needs to realize Dave isn't going to hurt you."

"Is that what he was doing?" Hannah questions.

"I think so. Probably wanted to keep a close eye on our girl." I swing closer to her, kissing her cheek.

"Our girl?" she remarks.

"Yep," I reply, leaving no room for argument. "We're a package deal, me and him."

"A two-for-one special?" she teases.

"Exactly, freckles. Want to head inside?"

She agrees, and I reach out, taking her hand and leading us inside. The burner phone sits in the middle of the small kitchen table. I grab it and turn it on, hoping that there is a new text from Elena.

At first, nothing comes through, then the phone buzzes in my palm with a message. "Han, there's a message," I call to her.

She's at my side in an instant. "What does it say?"

I shift the phone so we can both read her message.

ELENA

> Sorry it's been so long without an update. We have been slowly working on the investigation, and arrested three suspects last night. I don't have much more than that, but it's something. Hope to have you two home in the next few weeks.

> You can contact your families today, but then turn the phone back off as soon as you're done. With the arrests we made, we have more confidence that the people intending to harm you are behind bars. Everyone in your families is safe, and Henry is recovering well.

I let out a heavy sigh of relief, knowing that both our families are well, and that Henry is recovering. Hannah does the same, her hand trembling as she clutches her chest.

I set the phone on the table, and take her hands in mine. "Hey, we're okay. Everyone's okay."

Her eyes well with tears as she looks up at me. "I don't know why I'm emotional. We haven't even called them yet."

"Probably because you've been worried for nearly two weeks, and having that confirmation settled your nerves," I explain, pushing her hair behind her ear and cupping her cheek. "Come on, let's call your grandma. It will help."

I help her sit at the table, scooting my chair close to hers and wrapping an arm around her shoulder, hoping to provide comfort. If I had it my way, I would pull her into my lap, but I'm not sure she'd like that right now.

I hand her the phone and tell her to dial. The line rings and rings, until it picks up. "Hello?" a woman's voice comes on the line.

"Grandma?" Hannah greets, her voice shaking.

"Hannah, is that you?"

"Yes," Hannah responds.

"Oh, my sweet girl. How are you? Are you okay?"

"I'm okay. We got the okay to call you today, and I needed to check in. Are you okay? Are you safe?"

"I'm safe," her grandma replies. "Julia and Tiff have been staying with me, even though I've told them a million times I'm fine. I think they need me more than I need them."

That makes Hannah chuckle, and I'm glad to see her humor returning. "I'm glad they're staying there. Are they there now?"

"They're out back. I'll yell at them." In the background, there's scuffling, and then the distant sound of her grandma yelling Tiff and Julia's names. "Here they come."

"Hannah?" Julia's voice is next on the line. "Oh my god, we've been worried sick. Are you okay?"

"I'm fine," Hannah says. "Thomas is taking really good care of me. We're in a nice little cottage, and the people hosting us are so sweet."

"Thank goodness," her grandma says. "It's so good to hear your voice, Hannah."

"Yours too," Hannah replies, her entire body relaxing. They chat for a few minutes, asking me how I am before Julia asks Hannah to step away for a private conversation.

I shift my arm off of her and stand. "I'll go outside. Let me know when you're done, and we can call my family next."

Hannah looks up with me, and nods. "Thanks. It won't be long."

I lean down, kissing her lips quickly. "I'll be outside if

you need me, freckles." With that, I head outside, leaving Hannah some much needed alone time with her family.

I wish it was a Sunday morning so I could know that all my family was together at Sunday brunch, but it's okay. Whoever I can get a hold of will be great.

## 32

## HANNAH

As soon as the door audibly clicks behind Thomas, Julia is hounding me. "Tell me *everything*," she says.

"I can't," I murmur. I am not about to let my grandma hear all about how I am about ready to climb Thomas like a tree and beg him to touch me. We haven't touched since the night on the couch, and I need more. Arson is tangled in my feet, snoring loudly.

"What do you mean, you can't? Grandma excused herself to give us a minute. It's only Tiff and me now."

Tiff says a quiet affirmative, letting me know my sister was telling the truth. I take a deep breath, thankful that I have this alone time with them. I've needed this, needed their advice. On my exhale, I tell them everything.

I tell them all about how I wasn't sleeping, and how Thomas was my first kiss. Then, I emphasize how comfortable and safe I feel with him, how we've done more than kiss now too, and how nervous I am for the next step, even though I feel ready.

They listen intently, only popping in the occasional reactionary noises and affirmations as they do.

"And now, I can't stop drooling every time I see him, especially when he wears his glasses at night," I finish with a groan.

"Oh, you've got it bad," Tiff says with a laugh.

"I do," I confirm, dropping my head into my hands.

"And you're comfortable with him?" Julia asks, ever the big sister.

"As comfortable as I've ever been with someone. I'm sure I'll be anxious and stuff, but I want to take this next step. I'm ready for the intimacy with him."

"Then go for it. I can't say that your first time is all that amazing, at least mine wasn't. Then again, it was with a man," Julia jokes. "But seriously, Han. If you're comfortable with him, and are ready to have that connection with him, then go for it. You deserve a good dicking down."

"You did not just say that," I laugh.

"I did! And it's true! You deserve it. Thomas is a great guy, Hannah. He'll take care of you."

"He already does take care of me," I reiterate.

"Yes, but he'll *take care of you*," Julia says, enunciating her words.

I groan into my palm. "I know."

"Good. Now, what else?" she questions.

She helps talk me through some of my anxieties as best she can, but then our time is up. It's Thomas's turn to talk to his family, and as much as I wish I could stay on the phone with mine, it's time.

I say goodbye to my sisters and grandma, holding back my tears the entire time. I sit in the silence for another minute, letting myself try to handle this pain of missing them, while also enjoying my time with Thomas.

After a few minutes, I stand, taking the phone with me

and heading outside. Arson follows, darting across the lawn to Thomas in one of the swings by the pond.

Thomas stands, crossing the lawn to meet me in the middle. I wrap my arms around his torso, melting my body into his. "Thanks for that," I say. "I didn't realize how much I needed it."

Thomas tilts my face to meet his. "I'm glad you got that time with them."

"Now, it's your turn," I reply, passing him the phone as we separate. "Do you want some alone time?"

He shakes his head. "No, I think I want you there with me. It might be easier."

"Okay," I respond, taking his hand in mine as we head back to the house.

When we're inside, we take the same spots as before at the kitchen table, only this time, Thomas surprises me by pulling me into his lap. I tense for a moment until I settle into him. He feels so warm, and I can't help but soak up the comfort that he gives me and hope that I can provide that for him as well.

He dials the number, and whoever he's calling picks up on the third ring. "This is Jason," he answers.

"Jase," Thomas breathes. "It's Thomas."

"Holy crap, Tommy, are you good?"

"Yeah. We're good. Are you with anyone?"

"Yep. There's an event at the brewery today, and everyone is here. Give me a minute and I'll round everyone up."

There's a lot of rustling and conversation and a few minutes later, Jason is back. "Tommy? I've got everyone in here."

A cacophony of voices breaks out across the line, all of them fighting to be the one to speak first.

"Everyone chill," Thomas says with a laugh, his earlier nervousness softening. "Hannah and I are fine. I'm sorry I had to leave so abruptly, but we're fine."

"Oh thank god," a feminine voice says. "When are you coming home?"

"I'm not sure, Mom. Hopefully, only a few more weeks, but there's no way to know for sure. Did Josie have the baby yet?"

Andrew's voice pops in. "Nope. She's convinced she's going to hold out until you get home, but there's only two more weeks until she's due, so she could go anytime."

"I'm sorry. Josie, don't worry about it. I'll meet him as soon as I get home." Thomas runs his hand down my thigh, like he needs my touch to anchor him right now. I lean my head into the crook of his neck.

"I don't want you to miss it," Josie says, sniffling. "He's your nephew. You should be able to meet him right away with everyone else."

"I know, and I want that too, but if I miss it, it will be okay. Take lots of pictures for me, okay?"

"We will," Andrew agrees.

The family catches up for a few more minutes, Jason's two daughters chiming in with things they've been up to this summer, until Thomas's grandpa chimes in.

"What's this I hear about you and Hannah being engaged?" he says, his voice gravely and filled with humor. I stiffen and lean back, trying to slide away, but Thomas's grip tightens around my waist.

Thomas tilts his head back, taking a deep breath. I'm about to say something, tell them it's all a joke, but Thomas clamps a hand over my mouth before I can. "Yes, we're engaged. Right, Hannah?"

I roll my eyes at him, and he narrows his at me. When

he seems convinced I won't tell them it's fake, he drops his palm from my mouth. "Yes, we are. It's fast, but it makes sense for us." The lie slides from my lips easily, and I wish I could believe it as much as he does.

"Hmm," Gramps mumbles. "I'm happy for you two. Sounds like we have a wedding to plan when you get back. Thomas, you got that ring?"

Thomas chokes, letting out a rough cough. "Yep," he says tightly.

*He has a ring?*

"Good. Then you're set."

"I guess so."

The family wraps up their conversations, and a few minutes later, we're saying goodbye and hanging up the phone. Thomas shuts the burner phone off again, sliding it across the kitchen table until it lands in the middle.

"How are you?" I ask. I purposefully avoid the subject of the ring, because it's not like a potential family heirloom is any of my business. We aren't really engaged. It's going to be messy when we get home, but for now, it is what it is.

"Better. It was good to hear their voices. I wish Josie wasn't so close to delivery, but there's nothing I can do about it right now," Thomas says.

I rest my palm on his chest. "You're close with her, aren't you?"

"I'm close with all my siblings and their partners. They're my best friends."

"I understand. I'm super close with Julia and Tiff too."

"I hope you can become friends with my sisters-in-law when we get back too. They're all great," Thomas says, his smile growing.

"What are you smiling about?" I question, poking the dimple in his cheek. His face flushes.

"Thinking about what it will be like to have you really get to know my family."

My heart swells and cracks painfully all at the same time. I want to give into the fact that this can work when we get home, but how can I? We're living in a safe house, secluded from the entire world. Of course, things are going to seem perfect and like a fairytale here. But as soon as we get home, he will get sick of me, I know it. I'm a lot to handle, and I'm surprised he isn't sick of me already.

But that's another day's problem. For now, I can soak up the time that we have, and let myself experience a relationship, no matter how fake it may be.

"That will be nice," I reply to placate him.

"I agree. They're going to love you, Han." He presses a kiss to my lips, and it isn't long before the kiss turns deeper.

I shift in his lap so I can face him, and my thigh brushes against a growing bulge between his legs. Before I can second guess myself, I reach down, laying my palm over top of it and gently squeezing. Thomas moans into my mouth, and the sound is so sinful that it makes my confidence grow tenfold.

"Fuck, Hannah," he groans. He moves a hand down to my palm to guide me over his cock again, showing me how hard to squeeze. He moves my palm up and down the length of his hardening cock beneath his shorts, and I can't stop the tingly feeling budding in my lower belly. This is the sexiest thing I've ever done.

Thomas shifts me, tugging my hand off his length. I whimper, wanting to be touching him again, but he pulls my legs around his waist. His fingers dig into my thighs as he stands, carrying me. He walks us over to the couch, laying me down on my back. Thomas pushes my legs apart with his knee, his thigh resting at the apex of my thighs, rubbing against my already soaking pussy through my clothes.

I don't want to feel him through my clothes though, I want to feel him skin to skin.

Thomas's lips find mine again, his hands caressing my hips, up to my breasts. He cups my breasts through my clothes. My body is experiencing sensation overload, and I need *more*. I reach for him, sliding my hands under the hem of his shirt and tugging upward. Thomas helps, reaching behind his neck and yanking his shirt up and off of him.

He does the same with his shorts, leaving him in only his boxers. His blue eyes are dark as his gaze rakes over my still-clothed body. "Can I?" he softly asks, flicking his eyes to my shirt.

I frantically nod. His hands find my hips again, this time taking the hem of my top in between his fingers. A jolt of anxiety takes over. He's going to see me naked.

There's a brief moment of panic as he lifts my shirt over my head and throws it to the ground, but the absolutely hungry lust filled look in Thomas's eyes erases the unease. He squeezes my ample hips, hands dragging up my sides and over my stomach until they reach my breasts.

He traces the edge of my bra, his fingertips smoothing over the roundness of my breast. Thomas bends down, taking my lips in his. For a long moment, that's all it is. He kisses me, devours me. His lips move from mine down my jaw, my neck, my collarbones, until his face is buried between my tits. Thomas groans, his hand squeezing as he tears the bra down, releasing my tits from the fabric.

I gasp, my eyes flying shut in anticipation. I don't know what comes next, but his mouth is covering the skin in kisses and licks until he's sucking my pebbled nipple into his mouth, flicking with his tongue. "Thomas," I cry, the sensation overloading me, sending heat shooting straight to my clit, which is thrumming with need. I never knew that it could feel this good. I've never liked playing with my breasts or my nipples when I'm on my own, but apparently when someone else does it, it drives me wild.

"Tell me, baby," Thomas moans, switching to my other breast, repeating the motion while using his fingers to continue his teasing on the first one.

"It feels so good," I groan.

He continues to suck and play with my tits until I can't take it anymore, and I need something more to ease this building ache. Thomas must sense this, as he draws his hand down my body, flattening his palm over my belly. He slides his hand into my shorts, over my underwear, and the sensation is so mind-blowing that I don't know what I'm going to do when he's inside of me.

"Do you want this?" he asks, hesitating. My eyes fly open when he stops all movement. His blue eyes hold my own, and despite the lust and heat burning in them, I can see the clarity there, too. He will stop if I say so, if I need him to. I trust him.

"Yes, please," I say, threading my hand into the hair at the nape of his neck and kissing him roughly.

His fingers push down on my waistband, and I help him shimmy them off, leaving me in only my underwear and bra. I always thought that at this moment, I would be panicking, that I would be scared of what he thought of my body, but I'm not. I can see the heat in his eyes, can see the way he's looking at me, and it makes me feel incredible. His gaze traces down my body slowly, like he's appreciating every inch, every curve and roll I have. It makes heat burst in my core, and I feel more treasured than I ever have. He's called me beautiful since the day we went on our first date, but the look in his eyes shows me how much he means it.

"We'll start slow," Thomas promises, and even though I want it so badly, I'm grateful.

"Thank you," I murmur, kissing him again.

Thomas's fingers tease the edge of my underwear, and I let out a shuddering breath. His fingers slide underneath, and his skin meets mine. My body tenses in anticipation, and when they find the wetness between my folds, Thomas groans loudly.

"Fuck, baby, you're soaked," he murmurs. "So perfect for me. So beautiful."

The words of praise send a shiver through my body. "Thomas, I need more," I breathe, clutching at his shoulder blades.

His fingers trace and circle as he finds my clit. When he does, he puts the softest pressure on it, rubbing in a circular motion. "Oh, god," I breathe. This feels so different than when I do it myself or when I use my toys. It feels ten times better.

Thomas replaces his pointer finger with his thumb, while the long finger moves downward to my entrance. He circles the wetness there, looking at me for permission. I nod, and he slides his finger inside me slowly, as if he's afraid he'll hurt me.

"*God*, you're tight," he says, the words coming out strained. He adjusts his hips, and I shift one of my legs up and hooking around his waist, opening myself to him.

The intrusion of his finger inside me is welcome, and so good. He hooks the finger, curling it against a spot that I've never been able to find myself. "Thomas!" I wail as he adds a second finger, stretching me in a way I've never experienced. He pumps his fingers in and out, my wetness easing the slight ache to this new feeling.

My clit pulses as he circles it with his thumb, the dual sensation sending me up and up toward a climax I never expected. Only, I can't get there. I'm searching for it, needing something more to fall over the edge, but I can't get there. This happens sometimes when I'm at home with my vibrator, and I usually give up. My stupid anti-depressants and getting in my own head can make it so hard for me to come sometimes.

I grind my hips against his hand, but it's not helping. I'm overthinking it now. Is it taking too long? Is his hand tired? Now I'm thinking about the sounds I've made. Does he like them? Or does he think they're weird?

I've ruined this.

All the earlier anticipation and build-up is gone, and I don't know what to do. Thomas takes his other hand, caressing my body in a way that two minutes ago felt amazing, but now all I can think about is how bored he must be. My eyes are shut, and I furrow my brow. Clenching down on his fingers, I let out a forced cry as I fake my orgasm. I need to be done with this embarrassing moment, so I breathe heavily, make all the convincing noises and don't *dare* open my eyes.

# THOMAS

She's faking it.

She was enjoying it. I could tell. The cries falling from her beautiful lips were about to make me come in my pants yet again, but then, something changed. She tenses, her body freezing as her cries turn into a fake sound that I never want to hear again.

She's breathing heavily, her eyes squeezed tightly shut as she pretends to orgasm. I know she was close, I could feel it, could tell with the sounds she was making, but what caused her to freeze up?

I slide my fingers out of her soaked pussy, leaning back on my heels. I want to taste her so bad, but I don't deserve the satisfaction. She faked an orgasm. I don't deserve to taste her until I can make her come for real.

When she opens her eyes, she looks almost guilty.

"You faked it," I say, letting my sadness seep into my words.

"What?" She sits up, covering her breasts with her arm.

"You faked your orgasm. You didn't come. Was it something I did? Communication is one of the most important things about sex, Hannah."

She shrinks into her skin, and for a moment, I feel bad for calling her out, but I need to know.

"It wasn't you," she murmurs.

"Then what was it?"

"I'm defective," she mumbles. "I was taking too long, and I started overthinking. You shouldn't have had to do that for so long without me coming. I should have been quicker."

"That's bullshit," I state, scooting between her legs again. "I will stay down there as long as it takes, Hannah. Whether I am using my fingers or my mouth, I won't stop until you come."

"I can't expect you to stay down there that long—"

"You can and you will," I interrupt her. An idea pops into my brain, something I've never done before, but am willing to try. "Show me."

Hannah pushes herself up, scooting back into the couch, covering her beautiful body with her arms. "What do you mean?"

"Show me what you like, and I'll show you what I like. Make yourself come, and I'll do the same."

She furrows her brow and shakes her head abruptly. "No, I can't do that."

"Why not?" I genuinely ask, scooting closer to her again. "If you show me what you like, then I'll know for next time what you like, and how to make you feel good."

"You were making me feel good, Thomas, I got into my head, that's all."

"Show me anyway," I murmur, my cock throbbing in my boxers as she lays back again.

I can tell she's thinking about it, her body isn't as tense as it was a moment ago.

"You—You'll do it too?"

"Fuck yes," I confirm. "I'll even start if you want."

She nods rapidly, her wide blue eyes darting from mine to the bulge in my pants.

I lean forward, taking her lips in a quick kiss. I need one last taste of her if I'm not going to be able to touch her while doing this. I'll do anything she needs to be comfortable, and if taking a step back before we take another step forward is what she needs, then I'm happy to oblige.

When I pull back, her pupils are blown, and I think she's growing fonder of the idea with each passing second. I lean back onto my heels on the couch, moving my hand to grip my hard length through my boxers. I don't miss the shaky inhale of her breath as I do, or the way her eyes widen. It's hot as fuck to know that I have this effect on her.

I squeeze my cock harder, moving up my shaft as I do, then without waiting another second, I'm standing up off of the couch, shucking my boxer briefs down my legs and onto the floor. Hannah's eyes never leave my body with each movement, her mouth parted slightly as she breathes. She's still covering her body with her arms, her legs pressed shut, but my god if she isn't stunning like this. I settle back onto the couch, taking my cock in my palm again.

I move slowly, twisting my grip as I pump my cock the way I like. Her eyes are zeroed in on my hand, watching each movement with a calculating gaze. It's hot to see how intrigued she is by it all.

I continue to stroke myself, letting out soft groans as I do. This is the hottest thing I've ever done.

Hannah's lustful gaze holds mine, and I watch as her body slowly relaxes too. Her fingers start to play with her pointed nipples, her legs falling open as she pushes aside her underwear and shows me her glistening cunt.

"Fuck, Hannah," I groan, tugging harshly on my cock. "You're perfect. Look at that pretty pussy."

Hannah gasps, her fingers sliding down her body to circle her clit slowly, gathering her wetness and dragging it back to the little nub.

"Thomas," she cries, and I will never tire of hearing my name on her lips.

"That's it, baby, show me what you like."

I watch her fingers as she moves in perfect circles on her clit. I feel like a student studying for a final exam, but this is more important than that. This is *everything*. She's growing more confident and I can hear the difference in the noises she was making before when she faked it, to now. These are more breathless, less whiny, more... raw. Real.

My own climax tightens in my balls, but I won't come until she does. I squeeze my balls, tightening my grip on my shaft, doing whatever I can to stave off my release.

Her fingers strum faster, pace quickening as she chases her orgasm. Eyes closing, her mouth drops open in a silent cry as she comes. I watch her body writhe as she moans lowly, eyes flying open to watch me.

I jerk my hand up and down as she watches closely, her chest heaving as she catches her breath. I wait until her eyes are locked on my hands, and then I let myself go. I don't hold back from crying out her name as my climax hits, my cum spurting from my cock and landing on the couch between us, covering my hand and my thighs with it.

We catch our breath together, and I don't move my gaze from her. She's not covering her body anymore. Her legs are still splayed wide open, showing me her soaking pussy.

"How was that?" I ask, needing to know.

"It was perfect," she admits. "It helped me get out of my head."

"Good," I murmur, leaning forward to cup her cheek with my clean hand, kissing her. I rise from the couch. "Stay there," I tell her, and she doesn't move as I head into the bathroom, grabbing a washcloth and wetting it with warm water.

"May I?" I ask when I get back to the couch. She's adjusted now, scooting back and closing her thighs.

"Yes," she responds, her voice breathy and shaky.

I rest a hand on her knee, applying gentle pressure to open her legs for me. I clean her gently. Not that I got any cum on her, but it's still nice to clean her. It's another level of intimacy that I want with her.

"Better?" I ask when I'm done.

She nods, standing from the couch. "Thank you."

"Anytime, baby."

Hannah grabs her clothes from the ground and heads into the bathroom. I clean up the mess on the couch, hoping it doesn't stain because I'm not sure how I'd explain that to Dottie and Ron.

A relaxing warmth spreads throughout my body, and I can't wait to hold her in my arms again. I throw my own clothes back on, tossing the washcloth into the washer before I sit down on the couch.

A few minutes later, she comes out, a perfect pink flush covering her freckled cheeks and chest. "Come here, freckles."

She strides to me, trying to hide the smile tugging at her lips. I pull her onto the couch and into my side, kissing the top of her head as she curls up into my body. I love this closeness, the way she melts into me.

"Was that okay?" I ask, running my hand up and down

her arm.

"It was more than okay," she replies. "Thank you. I don't know how you knew what I needed, but it was amazing."

"Good. I'm glad. We can do that again whenever you want. I agree, it was amazing."

Hannah nods, then turns her head further into my chest. "Or we could do something else? Something... more?" she asks tentatively. She's embarrassed, and she has no reason to be.

I reach down, taking her chin between my fingers, tilting her head to look at me. "Look at me, baby."

Her blue orbs lock on mine. "We can do anything you want. Something more, something less, or something completely different. The options are endless."

Hannah nods, and I can see the wheels turning in her brain as it comes up with ideas. I'm doing the same. I can't wait to explore this new side of her, and explore it together as we become an *us*.

## 34

## THOMAS

A bead of sweat rolls down my cheek as I heft a shovel full of manure into the wheelbarrow. For the last few weeks, this has been my life. I start the day out with Hannah in my arms, then Arson and I head to the house and help Ron with whatever he needs. I've turned into his fix it man, and I don't mind a bit.

Hannah and Dottie are lounging on the porch today, watching us work. She keeps offering me shy smiles whenever I glance her way, and it's adorable.

"If you keep watching her instead of your feet, you're going to end up face first in horse manure," Ron says with a chuckle. I unwillingly rip my gaze from Hannah.

Every single day, she astounds me. In the five weeks we've been here, I've watched her open up to me, both body and soul. We spend our days with Ron and Dottie, then we spend our nights on the swings by the pond, talking for hours until we end up getting eaten by mosquitoes. Then, we go inside and cuddle up on the couch or in bed, and talk even more. Usually, it ends with her in my arms as we fall asleep.

I think she's still holding back, still holding a piece of herself from me. Sometimes, she shuts down, or ends a conversation before it really has the chance to get deep. I want to know every piece of her, even the stuff that hurts.

We've talked to our families a few more times since that first time, and based on our conversations with Elena, they are getting closer to tracking down the person who shot Henry, and the drug circles ringleader.

"I can't help it," I respond with a chuckle, focusing my gaze back to the task at hand.

Ron laughs. "I was the same way with my Dottie when we first met. Hell, I still am, only now, I've learned from my mistakes and I don't stare at her when I've got shit to shovel."

I shake my head as laughter rises in my chest. "Wise words, my friend."

We work in silence for a few minutes more before we head out of the barn. In the distance, I spot an old truck and an idea pops into my head. "Hey, Ron?" I question, pointing to the faded red truck. "Does that thing still run?"

"Hmm?" Ron questions, turning to look where my finger is pointing. "Oh, sure it does. We don't use it very often anymore."

"Think I can borrow it for a night?"

"Course," Ron says with a shrug. "It's not going to win you any races, but it will get you where you need to go."

"I was thinking of taking Hannah on a date. Not in town or anything, but maybe a drive to watch the stars." There are plenty of extra blankets and pillows in the cottage that we can use to lay in the bed if we want. I've been wanting to do something special for her, and I think this may be perfect. It's not like we can go into town and go for dinner or a movie, so this is a happy medium.

Ron and I finish up the day's work and he brings me out to the truck, handing over the keys and giving me a rundown on a few gimmicks the truck has. I've instructed Ron to keep Hannah at the house for an extra hour tonight if he can, so that I can get the truck cleaned up and ready to go with the blankets and pillows.

I get everything set up with extra fluffy blankets and all the pillows from the cottage. I have no idea why Dottie has so many pillows in the cottage, but I'm grateful for it if it means Hannah can be comfortable.

I close the bed of the truck as Hannah appears at the tree line, walking toward me. "Hey, freckles," I call when she gets closer. I lean against the truck, my eyes trailing up and down her beautiful body. She's gorgeous, so fucking gorgeous, I'll never get enough of her.

"Hey," she replies. "Where'd the truck come from?"

"It's Ron's. He offered to let us borrow it for the night."

"What for?" she asks curiously, reaching for me. I open my arms for her, loving how she automatically steps into my embrace and wraps her arms around my waist.

"We," I say, squeezing her tightly to me, "are going on a date."

"A date?" she questions, her blonde brows raising.

"Yep." I kiss the tip of her freckled nose. "We haven't been on a proper one since the street dance, and we deserve it."

"Where are we going?"

"Unfortunately, our options are limited, but you'll see. Go change, I'm going to feed Arson." I reluctantly let her go, and we walk together inside. She heads upstairs and I scoop Arson some food.

He's going to stay behind tonight. We need some time

to ourselves, and I don't want Arson to steal the cuddles from my girl anymore than he normally does.

Ten minutes later, Hannah floats down the stairs in a light pink swishy sundress. It's simple, no pattern or anything on it, but it's beautiful like her. When she reaches me, I pull her in for a kiss and run my hand up and down her spine. "Gorgeous," I mutter against her lips.

"Thank you," she mumbles shyly, her cheeks burning up the way I love.

"I'm going to change, and I'll be right back down."

I run upstairs to change, putting on a pair of Captain America boxers, and throwing on a pair of dark jeans and a light blue t-shirt. I add some fresh deodorant and a spritz of cologne as well.

I need luck tonight. I have a feeling tonight is going to be a pivotal moment for our relationship, and I cannot wait.

I practically race down the stairs, eager to get our evening started. "Let's go," I say, reaching out for Hannah's palm.

"Is Arson coming?" Hannah asks, turning back to where Arson is curled up on the couch.

I shake my head. "Nope. Tonight, it's all about us."

Hannah offers me a soft smile, but I can see the excitement burning in her gaze. We head out to the truck, and I help her in, making sure she's buckled before getting in the other side. Ron drew a map out to another section of their land for the best place to see the stars. The sun is starting to set in the distance, so it's the perfect time.

I grab the map off the dashboard where I stashed it and take another glance.

"Is that a paper plate with a map on it?" Hannah asks with a laugh.

"Yep," I reply. "Ron couldn't find a piece of scratch paper, so this was the best option according to him."

"I mean, whatever works, right?" she replies.

"Exactly."

I drive to the road that will take us past the main house, and when we pass, they are sitting out on the porch swings, waving and smiling at us. I follow the map to a field about a mile from the house. It's a bare field, only some tall grass with a tree line on the far corner. It's perfect for tonight.

Hannah shrieks as we drive straight to the middle of it, a smile growing wider as we bounce over bumps. When we reach a good spot, I shift the truck into park, turning the key and unbuckling my seatbelt to slide across the bench seat. I cup Hannah's cheeks in my palms and kiss her.

I care so deeply for her, and I know it's only a matter of time before I speak those three little words into existence. I can only hope that she's ready for them, and feels the same way.

## 35

# HANNAH

Thomas's lips on mine are starting to feel like home. I feel so safe in his arms, so protected and warm that the thought of being without him hurts. He's planned this amazing night for us, and I appreciate it more than he knows.

The last few weeks with Thomas have been magical. That's the only word I can use to describe it. He's made me feel things I didn't know were possible. He's made me feel more confident in my body, in my sexuality than ever before. I love who I am with him, and even though there's a niggling voice in the back of my brain telling me that it won't last, and that it's all temporary, I am soaking up every bit of it while I can.

Part of me wants to stay in this little bubble forever. I'm scared that once we go home, I'll be left behind in the dust. Left to my own devices again. He's done nothing to make me feel this way, but my brain won't stop telling me that's what will happen.

He's been the perfect gentleman too, ever since that night I faked it. He's making me come every chance he can with his hands. He's taking it slow, though, never pressing for more, or making me feel like he only is after one thing with me. He's taught me how to give him pleasure with my hands, and while I'm a bit nervous to do more, I'm also ready. I want him.

Thomas leans away from our kiss. "Come on," he says, scooting toward the driver's side door. He gets out and I follow, opening my door and meeting him on my side. "I have something else to show you."

He takes my hand, leading me to the bed of the truck. He opens the tailgate to reveal a little oasis. I can't believe I didn't notice this before. There's fluffy blankets and pillows piled high, leaving the space looking comfortable and cozy, and not at all like I imagined.

"Thomas," I breathe, a smile breaking out on my lips.

"You like it?" he asks.

"It's perfect."

"Hop in," he says, gesturing to the back. I do, and he follows, crawling up behind me. I lean up against the back of the cab, a pillow behind my back. Thomas sits right beside me, his arm automatically resting around my shoulders.

"Thank you," I tell him. "This is perfect."

"Just like you," he replies.

I shake my head, looking down at my legs.

"You know it's the truth," Thomas says, his finger finding my chin to get me to look up at him. His familiar blue eyes alight my soul, and I know he means it.

"Thank you," I repeat. He's helping me believe it more with each day that passes.

Thomas presses kisses to my nose and cheeks in rapid succession, making me giggle. "What are you doing?"

"Kissing every single freckle you have," he murmurs,

continuing to kiss me, moving down my jaw to my chest. "I love them so much."

"You're going to be kissing me for a long time," I shriek as he tickles my ribs.

"Worth it," he murmurs. We slide down so we're lying on our backs. My head rests on his chest as we catch our breath from our laughter.

"How long do you think we'll be here?" I ask, hoping that I don't pop the precious bubble.

"Probably a few more weeks. Hopefully not long, though. I know you miss your family."

I nod in agreement. "You miss yours too."

"I do. As much as I love this time with just us, it will be nice to be home."

I nod into his chest, resting my palm over his heart. The anxiety creeps in at the thought of going home and losing him, losing the constant time with him. Don't get me wrong, I want to go home, but I also don't want this fairytale to end.

"You're going to laugh," Thomas says, his voice rumbling in my ear. "I'm about to ask you the most basic question."

I chuckle. "Go for it."

"Where do you see yourself in five years?"

I let myself think, but I already know that I'm not going to tell him my real answer, or the answer that I so desperately want to happen. It all includes him, and that's not realistic for me. I can't keep pining over a future that may not happen.

Shrugging, I hide myself in his chest. "I don't know. Probably working, probably still in Ivy Ridge. What about you?"

Thomas shifts so he can look down at my face. "That's all? You don't see anything else for your future?"

I shake my head. I don't want to say it out loud. I can't risk the embarrassment of saying that I want to be married in five years. I don't want to say that not only do I want to be married, I want to be married to *him*. I want to have a family of my own, complete with the house, kids and dog, preferably Arson.

Thomas sighs. "Fine, my turn. In five years, I see myself married. Not only that, but I see myself married to a beautiful woman."

I catch my breath at his admission. He doesn't give me a moment to think on his words though, as he continues speaking.

"Someone kind, with a servant's heart. I see myself in our home, maybe with a kid, or one on the way. I see us going to Sunday brunches with my family, her becoming best friends with my sisters and brothers, being the best aunt to my nieces and nephews, and being a part of my amazing family."

He takes a deep breath, running his fingertips up and down the length of my arm. "I see it all with you, Hannah."

His admission hits me right in the chest. He's so confident, and for a moment, I sink into the fantasy. It's beautiful, like he said. I see it all with him too.

Instead of shutting down the fantasy, I let myself dream right along with him.

The sun sets in the distance as we hold each other, dreaming about a future that I can only dream about. We don't know what the future holds, but right now, it seems pretty amazing.

As the sky grows dark, the moon and stars illuminate the sky. We lie on our backs, pointing out constellations to each other. The air grows cooler, but we wrap up in the blankets Thomas brought, keeping us warm.

"Truth or dare," Thomas says, surprising me. We've been lying in comfortable silence for a while.

"Truth," I reply.

"Who's the most influential person in your life?"

I don't even have to think about the question for more than a moment before answering. "My grandma."

"Why?"

"She's been through hell. She should have had at least twenty to thirty more years with the love of her life, and it was cut off early. Then, she lost her child in a car accident, and had to finish raising her granddaughter." My eyes burn at the mention of her.

"She taught me everything. I already wasn't a fan of driving, so when my parents died in a car accident, I wanted nothing to do with cars. She helped me get over that anxiety, and taught me how to drive. She got me into therapy, helped me get my license, and basically helped me figure out how to be an adult. It's still hard. I have a lot of anxiety as you know, a lot of it stemming from my grandfather and my parents' death, but she's been there for every step."

"She seems amazing," Thomas replies, squeezing me tightly against him. "I bet she's proud of the woman you've become."

I shrug. "She's probably more proud of Julia. She's accomplished so much more than me, she's married, has an amazing job, and works hard." Her success is always something I've envied.

"And you don't work hard?"

"I mean, I do, but it's different," I reply, trying to shift away.

Thomas doesn't let me move. "How is it different?"

"I don't know, but it is. She didn't have to watch Julia

fall apart at the seams. She didn't have to help put her back together."

"Baby, that's not a bad thing. That's what family is for. Whether it's blood or chosen, they're the people that are there to help put you back together. I can't tell you how many times my brothers have put me back together."

I shake my head. "That's different."

"How?" he interrupts. "We all experience things, and we have to lean on our people to get through it. No one should have to do things alone."

"But I should be able to do things on my own, I shouldn't need Miles to coach me on how to pick up a coffee from a coffee shop, or my grandma to put together my pieces, or you to help me sleep with my stupid anxiety. I shouldn't *need* to sleep in your arms every night. I shouldn't be so weak." Tears stream down my cheeks as the dam bursts.

Thomas swipes at my cheeks, kissing my tears away. "You are not weak, Hannah Pearson. You are incredible. Having to fight through what you've been through and ask for help doesn't make you weak. It makes you strong."

He presses his lips to mine, palms cupping my cheeks, like he's trying to pour all of his strength into me through a kiss. I moan into the kiss, losing myself in him. It doesn't take long before my tears have dried, and he pulls away from my lips.

"Do you believe me?" he asks.

"Yes," I reply, and I do. It might take a while for me to *fully* believe it, and not revert back to my usual anxieties, but I do believe him.

"Good."

I shiver as the breeze picks up, and Thomas wraps me

up further in the blanket. "Should we go back?" he questions.

I really don't want to, but even with the blankets, I'm getting chilly. "Probably."

Quickly, we fold up the blankets and get out of the bed, putting them in the front seat of the truck. The massive pile of pillows and blankets is between us, and I wish it weren't. I want to be curled up in his arms again.

Thomas glances over at me as we drive out of the field. "Well, that's unfortunate," he grumbles.

"What?"

"That you're so far away, and all the blankets are between us. I want to snuggle you more."

I laugh, "I was thinking the same thing." With some shuffling around, I push the blankets and pillows to the window, and within a minute, I'm curled up against his side the way I want.

"Better," he says.

I hum in response as he squeezes me tightly, his fingers tracing circles on my arm. I love his touch, crave it even, something I never thought possible. Something I never would have anticipated. It took a minute to get used to, but now I love it. He's such a physical touch kind of guy.

Five minutes later, we are pulling into the Graff's driveway, passing by the dark house and making our way to the cottage. The soft glow of the lamp illuminates the pointy ears of Arson, waiting for us in the front window.

"I think he missed us," I say, pointing him out to Thomas.

"In his defense, he's been with one of us at all times for a month now."

"Good point," I reply, reluctantly pulling away from Thomas as he parks the truck.

"Wait," Thomas says, already pulling me back into him. He takes my face, kissing me deeply. "Thank you for opening up to me tonight. We never really finished our game of truth or dare, but if you want to, we can."

I shake my head. "Maybe later."

Together, we head inside, and Arson skips around our feet, talking to us in dog howls. Thomas lets him out to go to the bathroom, while I head upstairs to change out of my dress.

A few minutes later, Thomas and Arson bound up the stairs. I'm sitting on my side of the bed in my pajamas, feeling anything but tired. Something I've learned since starting to be intimate with Thomas is I have no idea how to initiate things. I want more, I need it, *crave* it, so why can't I get over myself and ask for it? Show him what I want?

"Ready for bed?" Thomas asks, taking in my pajamas. He's still in his clothes, but he must have taken his contacts out since he's wearing his glasses now.

"I guess," I say with a shrug. Thomas takes his shirt and pants off so he's in only his boxers. These aren't his normal boxers, though. They are a pair of superhero underwear. The underwear he wears when he needs luck. Did he wear them for me? For tonight?

I stare at the underwear. My heart pounds a heavy beat in my chest. He may not even realize how sweet the gesture is, or what it means to me that he wore something he considers lucky on our date. I want this man more than my next breath.

Shocking myself, I blurt, "Truth or dare."

## 36

## THOMAS

"Truth or dare."

Hannah stares at me with more heat in her eyes than I've ever seen.

"Truth," I reply, my eyes widening.

"What turns you on?" she asks, her voice shaking.

"You," I reply without a second thought.

Hannah scoffs, a blush rising up her cheeks. "Be more specific."

"Fine," I reply, kneeling on the edge of the bed, resting my palms on my thighs. "You, in the dress you wore tonight. You, in nothing at all. The noises you make when you come. The way you squeeze my fingers with your tight little pussy. You, Hannah. You turn me on."

Her mouth parts, pupils dilating as she stares at me.

"Oh," she breathes.

"Truth or dare, Hannah," I prompt, moving toward her, pushing her hair behind her ear.

"Truth," she replies.

"What turns you on?" I repeat her question to me, not because I can't think of something, but because I truly need to know. Anytime we've been intimate, it happened naturally, with no specific person initiating it. Is that what this is? Is she ready for more? I am. I want to be inside her more than my next breath. I want the closeness with her, the raw connection sex brings.

She swallows thickly. "When you kiss me, and you do that thing with your tongue."

"Hmmm," I reply, cupping her cheek and pressing my lips to hers. I gently bite down on her lower lip, swiping my tongue across the area. "Like that?"

"Y-Yes," she stutters. "And when you kiss my neck."

I do as she says, trailing down her jaw to her neck, pressing long, languid kisses to her skin.

Before I get lost in the little noises she makes or the softness of her skin, she pushes me back by my hair, taking a deep breath and speaking, her voice clear. "Truth or dare."

Time to kick things up a notch. "Dare," I answer, narrowing my eyes, pushing my glasses up from where they slid down my nose.

With a sharp inhale, Hannah squares her shoulders and looks me in the eye. "I dare you to fuck me, Thomas."

Okay, that is totally not what I thought she was going to say. I thought she'd say, kiss me, or maybe something we haven't done yet, like eat her out, but I never thought she'd say that. I'm all in, of course I am, it just took me off guard.

"Are you sure?" I ask, all thoughts of our teasing game long gone. If she's serious about this, I want to make sure she's ready. This is all new for her, and I need to make it good for her.

"Yes, I'm sure," she replies. "I want it. I need you, Thomas."

Fuck, hearing those words leave her lips makes my cock thicken even more in my boxers. Once again, these boxers are lucky. At this point, maybe it's manifestation, but I'm not going to question it.

I slide my hand around her waist, locking my eyes with hers. "What did I do to deserve you?" I ask, not really waiting for an answer before kissing her again. Hannah whimpers into my mouth, and for a long while, I kiss her. We make out like teenagers, my body hovering over hers on the bed. In the distance, I hear the *click-clack* of Arson's nails as he goes downstairs, giving us some privacy.

My hand grips her soft waist as I lay her down, resting some of my weight on her. I slowly make my way down her body, kissing her through her thin pajama shirt until I reach the apex of her thighs. Heat radiates from her core, taunting me with her soaking pussy. I press a kiss to the fabric-covered heat, goosebumps breaking out on my flesh when she moans.

"This okay, baby?" I ask, looking up at her from between her thighs. She breathes heavily, her breasts rising and falling with each inhale and exhale.

She nods, her eyes glassy as she looks down at me. "Yes, please."

I slide my fingers under the waistband of her sleep shorts, prompting her to lift her hips. I push them down, revealing her glistening cunt to me. She's fucking soaked. She shimmies her thin top up and off, baring her breasts to me. My mouth is watering seeing her completely naked and knowing what is coming next. I adjust my glasses, fully aware that I could take them off, but wanting to see every-thing, every moment.

I slide my boxers down, freeing my throbbing cock. Just the thought of being inside her is making my brain short-circuit. Hannah glances down, watching my cock twitch, and bites her lip. *Fuuuck*, she's trying to kill me.

I kiss my way down her body again, not stopping this time when I reach her pussy, instead, sliding my tongue from her entrance to her clit, enjoying the taste of her for the first time. Hannah jolts under my touch, her body tensing and relaxing after a moment.

I take my time, letting my tongue explore her, my fingers moving to her entrance and sliding in. Her pussy tightens around them, and if this is a preview of what my cock is about to experience, we're going to be lucky if I make it more than three strokes.

Thrusting my fingers in and out of her, I soak up each moan, each breathy gasp and tense of her muscles. Her thighs tighten around my head as my tongue flicks and teases her clit. She's getting closer with each movement, her body showing me the signs that are growing all too familiar with each passing day.

"Come for me, baby," I order, needing to give her as much pleasure as possible tonight. I will make her feel good. This won't be some fumbled fuck in the back seat of a Honda Civic with a teenage boyfriend. Her first time should be amazing, and I feel honored that she's choosing me to be her first.

"Fuck," Hannah moans, her thighs shaking, squeezing my head even tighter as she reaches down to grip my hair, pulling at the strands.

I moan against her clit, giving her a little vibration, making her moan. I don't stop until she's shoving me off her. When I sit back on my heels, I wipe my mouth with my fingers, the ones that were just inside her. Not wanting her wetness to go to waste, I slide my fingers into my mouth, reveling again in her delicious taste.

"Holy shit," Hannah gasps. I smile as I let my fingers fall from my mouth to my cock, wrapping around the girth and stroking a few times. "Holy shit," she repeats, her mouth dropping open comically.

Stroking my cock is not enough, though, even with her eyes on me like they were the day we watched each other. I need more. Hannah surprises me, sitting up and leaning forward, her fingers grazing down my chest and stomach to cover my hand. "May I?" she asks delicately.

I swallow harshly. "Yes," I say through gritted teeth, anticipating her touch. No matter how much I anticipate and prepare though, it's never enough to lessen the pure bliss that hits me when she replaces my hand with her small fingers.

She tentatively strokes, squeezing my shaft the way I've shown her.

"Harder, baby," I coach, hissing when she follows my instructions. Hannah rises to her knees, matching my position. I reach out, cupping her heavy breasts in my palms as she strokes me with one hand. The other wraps around the nape of my neck, pulling me down to her lips.

## 37

## HANNAH

I have never wanted a person like this before. Never had someone want *me* like this. My hand wraps around his thick shaft, twisting and stroking him the way he showed me, and the noises he's making make me feel confident that he likes it.

Thomas slowly peels my hand free, murmuring against my neck, "If you don't stop, I'm going to come, and that's not what I want. Not yet, at least."

"Okay," I murmur, letting go of him and sitting back on my heels.

"Lie back, baby." Thomas helps me so I'm comfortable on the pillow, my hair fanned out behind me. He devours the sight of my body, his eyes tracing every inch of my skin. His gaze leaves me feeling achy and wanting. Self-consciousness doesn't get a chance to creep in, because the hungered look on his face would wipe it out immediately.

"I will never tire of this. Of you," he mutters, reaching out to trace his thumb across my bottom lip. "Do you feel ready?"

"Yes," I say. I don't know what is normal in situations like this, but I say it anyway. "I'm on birth control. I have an IUD, and I'm... well I'm clean."

Thomas nods, his finger tilting my chin. "I'm clean too, I was tested at my most recent physical and I haven't been with anyone in a long time. I'll still wear a condom, though."

Even though I trust him, having him say the words out loud relieves something in me. "Okay," I reply. Part of me wants nothing between us, but I know this is safest for now. An IUD is super effective, but I'm nowhere near ready to be a parent.

Thomas climbs off the bed and digs through his bag. "I didn't want to assume anything when we came here, but I also wanted to be prepared if something did happen." He produces a condom from the bag, climbing back onto the bed. He waves it in front of him. "I'm glad I was prepared."

"Me too," I answer, my tummy swooping as nerves start to build. I'm excited, of course, but there's also nerves. I have heard horror stories from others about losing their virginity. The pain, the blood, the lack of pleasure. So while I'm not expecting this to be absolutely incredible, I also know that Thomas will do his best to make it as amazing as possible.

I watch as he slides the condom on his hard cock, making sure it's on correctly, before he positions his body between my thighs. My heart pounds rapidly in my chest. This is finally happening. I'm about to lose my virginity, and it's to someone even better than I could have ever imagined. Thomas leans forward, his lips caressing mine once more.

It's not like I know any different, but the man is a *fabulous* kisser.

"I'm going to ask you one more time," he says, his body hovering over me, his weight pressing into me like a weighted blanket. It instantly relieves the rapid pounding of my heart, and the small inkling of anxiety. "Are you sure?"

I nod, wrapping my fingers around the back of his neck, taking his lips for another kiss. "I've never been more sure of anything in my life."

Thomas smiles down at me, his adorable dimpled grin making butterflies take over my body. His glasses are sliding down his nose, and I reach up, pushing them up, chuckling.

One of his hands slides down between us, gripping his hard cock and notching it at my entrance. The first feel of him against my pussy is surreal. With a gentle thrust, the head of his cock enters me.

We both gasp in unison at the feeling. It's something new and foreign, but at the same time, familiar, because it's him. I expect the pain to strike at any moment as he pushes further inside me, only... it never does. He checks up on me with each inch, slowly pulling out before easing back in. "Fuck, you feel so good, baby," he groans. "Are you okay?"

"Yes," I breathe, my body thrumming as he slides deeper inside me. "Don't stop."

"Never," he mumbles, leaning down to kiss my neck, his fingers tangling in my hair. Once he's fully inside me, he holds himself there for a long moment. "You need to tell me if this is too much."

He pulls almost all the way out before thrusting back, faster and harder than before. Even with how wet I am, there's the tiniest pinch, but it's gone as fast as it came, leaving only pleasure. Thomas's eyes are focused on mine, watching my every reaction and breath as if he's terrified of hurting me. "Feels so good," I say in an attempt to ease his mind. I reach up to caress his cheek, feeling thankful yet again that it's him I chose to do this with.

My legs open wider, one hooking up and around his hip

as he thrusts in and out of me, my body opening to him in a new way, and he groans in my ear. "You're incredible, Hannah. Thank you for trusting me." His mouth leaves hot kisses across my chest as he kisses the freckles.

"Oh, god," I moan as his other hand reaches between us, finding my clit. His fingertips caress it in the motion he's learned that I like, my body instantly reacting to his touch. It's so different from when he has his fingers inside me. I'm so full with him that the orgasm comes rushing in, bursting through my seams and careening down into pleasure within moments. My pussy squeezes him as I come, my body tightening around him.

"Fuck," he groans, pulling out and sitting up.

"What?" I breathlessly ask, pushing up on my elbows to look up at him.

"I wasn't ready to be done yet, and your pussy was squeezing the life out of my cock," he says with a chuckle, his cheeks painted red. He takes a deep breath, running his hands through his hair, fixing his glasses as he rubs his face.

I lie in front of him, smiling like a madwoman. *This man.*

"Lie on your side," he prompts. I do as he says, rolling to my side as he lies down behind me. It feels so natural to lie with him like this. This is how we fall asleep every night and wake up each morning. One of his arms wraps around my ribs, sliding up between my breasts to rest on my chest, while the other is above my head on the pillow.

"Lift your leg up and over my hip," he directs. I follow, opening myself up to him. The hand on my chest leaves for a moment as he guides his cock to my opening, sliding in again. "Just like that, let me in, baby."

"Oh, god," I cry. The angle is different in this position, not better or worse by any means, but still, different.

His hand moves back between my breasts, and I realize that I have the perfect angle to tease my clit. I reach down, sliding my fingers over the sensitive bud, my breathing hitching as the pleasure takes me by surprise.

Thomas's hips slap against my ass as his pace increases, his steady rhythm growing more frantic as he gets closer to his own orgasm. I tilt my head back to rest more on the pillow, angling my head so I can reach his lips.

The arm above my head reaches under my shoulder so both his arms are wrapped around my torso, and he's pulling me tighter to him, his hips grinding against me. I can't move my arms anymore with the way he's holding me, but the sensation of him moving in and out of me is enough.

"Thomas," I cry his name, my body lighting up. I can tell he's getting closer to his own orgasm, his breathing staggers as he whispers dirty words in my ear, groaning my name.

"Please," I beg, though I'm not sure for what.

Thomas thrusts three more times before I feel his cock jerking inside me, and not for the first time tonight, I wish there wasn't a condom between us. I wish I could feel his warm release filling me up, showing me the visible signs of his claim on me. He owns my body. He's the only one who has ever touched me like this, made me feel this way. Even if things don't work out between us, he will always hold this claim on me.

Thomas's movements stop as he holds me to him, his lips never stop caressing me everywhere. "Was that too much?" he breathes, still catching his breath.

"No, not at all. It was everything," I reply, kissing his cheek.

"I really don't want to let you go," Thomas says with a soft chuckle.

"Then don't," I simply say, as if it's that easy. He has to take care of the condom, and I need to use the restroom and clean up, but for now, this is what we need.

## 38

## THOMAS

Hannah shifts in her sleep, her legs intertwined with mine under the sheets. Arson is at our feet, snoring loudly. I've been awake for probably an hour now, completely unwilling to move.

Last night was... indescribable. It was perfect. Everything I dreamed of. She gave a piece of herself to me, trusted me with it, and for that, I will be forever grateful. If I wasn't sure of it, I am now. I love her. She's completely wrapped into my soul, and I know she's not ready for me to proclaim my love for her yet, but I will soon. Hopefully soon, we will be going home, and then we can start our lives as normal, together.

She moans, stretching her body as she slowly wakes.

"Morning, freckles," I murmur, leaning down to kiss her cheek.

"Mmm, morning," she replies, stretching her arms up above her head. We're both still naked, and her breasts pop out from the sheets, giving me a wonderful view.

"How do you feel?" I ask, gently wrapping my arms around her body. "Are you sore?"

She shakes her head. "My muscles are a bit sore, but not bad."

"Good," I reply, kissing her shoulder. She leans into my touch, letting out a relieved sigh. "What are you going to do today?"

Hannah sighs. "I think Ron and Dottie's son is coming today, isn't he?"

"Oh man, you're right." I'd completely forgotten about that. "I wonder what time. Ron wanted us to meet him, and have dinner with them."

Hannah yawns, rubbing her eyes as she wakes up a bit more. She tries to squirm away from me, but I pull her back into my chest. "We can lay here for a bit longer," I reply.

"I told Dottie I would help her get things ready. Do you know what time it is?" Hannah asks, successfully pulling away from me this time. I watch as the blankets fall from her naked body, revealing her perfect skin to me. I reach over, grabbing my glasses from the bedside table so I can thoroughly look at her. She pulls her hair off her shoulder and reveals a small hickey on her right shoulder.

"Oops," I murmur, my smile growing as she turns to face me. Her nipples are pebbled in the cool air, and she bends down to grab a blanket, yanking it from the bed to cover herself when she notices my gaze. My cheeks heat and my dick twitches, thickening under the sheet still covering me.

"What?" she asks, her blue eyes darting up and down my body.

I chuckle. "Let's just say, you might want to wear a t-shirt today." I gesture to her right shoulder.

She glances down, pushing her hair out of the way. "Thomas!" she shouts, rubbing at her shoulder as if that will make the hickey disappear.

"Sorry, freckles," I say, shrugging my shoulders. "Couldn't help myself." I lean back, my hands twined behind my head as she digs through her things to find an outfit. Arson hops off the bed to see what she's doing, and she scruffs behind his ears for a moment before continuing to dig through her things.

She throws a few things over her arm before glancing at me. "Are you going to come with me?" she questions.

I nod, letting my gaze roam over her. "I'm enjoying the view."

Hannah blushes a deep red, smiling as she turns to head down the stairs. "I'm going to shower."

"Be down in a minute," I call, watching her ass as she descends the stairs.

## 39

# HANNAH

My hands tremble as I scoop another dollop of batter into the muffin tin. Ron and Dottie's son will be here any minute, and to say I'm anxious would be putting it lightly. I mean, Thomas and I have invaded his childhood home, and the cottage is where he typically stays when we come to visit.

Thomas is outside with Ron, helping him with some yard work while I help Dottie in the kitchen. The beeping of the oven pre-heating pulls me out of my thoughts, and I finish scooping the last dollop of batter into the tin. I put the muffins into the oven, setting the dial timer on the counter to twenty minutes.

"Hannah, dear," Dottie calls from the kitchen sink. "Can you start a pot of coffee? He should be here any minute."

"Sure thing," I reply, wiping my hands on my apron.

The front door opens, and I hear the familiar tippy-taps of Arson's footsteps into the house. He rushes over to me, rubbing his face across my thighs. "Hey buddy," I greet. My hands still have some batter on them, so I don't give him any pets yet.

He follows me as I step in beside Dottie, washing my hands and filling the pot with water from the sink. Once the pot starts brewing, I squat down, taking Arson's face between my palms and giving him some love. He licks my face, surely finding some batter there. "Where's your dad?" I ask, not seeing Thomas near.

A moment later, I hear Thomas. "Right here," he calls. "Our boots got all muddy, so we left them outside."

"Thank you, sweetie," Dottie responds with a laugh.

Thomas enters the kitchen, his face red with splotches of mud on it. He strides over to me as soon as he spots me, a smile breaking out on his lips. "Hey freckles," he greets, taking my chin in his fingers and tilting so my lips are on his. He kisses me short and sweet, pulling away before it intensifies. My palm is on his chest, feeling his heart thump heavily beneath his skin. "Missed you."

The butterflies swoop low in my belly. "It's only been a few hours," I reply before tugging on his shirt to pull him back to my lips. I don't want to admit that I missed him too.

"You missed me, too," he teases.

I shrug, trying to play nonchalant, but inside, I'm giddy.

Of course, all that giddiness disappears instantly when a new voice joins in.

"I'm home!" a deep male voice calls from the entryway.

"Fletch!" Dottie shrieks, wiping her soapy wet hands on her own apron. Instantly, I'm glancing down at my messy apron, pulling it up and over my head, smoothing my hands over my light pink sundress. I catch a quick glimpse of Fletcher, meeting his eyes briefly. I start picking at the skin around my fingernails to distract me from the churning fear.

"Hannah, you look perfect," Thomas says, grabbing my

hands to stop me. I look up at him, my anxiety brimming. He can see it, and instead of trying to calm me with words, he does what he knows works. He kisses me senseless. I should be embarrassed that this is Ron and Dottie's son's first impression of us, but at this moment, I don't care. He helps me in the way he knows works.

When he pulls away, I catch Fletcher's eye. A sly grin takes over his face as he takes us in.

"Hannah and Thomas?" he asks, brown eyes lit up in happiness. "I'm Fletcher, but you can call me Fletch."

He crosses the room, thrusting out his hand. We both shake it as Thomas formally introduces us.

"Hi," Thomas greets, his dimpled smile flashing. "I'm Thomas, and this is my fiancée, Hannah. We've been staying here for a few weeks in the cottage out back, and this is our dog, Arson."

Hearing him introduce me as his fiancée sends a thrill down my spine. It's not the first time he has, since he introduced me as it to Ron and Dottie, and we've been playing this part for a month now. It doesn't stop the feelings associated with it, though. I love that a little part of me is his, even if it's only temporary.

"It's so nice to finally meet you two," he says. "My parents have told me all about you, and selfishly, I was hoping you were still here when I came so I could meet you."

Some of the tension in my body melts away at his words. He was excited to meet us?

"It's a pleasure to meet you too," Thomas says. Fletch heads to the kitchen table, sitting down and gesturing for us to sit too. Dottie pours us all a cup of coffee.

"So, you're from Minnesota, too?" he asks, taking a sip of her coffee.

"Yeah, I'm not sure if we can tell you where, what with the circumstances of us being here, but I can tell you that much," Thomas explains.

Fletcher waves a palm. "No worries. I know how it is when my parents have 'friends that come to visit.' I'm in a suburb outside of the Twin Cities."

"We're a little further North than the Twin Cities," Thomas says ambiguously, reaching for the frame of my chair to scoot closer to him so he can wrap an arm around me. The simple touch helps me more than I realize. I was tensing up again and didn't even know.

"Well, when you get home, if you ever want to meet up, let me know. I tend to have a busy schedule once fall starts, but we can work something out."

I swallow thickly, mustering the confidence to join the conversation. "Your parents said you're playing for a hockey team?"

He nods. "Yep, I play for the MBH."

Thomas asks, his eyes widening. "The Minnesota Blue Herons?" Thomas asks, his eyes widening.

His smile widens. "You guessed it."

"Wow, that's cool," I respond. I've never been a huge hockey fan, but it's clear Thomas is.

"You like hockey?" Fletcher asks.

Thomas nods, while I shake my head, saying, "It's not that I dislike it. I just haven't really watched it much."

"I'm sure we can make a convert out of you," Fletcher says, his brown eyes focused on me. His focus is so intense that it takes me by surprise.

"We will have to go to a game when we get home," Thomas says, eyes locking on mine. His fingers trace a circle on my shoulder, distracting me from his statement.

I nod. PDA isn't something I'm used to outside of the

comfort of the cottage. Ron and Dottie have seen it a few times, but Thomas isn't usually this touchy with me around them, and it makes me wonder what the difference is.

Fletch interjects. "I can get you guys tickets, any game you want, let me know."

"Really?" I question. "We don't want to get you in trouble or anything."

He waves off my question. "No way. I can talk to my director. We all have access to tickets and suites, and honestly, the only one that uses them is my best friend."

"I could take you out for a real date," Thomas suggests, kissing my cheek and brushing my hair from my face.

I blush furiously, looking away.

"Fletch, have you talked to your brother lately?" Dottie asks, directing the conversation away from hockey and dates. Fletcher talks with his mom and dad while Thomas and I listen, enjoying their company and laughing at some of the stories they tell about Fletcher and his siblings' childhood.

Thomas never leaves my side, and most of all, he never stops touching me. His touch is constant, from our hands being tangled together on top of the table, to a hand on my thigh, or around my shoulders. He pulls me in for random kisses now and then, too. Arson doesn't leave my side either, his tail wrapped around my legs as he lies at my feet. Both of my boys are at my side, and the constant hum of anxious thoughts in my head dims.

There's less fear of him judging the way I look when I walk over to throw an apple core in the garbage an hour later, and no anxiety, only humor. Even when I tell a story about my childhood, and the time Julia and I were being watched by some friends who lived on a farm, their son convinced us to swim in the mud pile that turned out to be manure.

All of that fizzles away until it's a soft buzz, something that I can manage and not be overtaken by. This is what he does for me.

Many hours later when golden hour arrives and Fletcher yawns, Thomas stands from his chair, holding out a hand to me. "We should get going, freckles. Let's leave them to themselves."

Fletcher tries to protest, but Thomas shakes his head. "We've taken over your time with your parents, and I think Hannah and I are both tired."

I agree, nodding. I really am exhausted. Perks of being an introvert, I suppose. Constantly exhausted after social interactions. However, I've noticed that doesn't happen to me with Thomas. It's like he's exempt from that.

After one long Minnesota goodbye, Thomas and I are finally making our way to our temporary home. His arm is wrapped around my shoulders, one of my hands raised to twine our hands together as he pulls me into his body. We walk slowly.

"He was nice," I say, kicking a rock at my feet.

"Mhm," Thomas hums in agreement.

"Can I ask you something?" I ask, building up the courage.

"Hannah, you know you can ask me anything," he replies, stopping us by the old truck that's still in the area after the other night.

"Why were you extra touchy tonight?" Before he can reply, I blurt, "Not that I didn't like it, I always like when you touch me."

Thomas drops his arm from my shoulder, wrapping an arm around my torso and using the other to tilt my head up to look at him. "Oh, you like it when I touch you, do you, baby?" His voice drops an octave, and he nuzzles his face into my neck, kissing a line up to my jaw.

I suck in a gasp, my hands pressing against his chest as heat turns into embers in my core, waiting to burn. "Yes, but that's not what I meant." I lean away from his touch. "I mean, usually you're not quite that touchy around Ron and Dottie. You are at the cottage, but this was different."

"Because you're mine, and I needed to make sure he knew that."

"But... why?" I wonder.

"You clearly did not see the way he was looking at you, freckles. He wanted you."

I scoff. "No, he didn't."

"Yes, he did. The minute he saw you, he was trying to think of ways he could sweep you off your feet. And, he's a hockey player. They're good at that. It's what they're known for."

I look up at him, and I can tell he's serious. He really thinks that Fletcher was interested in me.

"Thomas..." I take a deep breath. This is going to be hard to get out. "Even if he is interested in me—which there is *no way*—I am not interested in him."

His blue eyes widen a little, and he turns me so we are face to face. "You're not?"

I shake my head. "No. I have no reason to be." I swallow hard. "Not when I have you."

A slow smile spreads across his lips as he tilts my chin between his fingertips. "You have me."

Nodding, I rise on my tip-toes to kiss him. His hands cup my cheeks instantly, drawing me into him. My chest presses against his, my hands sliding around the nape of his neck and gripping tightly.

Thomas leans against the old truck. We never brought it back where it was originally parked, so it's still in the makeshift driveway at the cottage next to the car we drove here. One of his hands glides down my body to my hips and squeezes at the flesh through my thin sundress. He yanks the fabric up, his warm skin meeting mine, sending a wave of goosebumps over me.

I giggle, pulling away from him. "Thomas, we can't do this out in the open."

"We can't?" he questions, nuzzling into my neck. "The only one who can see us is Arson, and he's seen worse at this point. Besides, he's over by the swings, ignoring us."

I groan, my core heating as Thomas slides his fingers under the waistband of my panties, migrating toward my already wet pussy. "Thomas," I plead, my voice unrecognizable in my lust. How is it that I've only had sex the one time, and already my body craves his touch this intensely?

His finger slides between my slit, and my head falls forward, my forehead resting on his chest as the jolt of pleasure floods my senses. Fingers find my clit, circling and bringing me closer to a fast, heated orgasm. "That's it, baby, how does it feel?" Thomas coaxes, his words tingling under my skin.

I cry out, breathing heavily, no words actually leaving my lips. My palms grip his broad shoulders, fingertips digging into his skin as I crest, my climax making my body shudder and pulse as he strums my clit like an instrument.

Thomas withdraws his fingers from my panties, and I miss his touch instantly. "I'm not done with you yet," he practically growls. I drag my heavy head from his chest, glancing up at him warily.

"You're not?" I ask.

"No," he says adamantly. Letting me go, he steps away

from me, dropping the tailgate and grabbing one of the blankets out of the front seat where we left them last night.

Thomas lays one of the fluffy blankets out to cover the metal, and gestures to it. "Come here." His voice is thick with lust and heat.

I take a step toward him, glancing at our surroundings to make sure Ron and Dottie haven't appeared out of thin air, but it's only us. Thomas pulls me into his embrace, kissing me deeply, before turning me to face the back of the truck. I'm pressed against him, my back to his front. His dick is pressed against my ass, hard as stone and ready. Thomas runs his hand up my belly, cupping my tits and squeezing. "Bend over," he whispers in my ear.

"What?" I gasp, my brain not fully processing his words, too lost in the haze of his touch.

"Bend over." His hand trails to the center of my back, pressing me down so I'm laid over the bed of the truck. My ass juts out on display for him, my feet on my very tip-toes as I try to find purchase on the ground.

I rest my arms out in front of me, gripping the blanket he laid out. My panties are pushed down my thighs, falling to the dirt below. Thomas's hand glides over my ass cheeks, lifting my dress to reveal my bare pussy to him.

"Fucking gorgeous," he groans. There's a shuffling noise, then the fan of his warm breath on my slit. Goosebumps blaze over my skin in anticipation of more of his touch.

"Thomas," I whimper, his name a plea. His tongue slides through my wetness in answer. Groaning, I rest my head forward onto my arm.

## 40

# THOMAS

This girl. She's opening up to me so well, and I couldn't stand not having another taste of her, not for another minute.

I find her sensitive clit with my tongue, swirling around and flicking it the way I know she likes. Massaging her round ass with one hand, I adjust so I can slide one finger inside her. She gasps, her body jolting under my intrusion. Biting back the smile on my lips, I press deeper inside, hooking my finger the tiniest amount.

The sound that comes from her lips can only be described as a whining scream. The sound makes my cock throb harder in my pants. I use my free hand to squeeze it. Now is not the time to finish in my pants again. I've got plans that don't include wiping cum from the inside of my jeans.

I add another finger to her tight cunt, desperate to give her as many orgasms as possible before filling her with my cock. Her core flutters around my fingers as she squeals. I don't stop my movements, needing to feel her orgasm the moment it hits her. I move my hand from my cock and trail it up the outside of her thigh, squeezing her ass. One day, I'll spank this perfect ass and make my mark on it.

Her entire body tenses, the climax hitting her intensely. "Fuck," she cries, legs shaking.

My mouth carries her through her orgasm until she's pushing back on my head, her fingers threading in my hair. I chuckle as I pull away, licking my lips. "Fuck, baby," I groan, rocking back on my heels before standing. Her feet flatten on the dirt ground once more and she rises, leaning back into my chest.

Oh, she thinks we're done. We're not. I still need to fuck her, and hopefully give her one more orgasm.

I tilt my head down, and nipping at her neck, I murmur, "I think you've got one more in you."

Hannah gasps, her head darting back to look me in the eye.

I eye her closely, raising my brow. My hands slink up her body, cupping her tits and squeezing through her thin bra. Her tight nipples poke through the light padding, and I tease them gently. "What do you say, baby?"

She nods, a doe-eyed look spurring me on even further. I reach into my back pocket for my wallet, pulling out a condom I put in there after our first time. Now that I've had her, I knew I wanted to be prepared for any circumstance.

I step back from her as she turns, her fingers finding the hem of my shirt and lifting it up and over my head. My shirt falls to the ground next to her panties, and Hannah reaches for my belt, unbuckling it and unzipping my jeans. They slide to my ankles, and she tentatively slides her fingers under the elastic of my boxers. Glancing up at me for permission, she pauses. I nod eagerly, and she shoves them down, freeing my hard as hell cock. She wraps her dainty fingers around my shaft, pumping me at a leisurely pace.

My head drops back, mouth opening on a groan when she swipes her finger over the pre-cum on the head.

"Can you put it on," I say through ragged breaths, her simple touches already bringing me closer than I'd care to admit. I hold out the foil package, sagging in relief when she takes it from my fingers. My relief is short lived though, when she takes my cock in hand again, sheathing my length with the condom. "Fuuuck."

She lets out a breathy laugh. "Now what?"

I tilt my head forward, taking her lips in a kiss. "Turn around," I murmur against her lips.

She does as I ask, turning around and leaning over the edge of the truck again. This time, she doesn't bend over completely, leaning on it rather than folding her body over it. I flip the bottom of her dress up again and bite my lip at the view. Hannah looks back at me with a devious smile. My little Miss Innocent isn't so innocent anymore.

Notching the head of my cock at her entrance, I thrust in, savoring the way she grips around me with each inch.

"Ah," she cries, voice high pitched as I pull back.

"I've got you, baby," I reply to her noises, gripping her hips tightly as I rock in and out of her. She loses her strength, bending over the truck more with each thrust.

I reach around, flicking her clit with my fingers. I know I can get one more out of her, and I'm aching to feel her squeezing tightly around my cock when she finishes.

"Oh god," she nearly screams.

Each thrust is like coming alive. I've never felt more like myself, more alive and ready for life as I do when I'm with her. She's everything I want for my life and I can't wait to have these moments for the rest of it.

Her already tight cunt squeezes me like a vice as she orgasms a third and final time, and I take pride in wringing this much pleasure from her. My own climax follows, and I can't wait for the day we don't have to use condoms anymore. I'd love to see my cum drip from her slit. Hell, I'd fucking lick her clean if I could. I would do anything to have my mouth all over her any chance I can.

I'm about to pull out of her, when I feel something behind me. A feather tickles my neck and I shout. Glancing down to my left shoulder, is fucking Dave. Leave it to the fucking emu to ruin the moment.

"Fucking hell, Dave," I curse, shifting back from my girl and pulling her dress down to cover her.

"What!" Hannah gasps, covering herself and standing, pushing back at me. Her eyes frantically dart around the clearing, finding nothing.

"Dave," she groans, running her hands over her pink, sweaty cheeks.

"How didn't we notice him coming?" I question, stepping away from his closeness. We must have been so lost in the moment, because we always hear him. I don't know why he felt the need to rest on my shoulder while I was clearly *busy*.

"I have no idea." Hannah breathes heavily as she catches her breath.

"He probably thought you were in danger or something. You were making some pretty great noises," I say with a wink.

Hannah swats at my bare chest. "I was not!" She glances around the clearing again, her eyes narrowing to make sure no one else heard.

"Yes, baby, you were. Don't worry, I liked it."

She bursts into laughter, and I join her. I cannot believe that the best sex of my life ended with an emu making an appearance.

## 41

## THOMAS

I swing our hands back and forth as we walk down the path to meet Ron, Dottie and Fletcher for coffee. After Dave left, we cuddled up in the back of the truck again for a while, making love one more time under the glow of the moonlight, then we went inside and passed out. I made us a huge stack of waffles early this morning because we deserved it after all the fucking we did last night. Then, we went at it one more time before we got ready to go this morning. She rode me for the first time, and it may be my new favorite position. Watching her from that angle, getting even deeper inside her was so intense I couldn't hold back for long before I was coming hard.

"You're not going to get jealous this morning, are you?" Hannah teases, her freckled cheeks flushing.

I grumble. "Depends on if he stares at your ass again when you turn around. I might have to punch him."

Hannah gasps. "Thomas! He was not staring at my ass. Don't be ridiculous."

"I'm not being ridiculous, freckles. He was staring at your ass." Don't get me wrong. He's a nice guy, and he's

Dottie and Ron's son, so I'm sure he's a wonderful person, but he was staring at my girl. He'd probably never act on it, but still. She's mine.

She shakes her head as if it's unbelievable. Do I want anyone else to be attracted to her? Fuck, no. Not when she's my girl. The engagement might technically be fake, but that doesn't mean our relationship is. When we get home, I can't wait to take her out and show her off to my family and friends. Show them how lucky I am to have her by my side.

"It doesn't matter who looks at you. If they aren't me, I'm going to get jealous, baby." I shrug. "It is what it is."

"You're dramatic," Hannah tries to say, but I shake my head.

"Dramatic would be punching him out for looking at you. A little jealousy is nothing."

I lead her up the creaky front steps of the house, not bothering to knock as we walk in. After over a month of being here and being told many times not to bother knocking, we've gotten used to it.

"Good morning," I call into the house. The smell of bacon, cinnamon rolls, and coffee invades my senses. My mouth waters. Even though we had a shit ton of waffles, I'm already hungry again. Dottie is one hell of a cook, and her cinnamon rolls are my favorite. She's taught Hannah the recipe too, so once we get home, we will keep making them.

"Morning kids," Ron calls from the kitchen. Hannah and I kick off our shoes, heading down the hall.

Ron, Dottie, and Fletcher sit around the kitchen table, empty plates and half-empty coffee cups surrounding them.

"Sorry, we didn't wait," Dottie exclaims. "We weren't sure if you two were coming."

"No, don't be sorry," Hannah rushes to say. "We're sorry we are late. It's so rude but we overslept."

Ron guffaws. "Now, don't be silly. Since when have we eaten breakfast at a set time, sweetie?" He stands, kissing Hannah on the cheek. "Dish up. I'll get you both some coffee."

I reluctantly let go of Hannah's hand, grabbing her a plate and putting a cinnamon roll and some bacon on it for her before handing it to her. I fill myself a plate and sit down beside her at the table. It appears Fletcher got the hint last night, because his gaze is much friendlier this morning.

"Did you two get any sleep last night?" Ron asks, his eyes full of humor. "There were some coyotes making a lot of noise at dusk. We drove around in the side by side a little later when we heard them again, but couldn't find any. Did you hear them?"

The coffee I'm drinking goes down the wrong pipe, causing me to cough and splutter. Hannah's eyes drop to her plate, her entire face and chest a new shade of red that I haven't had the pleasure of seeing yet. I swallow the lump in my throat, clearing the coffee that trickled down my windpipe. "No, we didn't. We went to bed early, and must have been sleeping hard."

I scan the table, noting the way Fletcher is smirking at his coffee cup. They totally heard us last night. Trying to stay quiet was near impossible, and never in my wildest dreams did I think our noises would carry all the way to the house. I'm not embarrassed, but I know Hannah isn't exactly comfortable with other people hearing us.

"Those darn coyotes," Dottie says with a frown. "Hopefully they don't hurt our chickens. We can't lose any of our flock."

"We'll keep a closer eye on it," I mumble, taking a bite of my bacon. "Can't have you losing any of the chickens. Is Dave okay? Should he be kept in the barn?"

Ron shakes his head, waving me off. "Nah, he can hold his own."

We talk for a little longer, finishing up our breakfasts. The entire time, my hand is resting on Hannah's thigh. When she's done eating, I hold her hand on top of the table, drawing circles on her skin.

After a while, we say goodbye. The sky is a dark gray, with heavy clouds that make me think it's about to rain, so Hannah and I decide to get back to the cottage sooner than later. Fletcher is leaving tomorrow morning early, as he has to get back for the start of training camp, so we're unsure if we will see him again. My jealousy faded as the morning went on. He stopped staring at Hannah as if she was a conquest, and I enjoyed his presence a lot more. I might even take him up on tickets for a game this year. I'd love to take Hannah to one.

"THERE HASN'T BEEN anything on the phone, right?" Hannah asks, curled up against my side. We're on our third movie of the day. The only thing we've done today was have our late breakfast and then come back here, only leaving the couch for snacks and bathroom breaks. The rain we expected never came, but it's still gloomy, the perfect day to be lazy and cuddle.

"Not yet," I reply. The burner phone is sitting on the side table, and both of us are waiting for it to ring. Elena didn't give me a time the last time I spoke with her, only a date to have the phone on. A nervous thrum runs through my body. I'm ready to get home.

"Okay," Hannah murmurs. She's as anxious as I am to

hear. She's lying between my legs, her back to my front, her head resting on my chest. Arson is at our feet, curled up and snoring. I should take him for a run or something later.

The phone starts to buzz obnoxiously, and Hannah and I jolt apart as I reach for the phone. Hannah moves so she's sitting in front of me as I answer the call and put it on speaker.

"Hello?" I answer.

"Thomas?" Elena's voice carries through the line.

"Yes, hi, Elena."

"I have good news," she says, a hint of excitement in her tone. "We've arrested Chaz, and have a warrant to search the house he was living in. You should be able to come home early next week."

All the air whooshes from my lungs as I sigh in relief. "Really? Next week?"

"Yep. We have a few things to straighten out, but once I get the all clear, I'll give you a call. Feel free to call your families and let them know you'll be home soon."

We chat another minute longer about Henry and his recovery, but with each passing minute, it's like the reality of it is hitting us both. Hannah is shrinking further away from me into the couch, and I can tell she's pulling away from me. Physically and metaphorically. It hurts, knowing that we have come so far, only for one phone call to change it all.

"Thanks, Elena," I say as we hang up.

Hannah is picking at the skin around her fingernails. "Stop that." I reach out, taking her hand to keep her from making herself bleed. "Talk to me."

She shakes her head. "I'll give you some time alone to call your family." Without another word, she stands, stepping away from the couch to head outside. Arson follows her, glancing back at me like he's waiting for me to follow.

I wave him off. I should have stopped her, but I might have made it worse. She needs time to herself to process. I only hope she doesn't pull away from me.

I sit for a moment before I pull up Jason's contact and hit call. It rings twice before he picks up, only it's not his voice. "Daddy's phone," a familiar child's voice answers.

"Hey Lenners," I greet my niece.

"Uncle Tommy!" she yells, her voice raising an octave. "Are you coming home yet? Presley and I miss you."

"I miss you too, kiddo. Hopefully, soon," I answer her question. "Can I talk to your dad, or Fallon?"

Instead of acknowledging my question, the phone muffles, and there's a loud yell. *"Daddy!"* her shrieking voice calls, making me laugh.

In the background, I can hear Jason approaching. "Lennie, what did I say about answering my phone? It might be someone from work."

"Sorry, Daddy," she replies sweetly. "It's not someone from work. It's Uncle Tommy."

"It is?" There's static on the line, then my brother's voice. "Thomas?"

"Hey, man," I answer.

"Sorry about Lennie. Her new thing is answering everyone's phones," Jase explains.

"No problem," I reply with a laugh. "It was good to talk to her for a second."

"Please tell me this isn't just another check-in," Jason pleads. "Please tell me you're coming home."

I take a deep breath and exhale the words. "We're coming home. We don't have a for sure date, but it's sometime next week, Elena says."

"Oh, thank god. Josie went into labor this morning. Andrew sent an update that they're keeping her at the hospital. It's really happening."

My heart twists. I'd wanted to be home when she went into labor so I could visit them in the hospital, but that probably won't happen now. The only thing stopping me from being angry is knowing that there's an end in sight. We got the official word that we're going home.

"How's Andrew holding up?" I ask with a laugh. Knowing him, he's probably freaking out.

"Marley went with, she's taking photos for them. According to her, he's not handling Josie being in pain well."

I imagine Hannah being in that much pain and sympathize with my youngest brother. "I can understand that. I don't know how I'd handle seeing Hannah in that much pain," I say.

"Speaking of, how are things with your *fiancée?*" Jason asks curiously, enunciating the word fiancée.

"Ten minutes ago, I would have said amazing," I reply with a sigh, running a hand over my face. "Now, I'm not so sure. As soon as we got the call that we could go home, she distanced herself from me. She left as soon as we hung up the phone to give me space to call you guys. But I don't want space. I want her to be part of this, part of the family."

"I mean, maybe she thought she was being respectful," Jason tries to say, but I'm shaking my head, even though he can't see me.

"Sure, maybe that was part of it, but you don't know her like I do. I've spent the entire time we've been here getting to know her, falling in love with her, and trying to show her that this isn't temporary, but I'm worried she doesn't see that like I do."

"So, show her, then. Don't let her get away from you. Do you want her?"

"More than I've ever wanted anyone," I reply without having to think about it. "I want forever with her, Jase."

"Then, don't let her panic. Show her you're here to stay."

"I can do that," I say. We talk for a few more minutes about random things, and I tell him I'll let him know when we leave.

We hang up, and I stand from the couch, heading to the front door of the cabin. When I open the door, I spot Hannah in the distance on the swings. She sways back and forth slowly, Arson at her side. One of her hands holds the rope, while the other rests on Arson's head.

"Hey freckles," I say as I walk closer. I don't miss her sniffles or the way she wipes at the tears on her cheeks. Instead of taking my usual swing next to her, I crouch down in front of her. "Don't cry."

She waves me off, turning her face away. "I'm fine."

"No, you're not." I swipe at a few of the tears on her cheeks.

She shakes her head back and forth. "It's stupid."

"It's not stupid."

"Yes, it is. All we've wanted the entire time we've been here is to go home. Now, we get the call that we can soon leave, and all I want to do is stay," she mumbles, tears still streaming. "Everything is going to change. What happens to us?"

"I feel the same." My heart is cracking. All I want to do right now is hold her, tell her I love her and that I'll never leave her, but I worry that it's going to be too much. Now certainly isn't the time to tell her I love her for the first time,

I know that much. "We have to figure out a new normal when we get home, Hannah. That's all."

She nods, but she's not hearing me. She's stuck in her head.

"Do you want to call your family?" I ask. She nods, and I pass her the phone. "I'll leave you to it."

Hannah nods again, looking down at the phone in her hand.

## 42

HANNAH

Thomas's footsteps crunch as he walks away, leaving me alone to my thoughts. The phone sits in my hand like a weight, taunting me. The blank screen begs me to make the call, to hear my grandma's or my sister's voice, but yet, I can't seem to do it.

How is it possible that after such a short period of time I've come to rely on someone more than I ever have before? Sure, I've relied on my grandma and sister for a long time, but I'm also very independent. I had to be. I've lived alone for eight years, and now the thought of going home to my small apartment without having Thomas at my side every night is petrifying. I don't want to be alone anymore, but yet, at the same time, I know what we have can't continue. We will get back to reality, and he will forget all about me.

Another minute passes before I build the courage up to dial my grandma's number. She answers on the third ring.

"Hello?"

"Grandma? It's Hannah."

"Oh, hi, honey." Her soft voice soothes me instantly.

"I'm coming home," I say, my voice cracking as tears stream down my cheeks again.

"Really?" she cries, her voice breaking the same as mine. "That's wonderful. Julia isn't here. You have to call her too."

"I will."

"When will you be home?" Grandma asks eagerly.

"We don't know for sure. We got word that it will be early next week." I sniffle and wipe at my eyes as tears continue to roll down my cheeks.

"That's wonderful," she says tentatively. "Why do you sound so sad then?"

Shaking my head, I let out a watery laugh. I'm so ridiculous. "We have a routine here. And now it's all going to change. I don't want it to change. I want to go home more than anything. I miss you, I miss my life, and Julia and Tiff, but I'm going to lose Thomas."

"Who says you're going to lose him?" Grandma asks.

"It only makes sense that I would." I take a deep breath and change the subject. I can't talk about this anymore. "You would love Dottie, the woman we've been staying with."

Grandma sighs, sensing my avoidance of it, but doesn't bring it up. "Tell me about her," Grandma says. I tell her all the ways she reminds me of my mom, and how she's been teaching me to cook and bake. After a few more minutes, I reluctantly say goodbye to her, with a promise to call when we're on our way home.

I dial Julia's number next, feeling a bit more confident now. Thankfully, she answers right away.

"Han, is that you?"

"It's me," I reply. A smile crosses my face as I hear yelling.

"Tiff, it's Hannah!" Julia calls.

"Hannah!" Tiff shrieks my name, her voice joining Julia's.

"Hi guys," I say through laughter. "I have good news."

"You had sex!" Julia cries.

Heat floods my veins. "Um—" I start, but she interrupts me.

"I knew it. Tell me *everything*. How was it?"

"Let the girl talk, sweetie," Tiff coaxes.

My heart pangs. I miss them so much. "That's not why I'm calling. We get to come home."

A loud scream pierces my eardrums.

"Thank goodness," Julia cries. The sound of her tears makes my throat thicken with emotion.

"Yeah," I blubber.

"When?" Tiff asks. "Now?"

I shake my head, even though they can't see. "Early next week." I wipe at my nose, trying to rid the snot.

"Holy shit, Han," Julia breathes. "How are you? Are you excited?"

Sobs bubble up my chest and escape me before I can hold it back. "No."

"Wha— Hannah, what do you mean, no?"

"It's ridiculous," I wail. "All we've wanted since the moment we got here was to go home, and now the thought of going home terrifies me."

"How come? They wouldn't let you come home if you weren't safe," Tiff tries to say.

"It's not that." I take a deep breath. "I'm not ready for this to end. Whatever Thomas and I have, it has to stay here, in this little bubble."

"Did Thomas say that?" Julia asks, her voice growing angry.

"No, no." I rush to defend him. "But I know it has to stay here."

"Why?" Tiff wonders.

"I mean, the whole reason I'm here is because he wanted to keep me safe."

"And? Why does that mean it has to end?"

"The need to pretend and keep us safe is gone, therefore, the relationship ends too. We both have demanding jobs, and when we aren't spending twenty-four-seven together, it will fizzle out." I lean against the gritty rope, trying to force myself to keep that logic. If I am prepared for it to end, then it won't hurt as bad. Right?

"Hannah..." Tiff starts. "You know I love you—"

"You're being an idiot," my sister interrupts her wife. "You can't seriously tell me that man does not have feelings for you, or that he doesn't want whatever is happening *wherever* you are, to continue at home?"

"I don't know!" I shriek, my heart cracking. "Of course I don't want this to end. But what if he does? I'm trying to prepare myself, Julia."

"Prepare yourself for what? You don't have to prepare for every possible outcome, Hannah." Julia lets out an indignant noise.

Irritation blooms in my chest, though I know she's right. "I can't help it, Julia. You know this."

"Yes, I do, but you didn't see the way that man looked at you that night. *I did.* I haven't even been with you in over a month, and I know he will do anything for you. I mean, the man told everyone you were engaged to keep you safe! Who does that? A man who knows who he wants. And that's you, Hannah," Julia finishes with a huff.

"I think what your sister is trying to say is, don't think that because you're coming home that it has to end. You never know what will happen, Hannah. Don't shut down the potential of something because of what you think might happen," Tiff finishes gently.

"I know, but I can't help it," I whisper. Why can't I be excited about going home? Why do I overthink everything and make things harder for myself and those around me? "I guess it's good I'm coming home. I need to see my therapist again," I laugh self-deprecatingly.

There's silence on the other end of the line.

"That was supposed to be funny," I state.

"Oh," Julia murmurs. "I mean, you're not wrong, though. Seeing your therapist won't be a bad idea."

"I know," I say with a sigh.

"Now, enough of the heavy. Tell me. Did you have sex? Was it amazing?" Julia asks, her voice lighthearted and excited again.

Some of my own happiness returns. "We did." I smile, my cheeks heating at the memory. "I..."

"Ohh, she's speechless," Tiff squeals.

"I don't even know what else to say. It was amazing."

"You deserve happiness, Hannah. Now, focus on this feeling. Don't think about what happens next. Focus on the feelings he gives you right now," Julia says, as if it's that easy, but I'll try. I have to. I don't want to sabotage this thing we have.

"Wait until you hear this," I say, laughter bursting from me. I tell them all about last night, how Thomas got jealous of Fletcher, and how he fucked me hard against the truck bed. Then, I tell them all about how Ron and Dottie heard us, or rather, me, and pretended we were coyotes they'd heard.

Ten minutes later, we're all laughing, making plans to

all get together when I get home. Dinner with my sisters and grandma. It will be so nice to be home.

We hang up, and I'm left feeling relieved. A tip-tapping of footsteps come up behind me as I turn off the phone. I turn in the swing, expecting it to be Arson, but shriek when a large beak is staring me in the face.

"Jesus, Dave!" I clutch my palm to my chest. He leans down, resting his head on my shoulder. I tentatively reach out, brushing my hand over the top of his feathered head. The thumping sound I've grown familiar with echoes in my chest.

More footsteps approach, this time accompanied with a bark. "Arson, I'm fine, buddy," I call. Arson skids to a stop beside me, ready to protect me from this silly bird. Dave skitters back a step, ready to play. Arson tilts his head curiously.

Surprising me, they do a little playful dance around each other. Arson barks playfully, and the emu takes off, Arson chasing after it.

Thomas strides over to me, raising his brow. "Well, it only took five and a half weeks, but they're friends now."

"Apparently," I say with a laugh. I hand over the phone to him, and he puts it in the pocket of his shorts. "How are you?"

I take a long breath. "I'm okay, I think. How are you?"

He shrugs, sitting on his swing. "Honestly, I don't know. I'm so ready to go home. Really, I am, but at the same time, I love being here, the two of us."

"Me too."

"I don't want things to change," he says. "But, like I said earlier, we will have to find our new normal."

I nod, thinking about all the things I'm going to miss when

we get home. Sleeping in my own bed will be nice, but he won't be there to hold me as I fall asleep, or when I wake up in the middle of the night with a nightmare. I won't wake up in his arms, or hear him say "Good morning, freckles" every morning. No more lazy Saturday afternoons on the couch, or dinners with Dottie and Ron. How is it possible that I've gotten so used to this new routine in such a short period of time? And how can we find a new rhythm at home when we are both so used to being together in our own little bubble?

## 43

## THOMAS

I throw my toiletries bag into my duffel, cursing the fact that I'm fully packed up. It's officially time to go home.

We got the call early this morning, three long and bittersweet days after Elena told us they arrested Chaz. Hannah and I spent the remainder of our time together cuddled in bed, sitting on our swings talking, cooking and baking in the kitchen, basically anything to spend as much time together as possible. There were moments of sadness, realizing we wouldn't be able to meet Ron and Dottie for breakfast anymore, or help out on their little farm. But there were also moments of happiness, too. Realizing we built an incredible relationship with Ron and Dottie. We are going to stay in touch with them, and even plan to go to a Blue Herons game with them this winter. We've also gotten their phone numbers, with plans to FaceTime and visit when we can.

There was also happiness in the fact that whenever possible, we made love. The moments of pure bliss where I was inside her making her cry out my name as she came with her eyes squeezed shut, have been some of my favorites from our time here. She's grown and changed so much in her confidence in herself, in the way she carries herself around me, and opens up to me, and I'm so proud of her.

Both Hannah and I have been quiet, avoiding the elephant in the room. What happens when we get home? I know what I want. Sure, we may not have to play engaged anymore, at least in the eyes of the investigators, but I still want her to be mine. Anytime I've tried to bring it up, Hannah shuts down.

If I didn't think it would scare the shit out of her, I would propose to her for real, the minute we got home. I know that she's not ready for that though. I am. Perhaps it's too soon, but I know who I want alongside me for the rest of my life, and it's her.

Thinking of proposing reminds me of the ring in my dresser. Gramps gave it to me years ago. I'm not sure why he chose me out of my three other brothers to give Grandma's ring to, but it's perfect. A yellow gold ring with small white diamonds nestled around a single pearl.

I shake off the thoughts of an engagement ring that isn't quite ready to be used yet, and turn my attention elsewhere.

"Han?" I call. She's upstairs packing her things. Last I checked, Arson is with her, snuggled up on the bed. If we get packed up quick enough, we will start the drive today. The sun has barely risen, but we are up and at 'em.

"Yeah?" she calls back.

"I'm going to run a few things out to the car," I tell her, hauling my bag over my shoulder and grabbing Arson's bed from the living room floor. A plume of fluff erupts from the bed, and I groan. I'll make sure to vacuum everything twice before we leave.

Hannah calls an "okay" and I head out the front door into the early morning. The sun peeks through the trees, casting a glow over the dew-covered grass. I'm really going to miss the serenity of this place.

I throw the bag into the back of the vehicle, then decide to take a minute to myself. I stride over to the swings where Hannah and I have spent many hours learning so much about each other. Sharing vulnerabilities, stories, and all around, spending the time together.

I sit down on the swing that has been unofficially designated as mine, rocking back and forth as I take in the view one last time.

As I sit, I ponder over our time here. Looking back, it feels like it was yesterday that we arrived. When we arrived, I was terrified. Terrified that I made the wrong choice by taking Hannah with me, that it was selfish of me, but now, I don't regret it. I did what I had to do to keep her safe, and in doing so, I got to know her better than I might have if we were at home. This uninterrupted time with her has been a gift, one that I won't take for granted.

It hurts, knowing that things will change, but I think it will be a good change. It will be good getting back to real life, and our normal routines.

Footsteps alert me to her arrival before I see her.

"You okay?" she asks, sitting down on her swing.

"Thinking," I reply, offering her a smile.

"What about?"

"I'm going to miss this place. It's so peaceful."

Hannah nods. "I agree."

"Are you all packed up?" I question.

"Yeah. We have to clean a bit, but otherwise, I'm ready." Her voice is somber.

"Arson left a pile of dog hair behind his bed." I chuckle.

"He left some under the kitchen table, too," Hannah replies with a soft laugh.

"Sounds about right. I swear, I could make two whole other dogs with the amount of dog hair I find and vacuum up at my house."

She laughs again. I'll do anything to make her laugh. Anything to keep her smiling.

"Remember our first date?" I ask, already knowing the answer.

She gives me a look, raising her brows. "Are you serious?"

"Roll with it," I suggest.

Hannah tilts her head with a smile. "Yeah, Tommy, I do."

Oh, fuck, she called me Tommy. My family and some close friends are the only ones who have ever called me that, so hearing it from her lips is incredible. Not that I've ever been huge on the nickname. My brothers started calling me Tommy after we watched *Rugrats*. But still. It makes me feel closer to her in a new way.

I can't stop the smile that breaks out on my face. "Dancing with you that night..." I trail off, taking a breath. "I knew that what we were starting was something special. Granted, I didn't know what was to come, of course, but I don't regret the way our relationship started."

Hannah looks down at her feet with a smile. "I don't either."

"I've had some guilt over the way I made you come with me, but I think it was worth it."

"I think it was too," she replies, looking up at me.

A bird sings in the distance, and I'm not ready for this moment to end. "Come here," I say, standing up and holding out my hand to her.

She places her small hand in mine, and I pull her into my arms, reminiscent of the night at the street dance.

Slowly, I begin to sway as I hum along to the song playing in my head.

The lyrics play in my mind on repeat. Hannah hums along with me, and I'm lost in this moment with her. This last peaceful moment of just the two of us before the chaos of real life. I love this girl, I know I do. We've had a backwards start, but the test will be life at home. I'm ready.

# HANNAH

After a long and tearful goodbye with Ron and Dottie and saying one final goodbye to the animals, we are on the long journey home.

Time has passed quickly this time around, each mile left behind us making me more and more sad, but also, so excited to get home.

Unsurprisingly, Thomas has had his right hand touching me at all times. Whether it was holding my hand, resting on my thigh, even grazing upwards toward my core and underneath the hem of my comfortable cotton sundress. Currently, he has his hand resting on the nape of my neck, playing with a piece of my hair that's fallen out of my messy bun.

There's only an hour left of the drive now. Talking has filled most of the hours, but also plenty of music and singing too. I even get him to sing along to all of the *Glee* songs he has on the iPod. He knows every single lyric.

We call all of our families on the way home, but tell them to expect not to see us until tomorrow.

Josie had the baby on Sunday afternoon after a long

labor. A little boy named Cooper. It sounds like everything went well, though, and both mom and baby are healthy and home.

The views of the Minneapolis city line appear in the windshield, lit up in the darkness, and both of us go quiet. It's fully setting in that within an hour we will be back in Ivy Ridge.

Thomas swallows thickly, his Adam's apple bobbing in his throat. "I suppose I should call Elena."

I nod, reaching into the glove box to pull out the burner phone. I turn it on and hand it over to him. He dials, putting it on speaker. While it rings, I look out the window at the familiar city.

"Thomas, so good to hear from you. Are you close?" Elena answers.

"Yes," he replies, glancing out of the window. "We are just getting onto six-ninety-four. We should be there in about an hour. Should we meet at the station? Or go home?"

"Meet at the station. We will have your phones ready for you, and give you a debriefing," Elena confirms.

"Great. We'll see you soon," Thomas responds. They say goodbye, and Thomas ends the call. A heaviness sinks in my gut.

The rest of the drive is made in silence, even as we reach the town limits, and our familiar hometown comes into view. Jason's brewery pops up on my right side, bringing back all the memories from our first date for the second time today.

We pass the street where Henry was shot, and I look away. I'm not ready to look at that. Not ready to see the scene where everything changed. Thomas squeezes my thigh tightly. How he knows what is on my mind, I'm not sure. But that's something he's good at. He knows me.

When we pull up to the police station, Thomas shifts the car into park, letting out a heavy breath. "We made it," he says, though he doesn't sound all that excited.

He turns off the car, and he leashes Arson. Both of us get out at the same time, and he rounds the car to take my hand before leading us inside.

The station is cold, the lights bright and unyielding as we enter. Arson's tail wags as he enters the familiar space, and Thomas leans down, unhooking his leash. The Chief is waiting for us in the lobby.

"Hey kid," he greets Thomas. Thomas lets go of my hand to shake Chief's, but his familiar touch is only gone for a moment, then he's taking my hand again.

"Chief," Thomas says gruffly.

"Nice of you to finally show up," a new voice calls from down the hall.

A huge smile appears on Thomas's lips, and his eyes glint with tears. "Fuck, man," Thomas mumbles, pulling me with him. When the person comes into full view, I realize it's Henry.

My hand is dropped once more as Thomas embraces Henry. I watch as Arson tries to greet him too, even barking to make his presence known. After their hug, Henry turns his attention toward me.

"Thank you," he says, holding his hand out to shake mine.

Confused, I shake it. "Thank you?"

"Yes. You both saved my life that night. I know you two witnessing me being shot is the reason you were sent away, but selfishly, I'm glad you were there. Had you not been, I wouldn't be here," Henry explains.

When I think about it, I realize he's right. I've saved

lives before. It's quite literally my job, but for him to be able to thank me for it, especially after everything, hits deep.

"Oh," I reply lamely. Thanks brain. Why can't I come up with things to say?

"We're glad you're okay," Thomas responds for the both of us.

"Heard the good news," Henry says, leading us down the hall. "Congratulations."

Thomas places his hand at the small of my back, swallowing a cough. "Thanks." He looks over at me, and I shrug. I'm not sure what the protocol is. Are we going to continue pretending?

We enter a familiar room, the same one Thomas and I shared our first kiss in. The same room where he told me he'd lied and said I was his fiancée. So much has changed since then. Am I even the same person anymore?

Elena is waiting to greet us with a smile. There's a manilla folder on the table, and I see my cell phone next to it. In all honesty, I haven't missed it. Maybe I should have, but I didn't. It was almost nice to have a break from it.

"Welcome home," Elena greets, telling us to sit. Of course, Thomas rests his hand on my thigh the moment we do.

Elena and Thomas volley questions and information back and forth, and Thomas nods his head, listening intently. Meanwhile, I'm sitting here lost and unable to focus. I should be listening, but I can't. My brain can't latch onto their voices or what they're saying. My breathing becomes shallow as I sit in the room where everything changed.

Thomas notices, because of course he does. "Can you give us a minute, Elena?"

"Of course." Her eyes soften as she takes me in. Clearly, she must see how much of a mess I am.

Once she and Henry leave us alone, it's like I can't breathe at all. "I'm sorry," I say through shuttered breaths.

"Hannah, stop," Thomas turns in his chair, cupping my cheeks in his large palms. "Take a deep breath with me, baby."

I try to follow him, taking long inhales.

"Good girl," he praises. "There you go."

After another minute of breathing, he slowly rests his palms on my shoulders. "What happened?"

I shake my head. "I don't even know. Being in this room brought back all the fear and anxiety I felt that night, and I couldn't think. I don't even know what Elena was saying."

"Nothing important. She was going over everything that's happened since we left. It's nothing you need to know. I can give you a rundown later."

Nodding, I take another deep breath. "Can we go home?" As I blurt the words, I realize I'm not sure what home is anymore. I feel so at home here, but it is the cottage itself, or is it Thomas?

"Soon. She has a few more things, but then, yes."

There's a soft knock on the door and Elena re-enters. "I brought some water for you two."

She passes us two cups of ice water, and I down mine, letting an ice cube slide between my lips to rest on my tongue. The cold ice helps me relax even more. Thomas keeps his palm on my thigh, and this time, I try to listen more when she explains what the next few weeks will be like, how we will more than likely have to testify in court when the time comes, and what they need from us.

Neither Thomas nor I bring up our engagement.

Though, I suppose in her eyes, it was never fake, so continuing it would only be logical.

Twenty minutes later, we both have our phones again, and we're walking out of the police station. Thomas opens the passenger door of the vehicle for me, closing it behind me when I'm in. He opens the back door for Arson who hops up and licks my face, similar to the first time I was in this car. All the similarities are sinking in, only this time, we aren't going to be ending up at a safe house together. I'll be back at my small apartment. Alone.

Thomas gets into the car and we leave the police station. With every passing second, I feel more and more like I'm about to burst into tears. I can't stand to look at him, because I know if I do, I will lose it.

I've fallen for this man, and I don't know if he will want to keep me. Once he sees who I am outside of the bubble we have been in, will he still like who I am in real life? Was it only due to convenience that he kept me as close as he has?

The evil voice in my head is telling me so, even though he's done nothing but protect, care, and... love me for who I am.

I look out the window at our small town, quiet at this time of night, and try to rationalize with myself. Thomas likes me for me. He's said that time and time again, so why can't I tell my brain to shut up and believe him?

He pulls into my apartment complex, and I grab my backpack at my feet, climbing out of the car before he can open the door for me. I open the back door, leaning in to give Arson some love. He won't be sleeping at my feet tonight, and leaving him behind might hurt most of all.

I wrap my arms around his soft fur, hugging him close. "Bye, buddy," I whisper. "Thanks for keeping me safe." Arson nuzzles in close, licking my cheek again.

When I pull away, I have to wipe tears from my cheeks. I shut the door, leaving him in the still-running vehicle. Thomas won't be gone long, so he will be fine for a few minutes. Thomas has grabbed my other bags from the trunk, leaving only my pillow and blankets. I grab them, and we head to the front door. I unlock the lobby door with my key, silently walking down the hall to my apartment.

When I reach my door, I unlock it and swing the door open, revealing my apartment. Nothing has changed in the time I've been gone. The mail I got that day is still sitting on the countertop, my throw blanket still strewn on the couch. My apartment has been frozen in time for six weeks.

I walk down the short hallway to my bedroom, throwing my backpack, pillows and blanket onto the bed. Thomas follows, setting the bags he's carrying onto the floor. We haven't said more than three words to each other in the last twenty minutes. I don't even know what I would say.

Thomas is the one to break the silence first. "Do—do you want me to stay?"

I'm shaking my head before my heart even has time to process. My heart wants to say yes, of course it does, but my brain is saying no. "No, I should get some sleep," I say, as if that isn't what he would want to do here.

"Hannah," he breathes my name, stepping up to me. His hand slides around my neck, the other tilting my chin so I'm forced to look at him. "Can I stay? I want to be close to you tonight."

"I'll be fine," I say, but even I can taste the lie as it leaves my lips.

"That's not what I asked," he mutters, squeezing his eyes shut. "Freckles, I can't stand the thought of not sleeping by your side tonight."

I rest my head on his chest. I have to do this. "I... I think some time apart would be best."

"Time apart?" he questions, pain seeping into his voice.

"Not a lot. I don't think we need to be together all the time. Sleeping apart might be good for us," I explain. I don't look at him, because I know I'll break. I'll tell him to stay and never leave my side. "We spent six weeks together. With each other nearly every moment of the day. Don't you think a break is good?"

"No," he says, voice cracking. "I don't. Don't pull away from me, baby."

"I'm not," I try to say, but Thomas pulls my face from his chest to look him in the eyes. His beautiful blue eyes are filled with tears.

"I don't want this to end, Hannah."

"It's not ending," I say. "I want to sleep alone in my bed tonight, is that so bad?"

Thomas looks up at the ceiling, swallowing harshly. "You promise you aren't pulling away?"

I shake my head. Can I really make that promise? I don't want to pull away, but yet aren't I doing exactly that?"
"I promise."

"I will give you some space, but Hannah, trust me when I say I am all in with you. I don't want to leave tonight, but if that's what you want, then I will."

"I think a night or two apart is good, Thomas."

"I disagree, but okay," he concedes. "Do you need anything before I go?"

I shake my head, willing myself to keep it together for a few more minutes.

"Okay. I'll talk to you in the morning." He cups my cheeks, taking my lips in a deep kiss. He pours all his emotion into this kiss, and by the end of it, I'm ready to throw in the towel. Make him stay and hold me all night long so I don't have to feel the way my heart is being ripped out of my chest as he tears our lips apart, kissing me one final time on the forehead. I don't though. I need to start getting used to being alone again. I can't always rely on him.

"Goodnight, Hannah," he whispers, turning and heading to my front door.

"Goodnight, Thomas," I reply, watching him leave and instantly regretting it.

## 45

## HANNAH

My bed is so cold without another person to keep me warm. I should have let him stay. He texted me when he got home, and I said thanks. All I wanted to do was tell him to come back, but I didn't. I couldn't.

I can't sleep. My mind is whirring a million miles a minute. What if they didn't get all the people working for Chaz, and they know we're back in town? What if they hurt Thomas? What if they hurt me?

I haven't needed to take my anxiety medication to sleep in over three weeks. The realization surprises me, but I know that I only have Thomas to thank. He's the reason I was able to stop taking it without even knowing it. If I want to get a wink of sleep tonight, I need it. I get out of my cold bed and stride over to my suitcases. I didn't bother unpacking, I can do that tomorrow. The only thing I did after Thomas left was take a quick shower to rinse off the day, and climb into bed. It feels weird not having Arson around to let out one more time before bed, or have him lying at the foot of the bed as he waited for me to change into my jammies.

How could six weeks alter my life so permanently?

I dig in my bag, searching for my toiletries bag. When I finally find it, I sag in relief against the wall. I find the pill bottle in the bag, sighing when I see there are only two left. I'll need to get a refill. I never needed to use it as much as I have recently, but then again, my life has never been as out of sorts as it has in the last six weeks.

Taking a pill from the bottle, I stand and head to my bed. Tears prick at my eyelids as I take the medication. I could be sound asleep in Thomas's arms right now, but no. I had to be stubborn.

I lie back down in my still cold bed and cry. I'm such a mess.

AFTER A NIGHT of minimal to no sleep, even with my medication, I wake to a text from Thomas.

THOMAS

Good morning, freckles. I missed you last night. What are you doing today?

I look through my phone, seeing the missed messages and calls from Julia. I hadn't gone through it last night after I got it back, but I have a bunch of messages from her. It looks like she was messaging me the entire time we were gone, even though she knew I didn't have my phone.

The most recent message was from her this morning.

JULIA

I know you're home.

Call me as soon as you wake up. I need to
see you!

I sigh, going back to the message from Thomas.

ME

> Not sure. I just woke up, but I'm pretty sure
> Julia and Tiff will break down my door if
> they don't hear from me in the next
> hour. You?

His reply is instant.

THOMAS

Josie and Andrew invited me over to meet
the new baby. Would you like to join? They
want to see you too.

ME

> Oh, no. That's okay. You spend time with
> your family today. I don't want to intrude.

THOMAS

You're not intruding, freckles. They invited
you. They want you there. I want you
there, too.

ME

> It's okay, really. I'll meet him another time.

THOMAS

Okay. Can I see you later?

ME

> I'm not sure.

THOMAS

Hannah, please. Don't pull away. I know
that coming home is a hard transition for us
both, but we can lean on each other.

ME

Okay.

THOMAS

Thank you. I'll come over after I'm done at Josie and Andrew's. Are you sure you don't want to come?

ME

I'm sure. Tell everyone I said hi.

THOMAS

I will.

I close the message thread and tap a few times to call Julia. It rings maybe twice and then she's answering.

"Oh my goodness, it took you long enough! Where are you? Are you at Thomas's? Should I pick you up? Tiff and I want to have breakfast with you."

"Jeepers, Julia. Calm down," I say with a soft laugh. "I'm at my place."

"Oh, did he drop you off on the way to work or something?" she questions.

"No, I stayed here. He dropped me off last night after we got home."

The line is silent for a moment. "Oookay?" she says questioningly. "Alrighty then. Should I pick you up? Or do you want to meet at the diner? We have so much to talk about."

"I can meet you at the diner in forty minutes. Does that work?"

"Yep. Tiff and I will pick up Grandma."

"Great," I reply. I'm surprised she doesn't stay on the phone the whole time I get ready and drive over, but she hangs up after a few minutes.

While I get ready, I call my therapist, Kimberly's office.

I definitely need to get in and see her sooner rather than later. I swallow down the fear of making a phone call. I hate making calls for appointments. Usually, I schedule online, but when I checked on the scheduling app, she's booked out for three weeks, which is not ideal in this situation, but I remember her mentioning that she always has emergency slots open.

I figure I'll leave a message with reception and see about getting an emergency appointment sometime in the next few days. I've never needed an emergency appointment, so hopefully it's not too hard to get one. I had Julia give Kimberly an update when we left and I missed my scheduled appointment, so hopefully she's aware of the situation.

The receptionist answers after a few rings. "Thank you for calling Ivy Ridge Health and Wellness, this is Laura, how can I help you?"

I shove down the anxiety brewing in my chest. "Hi, Laura. This is Hannah Pearson, one of Kimberly's patients."

"Oh, hi, Hannah!" she says happily.

"Hi," I say, swallowing the lump in my throat. "I was out of town for a while, but um, I'm wondering if Kimberly has any urgent appointments this week? I—I kinda need one."

"Let me take a look," she mumbles. She asks for my date of birth and a minute later, she's offering me an appointment this afternoon.

"I'll take it," I say without question. I need the appointment desperately.

"Great. We will see you at three," Laura says, saying goodbye and ending the call after I thank her.

A weight lifts off my shoulders as soon as that is taken care of, and I finish getting ready to head to the diner to see my family.

## 46

## THOMAS

"It's so good to see you, man," Andrew says as he hugs me, slapping me on my back. I sink into the familiarity of his embrace. I've always been close to all my brothers, but each of us have a different kind of bond. Even if I weren't here to see his brand new baby, I might have gone to him first after getting home. He can give great advice and I need that now.

Little baby Cooper is nestled in his mother's arms. Josie is sitting on the couch, and despite only giving birth a few days ago, she looks great. I can see the exhaustion in her features, but overall, she looks happy.

"Hey, Mom," I greet, leaning down to give my sister-in-law an awkwardly angled hug, trying not to squish my new nephew in the process.

Josie chuckles. "Hey. Where's Hannah?"

"She couldn't make it," I say regretfully, ignoring the pang of hurt in my chest. I wish she were here. "She's out with her family."

"Ah," Josie says. "Want to hold him?"

"Yes," I respond promptly, holding out my arms. I lean

down and she transfers the small bundle into my hands. I cradle him close, looking over his adorable features. He's the perfect mix of Josie and Andrew. I can see pieces of both of them in him. He's wearing a little hat, so of course, I can't see the color of his hair.

"Does he have your hair?" I ask Josie. Her red hair is pulled up into a messy bun, but in a way, I hope he has her hair.

"Take a look," Andrew says, reaching over and pulling off the small hat.

Wisps of red hair cover Cooper's head, and I smile. "I knew it."

Andrew laughs. "I wanted him to have red hair like his momma's so bad."

"It's amazing," I say, running my fingers over the soft fuzz of hair. "He's so cute you guys. Good job."

I sit down on the couch next to Josie, taking in the newest member of our family.

"Can we ask more about what happened, now?" Andrew asks, sitting down in the recliner beside us.

I sigh. "I can't really tell you much still, since it's an active investigation. But since we are back, I can tell you where we were."

Josie and Andrew nod, listening intently.

"We were in southern Missouri. They had us staying with an older couple, the Graffs, Ron and Dottie. They had a little cottage on their property that was tucked away, which is where Hannah and I stayed." I continue to tell them all about our time there, and how close Hannah and I got. I don't tell them that I was her first kiss, first everything, that would be betraying her trust. But I do tell them about my feelings for her.

"She's incredible. Once she opens up out of her shell

and shows you all the sides of herself, it's impossible not to love her."

"We never doubted that," Josie says, reaching out to place her hand on my arm.

"I know," I say with a shrug. "But I think she's pulling away. I think she's scared of her feelings for me, and I get it. It's hard when we've been in a separate world, away from reality for so long. I need to find a way to show her that I'm not letting her go, that she can trust me to take care of her."

"Do you have any ideas?" Andrew asks.

I shake my head. "Not yet. She wouldn't even let me stay with her last night. I slept like shit. Arson wouldn't stop pacing because he couldn't figure out where she was, and my bed was too cold without her."

"Oh, so you're like *in love* in love," Andrew says with a knowing smile.

I groan, squeezing my eyes shut and nodding. "Yeah. I am. But I can't come on too strong, because I'll scare her away."

"But I mean... aren't you engaged?" Josie asks.

I sigh. "For all intents and purposes, yes. For the public, yes. In real life? No. Not really. It was the only way I could get them to send her with me to the safe house."

"Oh," Andrew breathes.

"Yeah. But that doesn't leave this room. To the world, we are engaged."

"And I suppose proposing for real would be too much too fast?" Andrew wonders aloud.

"*Way* too much. She would run. She's not like you two, where you knew right away. She might think that I love her, but it scares her, so shoving her feelings down is the only thing keeping her calm."

"Hmm," Josie ponders. Cooper chooses that moment to let out a squawk, stirring in my arms. I adjust him to rest on my shoulder, and pat his small back gently. He soothes quickly.

"You're a natural," Josie comments.

"I'd hope so after being around all my nieces and nephews. I bet if we were around Presley as a baby, I'd be a pro."

"You're probably right," she says with a laugh.

Glancing down at the infant in my arms, I can't help but imagine what it might be like to have a little baby of my own. One with Hannah's eyes and freckles once they get older. The image is so real that I can't help but want to reach out and harness it.

I bet she'd be an amazing mom. I'm not getting any younger, and I always thought I would have kids by now, but Hannah's still young. All these things are something we need to talk about, but I'm scared to. I've never thought of our age difference as a hurdle for us, but the more I think about it, the more nervous I get. Age is a number, I know that, but what if we are at two completely different points in our lives?

There are too many unanswered questions, but I can't bombard her with all of them at once. She's already anxious about our relationship, I can't do that to her.

"Is she coming to Sunday brunch?" Andrew asks. I've never missed so many brunches in my life, and I miss it. It will be so nice to get back into the routine of things.

"I'll ask. I'd like her to, but maybe it's too soon," I say. We still have a few days before Sunday, so there's time.

"When the time is right, it will work out," Josie says comfortingly.

I can't help but hope that she's right. I am going to do

whatever I can to keep Hannah by my side, but I know it might take a lot of reassurance on my end. I'll do whatever it takes to keep her.

## 47

## HANNAH

"I missed you so much," Julia cries as she hugs me tightly.

"I missed you too," I reply, hugging her back.

We sit down at the table after I hug Tiff and my grandma.

"Tell us everything," Julia says, her eyes wide as she looks at me.

I narrow my gaze at her. I will not be telling them everything with my grandma present, and she knows that.

Tiff shoves gently at her wife. "Not everything. But what happened? Where were you?"

"I can't tell you why we were sent away," I say. I remember that much from the last bit of conversation last night at the station. "But we were in Missouri. We stayed with a really sweet couple who had a little cottage on their property." I tell them everything. How Dottie taught me so many new recipes, how she reminded me of mom. I tell them about how close Thomas and I got, and how special he makes me feel.

Then, I tell them about how scared I am now that we're

home. Julia and Tiff knew a bit about it, but they didn't know the extent of it.

"I don't know what to think. He told everyone we were engaged to keep me safe, but now that we're home, does that continue? Are we actually engaged?" I let out a heavy breath as I finish.

"Hannah, talk to him," Tiff encourages. "This is all stuff that could be answered if you talk to him."

"I agree with Tiff," Grandma says, reaching across the table to take my hand.

"I'm so scared. What if he doesn't want me anymore outside of the girl he knew at the cottage?"

"Stop that," Julia says tersely. "He is one of the nicest people I've ever known. If things end, we will take that as it comes. And like I said before. Thomas really likes you, even loves you. Look at the lengths he went to to keep you safe, Han. That's not a man who is going to drop you as soon as you get home. Give him a chance. You are the same girl you were at the cottage."

She's right. I know she is. Irritation with myself blooms in my chest, and I take a bite of my food to distract myself.

"I have therapy this afternoon, so hopefully that will help me feel more settled," I say.

"You should still talk to him," Julia says.

"I know, I will."

She raises her brow questioningly.

"I will," I say firmly.

"Good."

The rest of breakfast feels like a normal day. Like I wasn't gone for six weeks and am fake engaged to the man who I think I might love. It's normal, and exactly what I needed.

I TEXT THOMAS AFTER BREAKFAST, letting him know I have therapy, and then he can come over. I want to see him. I miss him.

The day goes by slowly as I wait for my appointment, but thankfully, it's finally time. I drive across town to Kimberly's office, registering with Laura and taking a seat in the waiting room.

Even though I've been seeing Kimberly for years now, I still get nervous before each appointment. I shouldn't, the woman knows everything about me and has never judged me, but I still do. It's annoying.

"Hannah?" Kimberly calls my name from her office door, and I stand and head over to her. "It is so good to see you, Hannah. I've been worried about you."

"Thanks," I say with an awkward smile. I sit down on the couch where I've spent many hours, immediately getting comfortable and sinking in.

"Now, I know you might not be able to tell me everything yet, but tell me what you can," she starts.

I take a deep breath. "It's been a long few weeks," I say, bursting into tears. I grab a tissue from the table beside the couch, wiping at my face. "Sorry."

"You have nothing to apologize for, Hannah. Are you able to give me a little insight as to what's going on inside your head?"

Nodding, I start. "Thomas Cunningham asked me out on a date, and together we witnessed a detective get shot. The person who shot him made threats on Thomas's and my life, so we were sent to a safe house, only after Thomas told them we were engaged so that I could go with him. I'm pretty sure that now I'm in love with my fake fiancé, and I'm scared he's going to get sick of me and let me go."

I exhale heavily, wiping tears from my cheeks.

"Wow," Kimberly says. "Sounds like you've had an eventful few weeks."

"You could say that," I huff. "I had my first kiss and lost my virginity."

Kimberly doesn't say anything, simply waits for me to continue.

I tell her about my fears of him leaving me now that we're home, and the more I say it out loud, the more I realize how ridiculous it is.

"Has he given you any indication that he's going to pull away? Or that he's going to end things with you?"

I choke out a watery laugh. "No. I'm so ridiculous."

"No, you're not, Hannah. We've been over this. You have come so far since we first met, and I am so proud of you. This is a bump in the road. We have to change your goals, because you've accomplished most of your old ones. New goals are scary, but good. Now, what are some new goals you'd like to add to your list?"

I take a steadying breath and say the first thing that comes to mind.

"I want to tell Thomas I love him." The words fly off my tongue.

Kimberly doesn't speak for a moment, letting me process my own words.

"I want to date him, normally. We haven't had a chance to just be a normal couple, and while I want to be with him all the time, we need to get out of our bubble."

"Good, those are both great. What else?" Kimberly asks.

"I want him to meet my family." Imagining a day spent

with Thomas, my sisters and grandmother makes my heart flutter in excitement. I want that. The comfort of all my favorite people in one place.

There's a hint of nervousness when I think about it, because what if they don't like him when they get to know him? At the same time, I know how easy it is to know and love Thomas, so the fear disappears as soon as it appears. They also will love him because I do.

"What went through your brain just now?" Kimberly wonders.

"I got worried they wouldn't like him, but then I realized that if I love him, then they will, too. He's easy to love."

"Tell me more," Kimberly prompts.

"I want to meet his family. I've met some of them, but not his parents. It's going to be scary, but I know if he's what I want, then it's what I have to do."

"Those are very good goals, Hannah. Are there any more?"

"Not right now."

"Good. How are you going to achieve those goals?"

This is easier I suppose. "Go on dates, see if I can go to a Sunday brunch with Thomas, and coordinate something with my family to meet him as my partner."

"Wonderful. It seems like you have a good grasp on what you want, Hannah. I know how hard your anxiety can make things, but I'm proud of you, and how far you've come, especially with this huge change in your life."

"Thank you," I murmur, my cheeks flushing. It feels good to make a plan for a few things, and as always, there's still work to be done, but it's a good start.

## 48

## THOMAS

I knock on Hannah's apartment door, my nerves brimming on edge. We've been apart for less than twenty-four hours, yet it feels like days. She opens the door and within a second, I'm pulling her into my arms.

Having her back in my embrace feels right. All the fear and anxiety of her pulling away drifts off, leaving me in the here and now. "Hey freckles," I whisper against the top of her head.

"Hi," she mumbles, squeezing me tightly.

"I missed you."

"I missed you, too," she admits, and those three words help me breathe better.

I lead her over to the couch, sitting down and pulling her into my lap. "Where's Arson?" she asks, glancing around.

"He's at home. He and Travis, Andrew's dog, tend to get really playful, and we didn't want them to be too hyper in the house around the new baby," I explain.

"That makes sense. How is the new baby?"

"He's so adorable. I wish you could have met him, Han.

He has the same red hair that Josie does, and he looks like both of them."

"I bet he's perfect," she says with a smile.

"How was visiting your family?" I ask.

"Good." Hannah leans her head on my shoulder, her body melting into mine. "Can we talk?"

"Of course we can talk, baby. You know I'm always here for you." I brush some of her hair away from her face.

"What happens next with us?"

Sighing, I reply, "As far as being engaged? I'm not sure. But I know that I'm not done with *us*. Admittedly, I'm not sure I ever will be."

"Really?" Hannah questions.

"Really. I know it's probably way too soon to talk about things like our future, but Hannah, please know that I want it. Like I said that night in the bed of the truck. I want it all with you. I wasn't lying. I will say it however many times I need to in order to reassure you, and I will never get sick of it."

"I had an appointment with my therapist today, and we talked a lot about the future," she says quietly, turning her face into my chest. If what she needs is to not see me while we talk, that's fine. "It was hard, and I'm exhausted, but it helped a lot."

"I'm glad," I say. I won't pry into her business, but I would love to know more.

"Everything started so fast with us. Obviously, it's not a normal start to a relationship, but now that we are home, can we do things normally?" she asks hesitantly.

"Absolutely. We can start fresh. I can take you out for an official second date. We can slow things down if that's what you need, freckles."

She nods into my chest, and relief settles through my

body. Do I want to slow down? No, not really, but if it's what she needs, then I will do whatever it takes to keep her.

"My family wants to meet you," she says. "Like, officially. Obviously, you know Julia, and you met Tiff, but my grandma wants to meet you, as my boyfriend." She starts to stutter. "I–If that's what you are."

"I'm your boyfriend, freckles. Don't even doubt that for a second. I would love to meet your family. Would you be willing to meet mine too? Officially? I know Gramps is dying to see you again."

She takes a deep breath. "I would like that. I can't promise that I won't be quiet or anxious that day, but I want to meet them. Officially."

"I'll be by your side the whole time. And if it's too much, we can leave. I never want to make you uncomfortable, Hannah."

"What do we do about the whole engagement thing, though?" she questions.

I shrug. "I'm not positive. I think on the outside we may have to continue to play the engaged part, at least until things are through with the investigation. Are you okay with that?"

"I think so."

"That's the only part about us that isn't real, freckles. Everything else is real. You're mine, and I am yours. When I propose to you for real, it will be for us, no one else."

Hannah smiles and nods up at me, and everything feels right again. "Now, with this whole 'slow' thing. Does that mean we can't spend the nights together?" I ask with a laugh, though I'm completely serious. Last night was horrible. I slept like shit.

"I mean, we both work weird hours, Thomas. We aren't

going to be able to sleep in the same bed every night," Hannah replies, attempting to be logical.

"Fair, but when we can, I want you in my arms. Last night was the worst night of sleep I've had in months, and it's because you weren't there."

"You're sure it's not because you were stressed or something?"

"Nope," I reply, popping the p. "It's because I wasn't with you. Even Arson was stressed."

"He was?" she says, her voice upset.

"So you get upset over Arson being stressed, but not me? I see how it is," I tease, tilting her chin up to meet my gaze.

Hannah laughs, and the sound fills my soul with so much joy. "He's my favorite," she replies.

"I am hurt," I gasp, clutching my heart. "You stuck a dagger through me, baby. I won't make it." I dramatically flop backwards, groaning.

"Stop it," Hannah giggles, swatting at my chest. "Fine. I slept horrible without you, too."

I sit up straight. "You did?"

She nods, sobering. "I had to take a hydroxyzine, and it barely helped. It didn't feel right, not having you and Arson with me."

"I'm sorry, baby."

She shrugs. "It's okay. Can we go to your house? I want to see him."

"Will you stay the night?" I ask hopefully.

It takes a moment, but she nods. "Yes. I have to pack some things though."

"Part of me wants to tell you to pack everything, but I know you're not ready for that, yet," I say wistfully.

Hannah pauses as if she's fully considering it, then

replies, "I'm not. Maybe soon though. I mean, we did live together for six weeks already."

"We did," I confirm. Hannah stands from the couch, and I follow, pulling her into my arms for a quick kiss.

"Slow," she mutters against my lips.

"*Ish*. Slow-*ish*."

Hannah pulls away with another laugh, heading into her bedroom.

## 49

## THOMAS

"Time to wake up, baby," I whisper, kissing down Hannah's neck.

"Ten more minutes," she whimpers.

"I already gave you ten more minutes," I reply with a laugh. "We have to get going. Brunch starts in forty minutes."

Her body tenses.

"I'll be with you the whole time, freckles."

"I know you will. I shouldn't be nervous, I've met all of them before."

"You have, but that doesn't mean you can't be nervous. I get it."

Hannah sits up in bed, covering her body with the sheet. Since the day after we got home, she's been in my bed every night. I know she said she wasn't going to move in, but I'm not going to complain about her being here every night. I love it.

"Come on, freckles. You should wear one of those sundresses," I say with a wink.

"All of the ones I have here are dirty, Thomas. And we

don't have time to stop by my apartment. Oh god, we should have gone to my house yesterday. I don't have anything to wear but leggings and a stained tank top!"

"Breathe, baby," I chuckle, standing from the bed. I stride over to her, pulling her into my arms. "We have plenty of time to go to your apartment quick. It's no biggie. I can be ready in five minutes."

She takes a quick breath. "Okay fine, but we have to go fast. I can braid my hair on the way to my place."

"Deal." I pull away, only far enough to peck her on the lips before grabbing some clothes and darting into the bathroom to brush my teeth and hair.

Ten minutes later, we are in the car heading to Hannah's apartment. I decided to leave Arson at home since there will be a lot happening today. It's Cooper's first Sunday brunch too. It's a big day in the Cunningham family.

We pull up to Hannah's apartment and she starts climbing out. "I'll be back in like ten minutes, okay?" she says.

Ignoring her, I climb out.

"What are you doing?" she questions.

"Coming in," I say.

"Why?"

"Because," I say, reaching down to take her palm in mine. I lift it to my lips, kissing the back of her hand. "You will overthink every outfit you lay eyes on. I'm going to pick for you."

Hannah scoffs. "No, you aren't."

"Yes, I am."

"Thomas," she whines, but I notice she doesn't stop walking toward the building.

"Am I wrong?"

She groans. "Fine, you're not wrong, but you don't have to pick for me. I can do it myself."

"Alright, freckles. Either way, I'm coming. I'll help stop the inevitable overthinking."

She doesn't deny it as we walk into the building and to her apartment. When she opens the door, she leads us directly to her bedroom. I take in her apartment more as we walk. There's no real theme in terms of decor, but it's fitting for her. Lots of pictures of her with her family, including photos of her with her parents when she was younger. She doesn't talk about her parents much, but when she does, it's subtle things, like old family traditions, or the way her mom used to make a crazy cake every year on her birthday. All things that are important, but don't hurt Hannah too much to talk about.

Her bedroom is tidy, but the bed is unmade. I sit down on the edge of it, gesturing at her to look in her closet. She's wearing a pair of leggings and one of my T-shirts, and as much as I don't want her to change, I get it. She doesn't want to wear that to meet my parents, and I do love her in sundresses.

She pulls a light blue striped dress out of the closet and holds it up. "Too fancy?" she asks.

"Perfect," I reply, eager to see her in it.

"You would say that for anything I pick," she says with a roll of her eyes.

"True, but still. It's not too fancy. It's just right."

"I'll go change."

She heads into the bathroom, coming out a few moments later with the dress on.

I swear, my mouth waters and my cock throbs, growing hard in my jeans. "Oh, fuck," I groan.

"What? Is it bad?" Hannah panics.

"No, fuck no," I say, standing and adjusting myself. "It's gorgeous." Striding over to her, I grip her hips, pulling her to me. There's three buttons running vertically down her bust.

"Do these unbutton?" I ask, unable to tear my gaze from her cleavage.

Hannah laughs, swatting my hand from where it's trailing down the buttons. "No, you goon. They're fake."

"Damn," I say with a sigh. "You look beautiful, baby."

"Thank you," she says with a smile, tilting her chin and kissing my lips deftly. She put on a little mascara while in the bathroom, as well as a hint of light pink lipstick. It's gorgeous.

"Can you help me with the tie in the back?" she asks, turning around. I tie the bow at her back, and squeeze her delicious ass when I'm done.

"Maybe we can be a few minutes late," I say, pulling her into my body. Her back is to my front, and I press my hard cock into her ass. My hand runs across her soft belly, sliding up to cup her breasts. "I think I need a taste of you before we go."

"Thomas!" She pulls out of my hold. "We cannot be late."

"Yes, we can, they won't care! Plus, I think you could use a little stress relief," I argue, waggling my brows.

"*Thomas*," she whines. "We can't."

"Fine, fine," I say, adjusting my cock again. "Later."

"Later," she confirms, grabbing her phone from the bed and sliding on a pair of sandals before heading out of her bedroom. I hang back for *juuust* a second, watching the sway of her ass as she leaves. I can't help it.

My girlfriend is perfect.

## 50

## HANNAH

I don't live far from Thomas's parent's house, but with each house and block that goes by, my anxiety grows. I dig my fingernails into my palms, trying to stay visibly calm. If Thomas notices that I'm anxious, he'll do anything he can to stop it, and I'll feel bad. I shouldn't be this anxious to meet his parents and see his family again. They're all such nice people, and I don't want Thomas to think I don't want to meet his family. I do. My brain won't cooperate.

Thomas has his right hand on my thigh underneath the fabric of my dress as he smoothes his rough thumb over the soft skin.

I can sense my anxiety getting higher with each passing second, so I grab my water bottle from the center console, opening the lid and taking a drink of water, letting an ice cube slide between my lips. I'm not at the point where I usually would be when I need ice to ground me, but I can feel myself getting there, so I'm trying to get ahead of it.

I let the ice rest on my tongue, taking deep inhales through my nose.

"Hannah?" Thomas glances over at me.

"Hmm?" I ask, pushing the ice to the side of my mouth.

"Breathe for me, baby."

"I am," I mumble, inhaling sharply.

Thomas narrows his eyes at me, slowing the car and turning off the main road. "What are you doing?" I ask.

"You need a minute, so I'm giving you a minute," he explains. He turns in the opposite direction. "I'm going to help you calm down."

"What—" I'm not able to say another word as he covers my mouth, driving us a few miles until we're on a secluded dirt road that is covered in trees without a mailbox or driveway in sight.

"Lay your seat back," he instructs, removing his hand from my mouth and unbuckling his seatbelt.

"What?" I shriek.

Thomas gestures to my seat. When I don't immediately move, he leans over me, hooking the lever so I fly backwards.

"Oh," I breathe, the earlier anxiety replaced by confusion. Thomas flips the center console up, scooting over and unbuckling my seat belt.

"Take another drink of your water and grab me an ice cube, baby," he whispers, his eyes darkening as they roam my face.

I do as he says, taking a swallow of water and fishing a cube out. I hold it on my tongue, and Thomas cups my cheek, parting my lips so I can transfer the cold cube to his mouth. He trails his lips down my jaw, to my neck.

"Thomas, we should go," I try to say, but the words disappear on my lips as his mouth opens, letting the ice touch the sensitive skin on my neck.

I gasp, leaning into his touch. His hand reaches up to cup my breast through my dress, then slowly slides down my stomach to my pussy. He cups it through my dress, pressing the heel of his palm to my clit. "Someone could see."

"I don't care," he mumbles, licking a path across my breasts, his tongue frosty on my warm skin.

He slides his hand under the long hem of my dress, flipping it back over to cover my legs and pussy from sight. I instinctively spread my legs open further for him.

"Lift up, baby," he directs. I do as he says, and he shifts the backside of my dress up and my panties down. He presses me back down so my ass is directly on the cold leather.

Thomas takes the ice cube between his lips, using his other hand to pop it from his mouth. He holds it between his fingers, sliding over my folds where I'm already soaked for him. He presses it against my pussy. The cold sends a jolt through me, surprising me. It doesn't turn me off though. If anything, it makes me even wetter.

Fingers press into my wetness. The ice cube is being traced on my mound, the cold sending shivers up and down my spine as the unexpected pleasure takes over.

My pussy is dripping with both water and my own wetness. I'm probably going to have a wet spot on the seat, but at the moment, I don't care.

"How does it feel?" he asks, his blue eyes shining with so much lust.

"Amazing," I breathe, my head dropping onto the headrest.

"Good, now relax, and feel, baby."

The cold ice rests on my clit while his frigid fingers pump in and out of me. He moves the cube from my clit, strumming his thumb over the even more sensitive bundle of nerves.

He's right, though. I'm not even anxious anymore. Every ounce of anxiety is replaced with *need*.

The heat from my pussy melts the ice fast, replacing the cold with a building heat as I get closer and closer to orgasm. At this point, Thomas knows my body better than I know my own, and with each meticulous stroke of his fingers, I tense until finally, my climax takes over, my body shuddering into the seat.

When the aftershocks fade, Thomas slides his fingers out, sucking them clean. "Oh, fuck," I breathe. Every time he does that, it's such an erotic sight that my pussy thumps in delight.

"Feeling better?" he asks, a smile on his lips.

I nod. "I'm wet."

"Good, then I did my job," he says cockily.

"No, I mean, *yes*," I groan. "You did your job, but my ass is soaked from the ice cube."

"I have napkins," Thomas replies with a smile, digging into the glove box and pulling out a stack of napkins. He cleans between my thighs and then has me get out so he can round the truck and wipe the seat and my ass clean.

He helps pull my underwear back up, squeezing my ass and kissing me sweetly. "Ice works in many ways for you, it seems."

I blush furiously. I will never look at ice the same way.

## 51

# HANNAH

Thomas has his hand pressed against my back as we walk up the front steps of his parents' house. It's a cute two-story house with flowers decorating the front porch.

"I know this is hard for you," Thomas says, rubbing my back soothingly. "But I am here for you. I'll be by your side the whole time if you need me to."

"Thank you," I whisper, unable to raise my voice higher than that.

Thomas doesn't knock on the door, entering without any preamble. He guides me into the entryway where we kick off our shoes. The low chattering of voices gets louder as we walk into the living room.

The room is filled with people, some I recognize and some I don't. Gramps is sitting on the couch, Josie on his right side, and there's a small bundle in his arms, which must be the new baby. Two young girls are standing in front of him, wide smiles on their faces.

"Hey guys," Thomas greets.

All conversation ceases as heads swivel to us. I wince internally as eyes take us in.

I try to smile, to wave and greet them, but nothing comes out. Thomas reaches down, taking my hand. He squeezes my palm, looking down at me with a smile. He mouths, *"You've got this."* and I know that I do. With him by my side, I can do this.

"Thomas!" people call, and the two young girls run across the room to him, wrapping their arms around his legs in a giant hug.

He laughs, scruffing their hair and bending down to give them proper hugs. I let go of his hand for a moment, and step back, only to be met face to face with Thomas's mother.

"Hi, honey," she says gently, holding out her hand. "I'm Nikki."

"Hi," I reply, my voice soft as my heart beats loudly in my ears. "It's nice to finally meet you."

"You too." I shake her hand, but barely another moment passes and Thomas is by my side again.

"Mom," he greets, holding his arms out for her and giving her a hug. They embrace for a moment, and I stand next to him, too afraid to branch out even a little and say hi to the people I've met before.

Tears run down Nikki's cheeks as they pull apart, and she swipes at her cheeks. "Oh, my boy, I've missed you so much."

"I'm home now," Thomas soothes, stepping back and taking my hand again. We walk further into the room, and Nikki introduces me as Thomas's fiancée to the group.

There's a lot of people here, and while I recognize a lot of them, It's still a little nerve-racking. Nikki introduces me to her husband, Richard, and the neighbors, Gabriel and

Jane. They're both older couples, and it takes a moment to sink in that they more than likely knew my parents. Why wouldn't they? Julia and Thomas are the same age, and I think Marley has an older brother the same age as him, too.

The realization hits me harder than I expected.

Thomas sits down on an empty couch, pulling me down next to him. I sit on the couch beside him, wanting so badly to curl up into his body, but I don't. I sit straight, only holding his hand as I take in all of these people. Marley and Beau are in the corner playing with their twins, Fallon and Jason sit side by side on the floor against the other couch, and everyone relaxes into easy conversation. The focus isn't all on me, and for that, I appreciate them. Perhaps Thomas warned them about my social anxiety, or maybe they don't feel the need to interrogate me, but it's nice. I feel like I can slip into the conversations as they happen, and not feel pressured to be involved or come up with answers on the spot.

Everyone chats for a bit, every so often asking Thomas questions about our time away. He deflects to me a few times for answers, including me in the conversation, but otherwise, I stay quiet.

Fifteen minutes later, a timer goes off, and Nikki and Richard head into the kitchen, the two young girls who I've figured out are Fallon and Jason's daughters, Presley and Lennie, following. They call out to us and everyone starts to shuffle into the dining room. Thomas holds me behind, only speaking when everyone is out of hearing range.

"How are you doing, baby?" he asks, pushing a strand of hair away from my face.

I nod. "I'm okay, I think. It's a lot, but everyone is so nice."

"They are. They love you already."

I withhold the scoff that wants to escape. How could

they love me already? I've been here thirty minutes, and in that time, I have barely said ten words.

"Don't give me that look, Hannah," Thomas scolds.

"What look?" I retort, furrowing my brows.

"The look that says you don't believe me. It took me weeks to get you to stop making that face every time I called you beautiful, but don't worry. I'll break you of the habit here, too. They love you. How could they not?"

"They hardly know me."

"You're easy to love, Hannah." Thomas cups my cheek, swiftly kissing my lips, not giving me time to process his words before leading me into the large dining room.

A huge wooden table takes over the room, with more than enough room for everyone at the table, including high chairs. I have no idea how it's possible to make a table this big, but then I suppose Andrew made it, so it makes sense that he could do a custom size like this.

Thomas pulls out a handmade chair for me, and sits down beside me. A bowl of fruit is passed around, and Thomas scoops some onto my plate and his, passing it along to Jason on his other side. Gramps is on my right, pouring a very large amount of sugar into his coffee.

The ham and cheese egg bake is passed around, and everyone takes one or two squares, dishing up plates for the kids and Andrew dishes up for Josie, who is holding baby Cooper.

Once everyone is eating, conversation continues throughout the group again. I pick up on random bits and pieces of it as I munch on the food, trying not to draw attention to myself. Thomas chats with everyone, telling them about Ron and Dottie, and all the animals, including the chaotic Dave.

Everyone laughs, the young girls loving the stories. A

piece of me misses the safe house and the secluded world that Ron and Dottie provided, but an even bigger piece is loving being home. I'm loving the fact that Thomas and I are getting back to our normal lives, despite my earlier freak out about it. We both go back to work tomorrow, and I cannot wait. I've missed Miles, and I look forward to chatting with him and hearing what I've missed in these last six weeks.

"So, kiddo, you ready to get back to work?" Gramps asks, nudging my shoulder and pulling me out of my thoughts.

"Oh, yes," I reply, pushing the food around my plate. "I was actually just thinking about that."

"You're good at your job," he says with a wink.

"Thanks," I laugh. "Have you been staying out of trouble?"

"Sure have," he responds.

"You sure about that?" Thomas joins in.

"I'm offended," Gramps replies. "It's not my fault I have poor balance in the morning."

"I think you did it on purpose," Thomas replies, resting his arm around the back of my chair, his fingers resting on my shoulder, drawing patterns on my skin.

"You think I fell on my ass on purpose so I could get you out to my apartment with a pretty young girl who is perfect for you?" Gramps says, his voice feigning shock.

"I think you did, but I don't know how to prove it," Thomas states, pointing his fork at his grandfather. Meanwhile, I'm trying to hold back my laughter.

There's really no way he fell on purpose on the off chance that I was on duty and arrived at the scene with his grandson, but I suppose with a man like Earl, you never know what he's capable of.

After we clean up from brunch, we all make our way

back into the living room, and this time, Thomas and I sit next to each other on the floor. He pulls me into his body, and I lean against him. Josie strides across the room. "Do you want to hold him, Hannah?" she asks, and if she didn't say my name, I would honestly be questioning if she asked me, or not.

"Um, sure," I reply, holding out my arms. She places the swaddled infant into my arms, and I pull him close to my chest. It's been a long time since I've held a baby, but it all comes right back to me.

Cooper makes little noises, and I can't help but stare at him. Thomas rests his head on my shoulder, staring at his nephew. He's the perfect mix of Andrew and Josie, but I can see little hints of all the brothers in him. He has Thomas's nose, Beau's brow line, and Jason's ears. It's fascinating to see how genetics come into play.

"He's so cute," I whisper.

"Isn't he?" Thomas answers, kissing the side of my neck.

A new voice distracts me from staring at Cooper. "Are you going to be my new Auntie?"

Lennie. She's about six, if I remember correctly.

"Umm," I pause, unsure of what to say.

"Someday, Lennie," Thomas answers for me, but his reply only makes my heart stutter. He's said that he wants marriage and life with me, but hearing him say so casually that I'm going to be an aunt to his niece someday, really brings it all into focus, makes it real.

"Soon?" she questions.

Presley joins her at her side. She's a bit taller than Lennie, and her dirty blonde hair is wavier. They aren't sisters by blood, but they are in all the ways that count. "Hannah, you're really pretty," Presley announces, garnering the attention of the entire room.

I swallow thickly. "Thanks, Presley. So are you, sweetie."

"My mom said you were really pretty, but I didn't believe her until you were here. She was right."

"She's beautiful, isn't she," Thomas adds, kissing my cheek.

I wish I could hide away from the sudden attention, but I'm holding Cooper, so I can't even fidget with my hands.

I smile awkwardly, and Presley sits down at my right side. Her fingers twirl around the soft red hair on Cooper's head.

Arlo, one of Marley and Beau's twins, walks unsteadily toward us. He flops down into Thomas's lap, leaning over to place one of his tubby hands on Cooper's stomach.

"Baby," he says in his own baby talk.

"You're right," Thomas replies. "Baby Cooper."

Arlo scoots closer to me, and I think he's trying to get a better look at the baby, so I adjust him so he can see better, but instead, he tries to push Cooper from my arms. "My," he says, pushing at Cooper.

"Arlo, gentle hands," Marley says, scooting over to us.

"My," he repeats, this time, landing in my lap and settling in. I shift Cooper to one side, wrapping my arm around Arlo with my free arm. Arlo nuzzles his head into my chest. Did he want *me*?

I look up to Marley, who has a camera in her hands. "Can I?" she asks, and I nod, smiling. She takes a few pictures of us, all wrapped in Thomas's big arms. Arlo curls into me, repeating "my" every few minutes when someone tries to bring his attention elsewhere. Not even his sister can get him away from me. Marley takes Cooper, and I figure that Arlo will go with her, following wherever the baby goes, but instead, he curls further into me, his little fingers clasping at my shirt.

"I think I might have to fight my nephew for you," Thomas jokes.

"I thought he wanted the baby," I say.

"Nope. He wanted you. I knew he did. Like I said, you're easy to love. Everyone can see it."

## 52

# THOMAS

The last few weeks have been bliss. Hannah and I are both back to work and we have created some sort of a routine. On the days we both are off, we are together, going on dates, or spending time with her siblings or mine. When we both work a day shift, we go to her house or mine after work and have dinner together. Nine times out of ten we end up spending the night at one or the other's house, and every time, I wake up with her by my side. It can't get any better than this.

I've learned that Hannah is a bear on the days she has to flip to a night shift schedule. She gets crabbier than I ever could have expected, but it's nothing a few orgasms can't fix.

She's gone to a few more Sunday brunches as well, and has gotten more comfortable with my family. Arlo is still obsessed with her, calling her "My" every chance he can, since words aren't his strong suit yet.

I've gone to dinner with Hannah and her Grandma, and Hannah with Julia and Tiff. It's been wonderful getting to know them more, to know the people that helped raise the woman I love.

Hannah opened up more about her parents too in that time, and I've loved seeing her with her sister, telling stories about their childhoods.

I'm finishing up my shift, and then heading home for the night. Hannah is off shortly too, and I'm going to make us dinner at my place. I head into the station, walking down the halls to the offices. Henry is still on desk duty after getting shot, but soon should be back in the field investigating.

I haven't been involved in the investigation since I've been back, and I'm perfectly okay with that. After putting myself and Hannah in danger, I'm fine with stepping back from it.

I pass by Henry's office, offering him a wave, but he stops me. "Thomas, you got a sec?" he calls.

"Sure," I say, heading into his small office.

"I wanted to give you an update."

I sit down in one of the rickety chairs, waiting for him to continue.

"While we believe we arrested the main dealers and people associated with Chaz, we have reason to believe he has people that he's been communicating with on the outside."

"Okay," I say with a heavy exhale. This could mean many things. "So what now?"

"There hasn't been any mention of your name specifically, but a few of the undercover guys with the FBI have heard about plans to get back at the department for arresting Chaz and his inner circle."

A brewing fear starts in my chest. "Am I being sent back to a safe house?"

He shakes his head. "Like I said, we have no reason to believe that you—or Hannah— are being targeted this time.

We will keep an eye on it and keep you in the loop, but stay alert. That's all."

I nod, standing from my chair. I know I have to tell Hannah, but I don't want to burst this bubble for her. It seems like her anxiety has been so much better lately. I don't want to drag her right back to square one. "Thanks for the update, Henry. Let me know if you need anything from me."

"Will do."

I leave his office, trying to think this through. Do I tell her? Henry himself has said there is nothing to worry about right now, but then again, he said to keep an eye out, and I never want to lie to her or withhold any information. I'll tell her tonight, and then I'll hold her through any anxiety she may have.

A SOFT KNOCKING at my door makes me smile. She should know by now that she doesn't need to knock before entering my home, but it's adorable all the same. I wipe my hands on a towel before heading to the front door and opening it.

Hannah stands in front of it, her backpack slung over her shoulder and her pillow and weighted blanket in the other arm.

I lean forward, grabbing the heavy as hell blanket from her. She insists it helps her sleep, and I think I believe her. She didn't bring it along to Ron and Dottie's house, and the difference in her sleep is immense. She sleeps like a rock most nights. The only negative about it is that it can make it harder to cuddle her.

"You know you don't have to knock, freckles." I kiss her lips, cupping her cheek in my free hand.

She shrugs. "I'm a guest here, I should knock."

"Baby, you aren't a guest. You basically live here," I say, guiding her into the house and shutting the door behind her. After today's news, I feel a little on edge, so I glance around outside, noting nothing of consequence.

"I do not," she debates, and I raise my brow as I carry her blanket into my room.

"Yes, you do. If we aren't at your house, we are here. I don't mind one bit, but you also have a key."

"I do?" she questions, glancing down at her keys in her palm.

"You do," I state. "I put a key on there after we got home."

"You didn't tell me that," Hannah says quietly.

I shrug. "I guess I forgot."

"Thomas Cunningham, you have the memory of an elephant. There is no way you put a key to your house on my key ring, then *forgot*." She drops her bag onto the floor in the corner of my bedroom.

"Maybe it was my way of subtly trying to ask you to move in." I sit down on the edge of my bed. I didn't know I was going to bring this up again tonight, I thought maybe I'd give her some more time, but if tonight's the night, then I'm ready for it.

"You..." Hannah pauses, clasping her hands together and picking at the skin around her nails. "You said we could go slow."

"I did," I answer, standing to take her hands in mine, stopping their abuse on themselves. "But I also know what I want, Hannah. Just because you have a key to my house, doesn't mean that you need to move in right away. But it makes sense to keep things here. Unless you want me to move into your place?" I don't see how we would all fit in that tiny apartment, but we'd make do if it's what she wanted.

She shakes her head abruptly. "Don't be silly. We wouldn't fit. And I think my landlord is catching on to the fact that Arson is there often. We technically can't have pets."

"Then it makes sense to move in here."

"It does," she mutters, trying to pull her hands free from mine. I don't let her.

"It doesn't have to be right away," I reiterate, and she nods, leaning her head into my chest.

"My lease is up in two months, maybe we can talk about it again then?" she questions.

"Of course, baby. In the meantime, I'm getting you a weighted blanket to keep here. That thing is way too heavy to keep lugging around." I kiss the top of her head, holding her for another moment. Arson squeezes his way in between our legs, desperate for her attention. He really does love her more than me.

"Hi buddy," Hannah murmurs, pulling away from me and bending down to love on him.

"I made a roast for dinner. Are you hungry?"

"Starving," she replies, standing and following me into the kitchen where I dish us both up some roast and potatoes. We sit down at my dining room table, where she tells me about some of the calls she had today, and what her grandma has been up to this week.

Julia and Tiff are coming to town this weekend, so it will be nice to spend some time with them again. I think I'm going to invite them and her grandma to Sunday Brunch too. The table is getting very full, but we can always make room for family.

"How was your day?" she asks, finishing the last bite of her meal.

"Good," I reply. "Can't complain I suppose. I talked to Henry a bit."

I don't miss the tensing of Hannah's shoulders. "You did?"

"Yep. There's nothing to worry about," I say quickly. "But, there is some evidence that suggests the dealers that haven't been arrested yet are starting to plot something against the department. Nothing concrete yet, though."

Hannah doesn't look up as she wipes her face with her napkin. Her hands shake with the motion. "Baby, don't worry. We're safe. They don't foresee it being a problem."

"What about you?" she whimpers, finally meeting my gaze. Her blue eyes are full of watery tears. "They came after you once, what if they come after you again? What if they are successful this time? Thomas, I can't do this without you."

"You don't have to. I promise I'm safe. We are safe. They are keeping a close watch on it, and they have agents working undercover to assure that." I scoot my chair closer to her, and wrap my arm around her, holding her to me.

Her breathing is rapid and short, so I coach her through some deep breathing. Once her breaths match mine, I lean away to look into her eyes. "I am not going anywhere. You're stuck with me, and my annoying dog, too. I told you because you deserve to know."

"Thank you," she murmurs, wiping at her splotchy, tear stained cheeks. "As anxious as it makes me, I am thankful you told me. I appreciate it."

"Of course. Henry made sure to let me know we are

safe. We don't need to go back to Ron and Dottie's, or lay low. We can live our lives."

She nods, taking another deep breath. "Okay. I can work with that. I am going to have to get used to being scared every time I say goodbye to you, though."

"Your job is nearly as dangerous as mine is," I reply, pushing her hair from her face. "I worry about you too, you know. We both work in dangerous fields."

"I suppose that's true," she replies. "You more than me, though."

"Agree to disagree," I respond. "Now, are you okay?"

"I think so," she says, nodding her head.

"Want to watch a movie or something?"

Hannah shakes her head. "I actually had something else in mind…"

"Oh did you?" I question, with a hint of mischief in my voice, tilting my head.

She smiles, standing from the chair, taking her plate and glass and heading in the direction of my kitchen. "You'll have to wait and find out. We need to do the dishes first."

"You've turned into quite the tease, freckles."

"I learned from the best," she says, turning back to offer me a wink. I watch the sway of her hips with a groan as she strides into my kitchen.

## 53

# THOMAS

HANNAH

You stole my blanket last night

ME

I did not. 😧

HANNAH

Yes, you did! I woke up and you and Arson were hogging my blanket! I thought that's why we had separate blankets, so we don't have this problem anymore.

ME

Apparently I need to get myself a weighted blanket too.

HANNAH

Yes, you do. I'll add a second one to my cart now. 😊

ME

Thank you baby. Still on for tonight?

HANNAH

Yes, though I would be more excited if you
told me what we're doing. You know I don't
like surprises.

ME

I know, but this is a good surprise. I
promise. I'll pick you up at your house at
eight.

HANNAH

Sounds good. Gotta go

I don't question the abrupt end in conversation, both of us are constantly being called away for work, so it's not unusual for one of us to not respond for a few hours at a time, or send a text half crafted.

A jitter rolls through my body today as I think about what I have planned for this evening.

I've held off long enough, but it's time to tell Hannah I love her. Sure, I could have told her long before now, I mean we are still technically engaged to the outside world, and practically live together, and we have a plan to discuss it again in the near future, but we've never taken things at a normal pace. We're different, and that's not a bad thing. I do know that I can't hold back from saying how I feel about her for much longer, though. That's why, tonight's the night.

I have my trusty Iron Man underwear on, and a mental plan of how I want tonight to go. Sure, things don't always go to plan, but it can't hurt to be prepared.

Hannah left before I did this morning, so I was able to get my living room all set up. I have tea-light candles placed delicately around the room, and blankets organized in a comfy pile, and I have snacks and bubbly champagne in the fridge. Maybe it's a bit much for a confession of love, but we've done things a little bit backwards in our relationship, so I want her to know how special she is to me.

My radio beeps on the dash, pulling my thoughts away from plans for tonight.

"Possible overdose, 918 East Longview Avenue, age twenty-three."

"Fuck," I curse under my breath. "1831 responding."

I throw my vehicle into drive and turn the sirens on, listening as the dispatcher gives me what little information she has. They're in the backyard.

My heart sinks with each beat as I drive to the scene. I knew they didn't get them all. As I pull up to the scene with two other officers, I call out to Arson, "Stay here." He flops into a seated position in the backseat. I don't normally take him out of the car on calls like these. Throwing myself out of the car, I leave it running and slam the door behind me, already reaching for the Narcan I keep in my belt.

Officer Young is rounding to the back of the house where the gate is wide open. I run through the gate, assessing the scene before me.

Two people are hovering over a young man laying on the ground. I can't see his face, but his arms are limp at his side. "Ivy Ridge PD, we're here to help. EMS is on its way, can you tell us what happened?" I say with each step closer I take.

"I don't know man, one minute he was fine, the next he collapsed," the man on the right says.

I'm about to drop to my knees and start administering the Narcan, when everything changes. The sliding door on the back of the house flies open, revealing the two undercover officers held at gunpoint by two older men. I step back from the man who was laying motionless, but is now sitting up with a gun in his palm, pointed right at me.

I drop the Narcan from my fist, reaching to pull my own gun.

We can't move, can't even radio out to tell dispatch what is happening so we can call for backup, can't even warn EMS. My heart drops. Hannah's working today. There's a chance that she and Miles will be the one to arrive on scene any minute. I can't bear the thought of her near any of this.

The man in the back holding one of our undercover guys speaks first. "This is exactly what we wanted. Officer Cunningham, pleasure to see you again."

"What do you want?" Officer Young asks.

"To get revenge. You arrested our leader, the man who let us live like kings, and now, our time has come. Did you really think we were stupid enough to not know these two idiots were undercover?"

"Why lace the drugs you sell?" I ask, my gaze focused on him.

"Why not?" he shrugs.

"Do you not care about all the lives you've taken?" I question.

He shrugs again. "Enough with the questions. We brought you all here for a reason. I've had enough of this."

He points his gun in my direction, and before I can react, he pulls the trigger.

Pandemonium erupts around me as pain lances through my right upper thigh. I don't react to the pain, only focusing on what's happening around me. The two officers beside me respond, shooting the suspects, and freeing the two under-cover officers. It's quick, but we've taken back control of the situation.

I fall to the ground, my injured leg no longer able to bear my weight. I reach for my radio, shouting, "Shots fired, shots fired."

My head swims as I try to put pressure on my wounded leg. Blood seeps from between my fingers, rushing too fast for me to be able to stop it. My body feels heavy, too heavy as my consciousness wanes. The radio at my shoulder is too loud, the dispatcher desperately trying to get more information from me, but I can't answer. I'm fading, fast.

The only thing on my mind as I lay back into the grass is Hannah. Her beautiful soft smile, those freckles on her cheeks, and how much I love her. She's the person I want to spend the rest of my life with, and if this is it for me, I'm glad I found her.

## 54

## HANNAH

"Shots fired on scene, I repeat, shots fired on scene. Officer down."

My heart plummets with fear as the dispatcher gives us more information. They don't announce who the officer is, but somehow, I know. It's Thomas. Something in my gut is telling me that it is.

Miles glances over at me from the driver's seat, an understanding look on his face.

"I'm fine," I reply, adjusting my position in my seat. It's not like I can call or text him right now to be sure.

"Hannah," Miles says my name, and he must have the same feeling I do.

"Miles, I'm fine. Are we cleared to arrive on scene?"

He nods, accelerating the rig. We were already heading toward the scene for the possible overdose, but now, we're heading there for another reason.

I take a deep breath and the street comes into view, willing my heart to stop pounding, and my mind to manifest that it's not him. It can't be him. I just got him, I can't lose him now.

As soon as the bus is in park, I'm grabbing my bag and running toward the backyard, not caring about my safety. I have to get to him.

I fling open the gate, and what greets me will always and forever be engrained into my memory.

Multiple people are lying on the grass, some dead, some being tended to by one of the many officers on scene. A few are being handcuffed and led toward the gate, but I can only focus on finding him.

When I do, the breath is knocked out of my lungs. Thomas is lying on the grass with Officer Young holding firmly to his right leg. Blood is seeping through the white gauze. I run toward them, dropping myself onto the ground and grabbing more gauze as fast as my fingers can move.

"Is this the only wound?" I ask Officer Young as I take over, my gloved hands pressing down on his leg.

"Yes. No exit wound that we can tell. He's lost a lot of blood."

"Is he breathing?" I ask. I can't look at his face. If I look at his face, I'll break.

"Yes, breathing has been steady. "

I nod, focusing on his leg. Miles drops down beside me, hooking him up to the monitors and checking his pulse. "Hannah," he mutters my name, trying not to bring much attention to me.

"I'm fine," I say through gritted teeth, even as a tear slides down my cheek.

"You're *not* fine."

"If you try and take me away from him right now, I won't be fine. Right now? I'm fine. We need to keep him alive. I need him, Miles." My tone is sharp, and I've never spoken to Miles like this before, but I don't care. The man that I love has been shot and is lying unconscious on the ground in front of me as I tend to his bullet wound. That's more important than anything else.

Only once Thomas is hooked up to the monitor and I see the physical evidence of his heart beating do I take a full breath. Miles starts an IV and pushes some medication since I'm still holding pressure. I let go for a moment so we can get him onto the stretcher. We make our way to the rig, and Miles glances at me as I climb in with him, keeping pressure on the wound. The bleeding has slowed, but only a little.

"Are you sure you can handle this?" he asks.

For what seems like the hundredth time, I repeat, "I'm fine. Let's go."

Miles sighs, slamming the doors shut behind me and a moment later, the rig starts moving.

Using my free hand, I reach up to grab some shears to cut the leg of his pants off, knowing the hospital will need the access. With the bottom of his pants gone, I can get a better look at it.

The wound has mercifully slowed bleeding, but I keep pressure on it. Only now that it has slowed do I allow myself to look at his face. Glancing up his body, I notice the boxers that he's wearing. Iron Man is plastered on the front, and my heart drops. Why is he wearing these today? I thought he only wore his superhero boxers on days he is manifesting something good, or needs luck? I take a deep breath, knowing that he does need luck today. He *has* to survive this.

I take in his beautiful face as I continue to look over his body, checking for any other injuries we may have missed. He's so pale that he looks dead, but the sight of his chest rising and falling with each breath helps me acknowledge the fact that he's still with me.

Tears haven't stopped falling from my eyes since the moment I saw him, but now, they're in the way. I angrily swat them away, irritated that they're impinging on my view of him. "You can't die," I murmur, putting pressure on the wound again with both hands. "I can't live without you, Thomas Cunningham. You hear me?"

I know he's unconscious, but it doesn't stop the words from tumbling from my lips.

"You came into my life when I least expected it and made it so easy to fall in love with you. You made my life better than I could have ever imagined, and now I need you. I need you in ways I never thought. I was doing fine on my own, but then you made me realize how good life could be." I swallow down a sob. "I love you, and I need you to be okay, Thomas. I love you so much, okay?"

A groan pulls me out of my mumbled proclamation.

"Hey, freckles," Thomas says, his voice quiet and hoarse. His hand reaches up and presses gently on my arm. "I'm okay."

"No, you're not," I respond, staring into those familiar blue eyes. "You were shot, Thomas. You've lost so much blood."

He nods, groaning again. "Yeah, I'm not feeling too good."

I bite back the sarcastic comment on my tongue. "We're almost to the hospital and they'll get you taken care of there. There's no exit wound, so you'll probably need surgery."

Thomas doesn't acknowledge his possible need for surgery, instead saying my name. "Hannah." His voice is slurring, and his eyes are hazy, drooping closed. He's falling unconscious again. "Did you say that you loved me?"

His eyes fall shut as the words leave his lips. I'd panic, but I know that the combination of blood loss and medication he received is why he can't stay awake. I take a deep breath. I didn't want to tell him I love him this way. I wanted it to be a sweet moment between the two of us, and now, it's ruined.

Maybe his superhero boxers are bad luck now.

The rig slows to a stop in front of the hospital and Miles climbs out, opening the back doors. We pull the stretcher out and I keep pressure on his leg. The nurses meet us in the ambulance bay as I tell them about the GSW, and his vitals. I let them know that he regained consciousness briefly before passing out again about five minutes ago.

I switch hands with one of the nurses, watching as they wheel the man I love away from me. I can't follow them, I can only watch in disdain. My shirt, hands and arms are covered in Thomas's blood, so I head over to the sink, tossing away my dirty gloves and washing up. My hands begin to shake as the cold water turns red as it runs down my fingertips.

Miles comes up behind me, patting my shoulder. "You did good. I'm sure he will be in surgery for a bit, but why don't you call his family."

"Oh god," I murmur, my stomach turning. The thought of telling his mom that her son was shot is enough to make me sick. But I have to. Miles leads me to the front desk where I let them know that I'll be contacting his family.

Miles calls our boss, letting him know what happened, and that I won't be able to work the rest of my shift.

I sit down in one of the uncomfortable waiting room chairs, pulling my phone from my pocket. With a deep breath, I open up my contacts, and find his mom's number. Miles rubs my shoulders again. "I'm going to make sure someone brings Arson here," he says.

"Oh my god, Arson," I cry, looking around the room as if

he will suddenly appear. "Was he there? Did he get hurt, too?" My voice cracks in fear.

"I'm sure he's fine. I didn't see him at the scene, so he was probably still in the back of Thomas's car. I'll take care of him, and bring him here if I can."

"Thank you," I murmur. Miles leaves me alone to call Nikki.

I press the button to call her and bring the phone up to my ear, ignoring the pounding in my chest. Thank god we exchanged phone numbers at the most recent Sunday brunch.

Nikki thankfully answers right away. "Hi, Hannah, how are you?"

I clear my throat of the lump that's forming. "Hi, Nikki." My voice cracks, and tears slip down my cheeks again.

"What happened?" she immediately asks, her earlier pleasant tone replaced with fear.

"Thomas got shot," I say. "He went to a scene and they were ambushed and he was shot in his thigh. I think they're going to bring him back to surgery, but you need to come."

"Oh my god," she cries. I can hear Thomas's dad in the background, questioning her and comforting her all at once.

He takes the phone from her. "Hello?" he asks, his voice wary.

"It's Hannah." I don't give him time to reply before I continue. "Thomas was shot in the leg. They're taking him back to surgery soon."

"Fuck," he curses, "We'll be there as soon as possible. Are you okay?"

"Yeah," I reply, my voice shaking. Am I okay? Physically, yes. Mentally... yeah, probably not.

We hang up, and without thought, I'm calling my sister.

"Hey Banana, I thought you were working?" she answers.

"Thomas was shot," I blurt, the sobs breaking free.

"What?" she screeches, already yelling at Tiff in the background to get the keys. "Hannah, what happened? Are you okay?"

"I'm not hurt," I reply. "He was on scene and got shot in the thigh. He needs surgery, and he lost a lot of blood."

"Breathe, Hannah," Julia says, and I take a long inhale. "He wasn't shot in the chest or anything?"

"No," I reply. "But he lost so much blood, Julia."

"They will give him a transfusion while they try and save his leg."

"I told him I loved him," I say with a heavy exhale.

"You did? When?"

I pinch the bridge of my nose. "He was passed out, and I was trying to stop the bleeding and it all kinda slipped out. Then I think he woke up and caught the end of it."

"But you love him?"

I hiccup a sob and nod, words unable to leave my mouth.

"I'm going to take that as a yes," Julia replies. "We will be there in an hour. Does his family know?"

"Yes," I croak. "I talked to his parents, they'll be here soon."

"Good. He's going to be okay, Hannah."

"You don't know that," I reply. "I need him, Julia. I love him."

"I know you do."

She hangs up, leaving me alone in this cold hospital waiting room.

It's weird being on this side of things. Being the one waiting to hear information about their loved one. I don't like it. The door to my right bursts open and Nikki and Richard rush in. Nikki's face is red with tears streaming down her cheeks as she takes me in. I'm surely a mess, covered in her son's blood.

"Have you heard anything?" she asks, sitting by my side and pulling me into her. I relax into her touch, needing the contact right now.

"No. I'm not family, so they couldn't tell me anything."

Richard frowns as he steps away, heading toward the front desk.

"Do you know what happened?" Nikki asks.

I shake my head. "All I know is that we were called out for an overdose, and then we got the call that there were shots fired with an officer down. I knew somehow that it was him. We got there and I saw that I was right."

"Oh honey," Nikki croons, pulling me into her.

Richard comes back a few moments later. "They did a CT scan and he's in surgery, but doing well. They're giving him a blood transfusion to help with the blood loss."

"Thank you," I say. Nikki reaches out, taking her husband's hand as the door opens, more of Thomas's family running in.

Beau is first, one twin in his arm, while Marley holds the other. They rush over, firing off questions. Nikki and Richard fill them in, while I sink back into the chair, slowly numbing to the world around me.

He has to be okay.

## 55

## HANNAH

It's been hours with not many updates. Every second that passes I worry more. Shouldn't he have been out of surgery by now? Wouldn't they have more of a concrete update at least?

Josie brought me some fresh clothes to change into, and my sisters got here an hour ago. For now, we're all waiting. No one has been talking much, except to distract the kids. They've all been doing so well, even baby Cooper.

Miles texted me a while ago with information about Arson. He has him at his house, and I'll pick him up when I eventually leave here. He's even sent me a few pictures too, so I know he's really okay. I feel so bad. He is probably worried sick and knows something is wrong. I will have to make sure to give him extra love when I pick him up.

It's nearly nine at night, I'm sure everyone is exhausted. Fallon and Jason each have a kid laying in their laps fast asleep, and Marley and Beau are rocking the twins in the corner. Gramps snores in a seat a few seats down from me, his cane laying against his leg. Andrew has his arms molded around Josie, who has Cooper in a wrap around her chest.

We all love him so much that the thought of leaving is so hard to bear. I'm sure they all want to bring their kids home and put them to bed, but they're staying.

I stand from my chair, the anxiety eating at me. I've gone through more cubes of ice than I can count, and nothing is helping. I'm not going to take a rescue med because what good am I if I'm asleep? I need to be here when he wakes up.

An hour later, a doctor makes her way through the double doors. "Thomas Cunningham?" she questions, and every single one of us stands. She smiles softly at the show of family.

"How is he?" Nikki asks, her voice wavering.

"Good. We were able to get all of the bullet fragments removed from his thigh. He got lucky. An inch over, and it would have hit his femoral artery. He still lost a lot of blood, but the transfusions we gave him will help with that. He's in PACU now as he recovers, then will be transferred to the ICU after that. He'll be groggy for a while, but when he wakes up, you can see him. We try to limit visitors while a person is in the ICU, so one or two members of the immediate family only."

Her words strike me in the chest. I won't be able to see him. Heaviness sinks me back into the chair as I stare at the tiled floor.

The doctor says a few more things, but I can't focus on a word. I'm relieved that Thomas is okay. Of course I am, but I can't stand the thought of not being able to see with my own two eyes that he's okay. I won't be able to feel at ease until I see him. Feel the warmth of his skin under mine, hear his heart beating in his chest. I can't catch my breath as the anxiety rages.

"Hannah?" Nikki's soothing voice breaks through the

whooshing sound in my ears. Her hands wipe at the tears on my cheeks, cupping them gently. "Hannah, honey, can you take a deep breath for me?"

I try to do as she says, but it's hard. One or two more deep breaths later, and my vision clears and my eyes lock with hers. "Good job, sweetie. You're doing so good. Once we get the all clear, you and I are going to go see him, okay?"

I lift my gaze to see that the room around us has emptied besides my sister, Nikki, and Richard. How long was I spiraling?

"They said—"

"They said immediate family. You're his fiancée," Nikki interrupts me.

"But—" It was all fake. Nikki knows this. Everyone does.

"*You're his fiancée,*" she reiterates. She raises her brow at me, daring me to question her again.

"Right," I shakily nod. Julia is staring down at me, her face marred with an older sister's concern and care. "Where did everyone go?"

"They all decided to go home, especially with the kids. They will stop by tomorrow when he's hopefully out of the ICU," Julia explains.

Julia sticks around while we wait a bit longer, and then when we get the okay to see him, she hugs me tightly and says to call if I need anything. She and Tiff are staying at Grandma's tonight.

Once she's gone, I'm alone with Thomas's parents. "Are you sure it's okay for me to go?" I ask Richard.

He stands, pulling me in for a side hug. "I'm sure. You need to see him, sweetie."

"Thank you," I murmur as he releases me. Nikki takes my hand and together, we follow one of the CNA's as she leads us to the ICU. When we reach the doors to the unit, she holds the door open for us before leaving us with another nurse.

"Hi, who are you here for?" The new nurse asks.

"Thomas Cunningham," Nikki responds. "They said he was in room six."

"Oh, yes. He's down the hall here, follow me."

Twenty steps later, I'm standing outside of a sliding glass door. The curtains behind the glass are closed, so we can't see in, but I feel as though I need a minute to prepare myself. The nurse opens the sliding door, pushing the curtain back a bit and asking the other nurse inside if he's ready for visitors.

When they answer with a yes, I swallow the lump in my throat. She pushes the curtain back all the way, and I get my first glimpse of him.

His color is a bit better than the last time I saw him. There's a hint of pink in his cheeks. He has an oxygen cannula under his nose, and tubing coming out of his hospital gown at his chest. An oxygen monitor is on his pointer finger, and the blanket on top of him covers half of his body, his right leg uncovered, as the nurse checks the dressing on his thigh.

I stand in the doorway holding Nikki's hand, unsure of what to do next. Can I touch him? Sit by his side and never leave?

Nikki pulls me with her to the opposite side of the bed of his injury. She lets go of my hand, leaving me floundering with nothing to ground me. Nikki does what a mother does best and cares for him. She fixes his hair, making sure it's out of his face, while I stand here, scared out of my mind.

He's alive. There is proof of that. His heart is beating

and I can see him breathing. But I'm so scared. What if this happens again and next time he's not so lucky?

There's a chair beside his bed, so I pull it closer, sitting down. The hand by me is laying on the sheet, completely free of any wires or tubes. Tentatively, I reach out and take his hand in mine. The immediate warmth that his touch brings me is so soothing. A sob bursts from my lips at the contact. I want to climb into this bed and hold him, but I can't so for now, I rest my head on his hand, reveling in any sort of closeness I can get.

He's going to be okay. His recovery will surely be hard with lots of physical therapy, but he's here. We both are.

## 56

## THOMAS

My entire body is heavy as I try to pry my eyes open. I blink hard and try to take a deep breath. My mouth is dry, eyes crusty as brightness seeps through my lids. I squeeze my eyes shut against the offensively bright sunlight.

"Thomas?"

"Mmm," I answer. We must have slept hard last night because my entire body is stiff.

"You're awake?"

"Yeah," I grumble. My throat hurts, like I've been breathing with my mouth open all night. Hannah's not usually this talkative in the mornings. Usually, I'm the one who has to pry her up out of bed.

"Oh, thank god," she mumbles, her fingers fluttering down my cheeks.

Her words confuse me. I flick my eyes open again, this time blinking against the bright light instead of closing them. My surroundings flicker into view, and it's then I notice the tube under my nose and the steady beeping of a heart monitor. *Oh, fuck.*

Everything rushes back into my memory. I was shot. I look down at my right thigh where blood was spewing out the last time I saw it. Now, it's covered with a wrapped dressing around my thigh.

A hand pushes my hair back from my face. "Hannah," I breathe. "You're okay?"

"I'm the one who should be asking you that, you dummy." She lets out a watery chuckle, tears streaming down her cheeks. "I'm fine. I got to the scene once they had it under control."

"Thank god," I murmur, dropping my head to the stiff, crinkly pillow. "I was so scared you would be walking into an active scene."

She shakes her head. "No. How are you feeling?"

"Tired," I reply.

"How is your pain?"

I shrug. "It hurts, but it's not bad."

Hannah drops her hand from my cheek. "I'll go see when you can have more meds."

I reach out, wrapping my fingers around her wrist. "No, I'm fine. Stay, please."

"Thomas..."

"Please, Hannah." I pull her closer to me until she has to sit on the edge of the bed. She relents, curling up into my side. Wetness seeps into my hospital gown from her tears. "I'm okay, baby."

"I know," she cries. "I was so scared. You were bleeding so much and I was trying so hard to stop it, but it wouldn't stop. You were so pale."

I lift my head to press a kiss to her forehead. "Thank you for saving me," I whisper. Unfortunately, that makes her cry harder, so I have to come up with something to distract her.

"Who has Arson?" I ask. "And what time is it? What day is it?"

"It's early morning. Your mom went to go get some coffee. You got done with surgery at about midnight last night. Arson is with Miles. He got him from your squad car. I'll pick him up later, but he sent some pictures, do you want to see them?"

I shake my head. I need her close to me.

Is now the best time for a confession of love? Probably not, but if there's anything that this has taught me is that I'm not waiting a second longer to tell her how I feel.

"I remember waking up for a second in that ambulance," I say, and she tenses.

"You do?" she tentatively asks.

"Mhm. I need you, too, you know."

Hannah nods into my chest. "I hoped you didn't hear that."

"Why?"

"I shouldn't have waited to tell you. Then, I chose when you were unconscious to say it all. I was a chicken."

"I wasn't unconscious. I heard it all, Hannah."

"Really?" She lifts her head, turning to look me in the eyes. Her bright blue eyes are glimmering with tears, and with how swollen and red they are, she must have been crying a lot.

"I did. Remember that surprise I had planned?"

She nods.

"I love you, Hannah. I was going to tell you last night. Obviously, life had other plans for us, but it doesn't change how much I love you."

Hannah whimpers in my arms, leaning forward to kiss me. "I love you too, Thomas."

"If I have it my way, you'll never have to live without me."

"I'd like that." Hannah smiles, then scrunches her nose, pointing to the corner of the room where a plastic bag sits with my uniform in it. "We need to throw out every pair of your superhero underwear though. They aren't lucky anymore."

"What?" I bellow, coughing against the scratch of pain in my throat from the tube. "Yes they are."

"No, they're not! Thomas, the night of our first date, we saw Henry get shot. Then, you were wearing them yesterday for some reason, and you get shot. We're throwing them out."

"They are lucky," I say stubbornly. "Sure, some bad things have happened when I was wearing them. I can agree to that. But, even better things have happened because of them. That night, I got to take you on the best first date I've ever been on, my last first date to be honest. If I weren't wearing them, maybe Elena wouldn't have let you come with me. Then we wouldn't have had all that time together at Ron and Dottie's alone. I probably would have come home after six weeks to find you dating some guy named Luke or something."

Hannah scoffs. "Right."

"I'm serious, baby. I wore them the night we made love the first time. I knew that taking you on that date in the truck was going to be pivotal in our relationship. I didn't know how pivotal it would be, but still. I wore them yesterday because I planned to tell you I love you."

"How is where we are now, good luck though?" she asks, her voice filled with sass.

"I'm not saying it is. But, who knows. Maybe me getting

shot pushed you into telling me you loved me first, unconscious or not," I say with a shrug.

"You're ridiculous," Hannah breathes.

"*Ridiculously in love,*" I croon. I tilt her head up to meet mine. "I love you, Hannah. I'll say it as many times as it takes to make you believe it. I've loved you for a long time, but I knew you weren't ready to hear it, so I showed you instead. I will continue to show you how much I love you until the day I die. Fake fiancée or not, I intend to make it real someday, and after that, you will be my wife. The person I choose to love and show up for, no matter what."

Hannah leans forward, kissing me deeply. Her hand cups my cheeks gently, and I know she's afraid to hurt me, and I desperately wish we were home right now.

"Thank you for loving me, even when I was too scared to accept your love the way you deserved," she replies, kissing me again. "I will love you forever, Thomas."

Her words are better than any medicine that they could give me. A balm over the painful wound on my thigh, I sink into the uncomfortable bed, pulling her onto my chest. I run my fingers over her hair, twirling little pieces between my fingers.

No, this wasn't the way I planned it, but then again, nothing about our relationship has been normal.

"Baby, we have to leave in five!" I call from the living room.

"I know, I'm almost ready," Hannah yells from the bathroom.

In the year since I was shot, things have been a whirlwind in the best way. It's taken a long time to heal from the GSW, but I have, and I am officially off desk duty starting Monday.

Hannah's nervous for me to go back out in the field, and I get it. To be honest, I'm nervous too. But, we both have been in therapy since it happened, and it's helped a lot.

I also went through many months of physical therapy to help repair my leg. It gets sore and tires easily, but all things considered, I'm lucky. The bullet missed any major nerves or arteries, so most of my rehab was spent trying to get my muscle strength back up to the best it could be.

Two months after I was shot, Hannah officially moved in with me, and we haven't looked back. My brothers had to help with the move since I was still not putting much weight on my leg at the time, but we made it a fun time.

Things between us have been incredible. We make time to go on dates and spend time together with the two of us, but also with our families. Hannah has gotten close to all my sisters-in-law, and seeing her interact with my nieces and nephews is one of my favorite things.

Not long after I was shot, we confessed to everyone that the engagement was fake, and while everyone knew the whole time, it was nice to get it off our chests.

The trial for the trafficking ring ended a few weeks ago with Chaz getting twenty years to life behind bars, and the men who shot Henry and I getting the same. All the other accomplices have their sentencing in a few weeks, so hopefully that ends similarly.

Arlo is still as obsessed with her as he was the first day they met. Only now, instead of calling her "my", he calls her Auntie Nannah. It's adorable. We recently celebrated the twins' second birthday, as well as Cooper's first birthday.

Tonight is going to be something a little different. Hannah still hates surprises, but I think she's going to enjoy this one.

She strides out into the living room, and fuck if she isn't the most beautiful girl in the world. She has on a gorgeous rust orange tulle sundress on. Her hair is curled loosely and she has light makeup on, similar to the night of our first date. It's perfect, never covering her beautiful freckles that I adore so much.

"You look stunning, baby," I say, rising to my feet. I'm wearing a pair of dress pants and a nice button down shirt, fit for the occasion. "Ready?"

"I'd be more ready if you'd tell me what we were doing," Hannah replies, reaching out to take my hand.

"Can't do that, my love." I subtly pat the right pocket of

my pants to make sure I have it. Thankfully the outline is small, but it's there.

Arson follows us to the door, and we both give him some extra love before we leave. I take Hannah's hand in mine as I lead her to my truck, helping her up and in before getting in the other side.

"Thomas," she groans as we pull away from our house. "Surprises are not my thing."

"I know, baby. But you trust me, right?"

She glares at me. "Of course I do."

"So trust that I am taking care of you, and would never do anything to make you uncomfortable. Okay?"

She reaches over, taking my hand. "Okay."

I drive us out of town to a restaurant that isn't very busy, especially on a weeknight. The parking lot only has two other cars in it, but it's a nice restaurant, so I made sure to make a reservation anyway in a quiet corner where we will be able to talk.

I give the hostess my name, and she leads us to the far corner, seating us and offering a glass of wine. We both accept and she pours us each some white wine before excusing herself, leaving us to look at the menu.

"So, you brought me to a nice dinner? That was the surprise? You didn't need to get me all hyped up for that, Thomas," Hannah says with a small smile, taking a sip of her wine.

"Mhmm," I murmur, perusing the menu with my eyes, fully knowing that the real surprises are yet to come.

Not even five minutes later, I see them arrive from the corner of my eye. I jerk my head in our direction, letting them know to come. They get the message, and quickly walk to us. They stand at the table, and Hannah lifts her gaze from the menu with a smile, expecting it to be the waitress.

"Can we join you?" Dottie asks, a huge grin on her face. Ron stands at her side, an arm wrapped around her waist.

"Oh my god, what are you doing here?" Hannah shrieks, standing from the table to wrap both of them in a hug.

I do the same, acknowledging the pointed looks that they both give me while also giving one back. They know what my other surprise for Hannah is, but that won't come until later, when it's just us.

Ron and Dottie sit down with us and we spend the entire dinner talking. In the last year since we left Missouri, we have only seen them a few times when they came up to Minnesota for some of Fletcher's games.

We talk on the phone with them at least once a week where they update us on Dave's recent antics, and the new animals they have on their small farm. Dottie also shares recipes with Hannah, and some of the food that comes out of it is incredible. I miss the solitude of the farm somedays, but also wouldn't trade this life with Hannah for anything.

The entire evening is spent catching up with each other and making plans for the rest of the time they are in town. Both Hannah and I are off work the next five days, so it's perfect timing. They're going to stay at my parent's house and come to Sunday brunch this week. The Sunday brunch crew has grown since the addition of Hannah to our family. Now, her Grandma comes every week, as well as Tiff and Julia when they're able to.

My family has grown in size over the years, but I wouldn't change a single thing.

After we finish dinner, we say goodbye to them for now, and I take Hannah's hand in mine as we walk out to our vehicle. "Thank you," she murmurs, resting her head on my chest.

I press a kiss to her forehead. "Of course," I reply.

"That was a great surprise. I've missed them so much."

"I have too. We will have to go visit them soon, too."

"I'd love that."

"We have one more stop to make on the way home, if that's okay."

Hannah raises her brow as she gets into the truck.

I smile, kissing her cheek and getting in the driver's seat. I drive us back toward Ivy Ridge, but veer off at the signs for the state park.

"Where are we going?" Hannah asks, peering out the window. The sun is starting to set in the distance, leaving the world in a golden hue.

"You'll see," I say, pulling off the road to park. "We're getting out here."

She follows my lead, getting out of the car and taking my outstretched hand. "Do we have to walk far?" she asks. Her voice shakes a little, and I think she may have caught on to what's happening.

"No, not far." I lead her down the wooded pathway and to the clearing.

"Wow," she breathes as the trail clears to an empty area. Marley got here about an hour ago and set everything up beautifully. There's a quilt laying on the ground with fake tea-light candles around the edges, and polaroid pictures of us hanging on a tree branch nearby.

The view is spectacular. We're overlooking the river, surrounded by trees and bluffs that are the perfect backdrop for this moment.

"Thomas," Hannah sighs, the golden sunset lighting up her face so beautifully. Her cheeks are my favorite shade of red, her freckles prominently lit up and on display. I pull Hannah to the blanket, and take both of her hands in mine, turning her so we are face to face.

I cup her cheek in my palm, kissing her gently before reaching into my pocket and pulling out my grandmother's ring. I drop to one knee, holding the ring up for her to see.

"Hannah, I love you so much. Every day with you is a new adventure, and I find something more to love about you. Falling in love with you was the easiest thing I've ever done. Every moment with you is the golden hour. Everything is sunshine and glowy, you light up the world in a golden hue that makes everything shine brighter, simply by being you. I can't wait to spend every day by your side, watching you shine. Hannah Pearson, will you marry me?"

Tears fall down her red cheeks. She covers her mouth with one hand as she weeps, nodding her head frantically up and down. "Yes, I'll marry you," she murmurs, eyes focused solely on me.

I rise to my feet, wrapping my arms around her and kissing her deeply. "Thank you," I murmur between kisses. Hannah laughs, and the sound is music to my ears. I vaguely hear Marley clicking away on her camera in the background, but I'm so glad that besides her, this moment is private, and only ours. I knew Hannah wouldn't want it to be a huge affair. She wouldn't be able to fully enjoy it that way. The party with our families will come later, but for now, this moment is about us.

I've almost forgotten the ring still clutched in my fingers. I pull away, taking her left hand and sliding the ring onto her finger. I had it sized to fit her perfectly.

"I love you," I murmur, kissing her once more.

A dragonfly circles us, landing on the blanket at our feet. I smile, almost feeling as though the dragonfly is my grandmother's sign of showing her love for us at this moment. She was always fond of signs.

The engagement ring that once belonged to Grandma Irene rests on Hannah's finger, the single pearl surrounded in a set of diamonds resting on a gold band. The night of our first date, before things went wrong, I knew this was where we would end up someday. I knew that I'd found the love of my life, and it was only a matter of time until we could start our forever. Now, we are officially taking the first step toward a lifetime of happiness, family, and love.

WANT a sneak peek of what's next in Hannah and Thomas's story, and a glimpse into what comes next in the Alice Daniels world?

Scan the code to read the bonus chapters!

# ACKNOWLEDGMENTS

I'm going to be honest. This book means the absolute world to me.

Thomas and Hannah have lived inside my brain for a long long time. For nearly two years, their story was in the back of my mind, waiting to be written. I knew that Hannah would be a character that I resonated with, but I never realized how much. So much of myself lives in her character, and I hope you love her as much as I do.

I can't believe that this is the end of the Ivy Ridge Series. These four books changed my life in ways I never ever expected, and for that, I am eternally grateful. Thank you for reading my books and loving my characters.

Aria & Tiff- For constantly being there for me. I love you two more than you know and I am so freaking grateful for your friendship.

The Fat Writers Space- I fucking love you all. I have so many reasons to thank you all, but I'll keep it short this time around. Thank you for being there for me and hyping me up every second of the day. Also, it's Duck, Duck, Grey Duck.

My Beta Readers, Emily, Brittany, Abbey, and Jessica- your kindness and suggestions are so incredible. I appreciate you taking the time out of your busy lives to read and make this book better!

My ARC and Street Team- The fact that you are all so willing to take time out of your lives and days to read my books and hype me up will always be amazing. Each and every one of you mean more to me than you know!

My family and friends- for listening to me gush about my characters and stories, and being my biggest supporters.

Victoria- I'm doing it, Mr. Krabs! I love you.

HBC- Thank you for your constant willingness to help me with events, whether local or across the country, for the way you are always there for me and scream in excitement whenever I share exciting news.

# ALSO BY ALICE DANIELS

## Cinder Valley Series

*Tip Of My Tongue- Lainey & Colin*

*How Do I Tell You?- Mallory & Tyler*

*Give Me A Minute- Theo & Peyton*

## Ivy Ridge

*Flowers in Your Hair- Andrew & Josie*

*Never Really Mine- Beau & Marley*

*Can't Let You Go- Jason & Fallon*

*In Plain Sight- Thomas & Hannah*

## Minnesota Blue Herons Hockey Series

*TBA- Fletcher & Lydia*

# ABOUT THE AUTHOR

Alice Daniels is a born and raised Minnesotan who loves to write books based on the small town she grew up in. Her books are sweet, heartfelt, and sexy, with relatable characters.

As a child, she was an avid fiction reader, which evolved into a deep love for romance novels and the community surrounding them. She recently discovered a passion for putting her ideas into writing and decided to pursue her childhood dream of becoming an author.

She spends time with her family and friends when she's not writing, especially on the lakes or outdoors in the summer.

Follow Alice on Facebook, Instagram, and Goodreads for book updates, teasers, and future releases!

Join her Facebook Group, Alice Daniels Reader Group to get all the insider info, sneak peeks, and more!

https://alicedaniels.com/

amazon.com/author/alicedaniels

facebook.com/authoralicedaniels

instagram.com/authoralicedaniels

goodreads.com/authoralicedaniels

bookbub.com/authors/saylor-ann